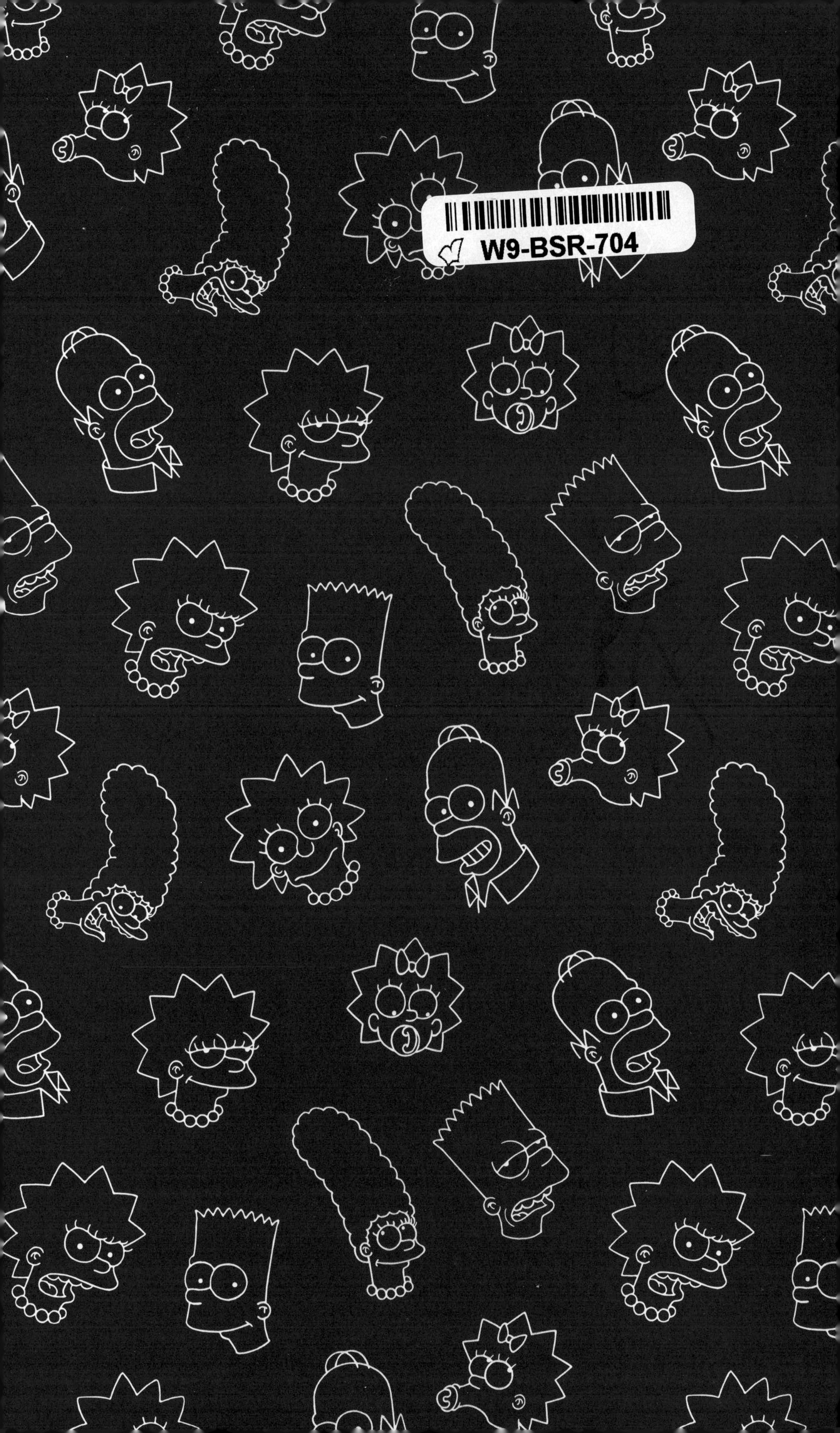

SIMPSONS™
COMICS EXTRAVAGANZA

Perennial

An Imprint of HarperCollinsPublishers

Dedicated to the memory of Snowball I:
Though you are gone, your claw marks
on our comic books remain.

The Simpsons™, created by Matt Groening, are the copyrighted
and trademarked property of Twentieth Century Fox Film Corporation.
Used with permission. All rights reserved.

SIMPSONS COMICS EXTRAVAGANZA.
Copyright ©1994 by Bongo Entertainment, Inc.
All rights reserved. Printed by World Color Press, Inc, St-Romuald, QC, Canada. 03/24/10.
No part of this book may be used or reproduced in any manner whatsoever
without written permission except in the case of brief quotations
embodied in critical articles and reviews. For information address
HarperCollins Publishers, Inc.,
10 East 53rd Street, New York, NY 10022.

HarperCollins books may be purchased for educational, business,
or sales promotional use. For information, please write:
Special Markets Department, HarperCollins Publishers, Inc.,
10 East 53rd Street, New York, NY 10022.

ISBN 978-0-06-095086-6

10 11 12 QWM 24 23 22

Publisher: MATT GROENING
Editors in Chief/Creative Directors: STEVE VANCE, CINDY VANCE
Managing Editor: JASON GRODE
Art Director: BILL MORRISON
Contributing Artists: TIM BAVINGTON,
PHIL ORTIZ, SONDRA ROY
Contributing Writers: DEB LACUSTA, DAN CASTELLANETA
Book Design: MARILYN FRANDSEN, DEBORAH ROSS
Publicity Director: ANTONIA COFFMAN
Legal Guardian: SUSAN A. GRODE

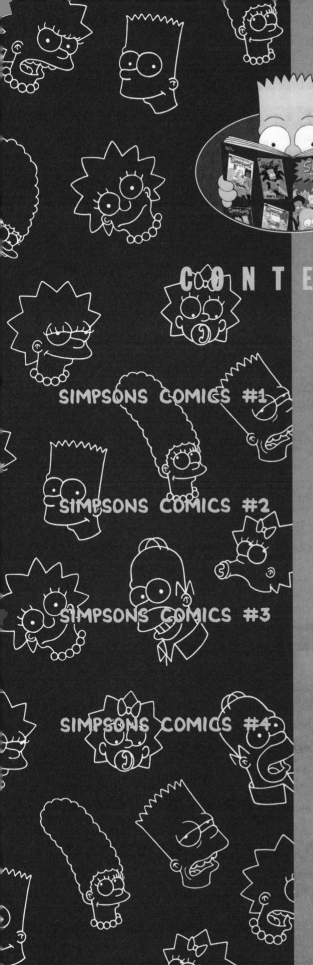

C O N T E N T S

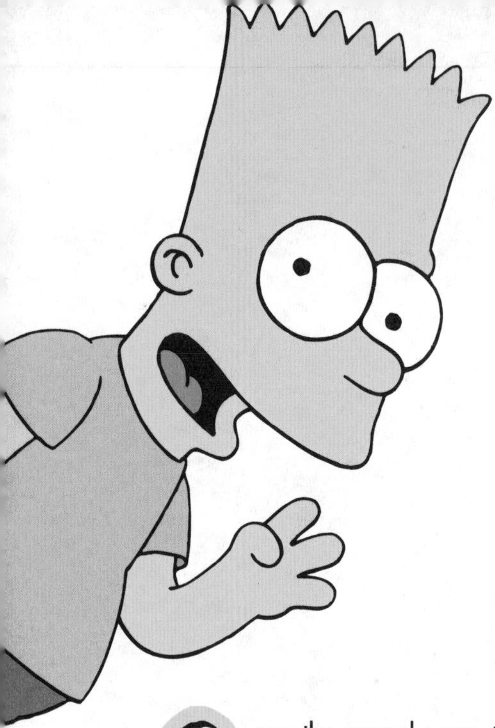

WELCOME TO SIMPSONS COMICS EXTRAVAGANZA, MAN!

Over the several years that the Simpsons have been cavorting on TV (since 1987, if you count the prehistoric shorts on the "Tracey Ullman Show"), we've gotten the kinds of compliments that cartoonists crave hearing: you're setting a bad example, you're corrupting youth, you're frightening Americans about nuclear power, you're hastening the downfall of western civilization. But my favorite prissy outrage at Simpsonian subversion came in 1990, when school principals, busybodies, and petty government officials across the land flipped out because of the Bart Simpson underachiever T-shirts—you know the ones, with Bart saying "And proud of it, man!"

The point of that T-shirt was that no kids call themselves underachievers—that's a label middle-achieving grown-ups slap on mischief-achieving kids. And the proper wisenheimer response to being labeled an underachiever, of course, is to be "proud of it, man!" Of course, none of the Simpsons critics gave us any credit when we followed up the Bart Simpson Underachiever T-shirt with a Lisa Simpson Overachiever T-shirt. But that may be because on that T-shirt we had Lisa saying, "Damn I'm good!"

Which brings me to the Simpsons Comics Extravaganza. This consists of the remarkable first four issues of Simpsons Comics, brought to you by the Bongo Comics Group, a small but overachieving band of merry artists, designers, lawyers, and publicists, namely: Steve Vance, Cindy Vance, Bill Morrison, Jason Grode, Susan Grode, and Antonia Coffman. Their work looks effortless, but believe me, the Bongo gang has shed several droplets of sweat, a few driplets of blood, and perhaps even a couple tears of joy in the making of these comics. Don't worry, however: All Bongo bodily secretions have been wiped off the original art so as not to distract you from your entertainment experience.

As Bart might say, We're proud of these comics, man. As Lisa might say, Damn, they're good.

And as Marge might say, I don't want you sitting up in that treehouse all day reading comic books! You'll ruin your eyes!

MATT GROENING
Bongo Comics Group

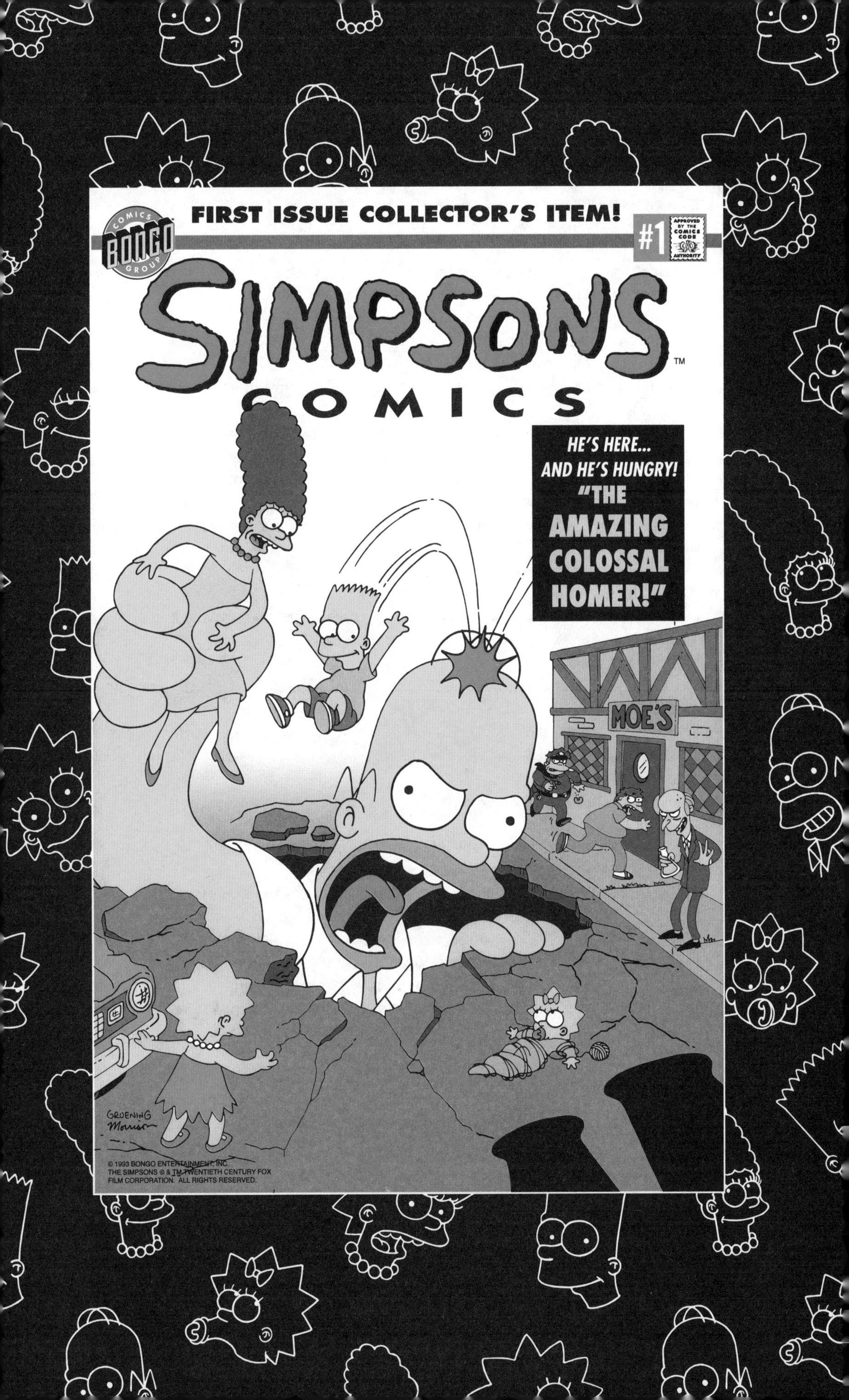
FIRST ISSUE COLLECTOR'S ITEM!
BONGO COMICS GROUP
#1
APPROVED BY THE COMICS CODE AUTHORITY
SIMPSONS™
COMICS
HE'S HERE... AND HE'S HUNGRY! "THE AMAZING COLOSSAL HOMER!"
MOE'S
GROENING Morrison
© 1993 BONGO ENTERTAINMENT, INC.
THE SIMPSONS © & TM TWENTIETH CENTURY FOX
FILM CORPORATION. ALL RIGHTS RESERVED.

BART'S BOTTOM 40

1. LISA'S SAXOPHONE
2. VEGETABLES THAT DON'T FLY WELL OFF YOUR SPOON
3. WRINKLED OLD GROWNUPS - - I HOPE I NEVER BECOME ONE
4. THE CHEAP LOUSY PRIZES THEY GIVE AWAY IN BOXES OF FROSTY KRUSTY FLAKES
5. HAVING NIGHTMARES THAT I'M A CHIP OFF THE OLD BLOCK
6. BEING CAUGHT RED-HANDED
7. THE HARDENED CRUST ON THE TOP OF MOM'S CASSEROLES
8. THE GOOEY STUFF UNDERNEATH THE HARDENED CRUST ON THE TOP OF MOM'S CASSEROLES
9. PRINCIPAL SKINNER'S SPECIAL FILE ON ME
10. THE "NO DRAWING ON THE WALL" RULE
11. THE FACT THAT OTTO HARDLY EVER LETS ME DRIVE THE SCHOOL BUS
12. CREAMED CORN
13. PARENTS WHO HAVE SIGNATURES THAT ARE REALLY HARD TO FORGE
14. ACCIDENTALLY FEELING GUM STUCK UNDERNEATH A RESTAURANT TABLE
15. SUCKING ON YOUR PEN IN SCHOOL AND HAVING YOUR MOUTH FILL UP WITH INK
16. NAMBY-PAMBY G-RATED MOVIES
17. DAD'S SNORING THAT YOU CAN HEAR THROUGH THE WALL EVEN WITH A PILLOW COVERING YOUR HEAD
18. STORIES WITH MORALS AT THE END
19. CARTOONS WITH NO FUN VIOLENCE AND PAIN
20. CARTOONS WHERE THEY RUN PAST THE SAME LAMP AND TABLE A ZILLION TIMES
21. THE STRAWBERRY AND VANILLA PARTS OF NEOPOLITAN ICE CREAM
22. GAS STATION RESTROOMS
23. MAKING BAD WORDS WITH MY ALPHABET SOUP AND HAVING LISA TELL ME THEY'RE MISSPELLED
24. ACCIDENTALLY DRINKING OUT OF THE GLASS WHERE GRANDPA KEEPS HIS FALSE TEETH
25. THE DIFFICULTY OF LOADING WATER BALLOONS WITH MAPLE SYRUP
26. SUGARLESS ANYTHING
27. BEING TRIED IN COURT AS AN ADULT
28. VENGEFUL BARBERS
29. THE HAUNTING THOUGHT THAT SIDESHOW BOB WILL GET OUT OF JAIL AGAIN
30. RIP-OFF CHOCOLATE BUNNIES THAT ARE HOLLOW INSIDE
31. COMIC BOOKS WITH INSUFFICIENTLY GIMMICKY COVER ENHANCEMENTS
32. PHLEGM (ALSO ON MY TOP 40 LIST)
33. WHEN MOM SAYS "IF ALL YOUR FRIENDS JUMPED OFF THE BRIDGE, WOULD YOU JUMP TOO?"
34. CARTOONS WITH REDEEMING SOCIAL MESSAGES
35. THE NONEDIBLE DECORATIONS ON BIRTHDAY CAKES THAT YOU ACCIDENTALLY TRY TO EAT
36. BRUSSELS SPROUTS
37. FORGETTING ABOUT THE CANDY BAR YOU PUT IN YOUR PANTS POCKET ON A REALLY HOT DAY
38. SWIMMING POOL BELLY-FLOPS THAT BOTH HURT AND LOOK DUMB
39. THE BOTTOMS OF YOUR SNEAKERS AFTER YOU COME OUT OF A PETTING ZOO
40. BEING AN "UNDERACHIEVER" - - TO TELL YOU THE TRUTH, I'M NOT EXACTLY SURE WHAT THE WORD MEANS

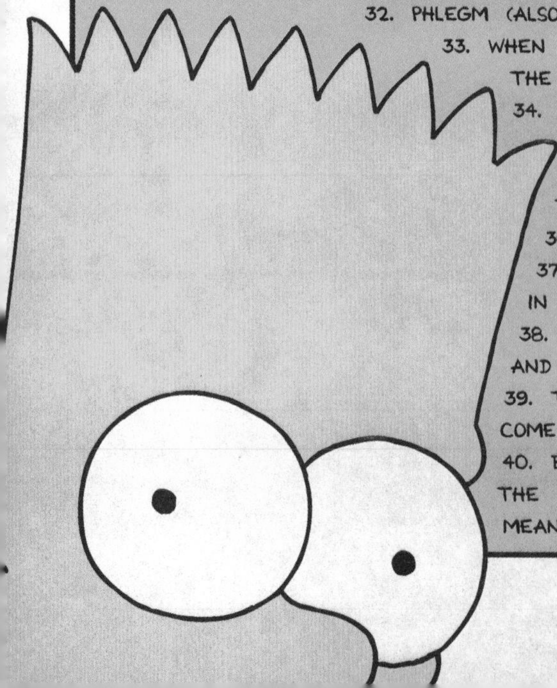

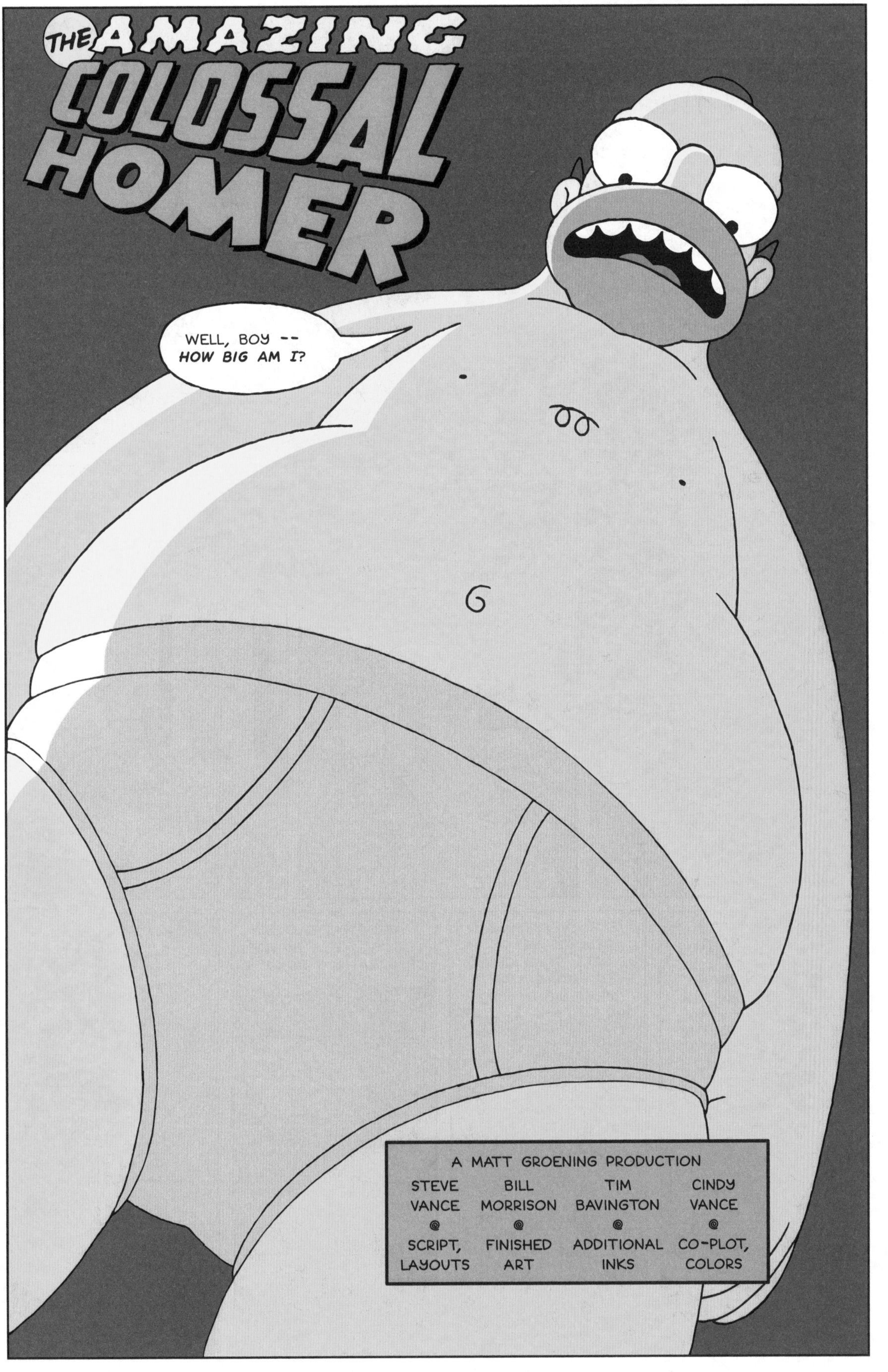
THE AMAZING COLOSSAL HOMER
WELL, BOY -- HOW BIG AM I?
A MATT GROENING PRODUCTION
STEVE VANCE SCRIPT, LAYOUTS
BILL MORRISON FINISHED ART
TIM BAVINGTON ADDITIONAL INKS
CINDY VANCE CO-PLOT, COLORS

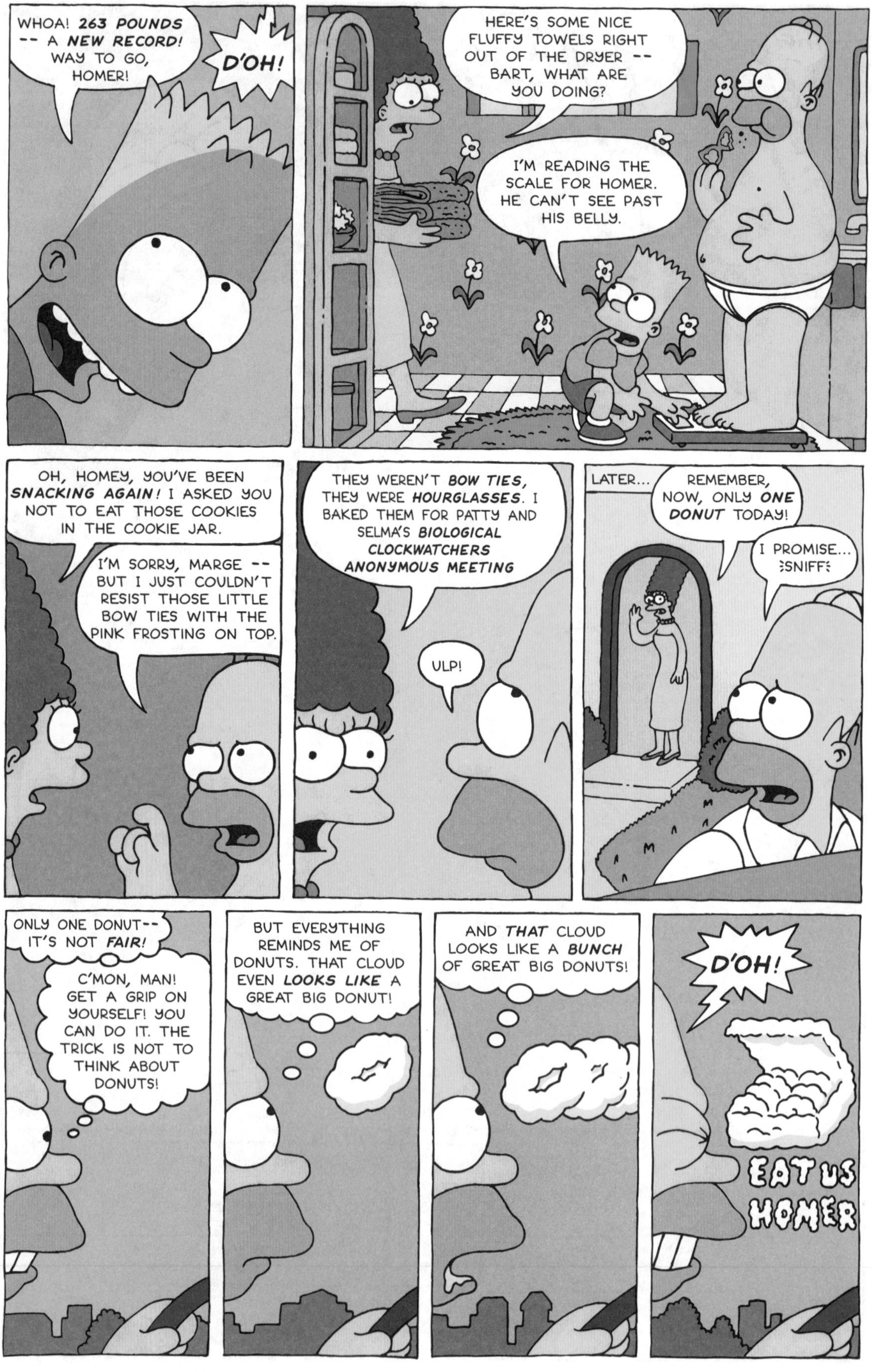
WHOA! 263 POUNDS -- A NEW RECORD! WAY TO GO, HOMER!
D'OH!
HERE'S SOME NICE FLUFFY TOWELS RIGHT OUT OF THE DRYER -- BART, WHAT ARE YOU DOING?
I'M READING THE SCALE FOR HOMER. HE CAN'T SEE PAST HIS BELLY.
OH, HOMEY, YOU'VE BEEN SNACKING AGAIN! I ASKED YOU NOT TO EAT THOSE COOKIES IN THE COOKIE JAR.
I'M SORRY, MARGE -- BUT I JUST COULDN'T RESIST THOSE LITTLE BOW TIES WITH THE PINK FROSTING ON TOP.
THEY WEREN'T BOW TIES, THEY WERE HOURGLASSES. I BAKED THEM FOR PATTY AND SELMA'S BIOLOGICAL CLOCKWATCHERS ANONYMOUS MEETING
ULP!
LATER...
REMEMBER, NOW, ONLY ONE DONUT TODAY!
I PROMISE... SNIFF
ONLY ONE DONUT-- IT'S NOT FAIR!
C'MON, MAN! GET A GRIP ON YOURSELF! YOU CAN DO IT. THE TRICK IS NOT TO THINK ABOUT DONUTS!
BUT EVERYTHING REMINDS ME OF DONUTS. THAT CLOUD EVEN LOOKS LIKE A GREAT BIG DONUT!
AND THAT CLOUD LOOKS LIKE A BUNCH OF GREAT BIG DONUTS!
D'OH!
EAT US HOMER

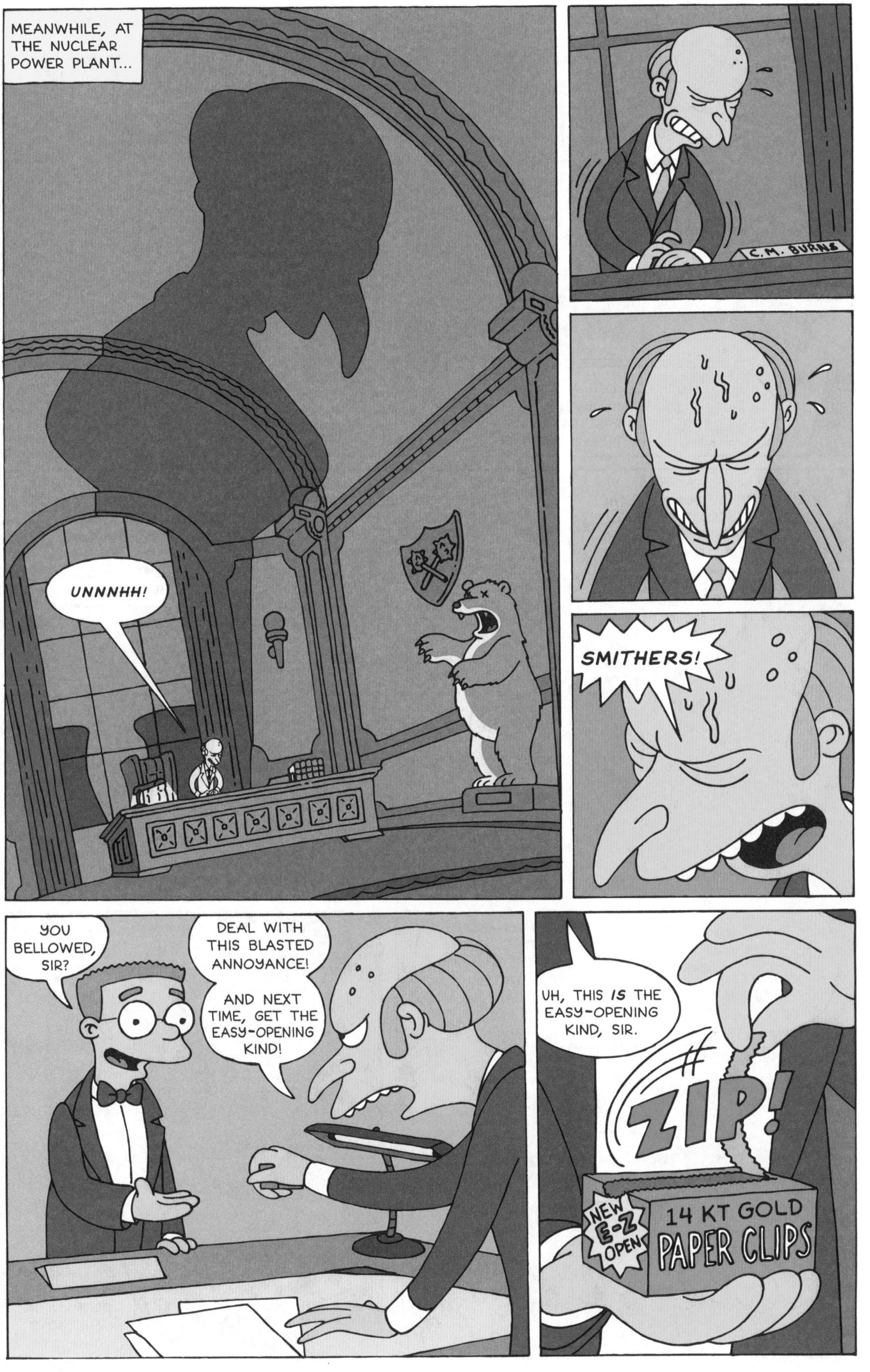
MEANWHILE, AT THE NUCLEAR POWER PLANT...
UNNNHH!
C.M. BURNS
SMITHERS!
YOU BELLOWED, SIR?
DEAL WITH THIS BLASTED ANNOYANCE!
AND NEXT TIME, GET THE EASY-OPENING KIND!
UH, THIS IS THE EASY-OPENING KIND, SIR.
ZIP!
NEW E-Z OPEN
14 KT GOLD PAPER CLIPS

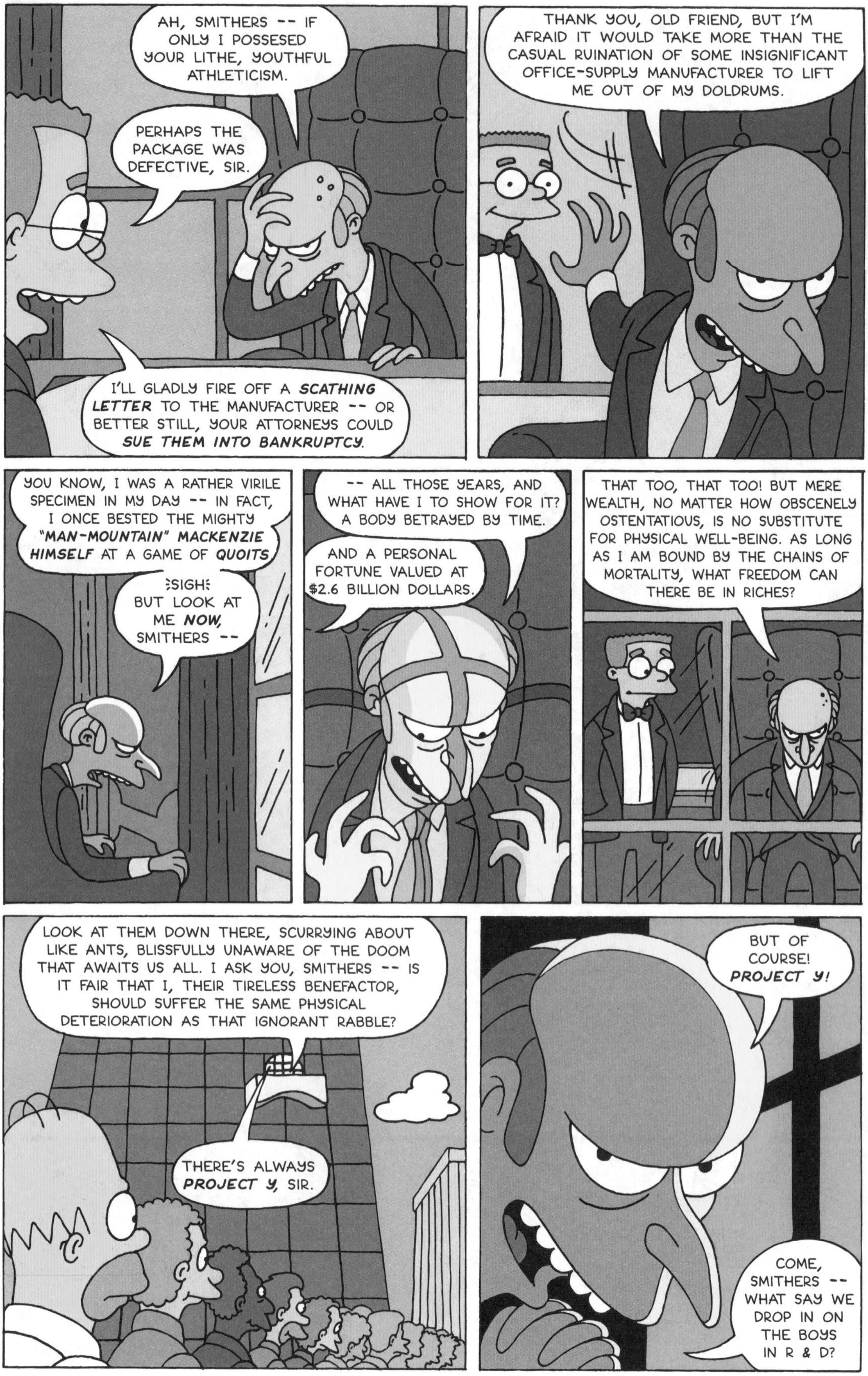
AH, SMITHERS -- IF ONLY I POSSESED YOUR LITHE, YOUTHFUL ATHLETICISM.
PERHAPS THE PACKAGE WAS DEFECTIVE, SIR.
I'LL GLADLY FIRE OFF A **SCATHING LETTER** TO THE MANUFACTURER -- OR BETTER STILL, YOUR ATTORNEYS COULD **SUE THEM INTO BANKRUPTCY**.
THANK YOU, OLD FRIEND, BUT I'M AFRAID IT WOULD TAKE MORE THAN THE CASUAL RUINATION OF SOME INSIGNIFICANT OFFICE-SUPPLY MANUFACTURER TO LIFT ME OUT OF MY DOLDRUMS.
YOU KNOW, I WAS A RATHER VIRILE SPECIMEN IN MY DAY -- IN FACT, I ONCE BESTED THE MIGHTY **"MAN-MOUNTAIN" MACKENZIE HIMSELF** AT A GAME OF **QUOITS**.
:SIGH: BUT LOOK AT ME **NOW**, SMITHERS --
-- ALL THOSE YEARS, AND WHAT HAVE I TO SHOW FOR IT? A BODY BETRAYED BY TIME.
AND A PERSONAL FORTUNE VALUED AT $2.6 BILLION DOLLARS.
THAT TOO, THAT TOO! BUT MERE WEALTH, NO MATTER HOW OBSCENELY OSTENTATIOUS, IS NO SUBSTITUTE FOR PHYSICAL WELL-BEING. AS LONG AS I AM BOUND BY THE CHAINS OF MORTALITY, WHAT FREEDOM CAN THERE BE IN RICHES?
LOOK AT THEM DOWN THERE, SCURRYING ABOUT LIKE ANTS, BLISSFULLY UNAWARE OF THE DOOM THAT AWAITS US ALL. I ASK YOU, SMITHERS -- IS IT FAIR THAT I, THEIR TIRELESS BENEFACTOR, SHOULD SUFFER THE SAME PHYSICAL DETERIORATION AS THAT IGNORANT RABBLE?
THERE'S ALWAYS **PROJECT Y**, SIR.
BUT OF COURSE! **PROJECT Y!**
COME, SMITHERS -- WHAT SAY WE DROP IN ON THE BOYS IN R & D?

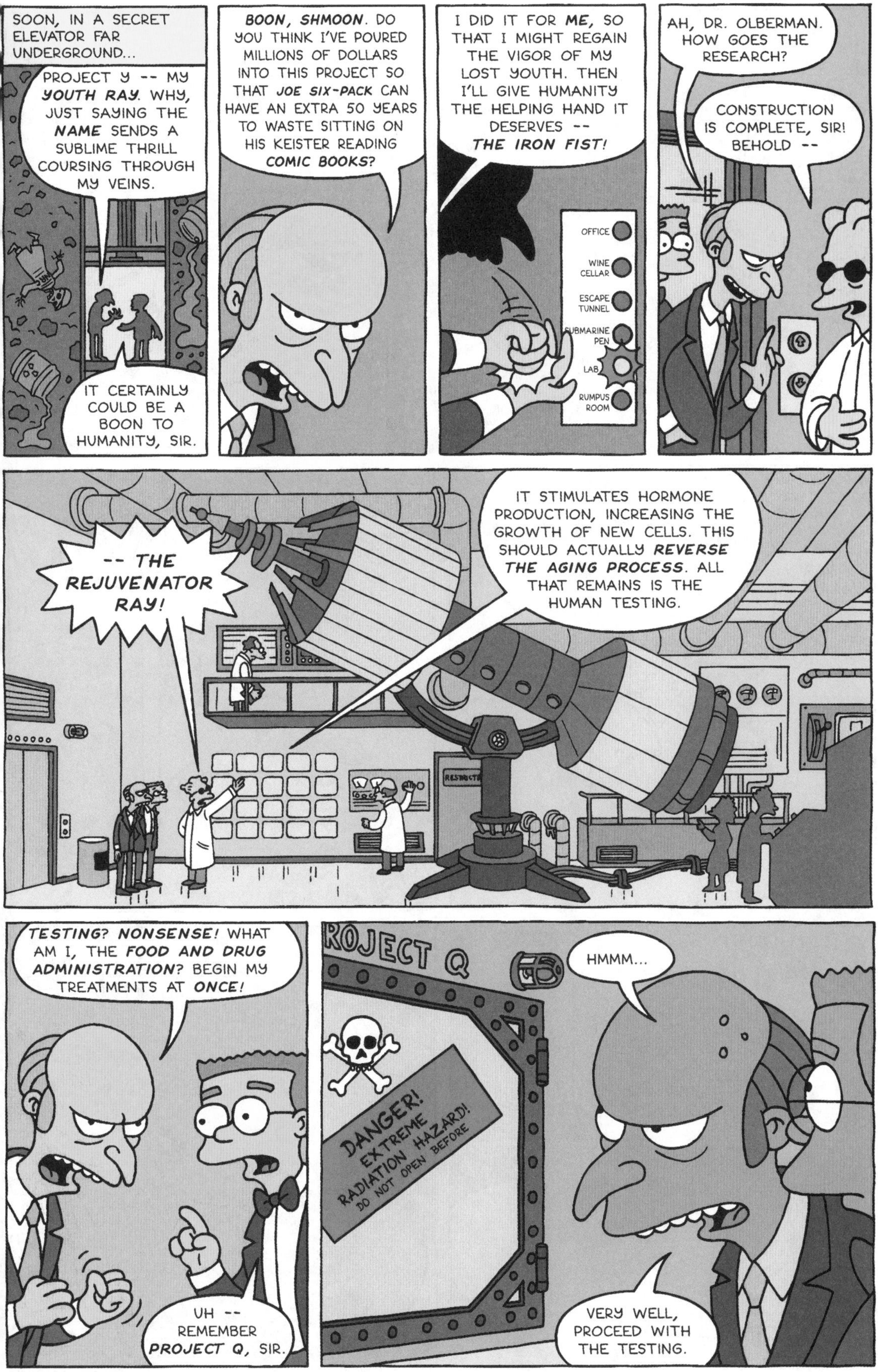

SOON, IN A SECRET ELEVATOR FAR UNDERGROUND...
PROJECT Y -- MY YOUTH RAY. WHY, JUST SAYING THE NAME SENDS A SUBLIME THRILL COURSING THROUGH MY VEINS.
IT CERTAINLY COULD BE A BOON TO HUMANITY, SIR.
BOON, SHMOON. DO YOU THINK I'VE POURED MILLIONS OF DOLLARS INTO THIS PROJECT SO THAT JOE SIX-PACK CAN HAVE AN EXTRA 50 YEARS TO WASTE SITTING ON HIS KEISTER READING COMIC BOOKS?
I DID IT FOR ME, SO THAT I MIGHT REGAIN THE VIGOR OF MY LOST YOUTH. THEN I'LL GIVE HUMANITY THE HELPING HAND IT DESERVES -- THE IRON FIST!
OFFICE
WINE CELLAR
ESCAPE TUNNEL
SUBMARINE PEN
LAB
RUMPUS ROOM
AH, DR. OLBERMAN. HOW GOES THE RESEARCH?
CONSTRUCTION IS COMPLETE, SIR! BEHOLD --
-- THE REJUVENATOR RAY!
IT STIMULATES HORMONE PRODUCTION, INCREASING THE GROWTH OF NEW CELLS. THIS SHOULD ACTUALLY REVERSE THE AGING PROCESS. ALL THAT REMAINS IS THE HUMAN TESTING.
TESTING? NONSENSE! WHAT AM I, THE FOOD AND DRUG ADMINISTRATION? BEGIN MY TREATMENTS AT ONCE!
UH -- REMEMBER PROJECT Q, SIR.
ROJECT Q
DANGER! EXTREME RADIATION HAZARD! DO NOT OPEN BEFORE
HMMM...
VERY WELL, PROCEED WITH THE TESTING.

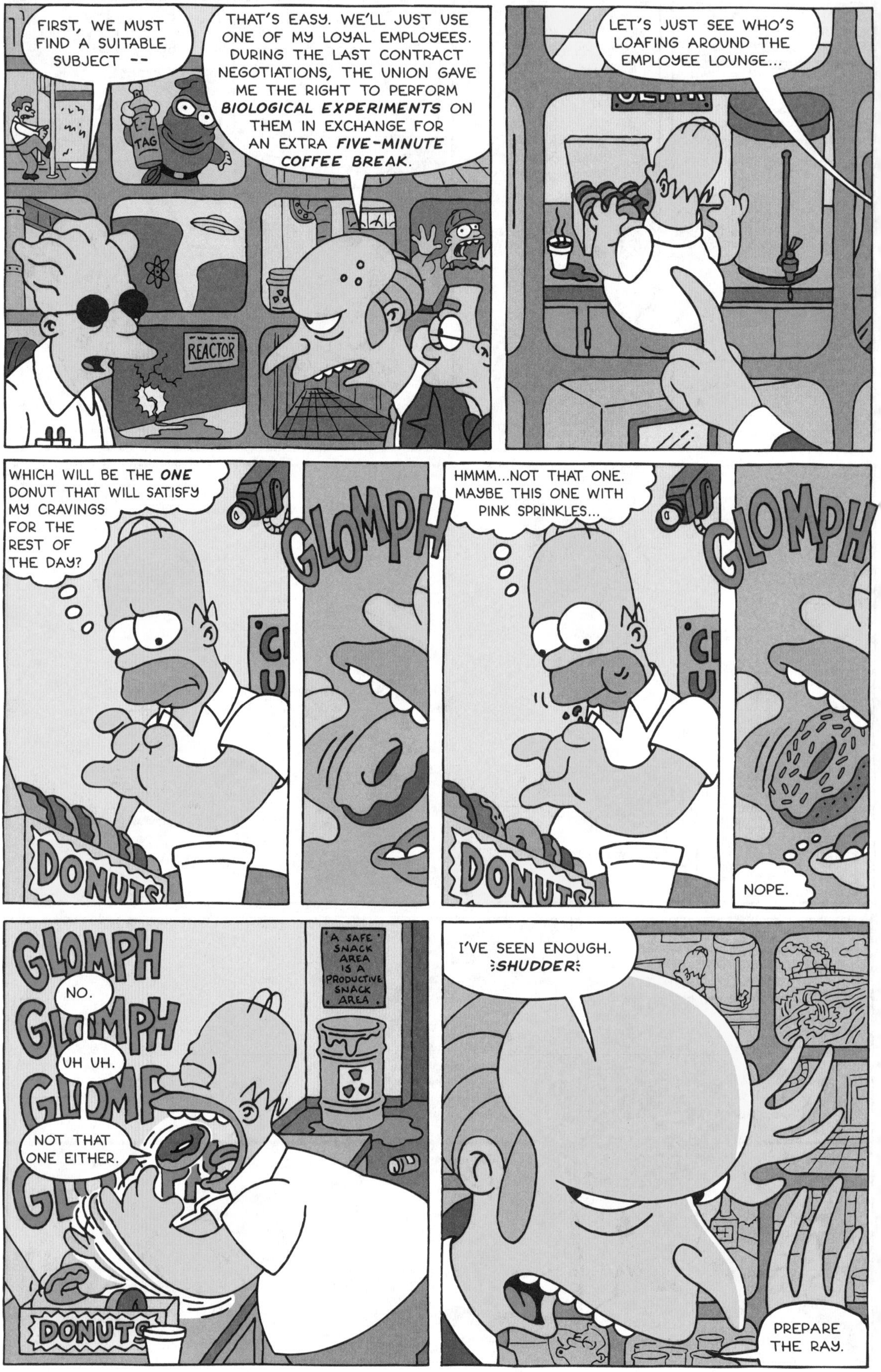
FIRST, WE MUST FIND A SUITABLE SUBJECT --
THAT'S EASY. WE'LL JUST USE ONE OF MY LOYAL EMPLOYEES. DURING THE LAST CONTRACT NEGOTIATIONS, THE UNION GAVE ME THE RIGHT TO PERFORM BIOLOGICAL EXPERIMENTS ON THEM IN EXCHANGE FOR AN EXTRA FIVE-MINUTE COFFEE BREAK.
TAG
REACTOR
LET'S JUST SEE WHO'S LOAFING AROUND THE EMPLOYEE LOUNGE...
WHICH WILL BE THE ONE DONUT THAT WILL SATISFY MY CRAVINGS FOR THE REST OF THE DAY?
DONUTS
GLOMPH
HMMM...NOT THAT ONE. MAYBE THIS ONE WITH PINK SPRINKLES...
DONUTS
GLOMPH
NOPE.
GLOMPH
NO.
GLOMPH
UH UH.
GLOMP
NOT THAT ONE EITHER.
A SAFE SNACK AREA IS A PRODUCTIVE SNACK AREA
DONUTS
I'VE SEEN ENOUGH. SHUDDER
PREPARE THE RAY.

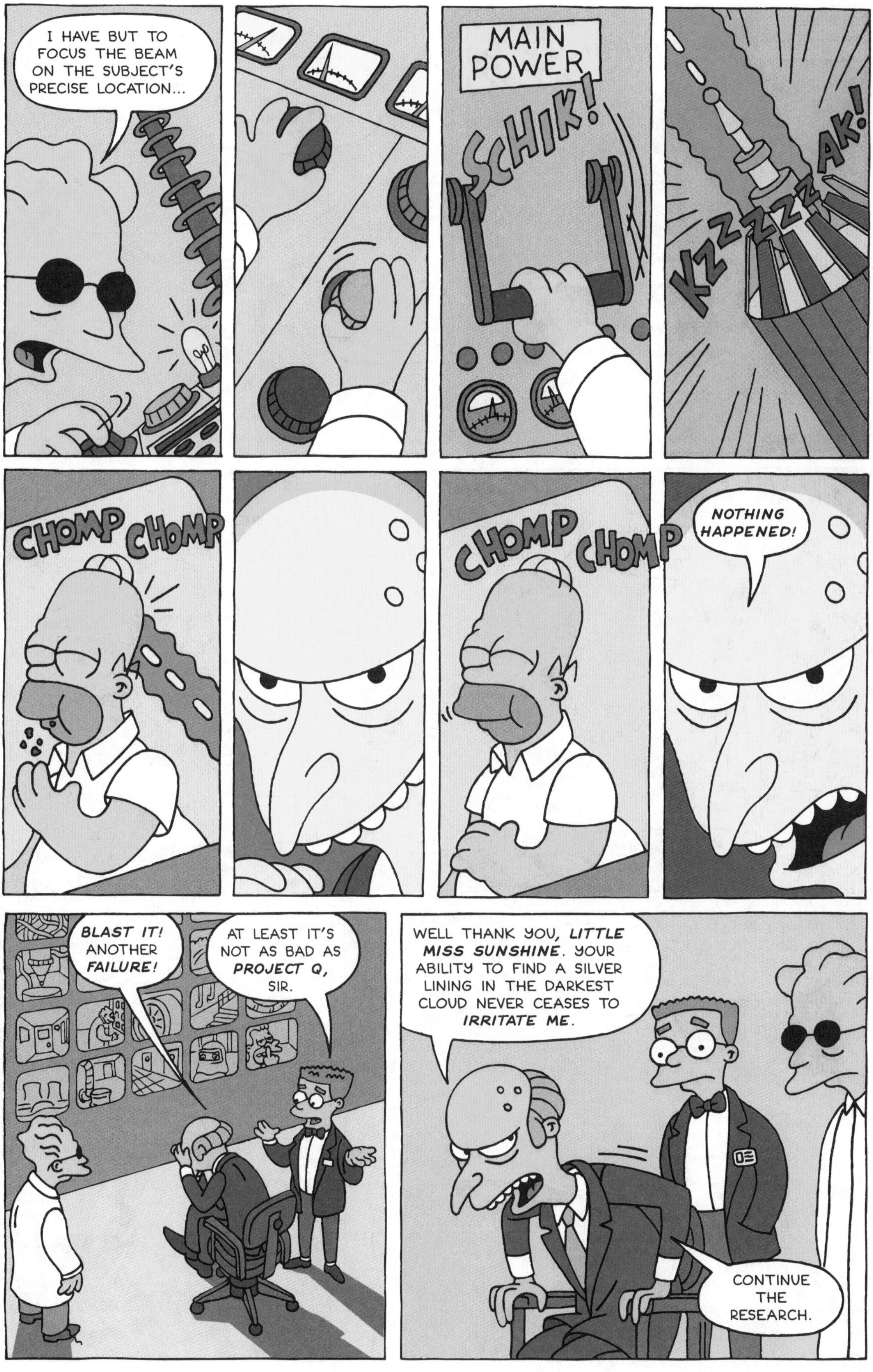
I HAVE BUT TO FOCUS THE BEAM ON THE SUBJECT'S PRECISE LOCATION...
MAIN POWER
SCHIK!
KZZZZZZZAK!
CHOMP CHOMP
CHOMP CHOMP
NOTHING HAPPENED!
BLAST IT! ANOTHER FAILURE!
AT LEAST IT'S NOT AS BAD AS PROJECT Q, SIR.
WELL THANK YOU, LITTLE MISS SUNSHINE. YOUR ABILITY TO FIND A SILVER LINING IN THE DARKEST CLOUD NEVER CEASES TO IRRITATE ME.
CONTINUE THE RESEARCH.

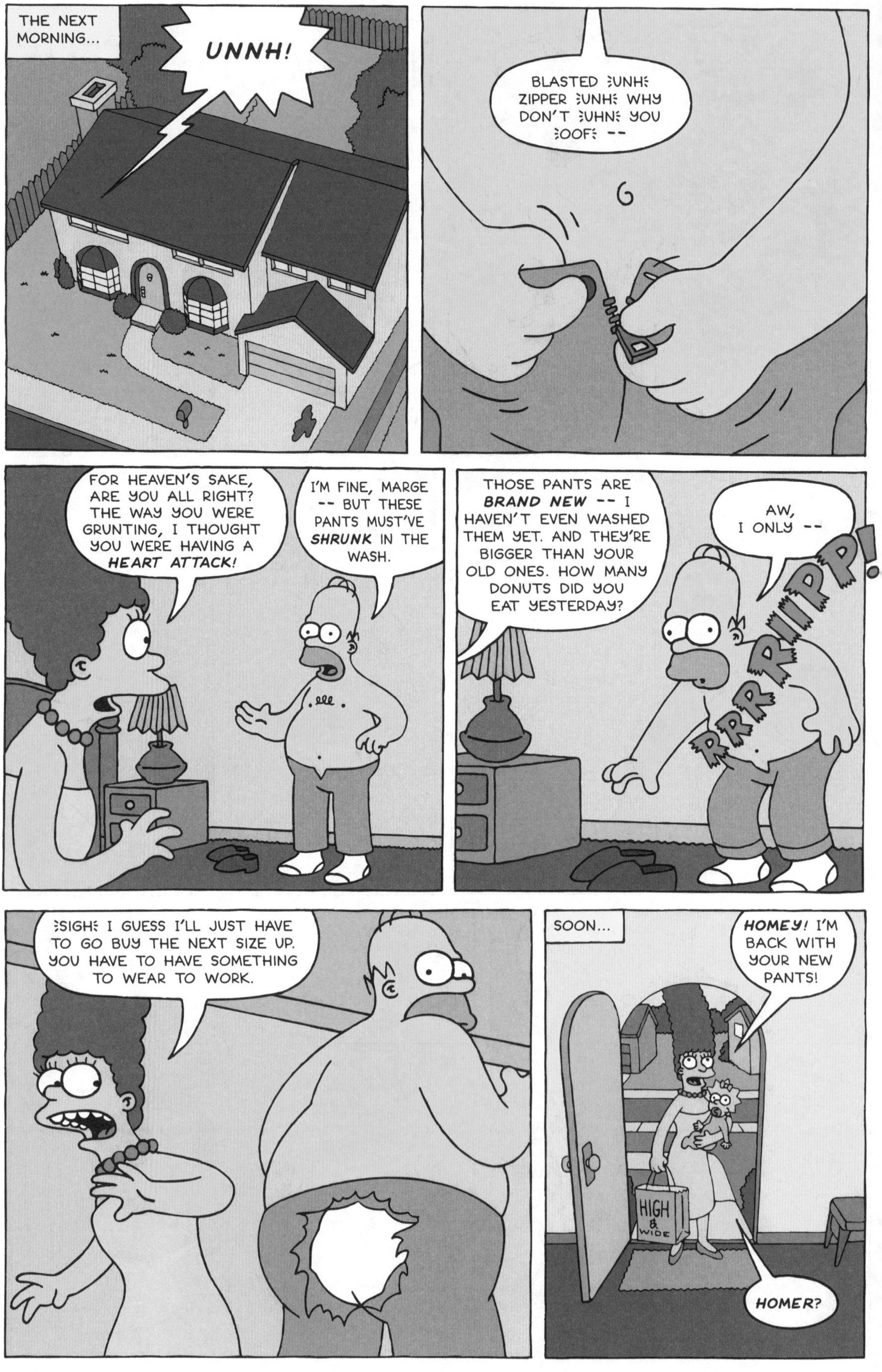
THE NEXT MORNING...
UNNH!
BLASTED ⁝UNH⁝ ZIPPER ⁝UNH⁝ WHY DON'T ⁝UHN⁝ YOU ⁝OOF⁝ --
FOR HEAVEN'S SAKE, ARE YOU ALL RIGHT? THE WAY YOU WERE GRUNTING, I THOUGHT YOU WERE HAVING A HEART ATTACK!
I'M FINE, MARGE -- BUT THESE PANTS MUST'VE SHRUNK IN THE WASH.
THOSE PANTS ARE BRAND NEW -- I HAVEN'T EVEN WASHED THEM YET. AND THEY'RE BIGGER THAN YOUR OLD ONES. HOW MANY DONUTS DID YOU EAT YESTERDAY?
AW, I ONLY --
RRRIIPP!
⁝SIGH⁝ I GUESS I'LL JUST HAVE TO GO BUY THE NEXT SIZE UP. YOU HAVE TO HAVE SOMETHING TO WEAR TO WORK.
SOON...
HOMEY! I'M BACK WITH YOUR NEW PANTS!
HIGH & WIDE
HOMER?

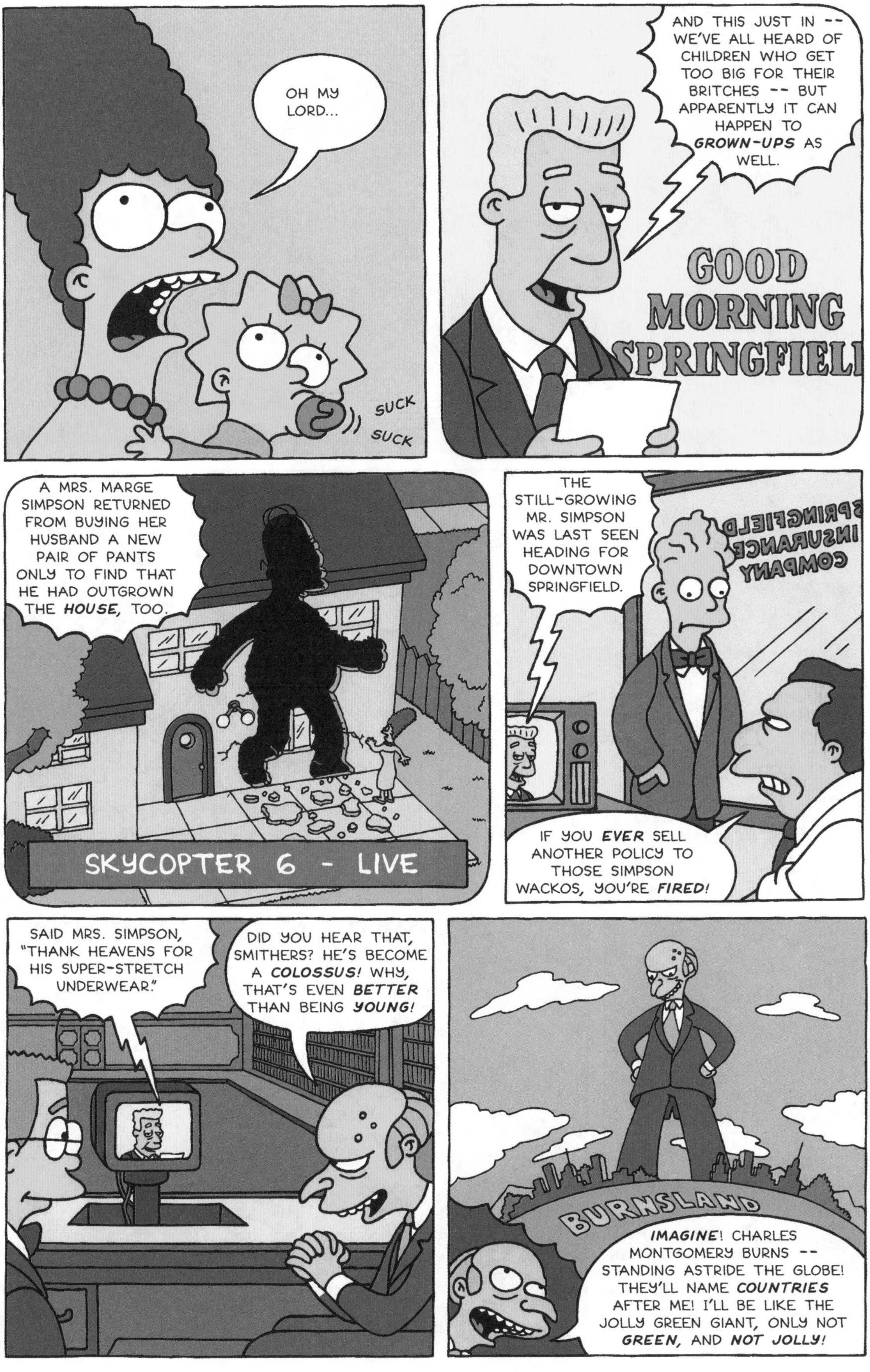
OH MY LORD...
SUCK SUCK
AND THIS JUST IN -- WE'VE ALL HEARD OF CHILDREN WHO GET TOO BIG FOR THEIR BRITCHES -- BUT APPARENTLY IT CAN HAPPEN TO GROWN-UPS AS WELL.
GOOD MORNING SPRINGFIELD
A MRS. MARGE SIMPSON RETURNED FROM BUYING HER HUSBAND A NEW PAIR OF PANTS ONLY TO FIND THAT HE HAD OUTGROWN THE HOUSE, TOO.
SKYCOPTER 6 - LIVE
THE STILL-GROWING MR. SIMPSON WAS LAST SEEN HEADING FOR DOWNTOWN SPRINGFIELD.
SPRINGFIELD INSURANCE COMPANY
IF YOU EVER SELL ANOTHER POLICY TO THOSE SIMPSON WACKOS, YOU'RE FIRED!
SAID MRS. SIMPSON, "THANK HEAVENS FOR HIS SUPER-STRETCH UNDERWEAR."
DID YOU HEAR THAT, SMITHERS? HE'S BECOME A COLOSSUS! WHY, THAT'S EVEN BETTER THAN BEING YOUNG!
BURNSLAND
IMAGINE! CHARLES MONTGOMERY BURNS -- STANDING ASTRIDE THE GLOBE! THEY'LL NAME COUNTRIES AFTER ME! I'LL BE LIKE THE JOLLY GREEN GIANT, ONLY NOT GREEN, AND NOT JOLLY!

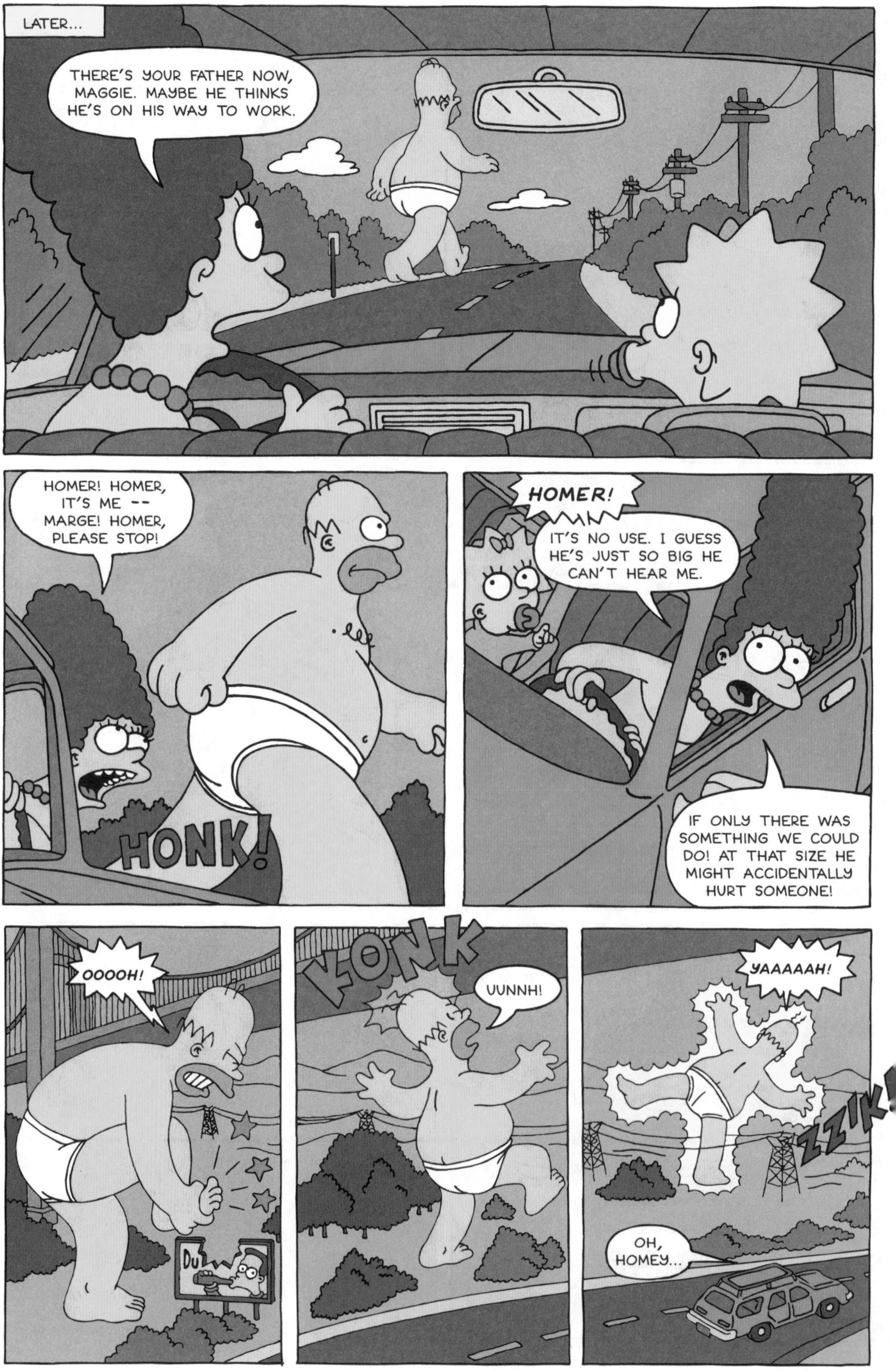
LATER...
THERE'S YOUR FATHER NOW, MAGGIE. MAYBE HE THINKS HE'S ON HIS WAY TO WORK.
HOMER! HOMER, IT'S ME -- MARGE! HOMER, PLEASE STOP!
HONK!
HOMER!
IT'S NO USE. I GUESS HE'S JUST SO BIG HE CAN'T HEAR ME.
IF ONLY THERE WAS SOMETHING WE COULD DO! AT THAT SIZE HE MIGHT ACCIDENTALLY HURT SOMEONE!
OOOOH!
KONK
UUNNH!
YAAAAAH!
ZZIK!
OH, HOMEY...

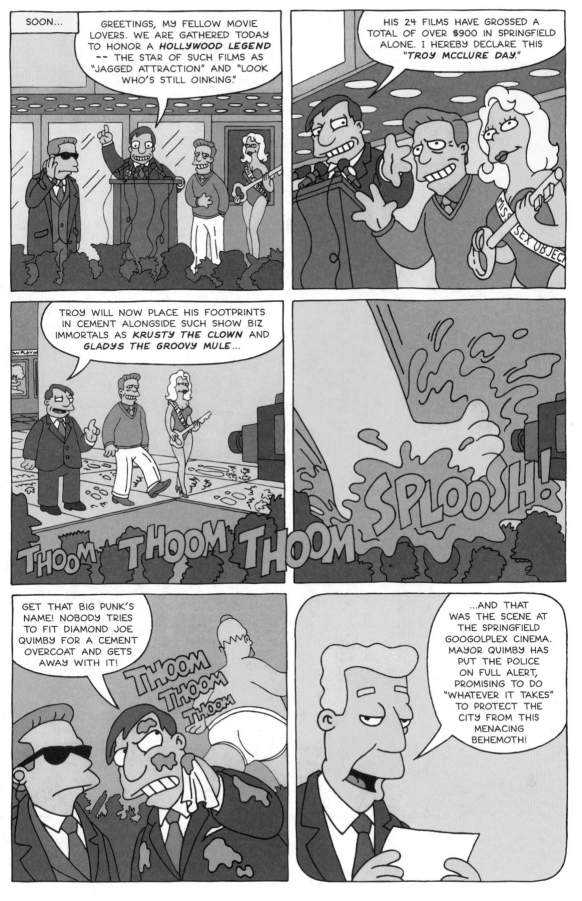

SOON...

GREETINGS, MY FELLOW MOVIE LOVERS. WE ARE GATHERED TODAY TO HONOR A **HOLLYWOOD LEGEND** -- THE STAR OF SUCH FILMS AS "JAGGED ATTRACTION" AND "LOOK WHO'S STILL OINKING."

HIS 24 FILMS HAVE GROSSED A TOTAL OF OVER $900 IN SPRINGFIELD ALONE. I HEREBY DECLARE THIS **"TROY McCLURE DAY."**

TROY WILL NOW PLACE HIS FOOTPRINTS IN CEMENT ALONGSIDE SUCH SHOW BIZ IMMORTALS AS **KRUSTY THE CLOWN** AND **GLADYS THE GROOVY MULE**...

THOOM THOOM THOOM

SPLOOSH!

GET THAT BIG PUNK'S NAME! NOBODY TRIES TO FIT DIAMOND JOE QUIMBY FOR A CEMENT OVERCOAT AND GETS AWAY WITH IT!

THOOM THOOM THOOM

...AND THAT WAS THE SCENE AT THE SPRINGFIELD GOOGOLPLEX CINEMA. MAYOR QUIMBY HAS PUT THE POLICE ON FULL ALERT, PROMISING TO DO "WHATEVER IT TAKES" TO PROTECT THE CITY FROM THIS MENACING BEHEMOTH!

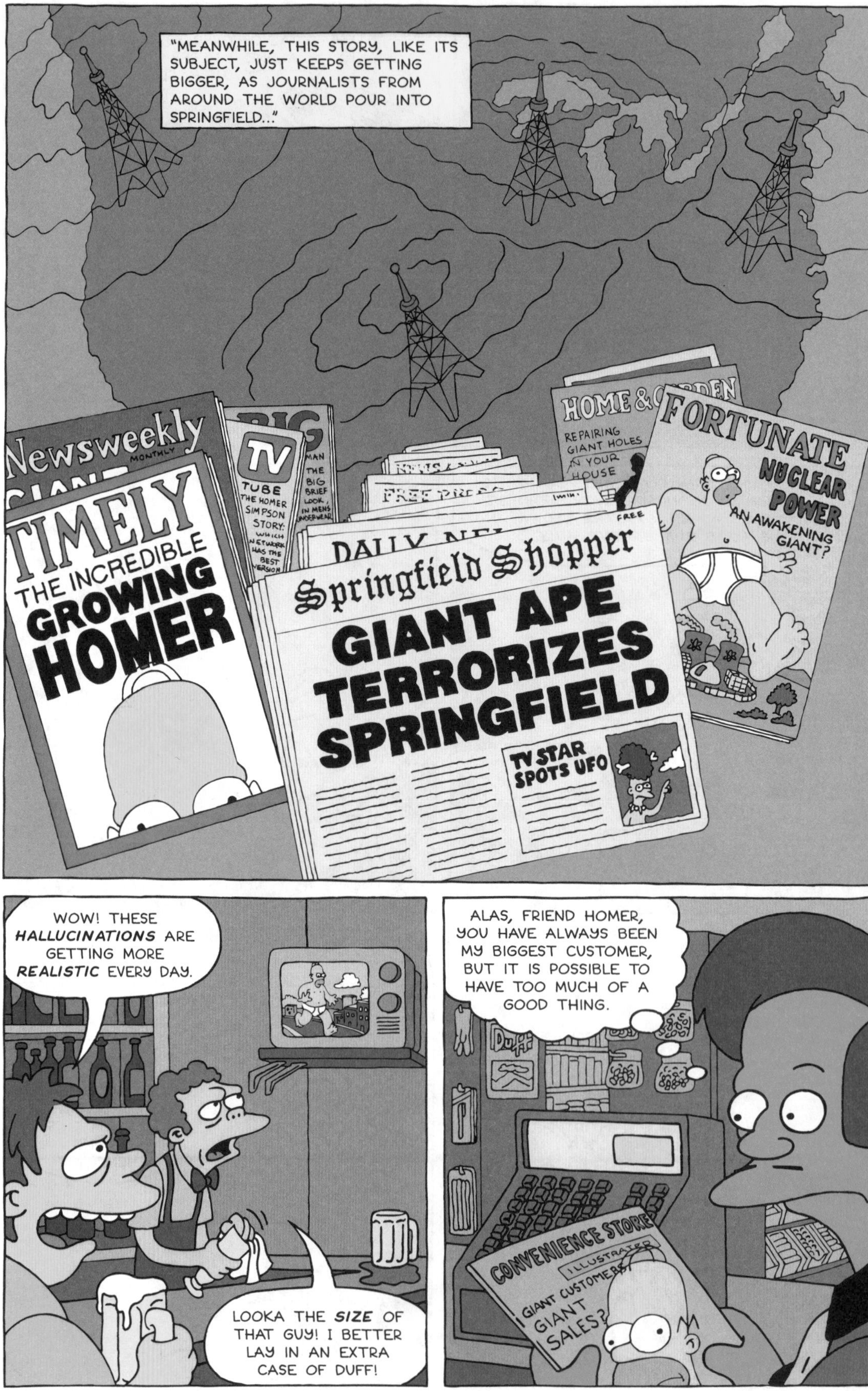
"MEANWHILE, THIS STORY, LIKE ITS SUBJECT, JUST KEEPS GETTING BIGGER, AS JOURNALISTS FROM AROUND THE WORLD POUR INTO SPRINGFIELD..."
Newsweekly MONTHLY
TIMELY
THE INCREDIBLE GROWING HOMER
TV TUBE
THE HOMER SIMPSON STORY: WHICH NETWORK HAS THE BEST VERSION
MAN THE BIG BRIEF LOOK IN MENS UNDERWEAR
REPAIRING GIANT HOLES IN YOUR HOUSE
FORTUNATE
NUCLEAR POWER
AN AWAKENING GIANT?
FREE
Springfield Shopper
GIANT APE TERRORIZES SPRINGFIELD
TV STAR SPOTS UFO
WOW! THESE *HALLUCINATIONS* ARE GETTING MORE *REALISTIC* EVERY DAY.
LOOKA THE *SIZE* OF THAT GUY! I BETTER LAY IN AN EXTRA CASE OF DUFF!
ALAS, FRIEND HOMER, YOU HAVE ALWAYS BEEN MY BIGGEST CUSTOMER, BUT IT IS POSSIBLE TO HAVE TOO MUCH OF A GOOD THING.
CONVENIENCE STORE
ILLUSTRATED
GIANT CUSTOMERS GIANT SALES?

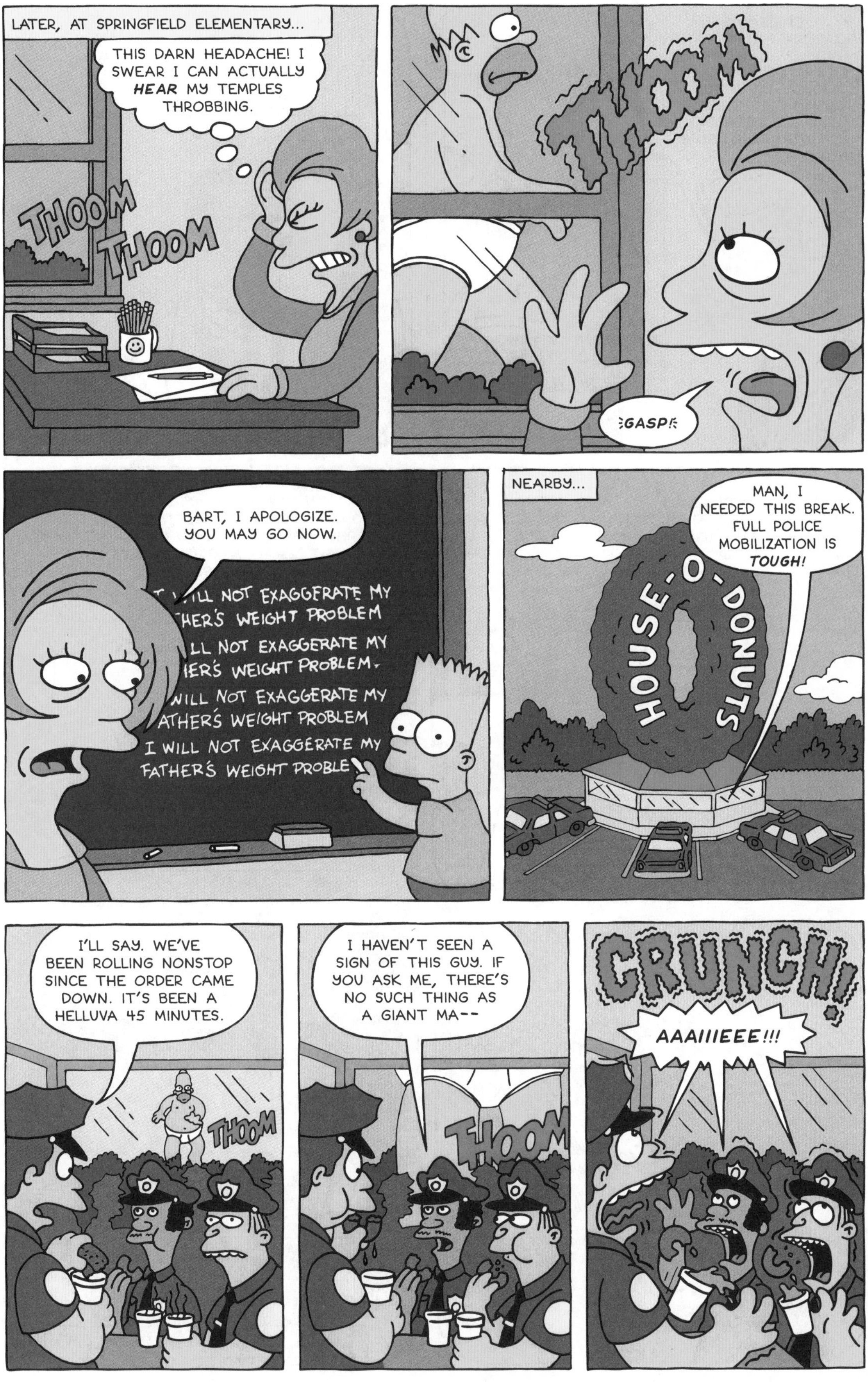
LATER, AT SPRINGFIELD ELEMENTARY...
THIS DARN HEADACHE! I SWEAR I CAN ACTUALLY **HEAR** MY TEMPLES THROBBING.
THOOM THOOM
THOOM
GASP!
BART, I APOLOGIZE. YOU MAY GO NOW.
I WILL NOT EXAGGFRATE MY FATHER'S WEIGHT PROBLEM
I WILL NOT EXAGGERATE MY FATHER'S WEIGHT PROBLEM.
I WILL NOT EXAGGERATE MY FATHER'S WEIGHT PROBLEM
I WILL NOT EXAGGERATE MY FATHER'S WEIGHT PROBLE
NEARBY...
MAN, I NEEDED THIS BREAK. FULL POLICE MOBILIZATION IS **TOUGH!**
HOUSE-O-DONUTS
I'LL SAY. WE'VE BEEN ROLLING NONSTOP SINCE THE ORDER CAME DOWN. IT'S BEEN A HELLUVA 45 MINUTES.
THOOM
I HAVEN'T SEEN A SIGN OF THIS GUY. IF YOU ASK ME, THERE'S NO SUCH THING AS A GIANT MA--
THOOM
CRUNCH!
AAAIIIEEE!!!

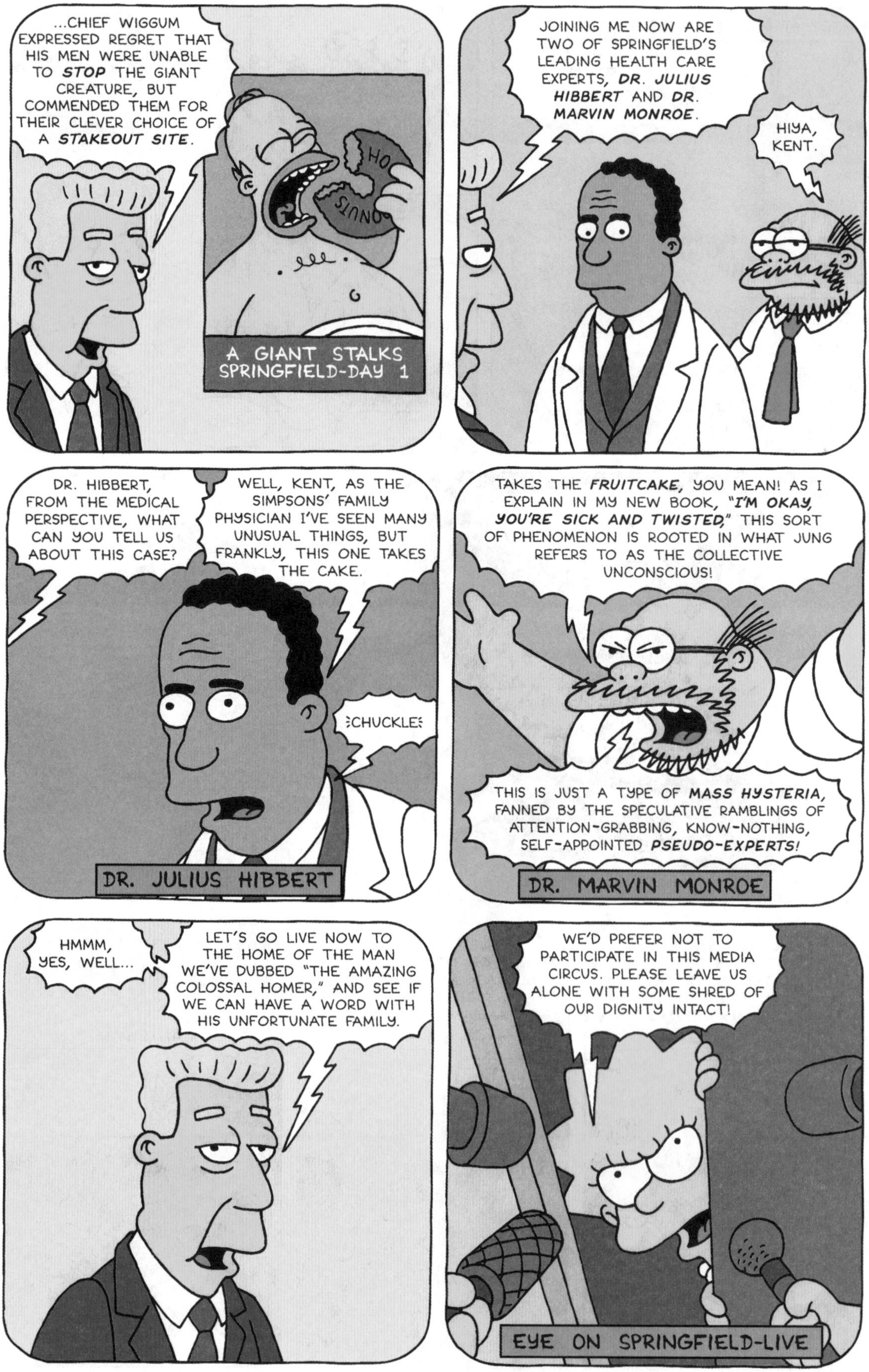
...CHIEF WIGGUM EXPRESSED REGRET THAT HIS MEN WERE UNABLE TO STOP THE GIANT CREATURE, BUT COMMENDED THEM FOR THEIR CLEVER CHOICE OF A STAKEOUT SITE.
A GIANT STALKS SPRINGFIELD-DAY 1
JOINING ME NOW ARE TWO OF SPRINGFIELD'S LEADING HEALTH CARE EXPERTS, DR. JULIUS HIBBERT AND DR. MARVIN MONROE.
HIYA, KENT.
DR. HIBBERT, FROM THE MEDICAL PERSPECTIVE, WHAT CAN YOU TELL US ABOUT THIS CASE?
WELL, KENT, AS THE SIMPSONS' FAMILY PHYSICIAN I'VE SEEN MANY UNUSUAL THINGS, BUT FRANKLY, THIS ONE TAKES THE CAKE.
CHUCKLE
DR. JULIUS HIBBERT
TAKES THE FRUITCAKE, YOU MEAN! AS I EXPLAIN IN MY NEW BOOK, "I'M OKAY, YOU'RE SICK AND TWISTED," THIS SORT OF PHENOMENON IS ROOTED IN WHAT JUNG REFERS TO AS THE COLLECTIVE UNCONSCIOUS!
THIS IS JUST A TYPE OF MASS HYSTERIA, FANNED BY THE SPECULATIVE RAMBLINGS OF ATTENTION-GRABBING, KNOW-NOTHING, SELF-APPOINTED PSEUDO-EXPERTS!
DR. MARVIN MONROE
HMMM, YES, WELL...
LET'S GO LIVE NOW TO THE HOME OF THE MAN WE'VE DUBBED "THE AMAZING COLOSSAL HOMER," AND SEE IF WE CAN HAVE A WORD WITH HIS UNFORTUNATE FAMILY.
WE'D PREFER NOT TO PARTICIPATE IN THIS MEDIA CIRCUS. PLEASE LEAVE US ALONE WITH SOME SHRED OF OUR DIGNITY INTACT!
EYE ON SPRINGFIELD-LIVE

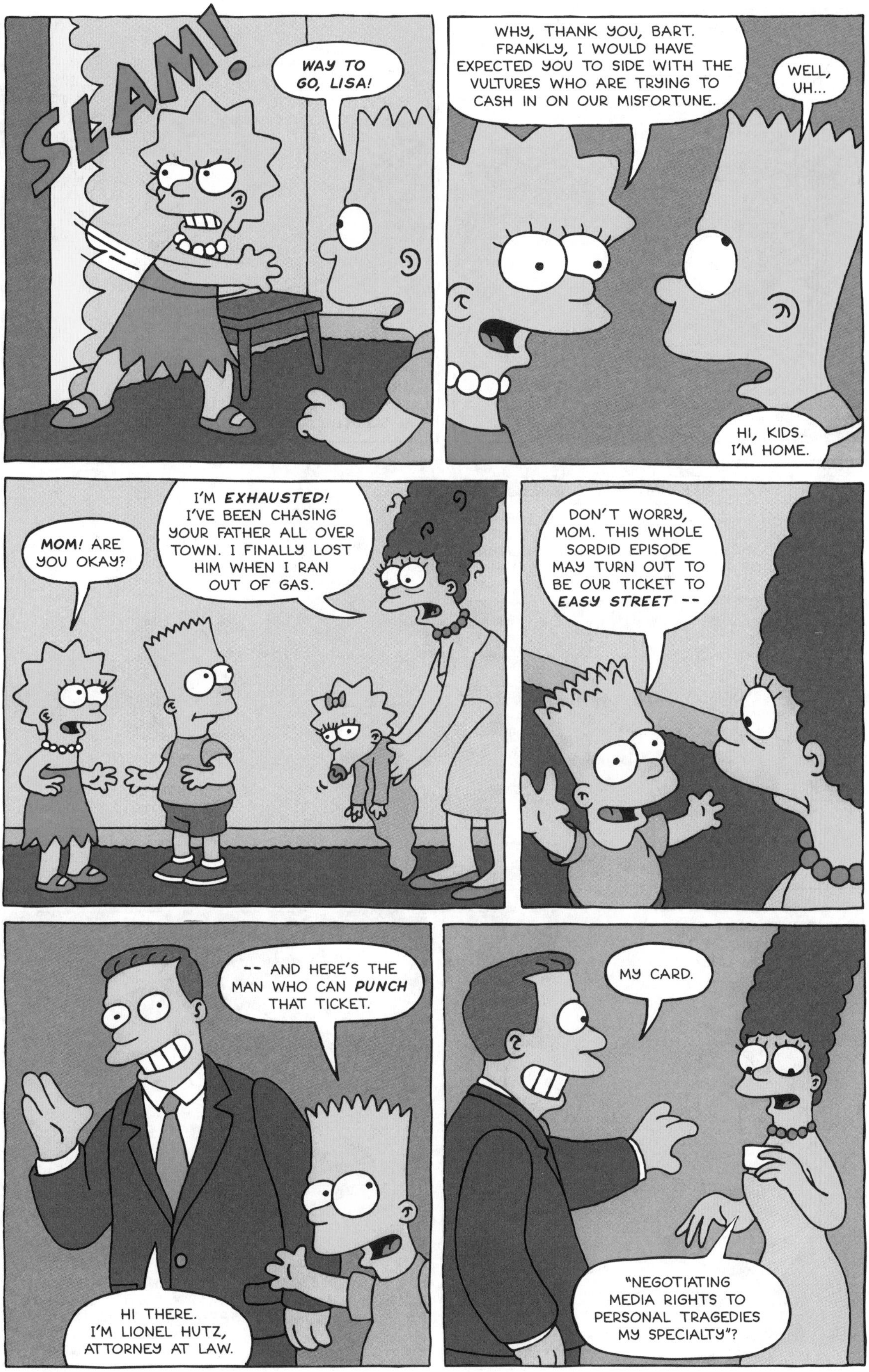
SLAM!
WAY TO GO, LISA!
WHY, THANK YOU, BART. FRANKLY, I WOULD HAVE EXPECTED YOU TO SIDE WITH THE VULTURES WHO ARE TRYING TO CASH IN ON OUR MISFORTUNE.
WELL, UH...
HI, KIDS. I'M HOME.
MOM! ARE YOU OKAY?
I'M EXHAUSTED! I'VE BEEN CHASING YOUR FATHER ALL OVER TOWN. I FINALLY LOST HIM WHEN I RAN OUT OF GAS.
DON'T WORRY, MOM. THIS WHOLE SORDID EPISODE MAY TURN OUT TO BE OUR TICKET TO EASY STREET --
-- AND HERE'S THE MAN WHO CAN PUNCH THAT TICKET.
HI THERE. I'M LIONEL HUTZ, ATTORNEY AT LAW.
MY CARD.
"NEGOTIATING MEDIA RIGHTS TO PERSONAL TRAGEDIES MY SPECIALTY"?

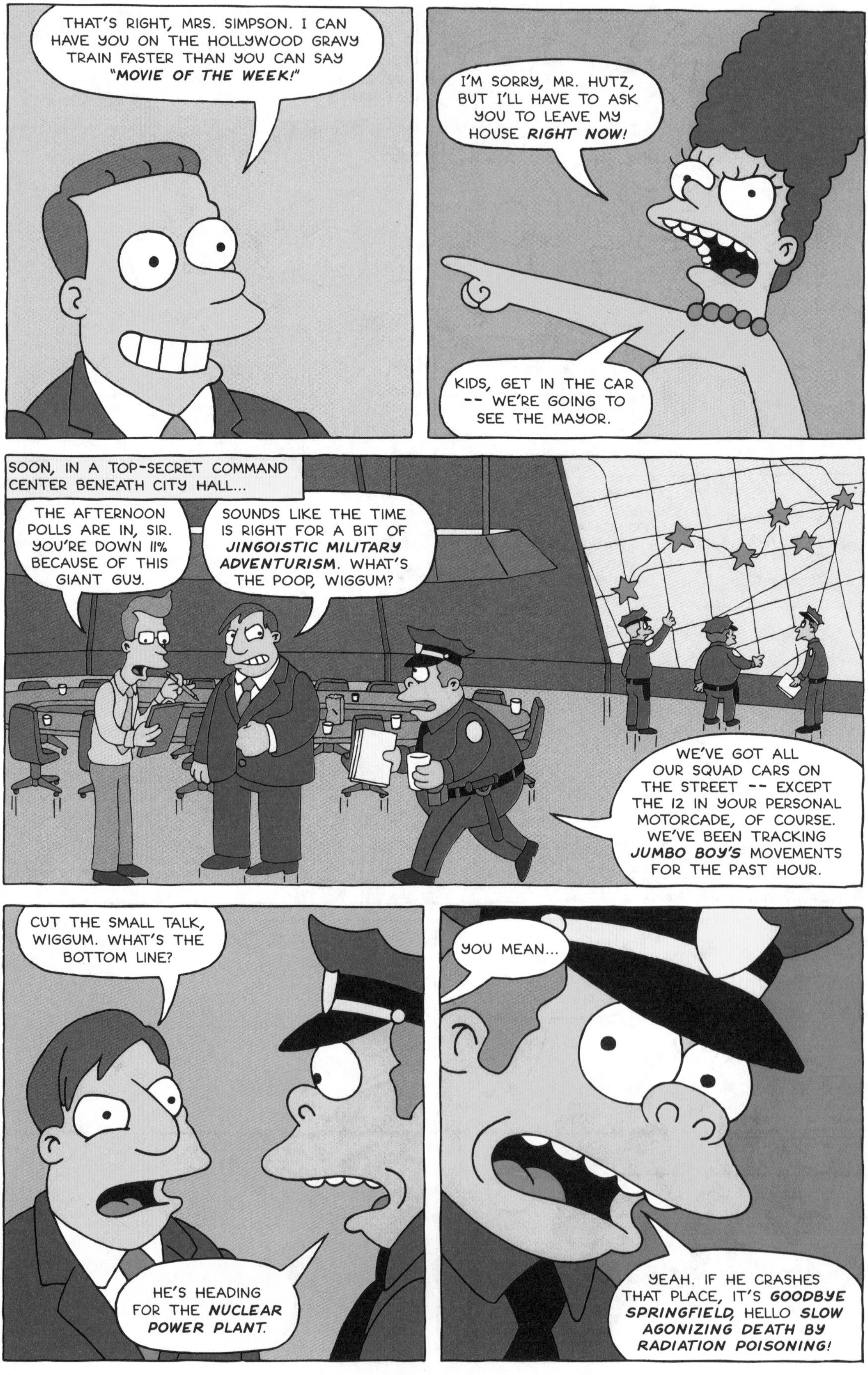
THAT'S RIGHT, MRS. SIMPSON. I CAN HAVE YOU ON THE HOLLYWOOD GRAVY TRAIN FASTER THAN YOU CAN SAY "MOVIE OF THE WEEK!"
I'M SORRY, MR. HUTZ, BUT I'LL HAVE TO ASK YOU TO LEAVE MY HOUSE RIGHT NOW!
KIDS, GET IN THE CAR -- WE'RE GOING TO SEE THE MAYOR.
SOON, IN A TOP-SECRET COMMAND CENTER BENEATH CITY HALL...
THE AFTERNOON POLLS ARE IN, SIR. YOU'RE DOWN 11% BECAUSE OF THIS GIANT GUY.
SOUNDS LIKE THE TIME IS RIGHT FOR A BIT OF JINGOISTIC MILITARY ADVENTURISM. WHAT'S THE POOP, WIGGUM?
WE'VE GOT ALL OUR SQUAD CARS ON THE STREET -- EXCEPT THE 12 IN YOUR PERSONAL MOTORCADE, OF COURSE. WE'VE BEEN TRACKING JUMBO BOY'S MOVEMENTS FOR THE PAST HOUR.
CUT THE SMALL TALK, WIGGUM. WHAT'S THE BOTTOM LINE?
HE'S HEADING FOR THE NUCLEAR POWER PLANT.
YOU MEAN...
YEAH. IF HE CRASHES THAT PLACE, IT'S GOODBYE SPRINGFIELD, HELLO SLOW AGONIZING DEATH BY RADIATION POISONING!

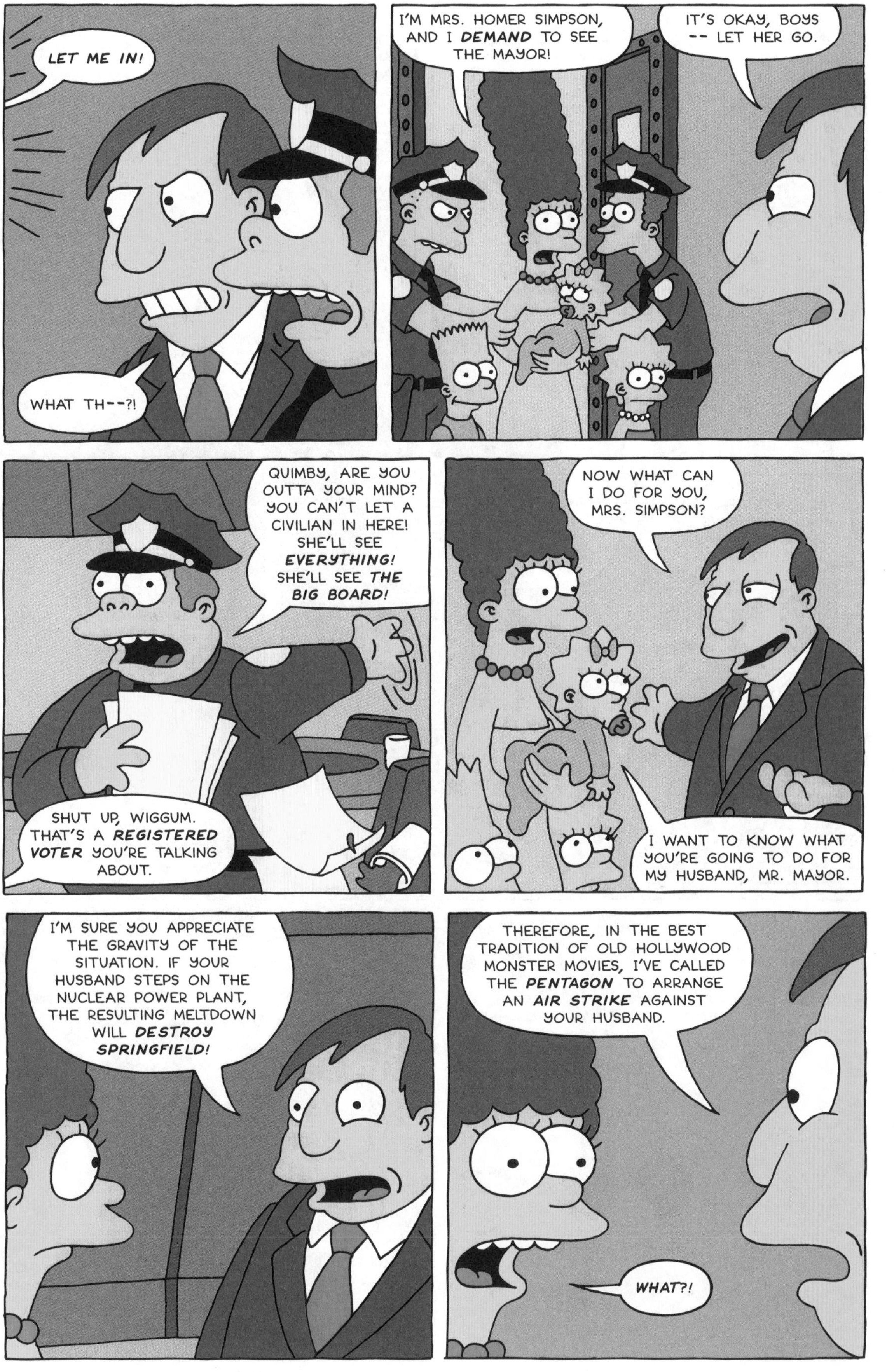
LET ME IN!
WHAT TH--?!
I'M MRS. HOMER SIMPSON, AND I DEMAND TO SEE THE MAYOR!
IT'S OKAY, BOYS -- LET HER GO.
QUIMBY, ARE YOU OUTTA YOUR MIND? YOU CAN'T LET A CIVILIAN IN HERE! SHE'LL SEE EVERYTHING! SHE'LL SEE THE BIG BOARD!
SHUT UP, WIGGUM. THAT'S A REGISTERED VOTER YOU'RE TALKING ABOUT.
NOW WHAT CAN I DO FOR YOU, MRS. SIMPSON?
I WANT TO KNOW WHAT YOU'RE GOING TO DO FOR MY HUSBAND, MR. MAYOR.
I'M SURE YOU APPRECIATE THE GRAVITY OF THE SITUATION. IF YOUR HUSBAND STEPS ON THE NUCLEAR POWER PLANT, THE RESULTING MELTDOWN WILL DESTROY SPRINGFIELD!
THEREFORE, IN THE BEST TRADITION OF OLD HOLLYWOOD MONSTER MOVIES, I'VE CALLED THE PENTAGON TO ARRANGE AN AIR STRIKE AGAINST YOUR HUSBAND.
WHAT?!

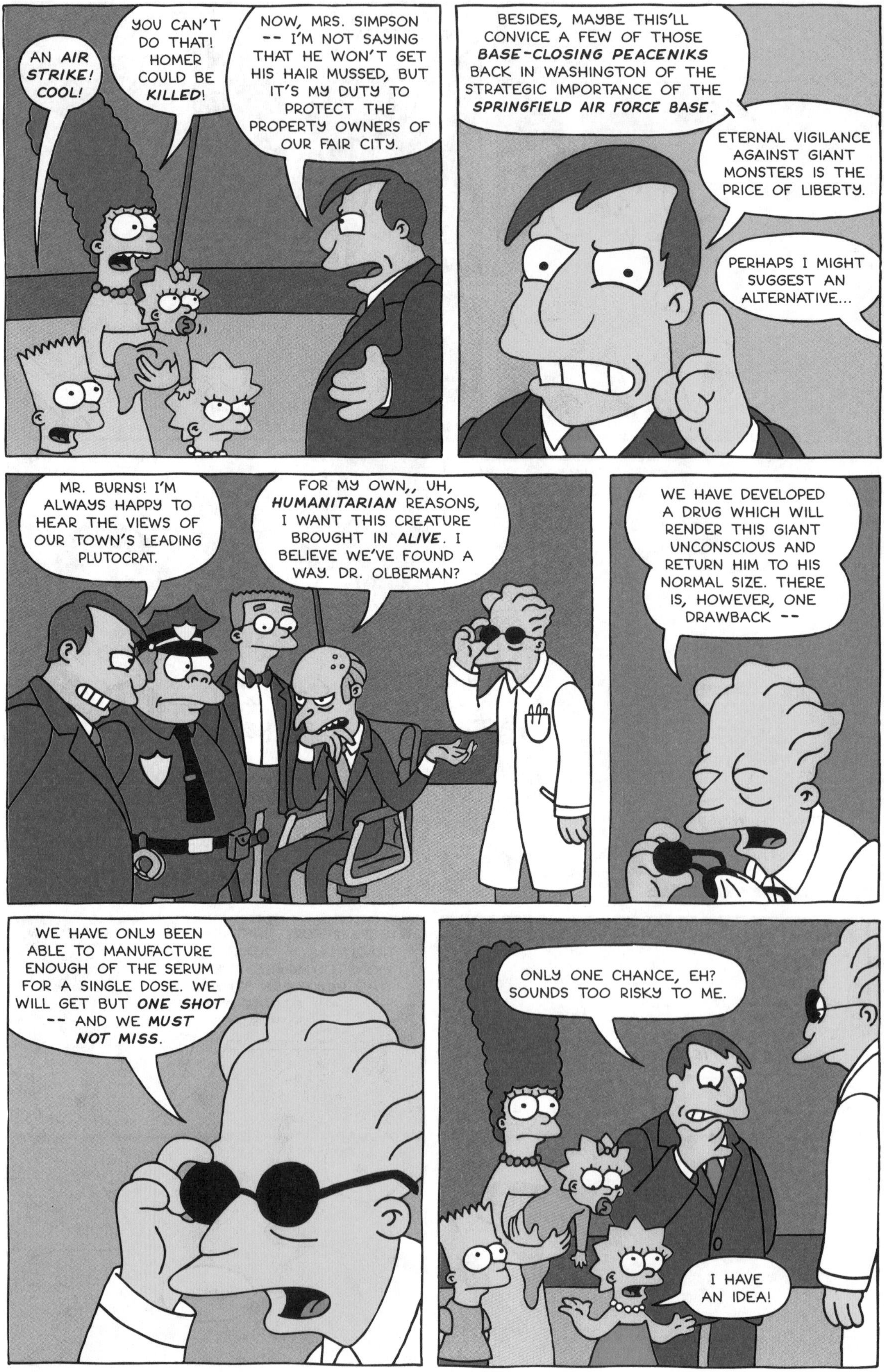
AN AIR STRIKE! COOL!
YOU CAN'T DO THAT! HOMER COULD BE KILLED!
NOW, MRS. SIMPSON -- I'M NOT SAYING THAT HE WON'T GET HIS HAIR MUSSED, BUT IT'S MY DUTY TO PROTECT THE PROPERTY OWNERS OF OUR FAIR CITY.
BESIDES, MAYBE THIS'LL CONVICE A FEW OF THOSE BASE-CLOSING PEACENIKS BACK IN WASHINGTON OF THE STRATEGIC IMPORTANCE OF THE SPRINGFIELD AIR FORCE BASE.
ETERNAL VIGILANCE AGAINST GIANT MONSTERS IS THE PRICE OF LIBERTY.
PERHAPS I MIGHT SUGGEST AN ALTERNATIVE...
MR. BURNS! I'M ALWAYS HAPPY TO HEAR THE VIEWS OF OUR TOWN'S LEADING PLUTOCRAT.
FOR MY OWN,, UH, HUMANITARIAN REASONS, I WANT THIS CREATURE BROUGHT IN ALIVE. I BELIEVE WE'VE FOUND A WAY. DR. OLBERMAN?
WE HAVE DEVELOPED A DRUG WHICH WILL RENDER THIS GIANT UNCONSCIOUS AND RETURN HIM TO HIS NORMAL SIZE. THERE IS, HOWEVER, ONE DRAWBACK --
WE HAVE ONLY BEEN ABLE TO MANUFACTURE ENOUGH OF THE SERUM FOR A SINGLE DOSE. WE WILL GET BUT ONE SHOT -- AND WE MUST NOT MISS.
ONLY ONE CHANCE, EH? SOUNDS TOO RISKY TO ME.
I HAVE AN IDEA!

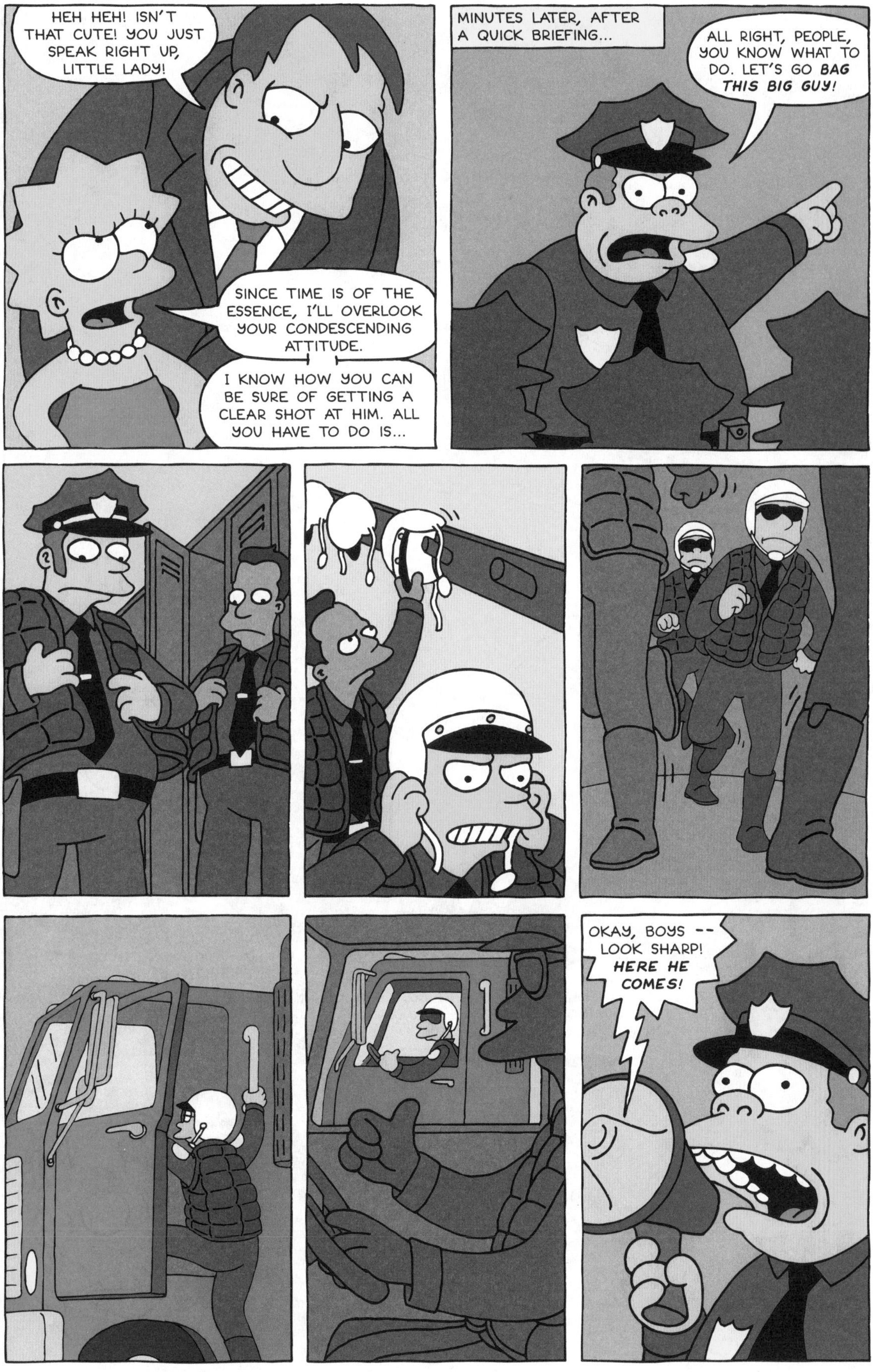

HEH HEH! ISN'T THAT CUTE! YOU JUST SPEAK RIGHT UP, LITTLE LADY!
SINCE TIME IS OF THE ESSENCE, I'LL OVERLOOK YOUR CONDESCENDING ATTITUDE.
I KNOW HOW YOU CAN BE SURE OF GETTING A CLEAR SHOT AT HIM. ALL YOU HAVE TO DO IS...
MINUTES LATER, AFTER A QUICK BRIEFING...
ALL RIGHT, PEOPLE, YOU KNOW WHAT TO DO. LET'S GO **BAG THIS BIG GUY**!
OKAY, BOYS -- LOOK SHARP! **HERE HE COMES**!

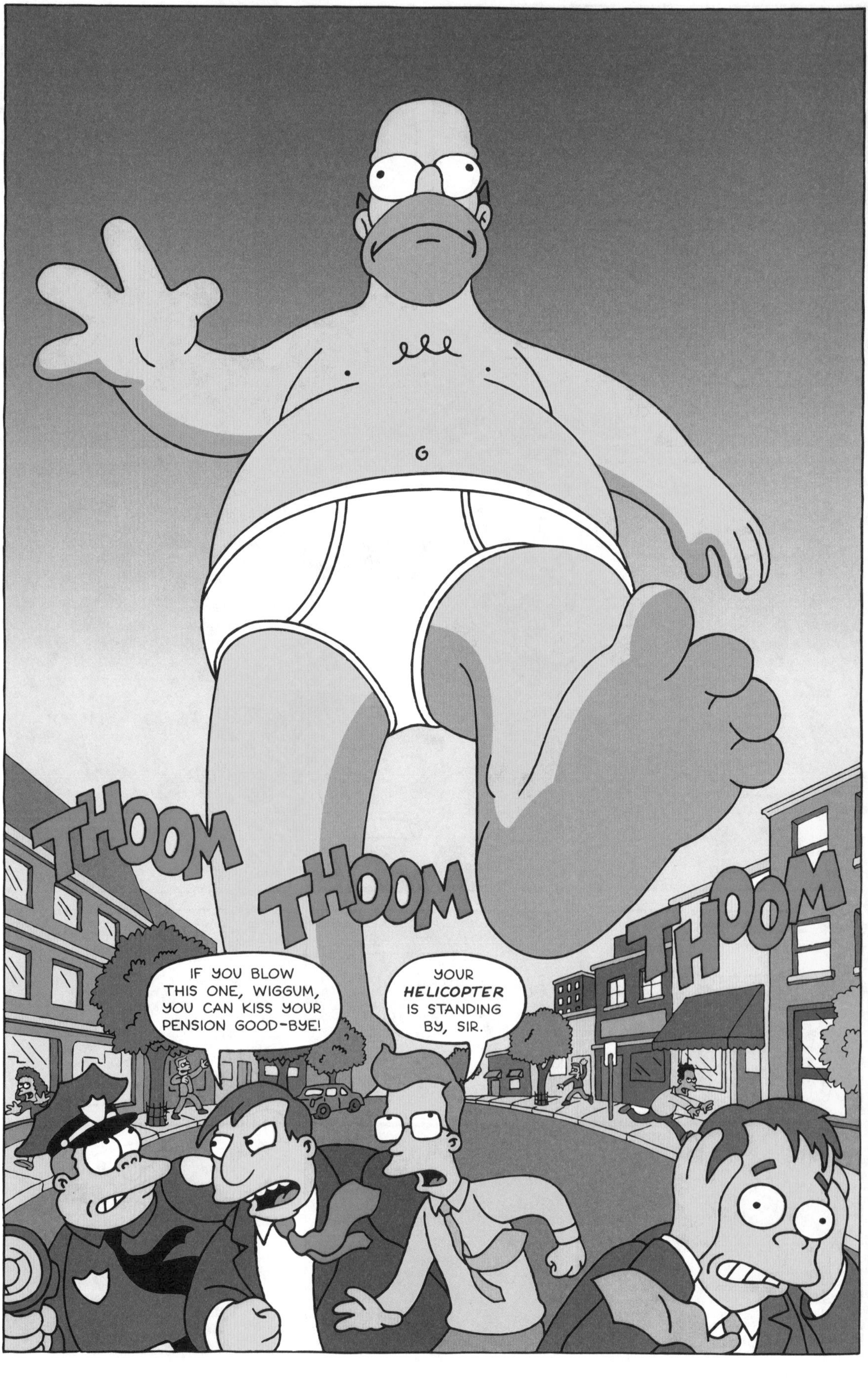
THOOM
THOOM
THOOM
IF YOU BLOW THIS ONE, WIGGUM, YOU CAN KISS YOUR PENSION GOOD-BYE!
YOUR HELICOPTER IS STANDING BY, SIR.

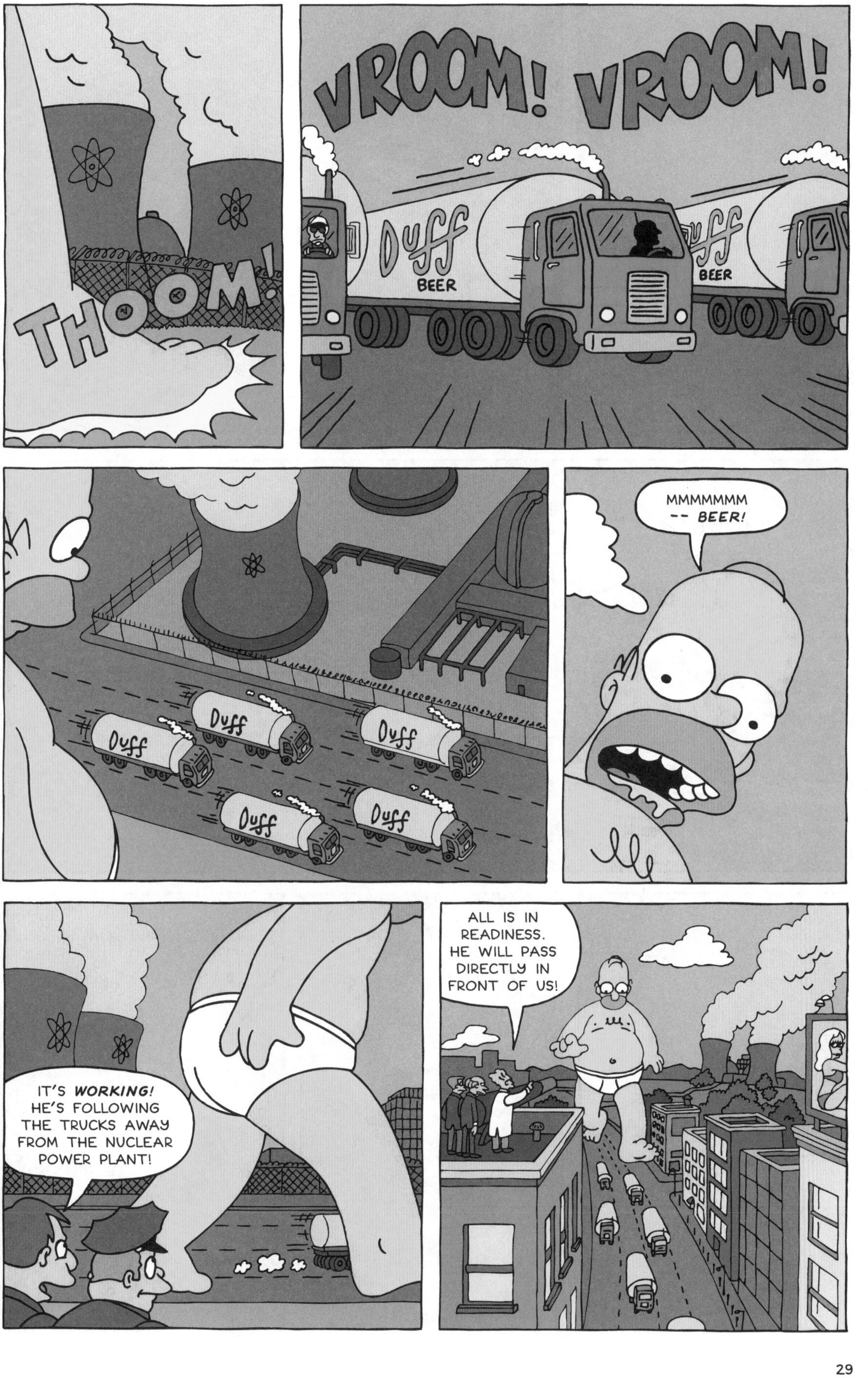
THOOM!
VROOM! VROOM!
DUFF BEER
DUFF BEER
Duff
Duff
Duff
Duff
Duff
MMMMMMM -- BEER!
IT'S WORKING! HE'S FOLLOWING THE TRUCKS AWAY FROM THE NUCLEAR POWER PLANT!
ALL IS IN READINESS. HE WILL PASS DIRECTLY IN FRONT OF US!

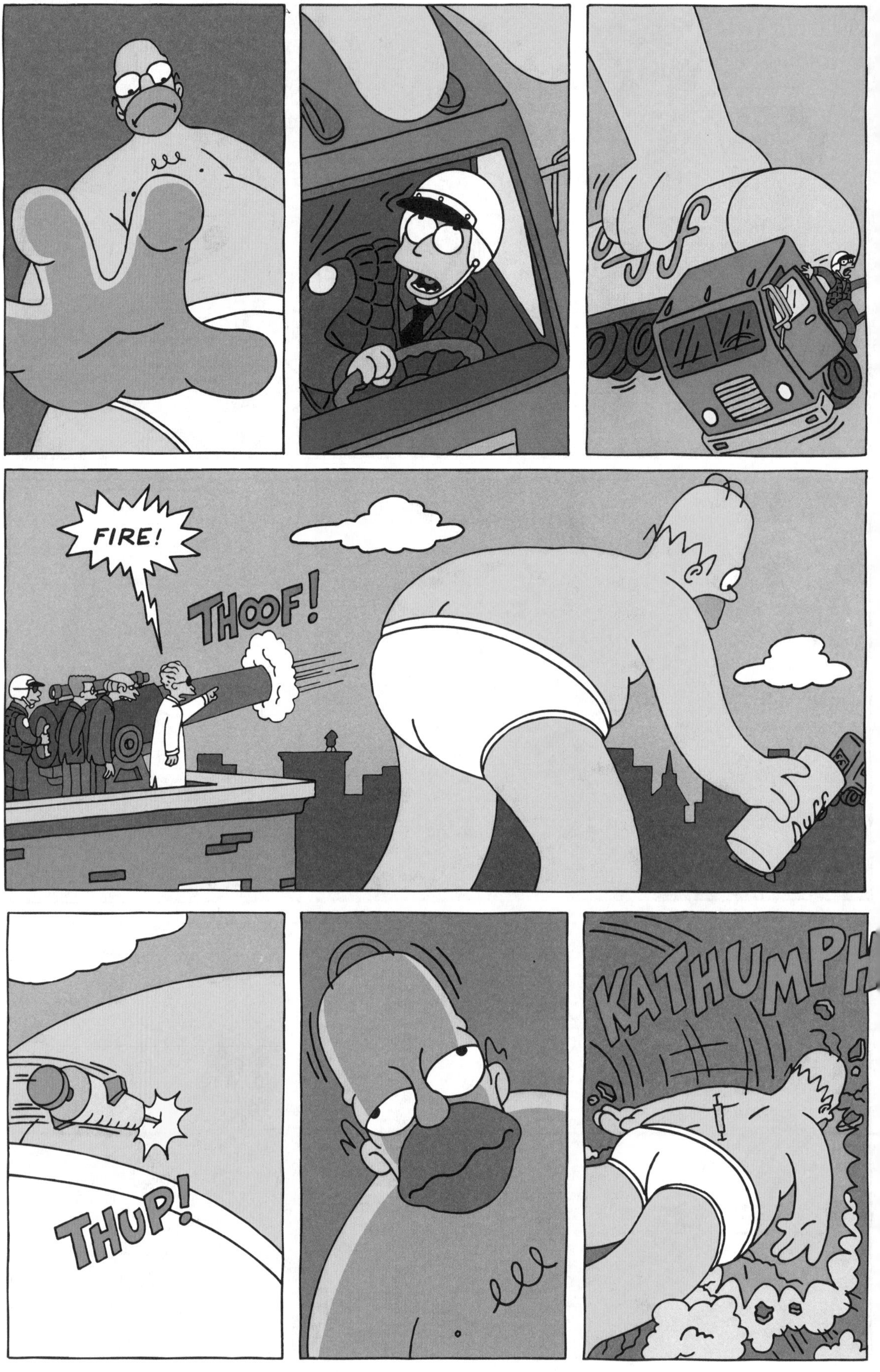
FIRE!
THOOF!
Duff
THUP!
KATHUMPH

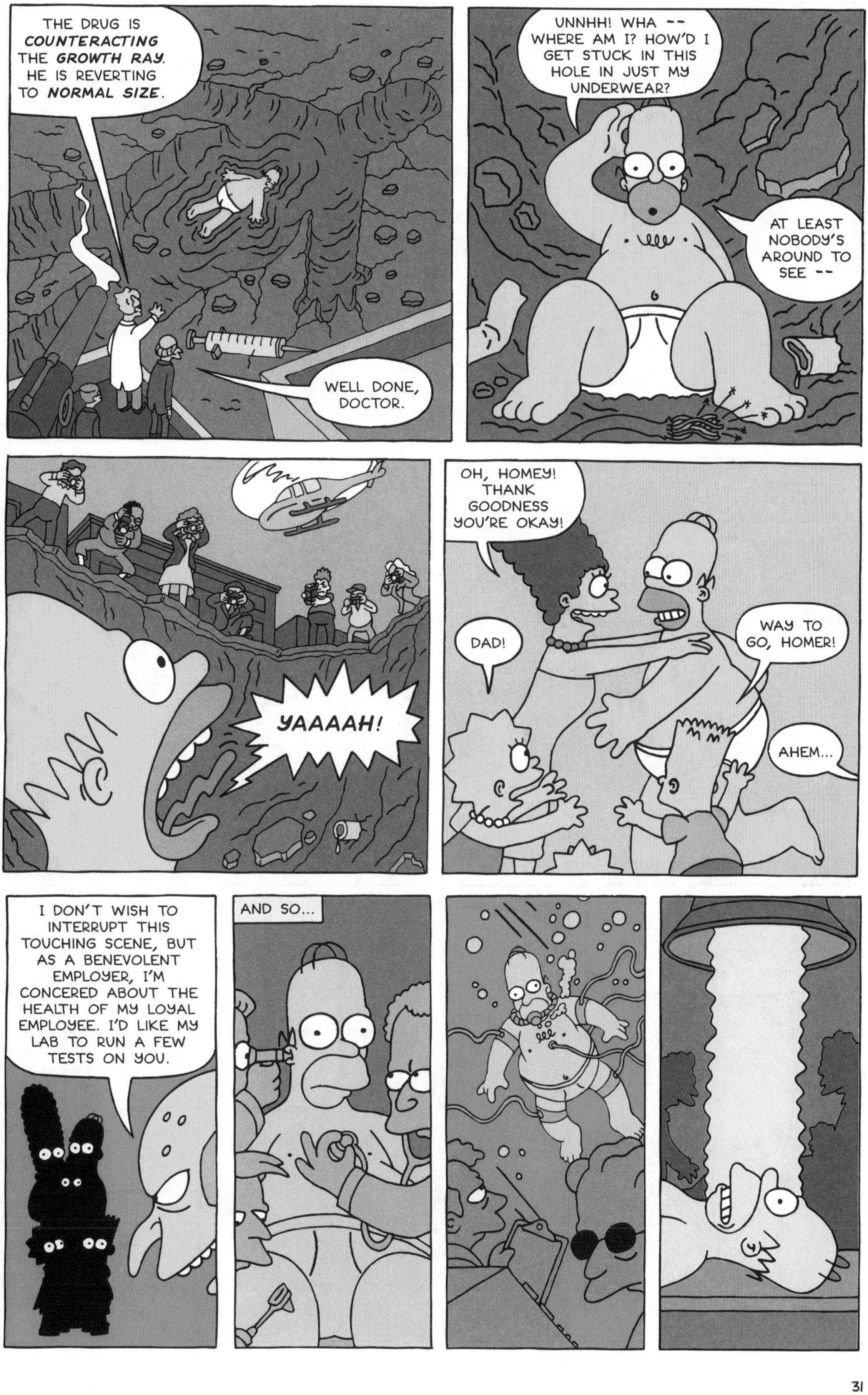
THE DRUG IS COUNTERACTING THE GROWTH RAY. HE IS REVERTING TO NORMAL SIZE.
WELL DONE, DOCTOR.
UNNHH! WHA -- WHERE AM I? HOW'D I GET STUCK IN THIS HOLE IN JUST MY UNDERWEAR?
AT LEAST NOBODY'S AROUND TO SEE --
YAAAAH!
OH, HOMEY! THANK GOODNESS YOU'RE OKAY!
DAD!
WAY TO GO, HOMER!
AHEM...
I DON'T WISH TO INTERRUPT THIS TOUCHING SCENE, BUT AS A BENEVOLENT EMPLOYER, I'M CONCERED ABOUT THE HEALTH OF MY LOYAL EMPLOYEE. I'D LIKE MY LAB TO RUN A FEW TESTS ON YOU.
AND SO...

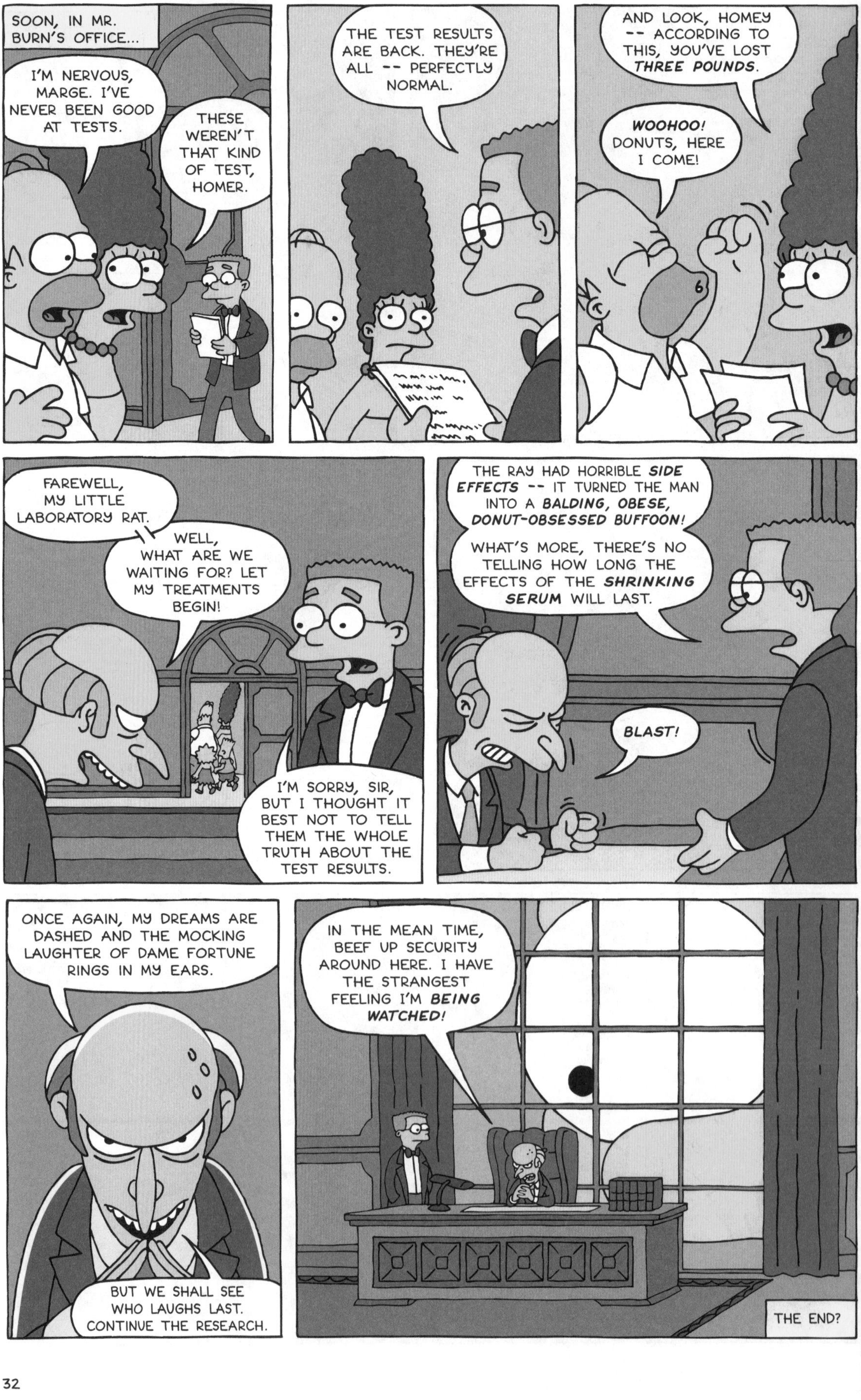
SOON, IN MR. BURN'S OFFICE...
I'M NERVOUS, MARGE. I'VE NEVER BEEN GOOD AT TESTS.
THESE WEREN'T THAT KIND OF TEST, HOMER.
THE TEST RESULTS ARE BACK. THEY'RE ALL -- PERFECTLY NORMAL.
AND LOOK, HOMEY -- ACCORDING TO THIS, YOU'VE LOST THREE POUNDS.
WOOHOO! DONUTS, HERE I COME!
FAREWELL, MY LITTLE LABORATORY RAT.
WELL, WHAT ARE WE WAITING FOR? LET MY TREATMENTS BEGIN!
I'M SORRY, SIR, BUT I THOUGHT IT BEST NOT TO TELL THEM THE WHOLE TRUTH ABOUT THE TEST RESULTS.
THE RAY HAD HORRIBLE SIDE EFFECTS -- IT TURNED THE MAN INTO A BALDING, OBESE, DONUT-OBSESSED BUFFOON!
WHAT'S MORE, THERE'S NO TELLING HOW LONG THE EFFECTS OF THE SHRINKING SERUM WILL LAST.
BLAST!
ONCE AGAIN, MY DREAMS ARE DASHED AND THE MOCKING LAUGHTER OF DAME FORTUNE RINGS IN MY EARS.
BUT WE SHALL SEE WHO LAUGHS LAST. CONTINUE THE RESEARCH.
IN THE MEAN TIME, BEEF UP SECURITY AROUND HERE. I HAVE THE STRANGEST FEELING I'M BEING WATCHED!
THE END?

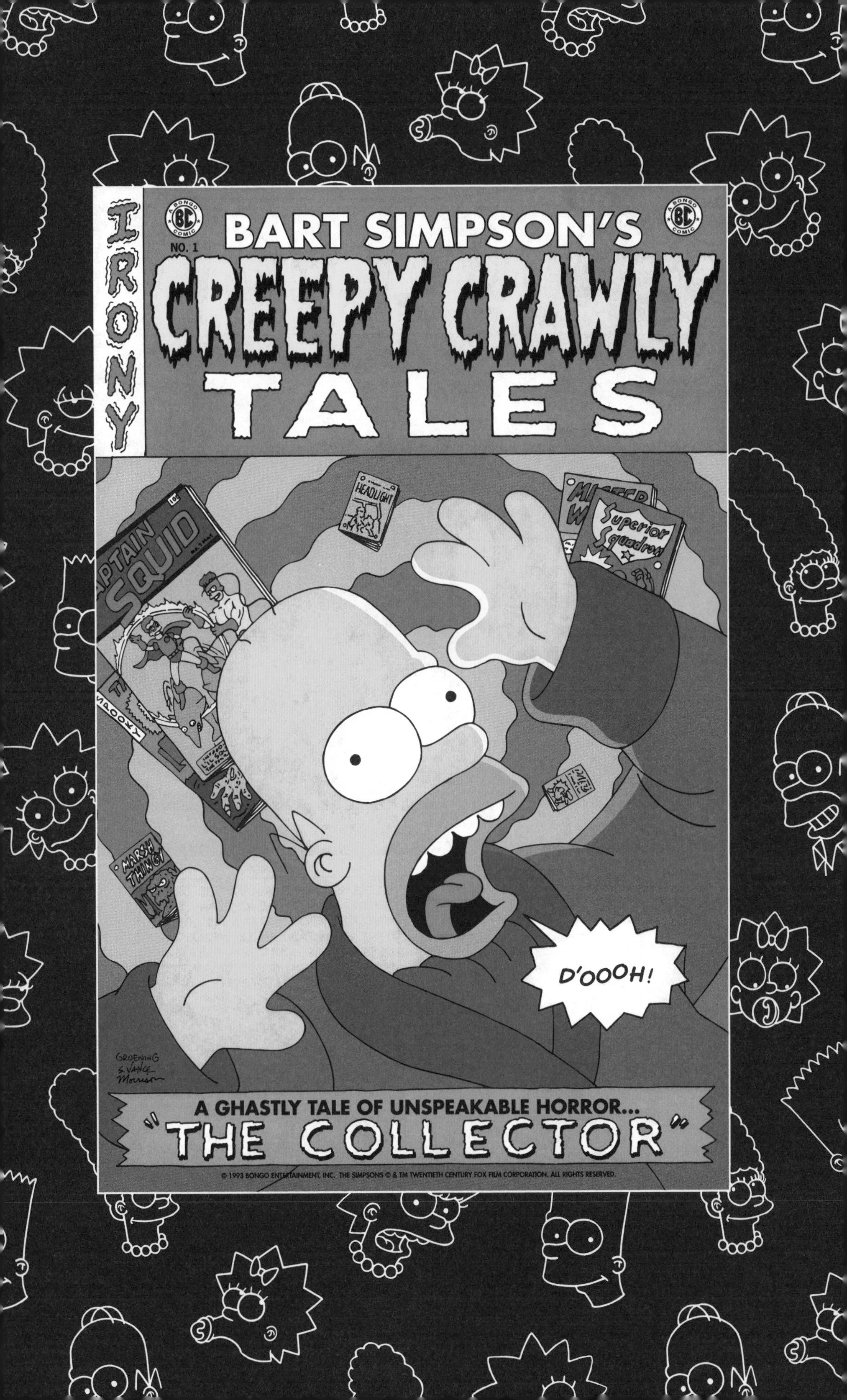
IRONY
BART SIMPSON'S
NO. 1
CREEPY CRAWLY TALES
HEADLIGHT
CAPTAIN SQUID
Superior Squadron
MARSH THING
D'OOOH!
GROENING
S. VANCE
Morrison
A GHASTLY TALE OF UNSPEAKABLE HORROR...
"THE COLLECTOR"
© 1993 BONGO ENTERTAINMENT, INC. THE SIMPSONS © & TM TWENTIETH CENTURY FOX FILM CORPORATION. ALL RIGHTS RESERVED.

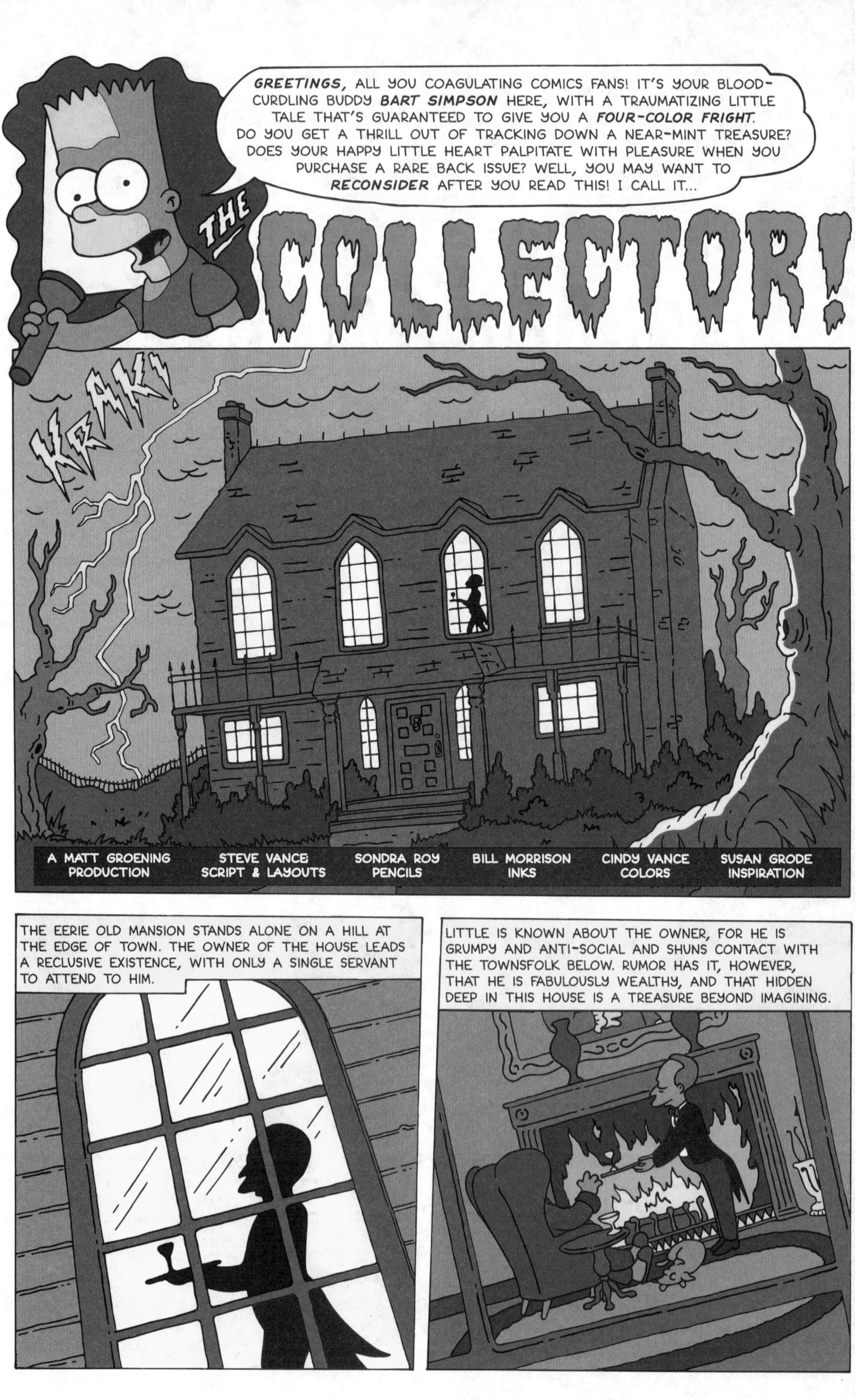
GREETINGS, ALL YOU COAGULATING COMICS FANS! IT'S YOUR BLOOD-CURDLING BUDDY BART SIMPSON HERE, WITH A TRAUMATIZING LITTLE TALE THAT'S GUARANTEED TO GIVE YOU A FOUR-COLOR FRIGHT. DO YOU GET A THRILL OUT OF TRACKING DOWN A NEAR-MINT TREASURE? DOES YOUR HAPPY LITTLE HEART PALPITATE WITH PLEASURE WHEN YOU PURCHASE A RARE BACK ISSUE? WELL, YOU MAY WANT TO RECONSIDER AFTER YOU READ THIS! I CALL IT...
THE COLLECTOR!
KRAK!
A MATT GROENING PRODUCTION
STEVE VANCE SCRIPT & LAYOUTS
SONDRA ROY PENCILS
BILL MORRISON INKS
CINDY VANCE COLORS
SUSAN GRODE INSPIRATION
THE EERIE OLD MANSION STANDS ALONE ON A HILL AT THE EDGE OF TOWN. THE OWNER OF THE HOUSE LEADS A RECLUSIVE EXISTENCE, WITH ONLY A SINGLE SERVANT TO ATTEND TO HIM.
LITTLE IS KNOWN ABOUT THE OWNER, FOR HE IS GRUMPY AND ANTI-SOCIAL AND SHUNS CONTACT WITH THE TOWNSFOLK BELOW. RUMOR HAS IT, HOWEVER, THAT HE IS FABULOUSLY WEALTHY, AND THAT HIDDEN DEEP IN THIS HOUSE IS A TREASURE BEYOND IMAGINING.

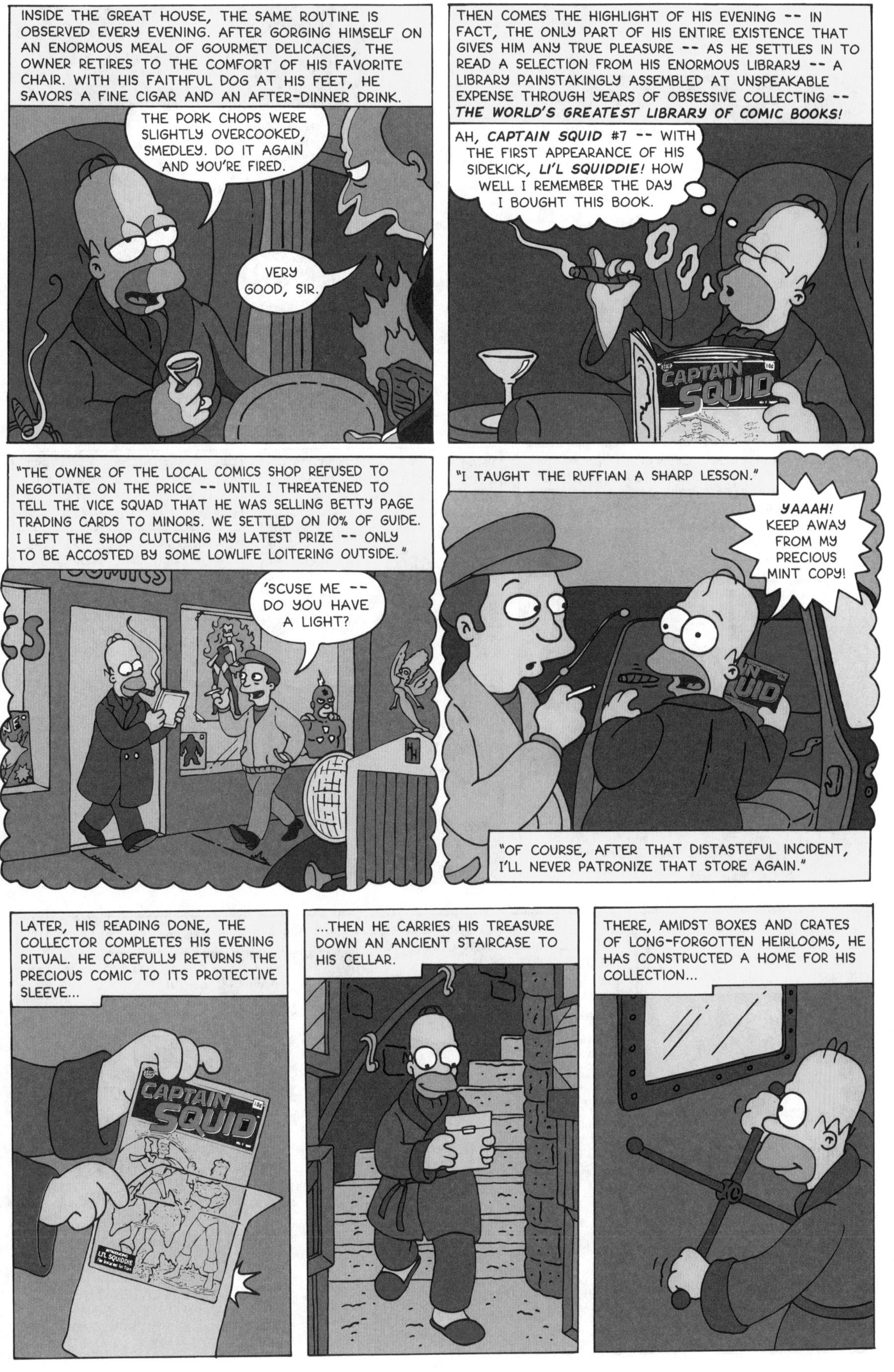
INSIDE THE GREAT HOUSE, THE SAME ROUTINE IS OBSERVED EVERY EVENING. AFTER GORGING HIMSELF ON AN ENORMOUS MEAL OF GOURMET DELICACIES, THE OWNER RETIRES TO THE COMFORT OF HIS FAVORITE CHAIR. WITH HIS FAITHFUL DOG AT HIS FEET, HE SAVORS A FINE CIGAR AND AN AFTER-DINNER DRINK.
THE PORK CHOPS WERE SLIGHTLY OVERCOOKED, SMEDLEY. DO IT AGAIN AND YOU'RE FIRED.
VERY GOOD, SIR.
THEN COMES THE HIGHLIGHT OF HIS EVENING -- IN FACT, THE ONLY PART OF HIS ENTIRE EXISTENCE THAT GIVES HIM ANY TRUE PLEASURE -- AS HE SETTLES IN TO READ A SELECTION FROM HIS ENORMOUS LIBRARY -- A LIBRARY PAINSTAKINGLY ASSEMBLED AT UNSPEAKABLE EXPENSE THROUGH YEARS OF OBSESSIVE COLLECTING -- ***THE WORLD'S GREATEST LIBRARY OF COMIC BOOKS!***
AH, ***CAPTAIN SQUID*** #7 -- WITH THE FIRST APPEARANCE OF HIS SIDEKICK, ***LI'L SQUIDDIE!*** HOW WELL I REMEMBER THE DAY I BOUGHT THIS BOOK.
CAPTAIN SQUID
"THE OWNER OF THE LOCAL COMICS SHOP REFUSED TO NEGOTIATE ON THE PRICE -- UNTIL I THREATENED TO TELL THE VICE SQUAD THAT HE WAS SELLING BETTY PAGE TRADING CARDS TO MINORS. WE SETTLED ON 10% OF GUIDE. I LEFT THE SHOP CLUTCHING MY LATEST PRIZE -- ONLY TO BE ACCOSTED BY SOME LOWLIFE LOITERING OUTSIDE."
'SCUSE ME -- DO YOU HAVE A LIGHT?
"I TAUGHT THE RUFFIAN A SHARP LESSON."
YAAAH! KEEP AWAY FROM MY PRECIOUS MINT COPY!
"OF COURSE, AFTER THAT DISTASTEFUL INCIDENT, I'LL NEVER PATRONIZE THAT STORE AGAIN."
LATER, HIS READING DONE, THE COLLECTOR COMPLETES HIS EVENING RITUAL. HE CAREFULLY RETURNS THE PRECIOUS COMIC TO ITS PROTECTIVE SLEEVE...
CAPTAIN SQUID
...THEN HE CARRIES HIS TREASURE DOWN AN ANCIENT STAIRCASE TO HIS CELLAR.
THERE, AMIDST BOXES AND CRATES OF LONG-FORGOTTEN HEIRLOOMS, HE HAS CONSTRUCTED A HOME FOR HIS COLLECTION...

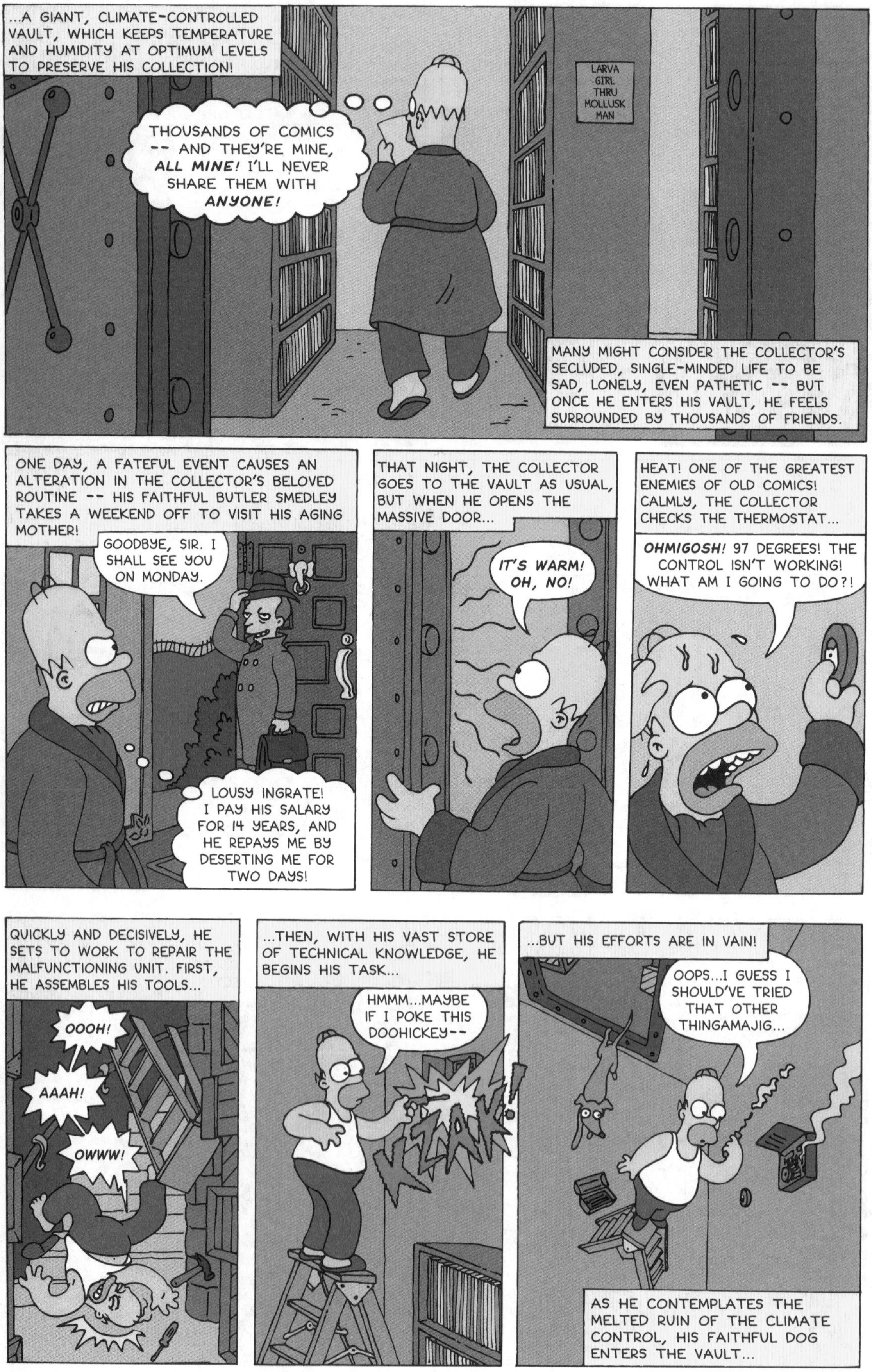
...A GIANT, CLIMATE-CONTROLLED VAULT, WHICH KEEPS TEMPERATURE AND HUMIDITY AT OPTIMUM LEVELS TO PRESERVE HIS COLLECTION!
LARVA GIRL THRU MOLLUSK MAN
THOUSANDS OF COMICS -- AND THEY'RE MINE, ALL MINE! I'LL NEVER SHARE THEM WITH ANYONE!
MANY MIGHT CONSIDER THE COLLECTOR'S SECLUDED, SINGLE-MINDED LIFE TO BE SAD, LONELY, EVEN PATHETIC -- BUT ONCE HE ENTERS HIS VAULT, HE FEELS SURROUNDED BY THOUSANDS OF FRIENDS.
ONE DAY, A FATEFUL EVENT CAUSES AN ALTERATION IN THE COLLECTOR'S BELOVED ROUTINE -- HIS FAITHFUL BUTLER SMEDLEY TAKES A WEEKEND OFF TO VISIT HIS AGING MOTHER!
GOODBYE, SIR. I SHALL SEE YOU ON MONDAY.
LOUSY INGRATE! I PAY HIS SALARY FOR 14 YEARS, AND HE REPAYS ME BY DESERTING ME FOR TWO DAYS!
THAT NIGHT, THE COLLECTOR GOES TO THE VAULT AS USUAL, BUT WHEN HE OPENS THE MASSIVE DOOR...
IT'S WARM! OH, NO!
HEAT! ONE OF THE GREATEST ENEMIES OF OLD COMICS! CALMLY, THE COLLECTOR CHECKS THE THERMOSTAT...
OHMIGOSH! 97 DEGREES! THE CONTROL ISN'T WORKING! WHAT AM I GOING TO DO?!
QUICKLY AND DECISIVELY, HE SETS TO WORK TO REPAIR THE MALFUNCTIONING UNIT. FIRST, HE ASSEMBLES HIS TOOLS...
OOOH!
AAAH!
OWWW!
...THEN, WITH HIS VAST STORE OF TECHNICAL KNOWLEDGE, HE BEGINS HIS TASK...
HMMM...MAYBE IF I POKE THIS DOOHICKEY--
...BUT HIS EFFORTS ARE IN VAIN!
OOPS...I GUESS I SHOULD'VE TRIED THAT OTHER THINGAMAJIG...
AS HE CONTEMPLATES THE MELTED RUIN OF THE CLIMATE CONTROL, HIS FAITHFUL DOG ENTERS THE VAULT...

HEY! GET OUT OF HERE! BAD DOG!

GO ON! SHOOOO

THE LADDER CRASHES TO THE FLOOR AND THE FRIGHTENED DOG RACES OUT OF THE VAULT, BRUSHING AGAINST A PRECARIOUSLY BALANCED STACK OF CRATES...

KRASH!

BUMP!

THE CRATES TOPPLE AGAINST THE VAULT DOOR, AND IT SLAMS SHUT -- LOCKED!

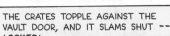

SLAM!

INSIDE THE VAULT, THE COLLECTOR COOLLY ASSESSES HIS SITUATION...

YAAAH! I'M TRAPPED!

WAIT -- CALM DOWN -- DON'T PANIC! THERE'S GOT TO BE A WAY OUT SOMEHOW. THINK, MAN -- WHAT WOULD RADIOACTIVE MAN DO IN THIS SITUATION?

I KNOW! HE'D CRUMPLE THE DOOR WITH A SINGLE ATOMIC-POWERED PUNCH!

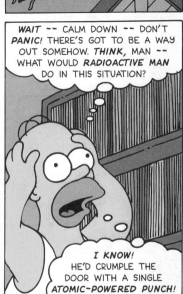

THE COLLECTOR IMMEDIATELY PUTS HIS PLAN INTO ACTION -- BUT TO NO AVAIL!

UNNNHH!! CRUMPLE, BLAST YOU!

WELL, WHADDYA KNOW -- I GUESS MAYBE USING BRUTE STRENGTH TO RESOLVE PROBLEMS DOESN'T ALWAYS WORK AS WELL IN REAL LIFE AS IT DOES IN COMICS.

LOOKS LIKE I'M STUCK HERE UNTIL SMEDLEY COMES HOME AND LETS ME OUT. OH WELL, I GUESS I'LL JUST HAVE TO SPEND MY WHOLE WEEKEND READING COMICS -- WHAT A SHAME! HEH HEH!

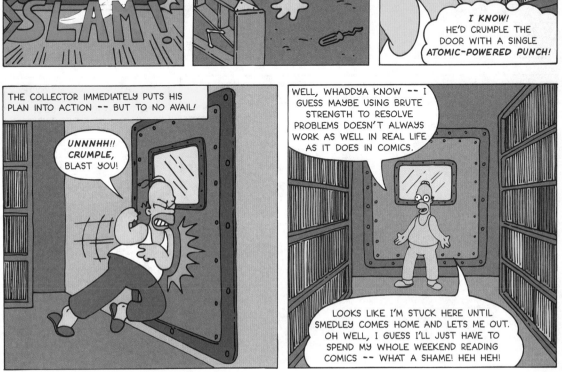

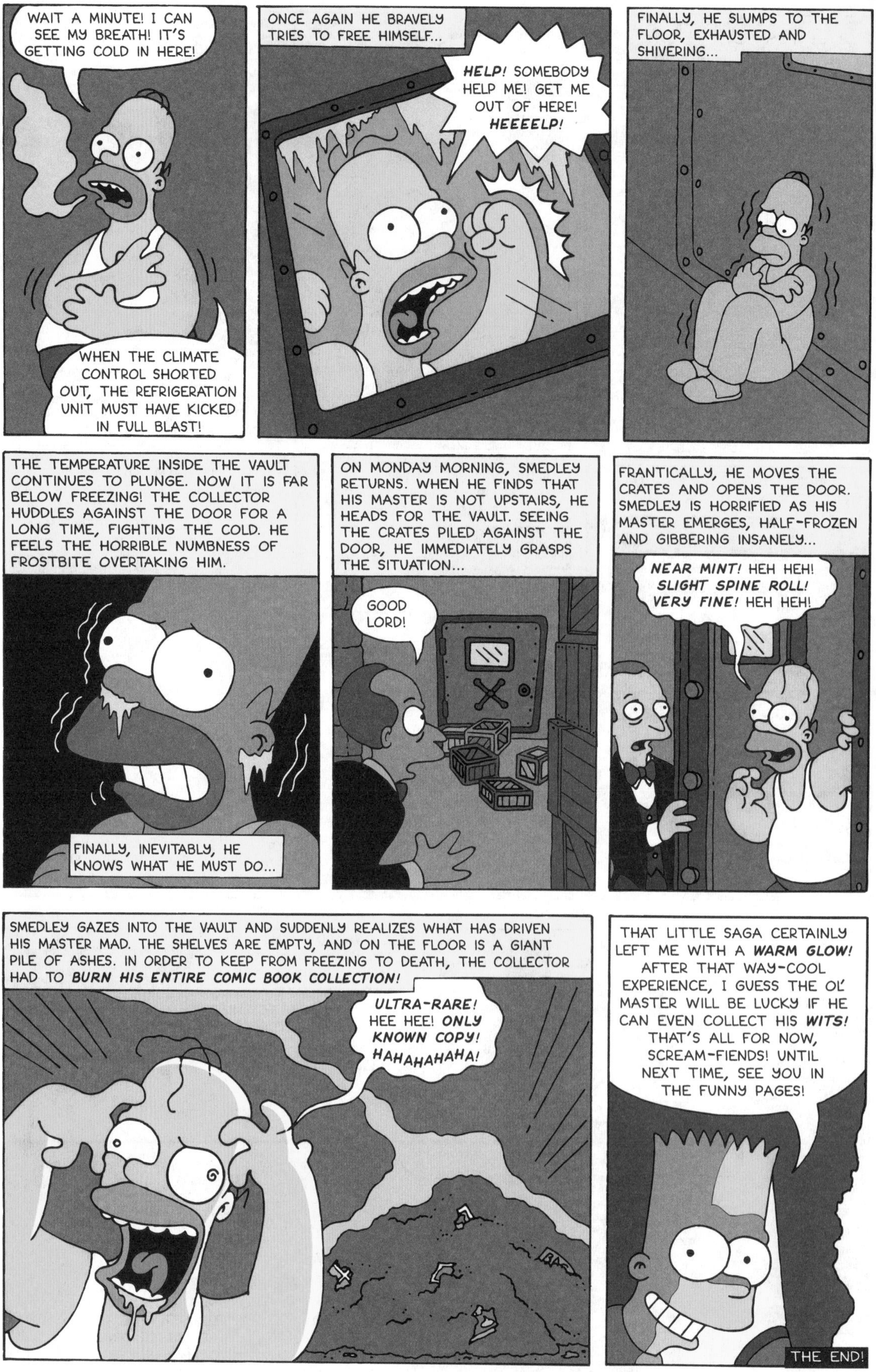
WAIT A MINUTE! I CAN SEE MY BREATH! IT'S GETTING COLD IN HERE!
WHEN THE CLIMATE CONTROL SHORTED OUT, THE REFRIGERATION UNIT MUST HAVE KICKED IN FULL BLAST!
ONCE AGAIN HE BRAVELY TRIES TO FREE HIMSELF...
HELP! SOMEBODY HELP ME! GET ME OUT OF HERE! HEEEELP!
FINALLY, HE SLUMPS TO THE FLOOR, EXHAUSTED AND SHIVERING...
THE TEMPERATURE INSIDE THE VAULT CONTINUES TO PLUNGE. NOW IT IS FAR BELOW FREEZING! THE COLLECTOR HUDDLES AGAINST THE DOOR FOR A LONG TIME, FIGHTING THE COLD. HE FEELS THE HORRIBLE NUMBNESS OF FROSTBITE OVERTAKING HIM.
FINALLY, INEVITABLY, HE KNOWS WHAT HE MUST DO...
ON MONDAY MORNING, SMEDLEY RETURNS. WHEN HE FINDS THAT HIS MASTER IS NOT UPSTAIRS, HE HEADS FOR THE VAULT. SEEING THE CRATES PILED AGAINST THE DOOR, HE IMMEDIATELY GRASPS THE SITUATION...
GOOD LORD!
FRANTICALLY, HE MOVES THE CRATES AND OPENS THE DOOR. SMEDLEY IS HORRIFIED AS HIS MASTER EMERGES, HALF-FROZEN AND GIBBERING INSANELY...
NEAR MINT! HEH HEH! SLIGHT SPINE ROLL! VERY FINE! HEH HEH!
SMEDLEY GAZES INTO THE VAULT AND SUDDENLY REALIZES WHAT HAS DRIVEN HIS MASTER MAD. THE SHELVES ARE EMPTY, AND ON THE FLOOR IS A GIANT PILE OF ASHES. IN ORDER TO KEEP FROM FREEZING TO DEATH, THE COLLECTOR HAD TO BURN HIS ENTIRE COMIC BOOK COLLECTION!
ULTRA-RARE! HEE HEE! ONLY KNOWN COPY! HAHAHAHAHA!
THAT LITTLE SAGA CERTAINLY LEFT ME WITH A WARM GLOW! AFTER THAT WAY-COOL EXPERIENCE, I GUESS THE OL' MASTER WILL BE LUCKY IF HE CAN EVEN COLLECT HIS WITS! THAT'S ALL FOR NOW, SCREAM-FIENDS! UNTIL NEXT TIME, SEE YOU IN THE FUNNY PAGES!
THE END!

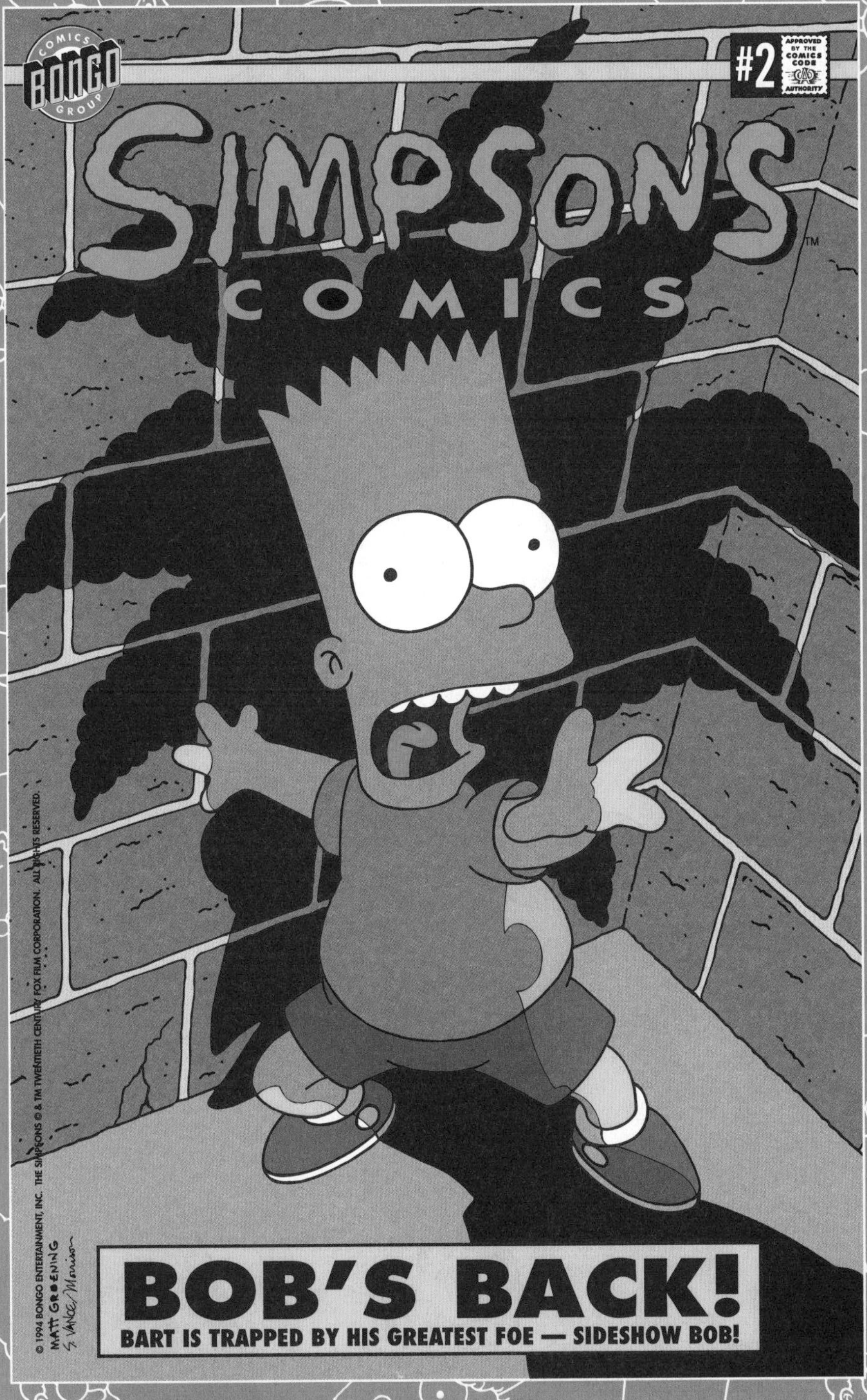

COMICS BONGO GROUP
#2
APPROVED BY THE COMICS CODE AUTHORITY
SIMPSONS™
COMICS
BOB'S BACK!
BART IS TRAPPED BY HIS GREATEST FOE — SIDESHOW BOB!
© 1994 BONGO ENTERTAINMENT, INC. THE SIMPSONS © & TM TWENTIETH CENTURY FOX FILM CORPORATION. ALL RIGHTS RESERVED.
MATT GROENING

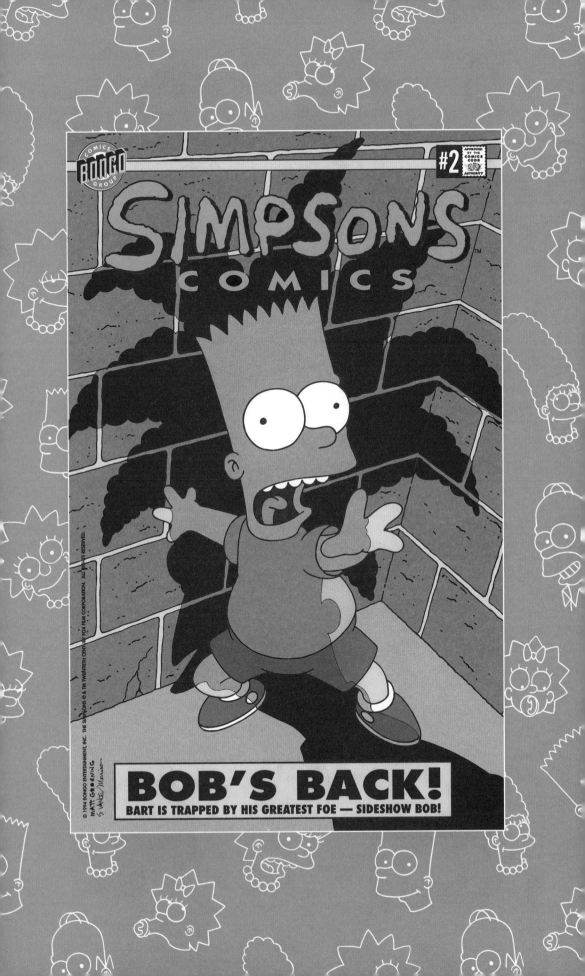

BECAUSE YOU DEMANDED IT, BONGO PRESENTS...

Patty & Selma's FASCINATIN' FASHIONS!

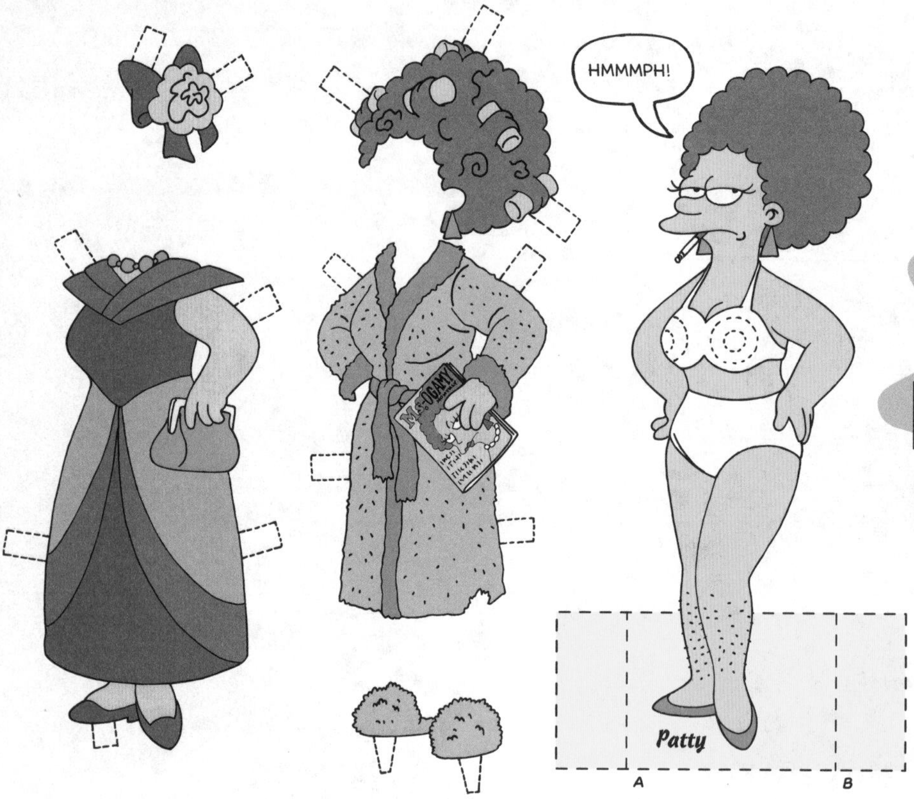
HMMMPH!
Patty
A
B

CUT OUT FIGURES (OR BETTER YET, USE A PHOTOCOPY!) AND PASTE ON LIGHTWEIGHT CARDBOARD. TO STAND, FOLD BASE AT ***A*** AND ***B***.

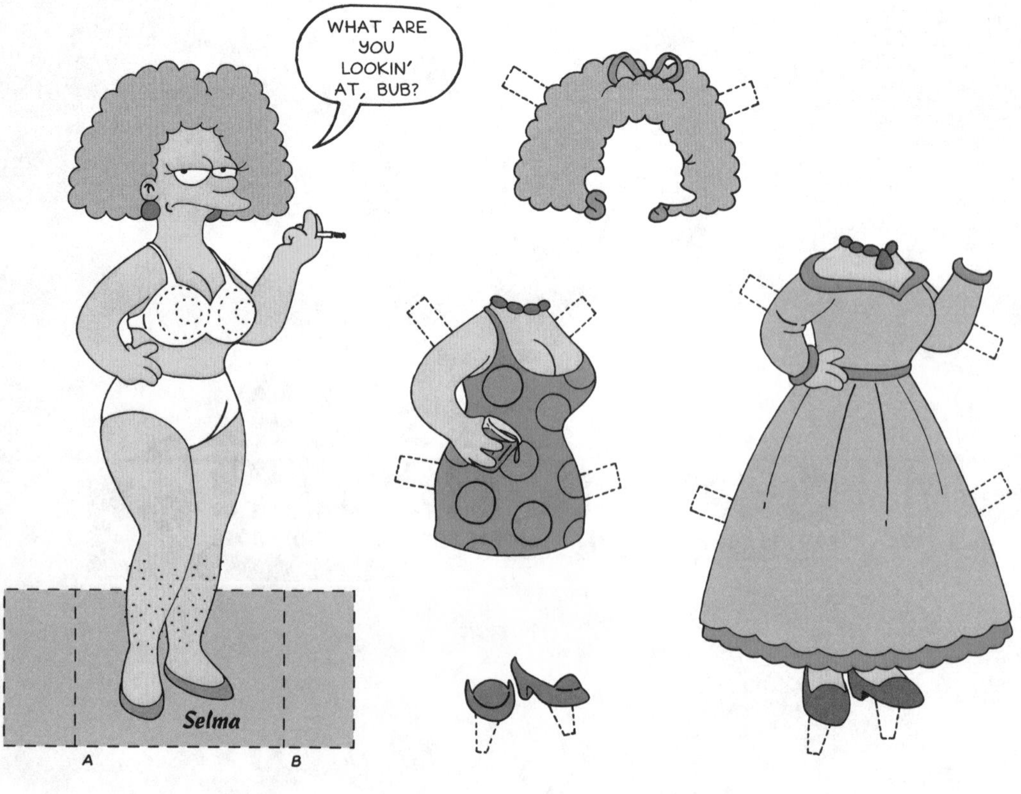
WHAT ARE YOU LOOKIN' AT, BUB?
Selma
A
B

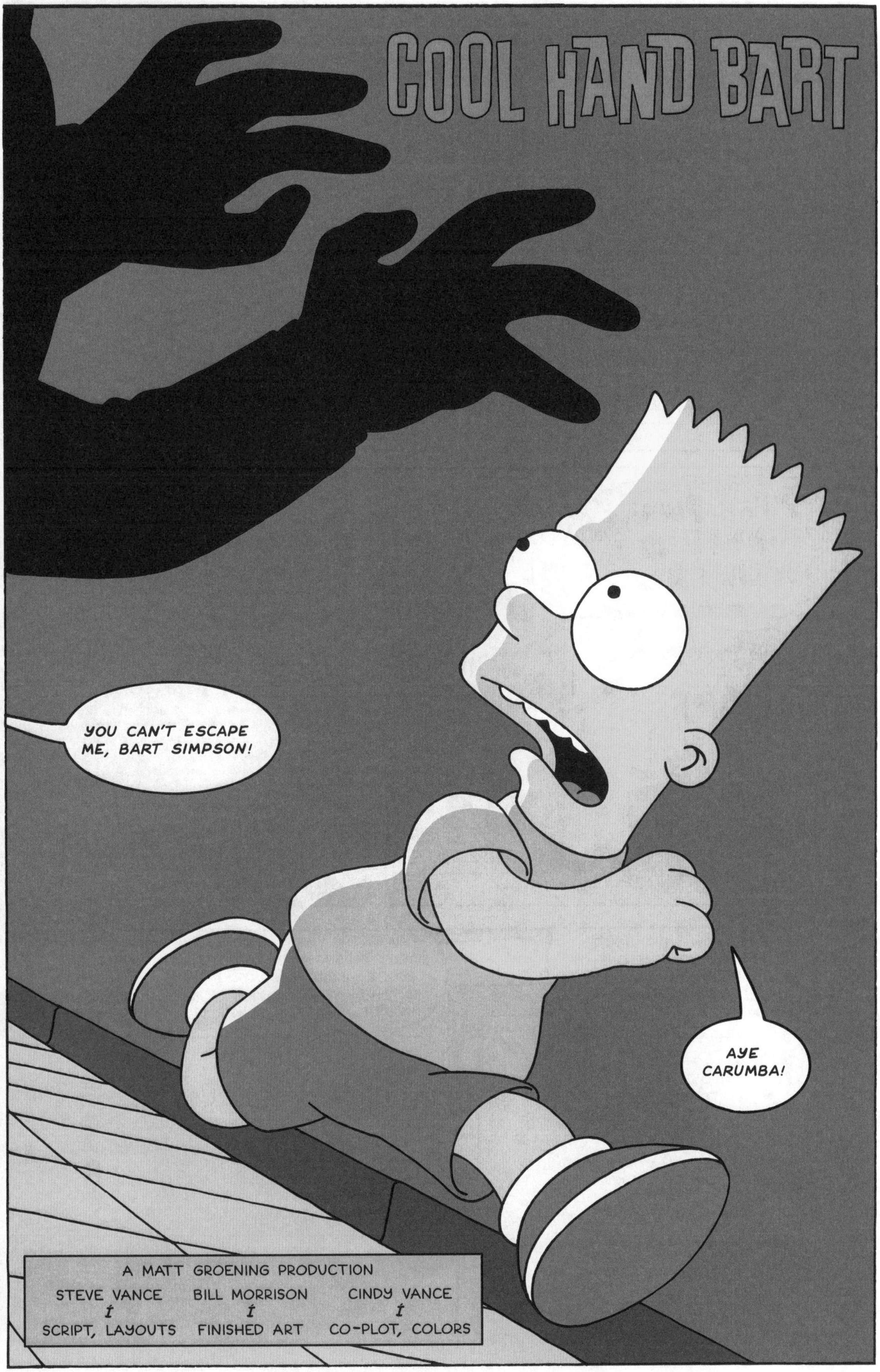
COOL HAND BART
YOU CAN'T ESCAPE ME, BART SIMPSON!
AYE CARUMBA!
A MATT GROENING PRODUCTION
STEVE VANCE SCRIPT, LAYOUTS
BILL MORRISON FINISHED ART
CINDY VANCE CO-PLOT, COLORS

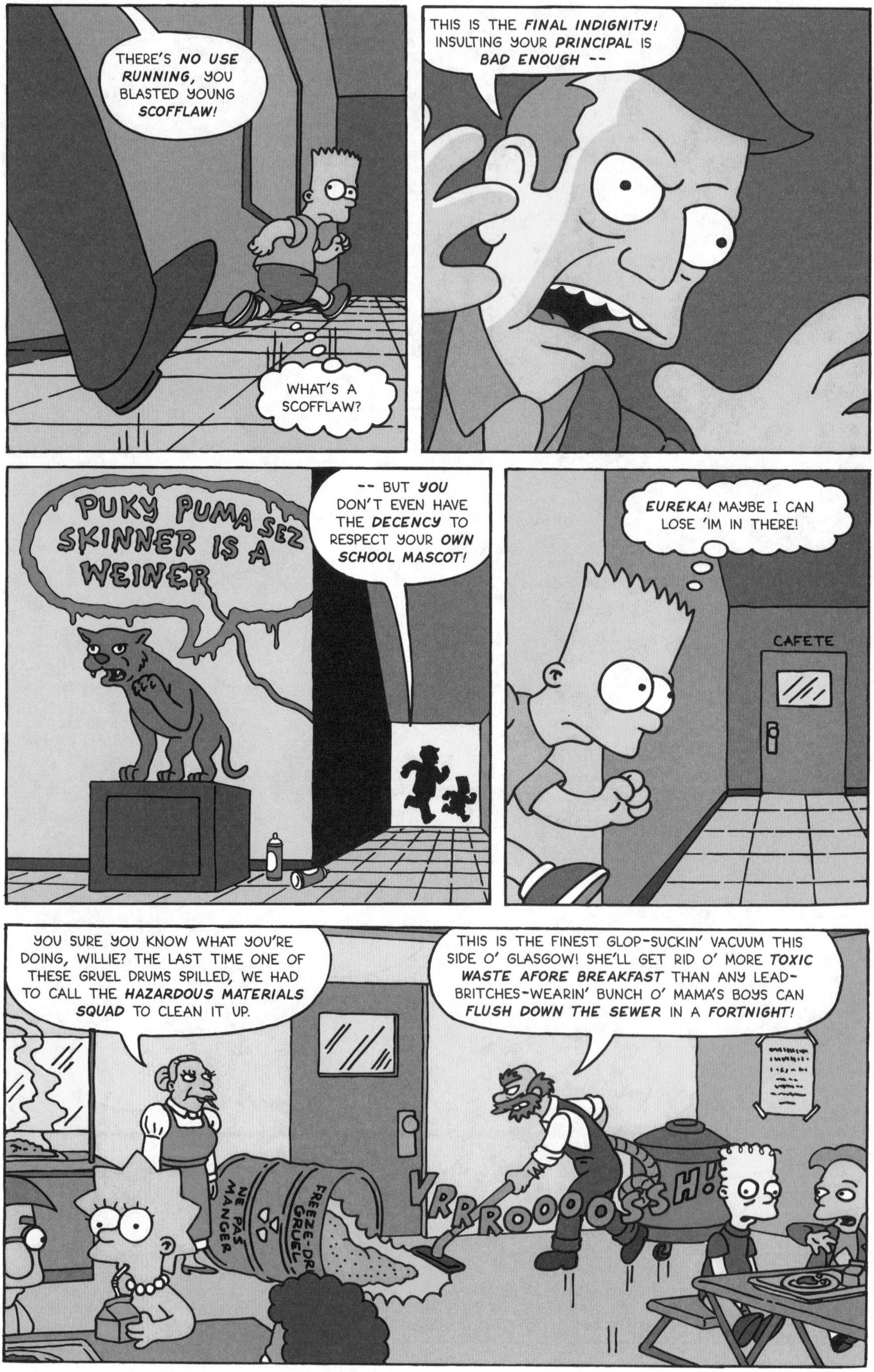
THERE'S NO USE RUNNING, YOU BLASTED YOUNG SCOFFLAW!
WHAT'S A SCOFFLAW?
THIS IS THE FINAL INDIGNITY! INSULTING YOUR PRINCIPAL IS BAD ENOUGH --
PUKY PUMA SEZ SKINNER IS A WEINER
-- BUT YOU DON'T EVEN HAVE THE DECENCY TO RESPECT YOUR OWN SCHOOL MASCOT!
EUREKA! MAYBE I CAN LOSE 'IM IN THERE!
CAFETE
YOU SURE YOU KNOW WHAT YOU'RE DOING, WILLIE? THE LAST TIME ONE OF THESE GRUEL DRUMS SPILLED, WE HAD TO CALL THE HAZARDOUS MATERIALS SQUAD TO CLEAN IT UP.
THIS IS THE FINEST GLOP-SUCKIN' VACUUM THIS SIDE O' GLASGOW! SHE'LL GET RID O' MORE TOXIC WASTE AFORE BREAKFAST THAN ANY LEAD-BRITCHES-WEARIN' BUNCH O' MAMA'S BOYS CAN FLUSH DOWN THE SEWER IN A FORTNIGHT!
NE PAS MANGER
FREEZE-DRI GRUEL
VRRROOOOOSSH!

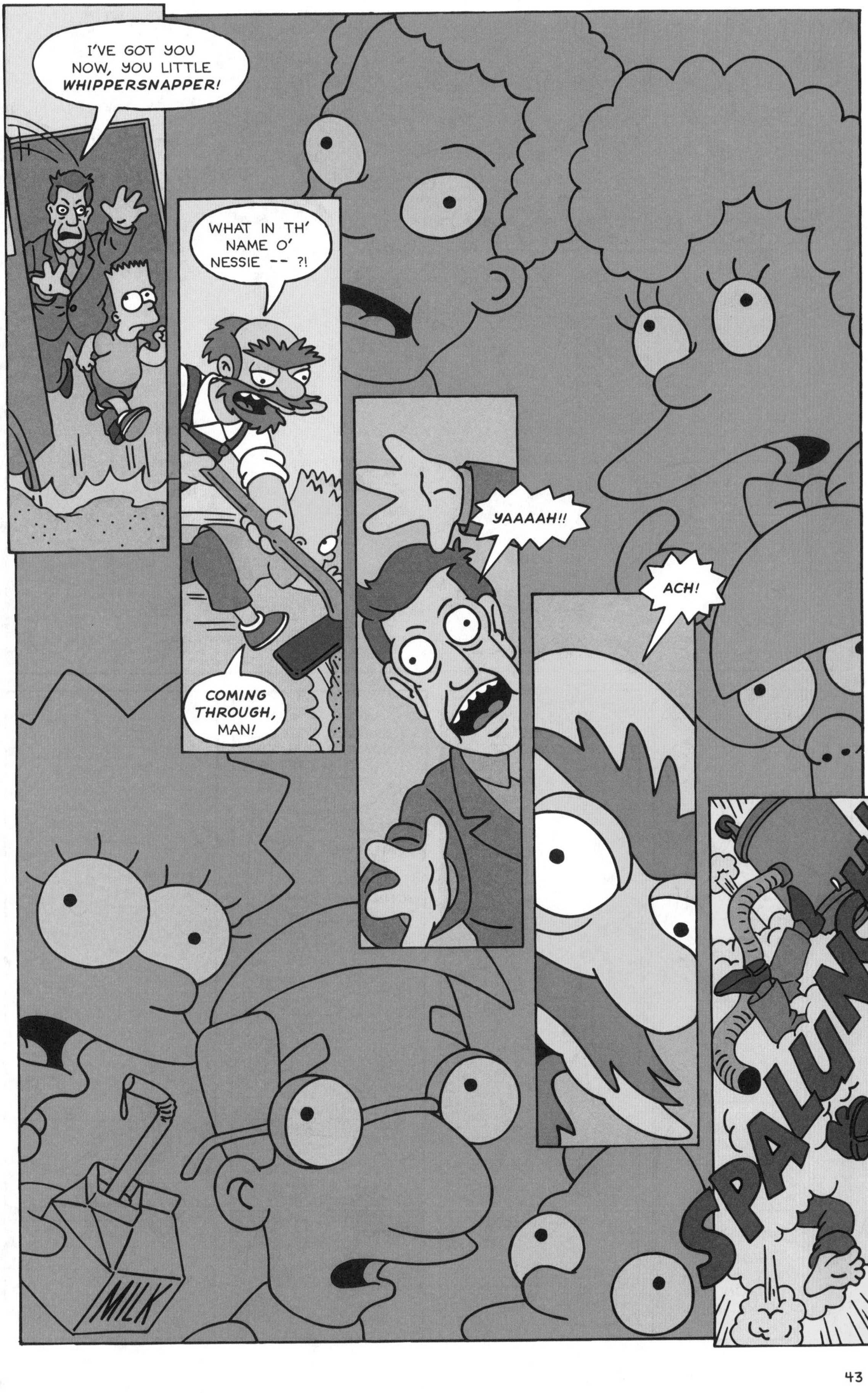

I'VE GOT YOU NOW, YOU LITTLE WHIPPERSNAPPER!
WHAT IN TH' NAME O' NESSIE -- ?!
COMING THROUGH, MAN!
YAAAAH!!
ACH!
SPALUNCH!
MILK

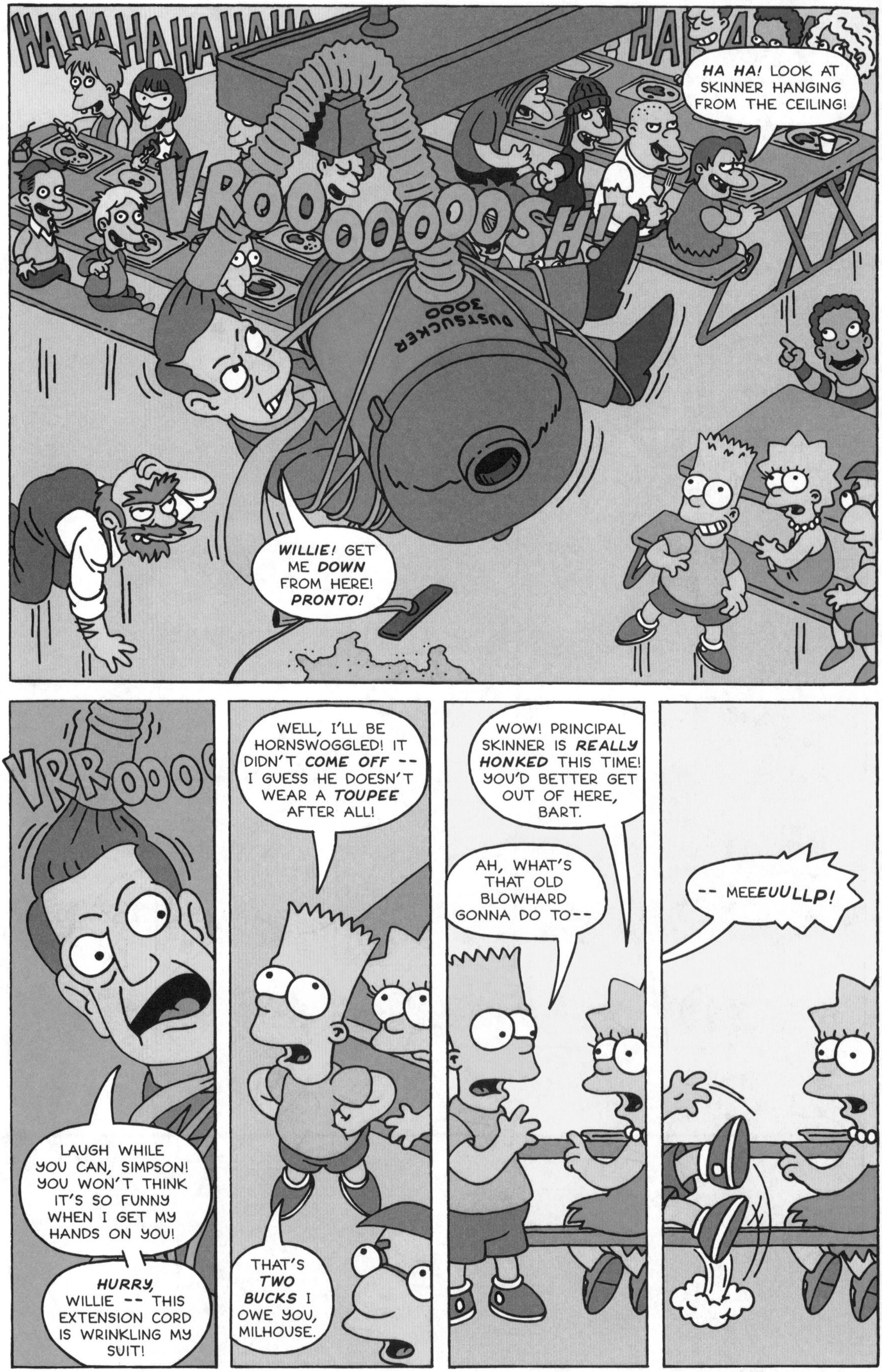
VROOOOOOOSH!
HA HA! LOOK AT SKINNER HANGING FROM THE CEILING!
WILLIE! GET ME DOWN FROM HERE! PRONTO!
LAUGH WHILE YOU CAN, SIMPSON! YOU WON'T THINK IT'S SO FUNNY WHEN I GET MY HANDS ON YOU!
HURRY, WILLIE -- THIS EXTENSION CORD IS WRINKLING MY SUIT!
WELL, I'LL BE HORNSWOGGLED! IT DIDN'T COME OFF -- I GUESS HE DOESN'T WEAR A TOUPEE AFTER ALL!
THAT'S TWO BUCKS I OWE YOU, MILHOUSE.
WOW! PRINCIPAL SKINNER IS REALLY HONKED THIS TIME! YOU'D BETTER GET OUT OF HERE, BART.
AH, WHAT'S THAT OLD BLOWHARD GONNA DO TO--
-- MEEEUULLP!

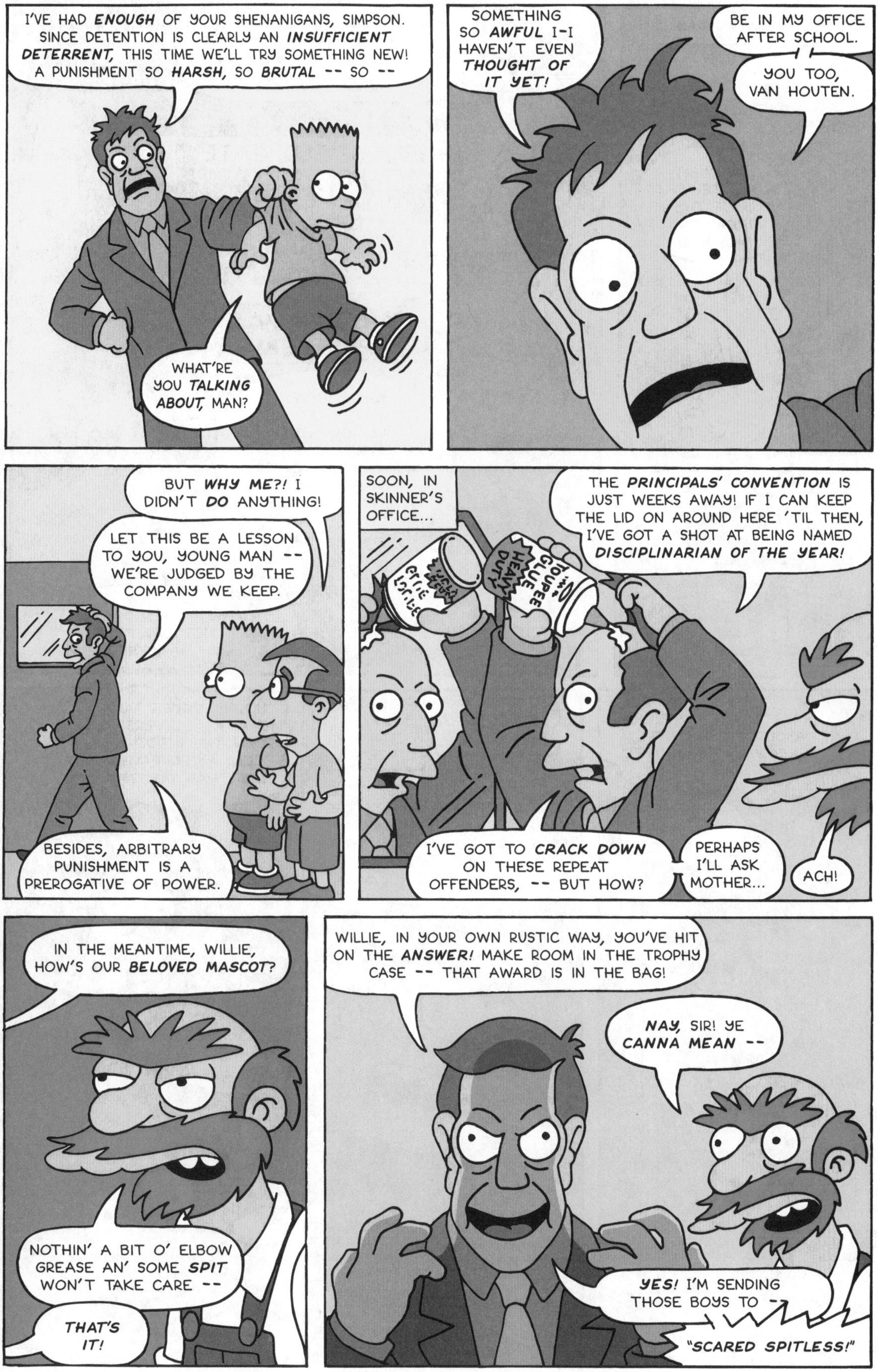

I'VE HAD ENOUGH OF YOUR SHENANIGANS, SIMPSON. SINCE DETENTION IS CLEARLY AN INSUFFICIENT DETERRENT, THIS TIME WE'LL TRY SOMETHING NEW! A PUNISHMENT SO HARSH, SO BRUTAL -- SO --
WHAT'RE YOU TALKING ABOUT, MAN?
SOMETHING SO AWFUL I-I HAVEN'T EVEN THOUGHT OF IT YET!
BE IN MY OFFICE AFTER SCHOOL.
YOU TOO, VAN HOUTEN.
BUT WHY ME?! I DIDN'T DO ANYTHING!
LET THIS BE A LESSON TO YOU, YOUNG MAN -- WE'RE JUDGED BY THE COMPANY WE KEEP.
BESIDES, ARBITRARY PUNISHMENT IS A PREROGATIVE OF POWER.
SOON, IN SKINNER'S OFFICE...
THE PRINCIPALS' CONVENTION IS JUST WEEKS AWAY! IF I CAN KEEP THE LID ON AROUND HERE 'TIL THEN, I'VE GOT A SHOT AT BEING NAMED DISCIPLINARIAN OF THE YEAR!
GLUPEE HEAVY DUTY
I'VE GOT TO CRACK DOWN ON THESE REPEAT OFFENDERS, -- BUT HOW?
PERHAPS I'LL ASK MOTHER...
ACH!
IN THE MEANTIME, WILLIE, HOW'S OUR BELOVED MASCOT?
NOTHIN' A BIT O' ELBOW GREASE AN' SOME SPIT WON'T TAKE CARE --
THAT'S IT!
WILLIE, IN YOUR OWN RUSTIC WAY, YOU'VE HIT ON THE ANSWER! MAKE ROOM IN THE TROPHY CASE -- THAT AWARD IS IN THE BAG!
NAY, SIR! YE CANNA MEAN --
YES! I'M SENDING THOSE BOYS TO --
"SCARED SPITLESS!"

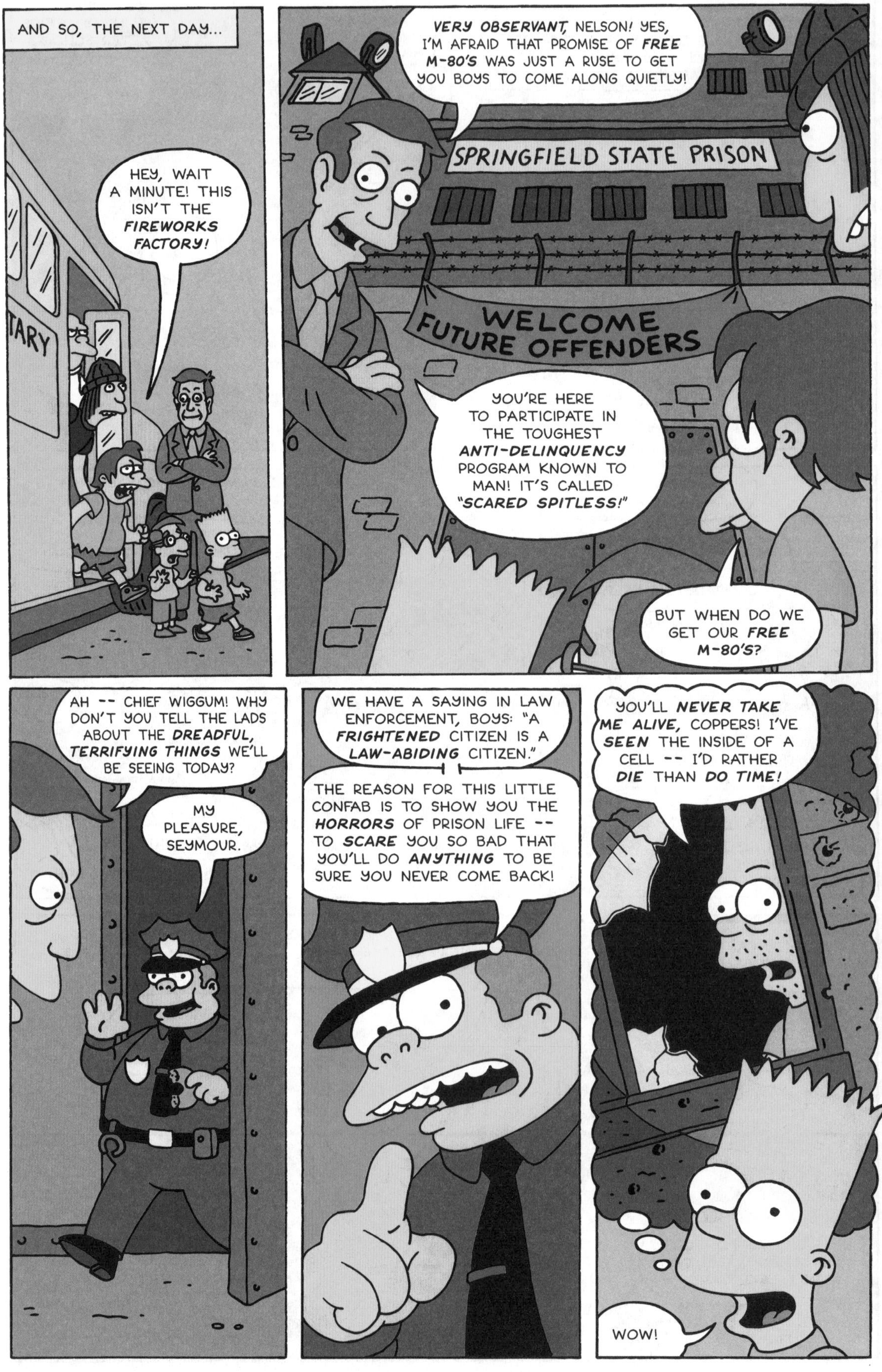
AND SO, THE NEXT DAY...
HEY, WAIT A MINUTE! THIS ISN'T THE FIREWORKS FACTORY!
TARY
VERY OBSERVANT, NELSON! YES, I'M AFRAID THAT PROMISE OF FREE M-80'S WAS JUST A RUSE TO GET YOU BOYS TO COME ALONG QUIETLY!
SPRINGFIELD STATE PRISON
WELCOME FUTURE OFFENDERS
YOU'RE HERE TO PARTICIPATE IN THE TOUGHEST ANTI-DELINQUENCY PROGRAM KNOWN TO MAN! IT'S CALLED "SCARED SPITLESS!"
BUT WHEN DO WE GET OUR FREE M-80'S?
AH -- CHIEF WIGGUM! WHY DON'T YOU TELL THE LADS ABOUT THE DREADFUL, TERRIFYING THINGS WE'LL BE SEEING TODAY?
MY PLEASURE, SEYMOUR.
WE HAVE A SAYING IN LAW ENFORCEMENT, BOYS: "A FRIGHTENED CITIZEN IS A LAW-ABIDING CITIZEN."
THE REASON FOR THIS LITTLE CONFAB IS TO SHOW YOU THE HORRORS OF PRISON LIFE -- TO SCARE YOU SO BAD THAT YOU'LL DO ANYTHING TO BE SURE YOU NEVER COME BACK!
YOU'LL NEVER TAKE ME ALIVE, COPPERS! I'VE SEEN THE INSIDE OF A CELL -- I'D RATHER DIE THAN DO TIME!
WOW!

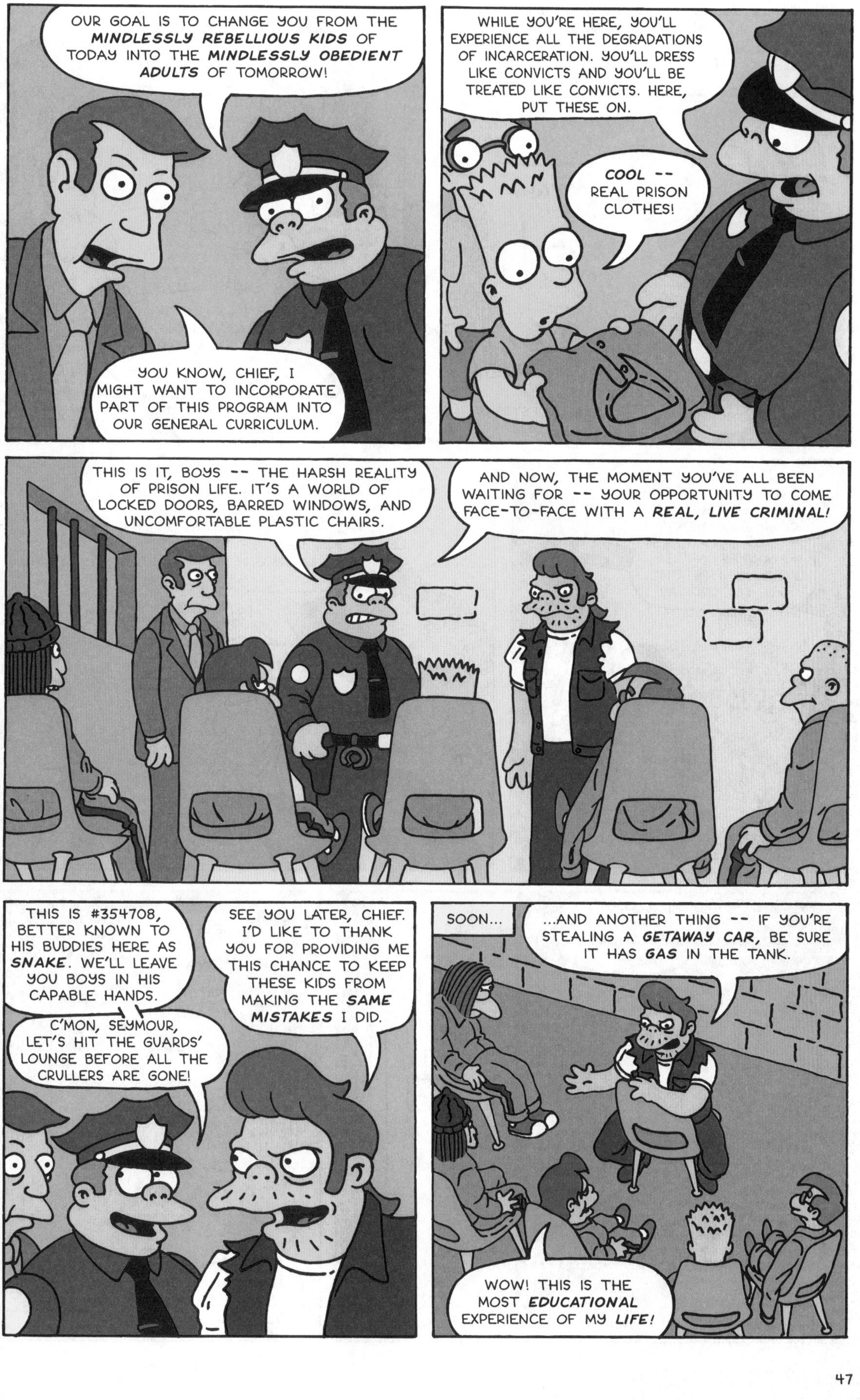

OUR GOAL IS TO CHANGE YOU FROM THE MINDLESSLY REBELLIOUS KIDS OF TODAY INTO THE MINDLESSLY OBEDIENT ADULTS OF TOMORROW!
YOU KNOW, CHIEF, I MIGHT WANT TO INCORPORATE PART OF THIS PROGRAM INTO OUR GENERAL CURRICULUM.
WHILE YOU'RE HERE, YOU'LL EXPERIENCE ALL THE DEGRADATIONS OF INCARCERATION. YOU'LL DRESS LIKE CONVICTS AND YOU'LL BE TREATED LIKE CONVICTS. HERE, PUT THESE ON.
COOL -- REAL PRISON CLOTHES!
THIS IS IT, BOYS -- THE HARSH REALITY OF PRISON LIFE. IT'S A WORLD OF LOCKED DOORS, BARRED WINDOWS, AND UNCOMFORTABLE PLASTIC CHAIRS.
AND NOW, THE MOMENT YOU'VE ALL BEEN WAITING FOR -- YOUR OPPORTUNITY TO COME FACE-TO-FACE WITH A REAL, LIVE CRIMINAL!
THIS IS #354708, BETTER KNOWN TO HIS BUDDIES HERE AS SNAKE. WE'LL LEAVE YOU BOYS IN HIS CAPABLE HANDS.
SEE YOU LATER, CHIEF. I'D LIKE TO THANK YOU FOR PROVIDING ME THIS CHANCE TO KEEP THESE KIDS FROM MAKING THE SAME MISTAKES I DID.
C'MON, SEYMOUR, LET'S HIT THE GUARDS' LOUNGE BEFORE ALL THE CRULLERS ARE GONE!
SOON...
...AND ANOTHER THING -- IF YOU'RE STEALING A GETAWAY CAR, BE SURE IT HAS GAS IN THE TANK.
WOW! THIS IS THE MOST EDUCATIONAL EXPERIENCE OF MY LIFE!

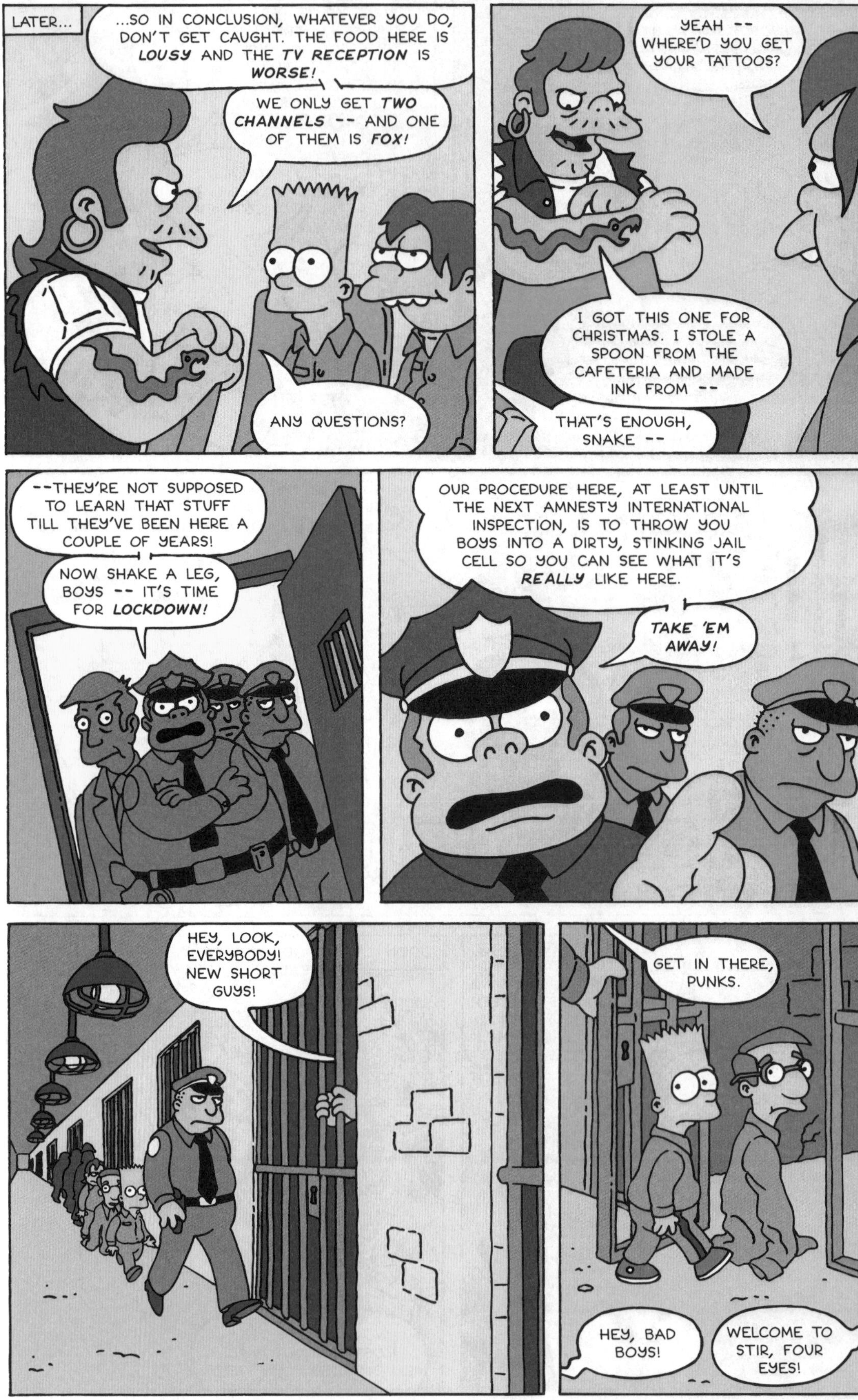
LATER...
...SO IN CONCLUSION, WHATEVER YOU DO, DON'T GET CAUGHT. THE FOOD HERE IS LOUSY AND THE TV RECEPTION IS WORSE!
WE ONLY GET TWO CHANNELS -- AND ONE OF THEM IS FOX!
ANY QUESTIONS?
YEAH -- WHERE'D YOU GET YOUR TATTOOS?
I GOT THIS ONE FOR CHRISTMAS. I STOLE A SPOON FROM THE CAFETERIA AND MADE INK FROM --
THAT'S ENOUGH, SNAKE --
--THEY'RE NOT SUPPOSED TO LEARN THAT STUFF TILL THEY'VE BEEN HERE A COUPLE OF YEARS!
NOW SHAKE A LEG, BOYS -- IT'S TIME FOR LOCKDOWN!
OUR PROCEDURE HERE, AT LEAST UNTIL THE NEXT AMNESTY INTERNATIONAL INSPECTION, IS TO THROW YOU BOYS INTO A DIRTY, STINKING JAIL CELL SO YOU CAN SEE WHAT IT'S REALLY LIKE HERE.
TAKE 'EM AWAY!
HEY, LOOK, EVERYBODY! NEW SHORT GUYS!
GET IN THERE, PUNKS.
HEY, BAD BOYS!
WELCOME TO STIR, FOUR EYES!

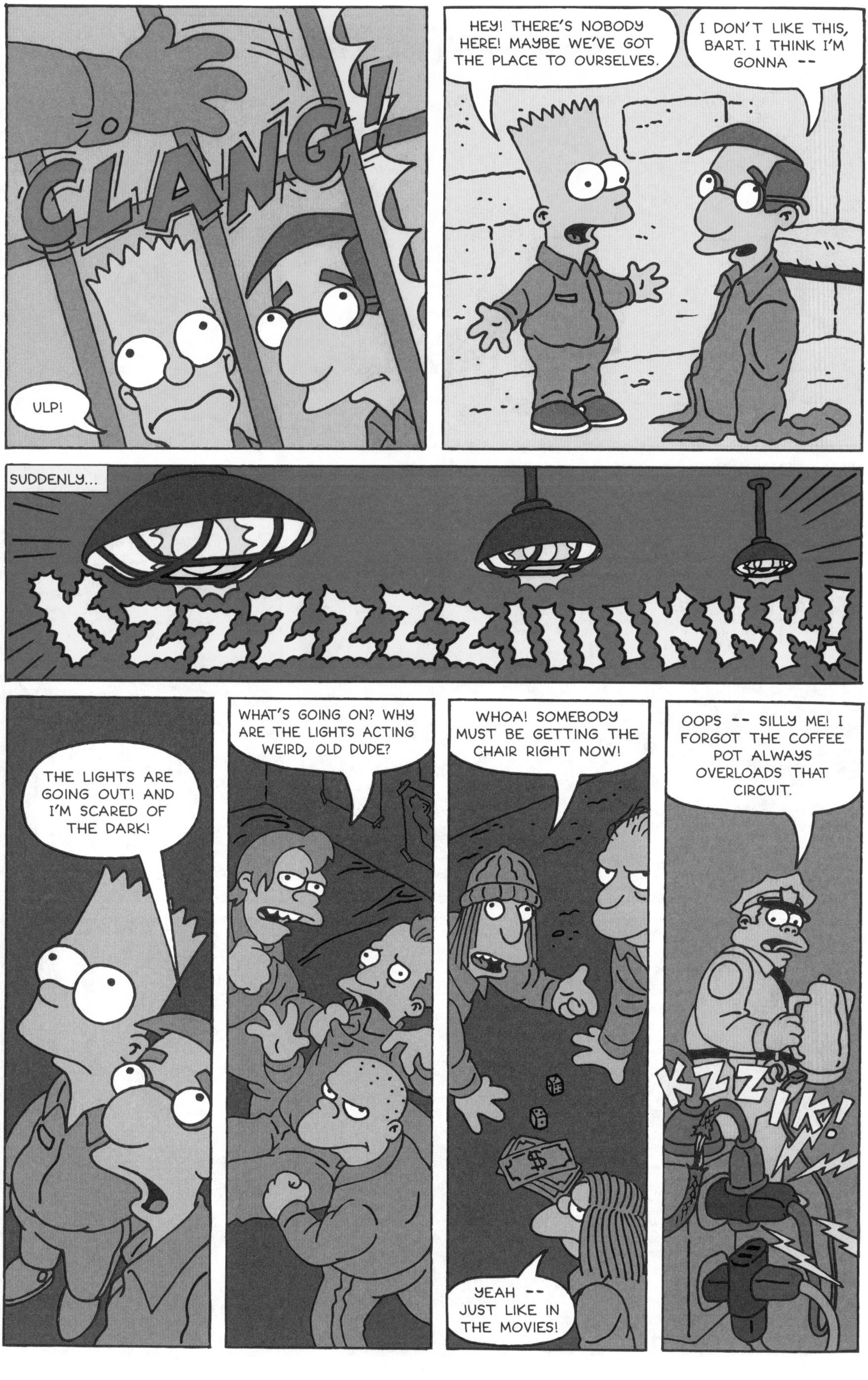
CLANG!
ULP!
HEY! THERE'S NOBODY HERE! MAYBE WE'VE GOT THE PLACE TO OURSELVES.
I DON'T LIKE THIS, BART. I THINK I'M GONNA --
SUDDENLY...
KZZZZZZIIIIKKK!
THE LIGHTS ARE GOING OUT! AND I'M SCARED OF THE DARK!
WHAT'S GOING ON? WHY ARE THE LIGHTS ACTING WEIRD, OLD DUDE?
WHOA! SOMEBODY MUST BE GETTING THE CHAIR RIGHT NOW!
YEAH -- JUST LIKE IN THE MOVIES!
OOPS -- SILLY ME! I FORGOT THE COFFEE POT ALWAYS OVERLOADS THAT CIRCUIT.
KZZIK!

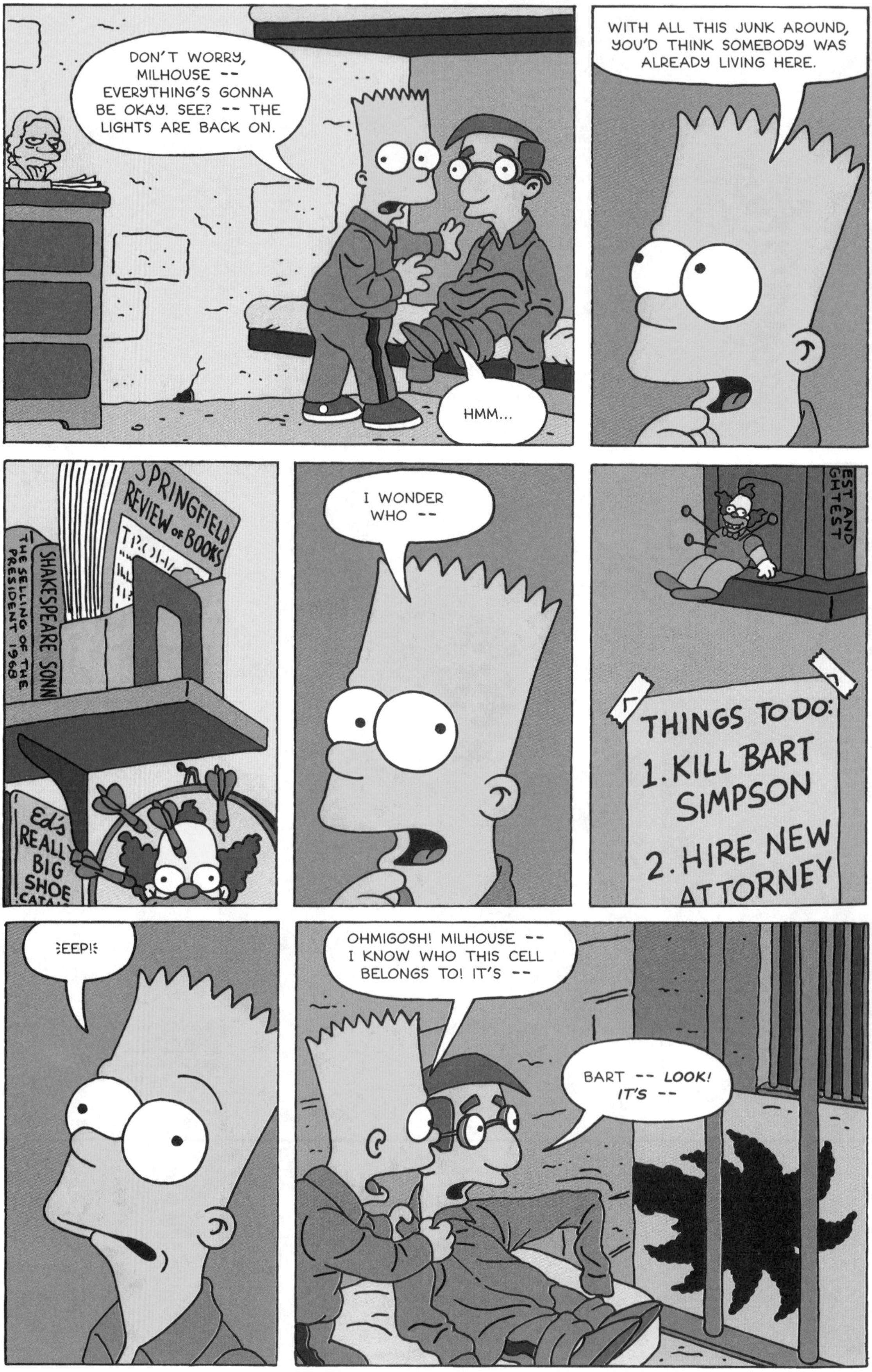
DON'T WORRY, MILHOUSE -- EVERYTHING'S GONNA BE OKAY. SEE? -- THE LIGHTS ARE BACK ON.
HMM...
WITH ALL THIS JUNK AROUND, YOU'D THINK SOMEBODY WAS ALREADY LIVING HERE.
SPRINGFIELD REVIEW OF BOOKS
THE SELLING OF THE PRESIDENT 1968
SHAKESPEARE SONN
Ed's REALLY BIG SHOE
I WONDER WHO --
THINGS TO DO:
1. KILL BART SIMPSON
2. HIRE NEW ATTORNEY
EEP!
OHMIGOSH! MILHOUSE -- I KNOW WHO THIS CELL BELONGS TO! IT'S --
BART -- *LOOK!* *IT'S* --

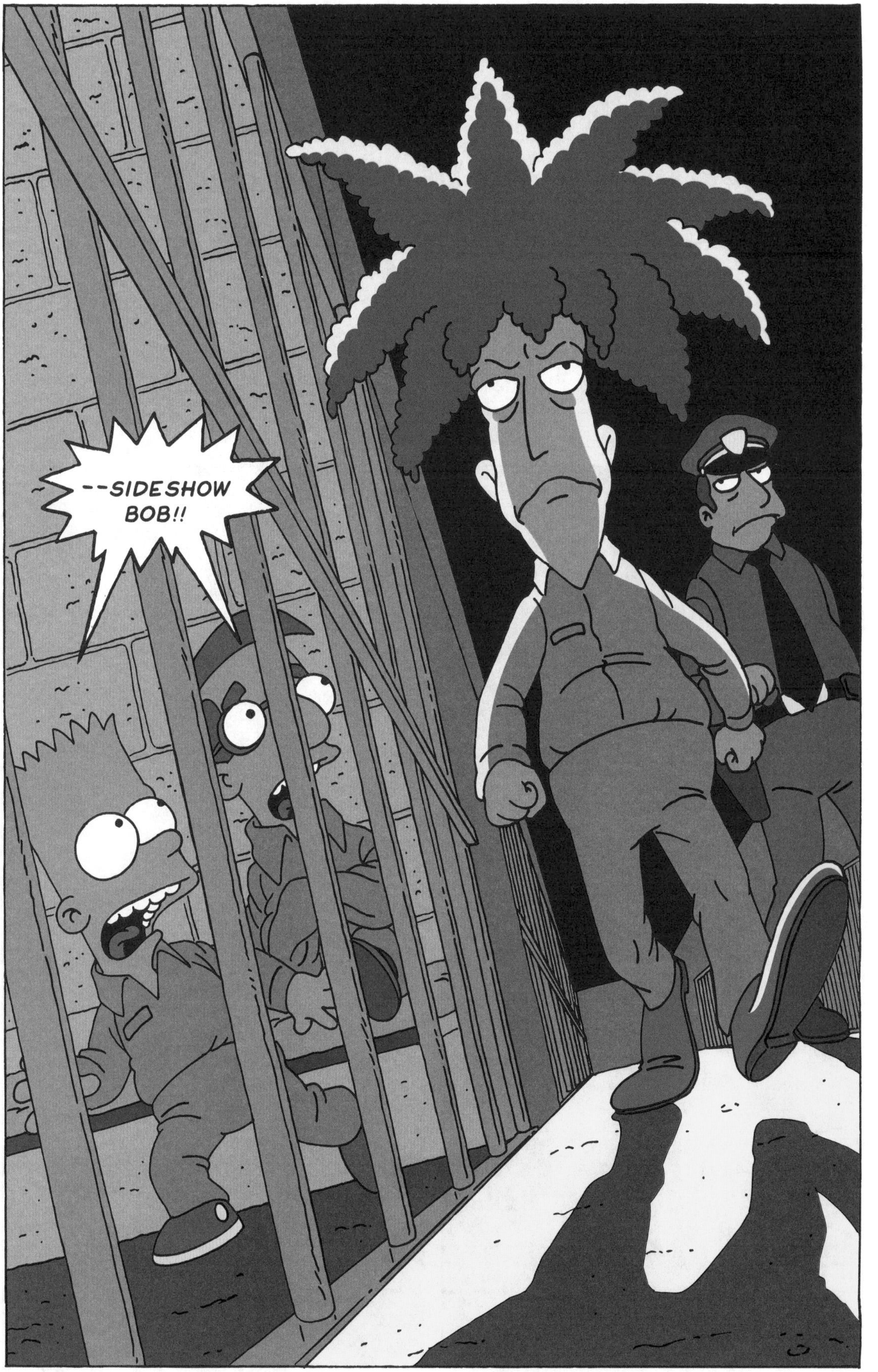
--SIDESHOW BOB!!

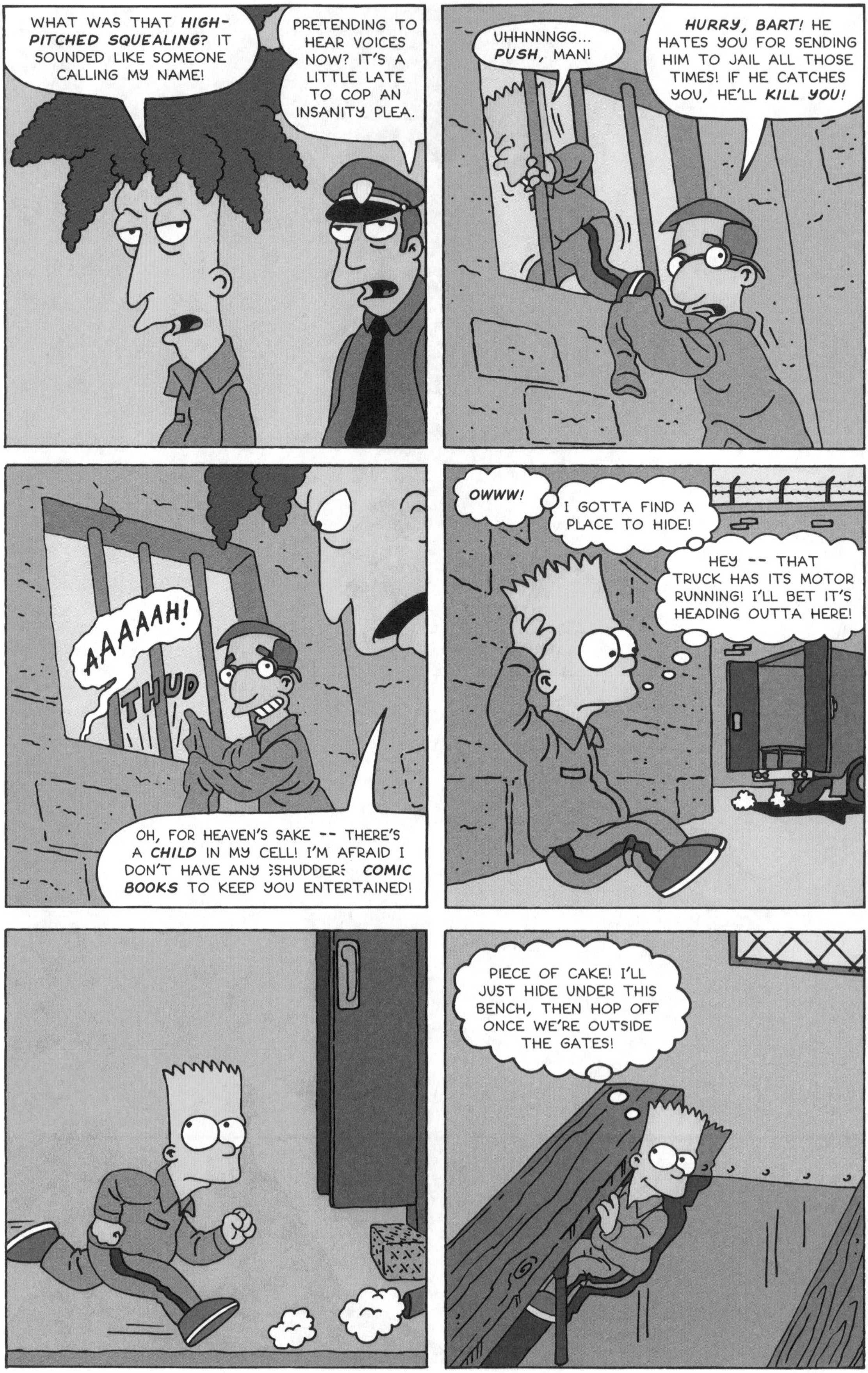
WHAT WAS THAT HIGH-PITCHED SQUEALING? IT SOUNDED LIKE SOMEONE CALLING MY NAME!
PRETENDING TO HEAR VOICES NOW? IT'S A LITTLE LATE TO COP AN INSANITY PLEA.
UHHNNNGG... PUSH, MAN!
HURRY, BART! HE HATES YOU FOR SENDING HIM TO JAIL ALL THOSE TIMES! IF HE CATCHES YOU, HE'LL KILL YOU!
AAAAAH!
THUD
OH, FOR HEAVEN'S SAKE -- THERE'S A CHILD IN MY CELL! I'M AFRAID I DON'T HAVE ANY :SHUDDER: COMIC BOOKS TO KEEP YOU ENTERTAINED!
OWWW!
I GOTTA FIND A PLACE TO HIDE!
HEY -- THAT TRUCK HAS ITS MOTOR RUNNING! I'LL BET IT'S HEADING OUTTA HERE!
PIECE OF CAKE! I'LL JUST HIDE UNDER THIS BENCH, THEN HOP OFF ONCE WE'RE OUTSIDE THE GATES!

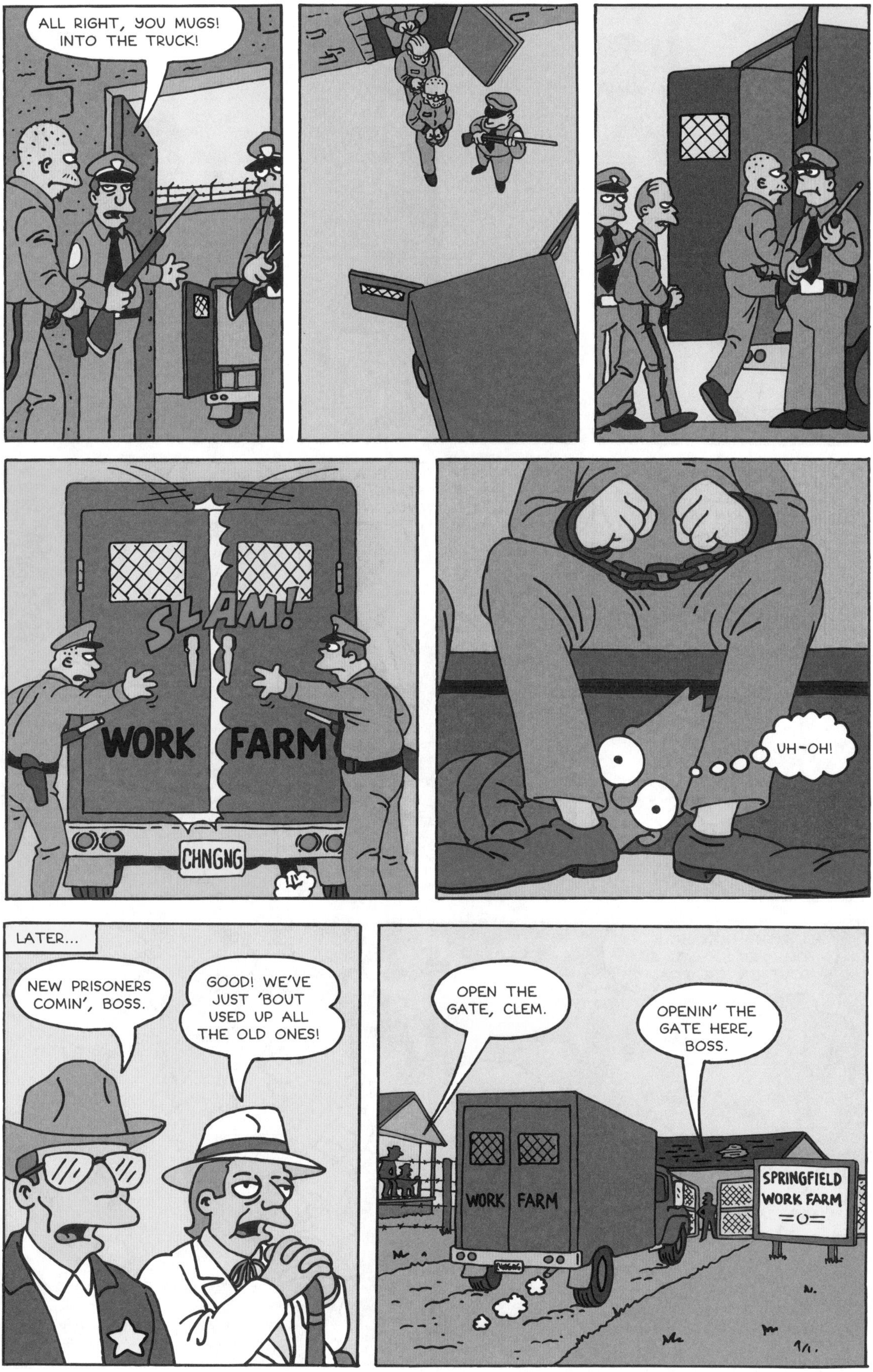

ALL RIGHT, YOU MUGS! INTO THE TRUCK!
SLAM!
WORK FARM
CHNGNG
UH-OH!
LATER...
NEW PRISONERS COMIN', BOSS.
GOOD! WE'VE JUST 'BOUT USED UP ALL THE OLD ONES!
OPEN THE GATE, CLEM.
OPENIN' THE GATE HERE, BOSS.
WORK FARM
SPRINGFIELD WORK FARM

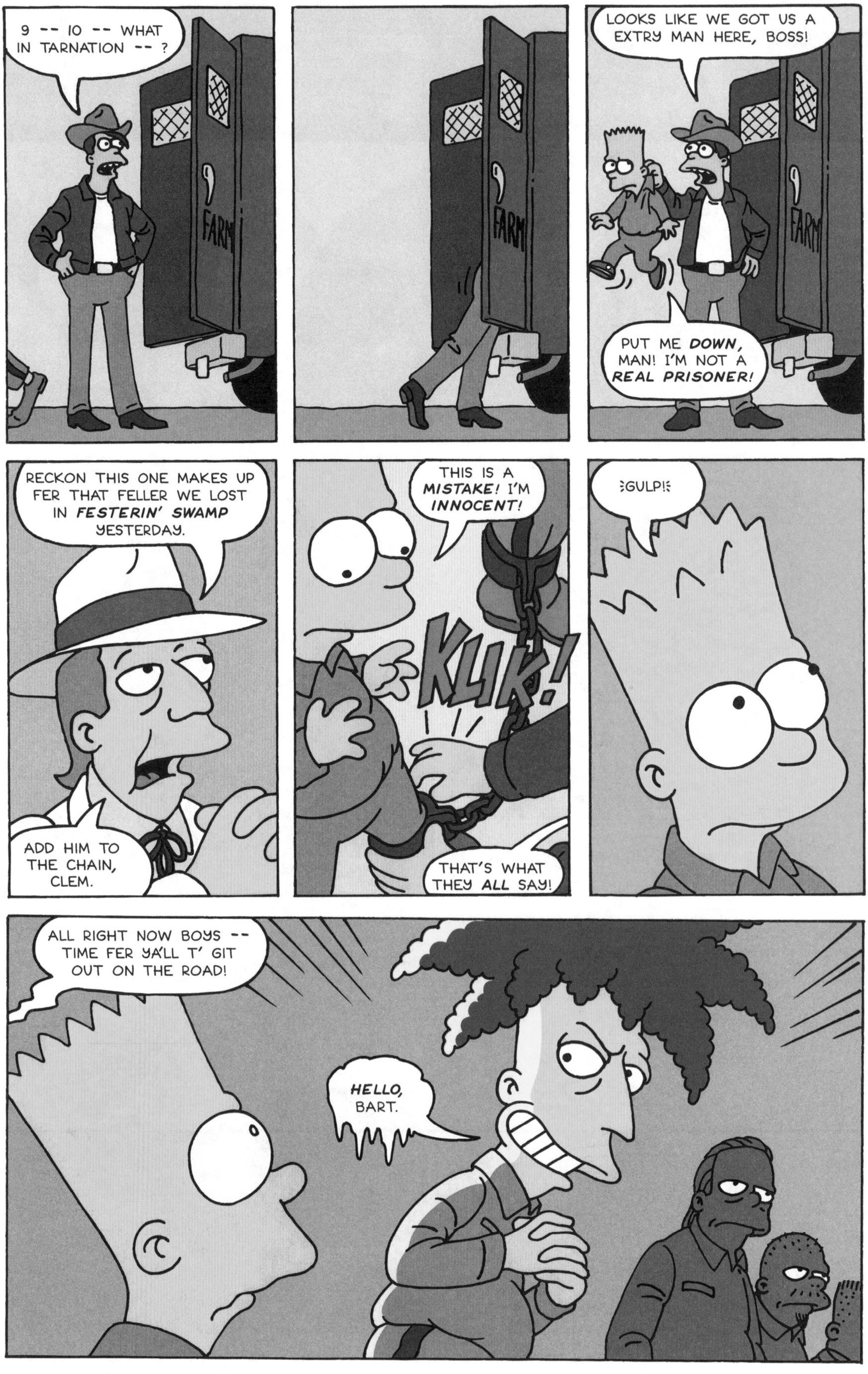
9 -- 10 -- WHAT IN TARNATION -- ?
FARM
LOOKS LIKE WE GOT US A EXTRY MAN HERE, BOSS!
PUT ME DOWN, MAN! I'M NOT A REAL PRISONER!
RECKON THIS ONE MAKES UP FER THAT FELLER WE LOST IN FESTERIN' SWAMP YESTERDAY.
ADD HIM TO THE CHAIN, CLEM.
THIS IS A MISTAKE! I'M INNOCENT!
KLIK!
THAT'S WHAT THEY ALL SAY!
GULP!
ALL RIGHT NOW BOYS -- TIME FER YA'LL T' GIT OUT ON THE ROAD!
HELLO, BART.

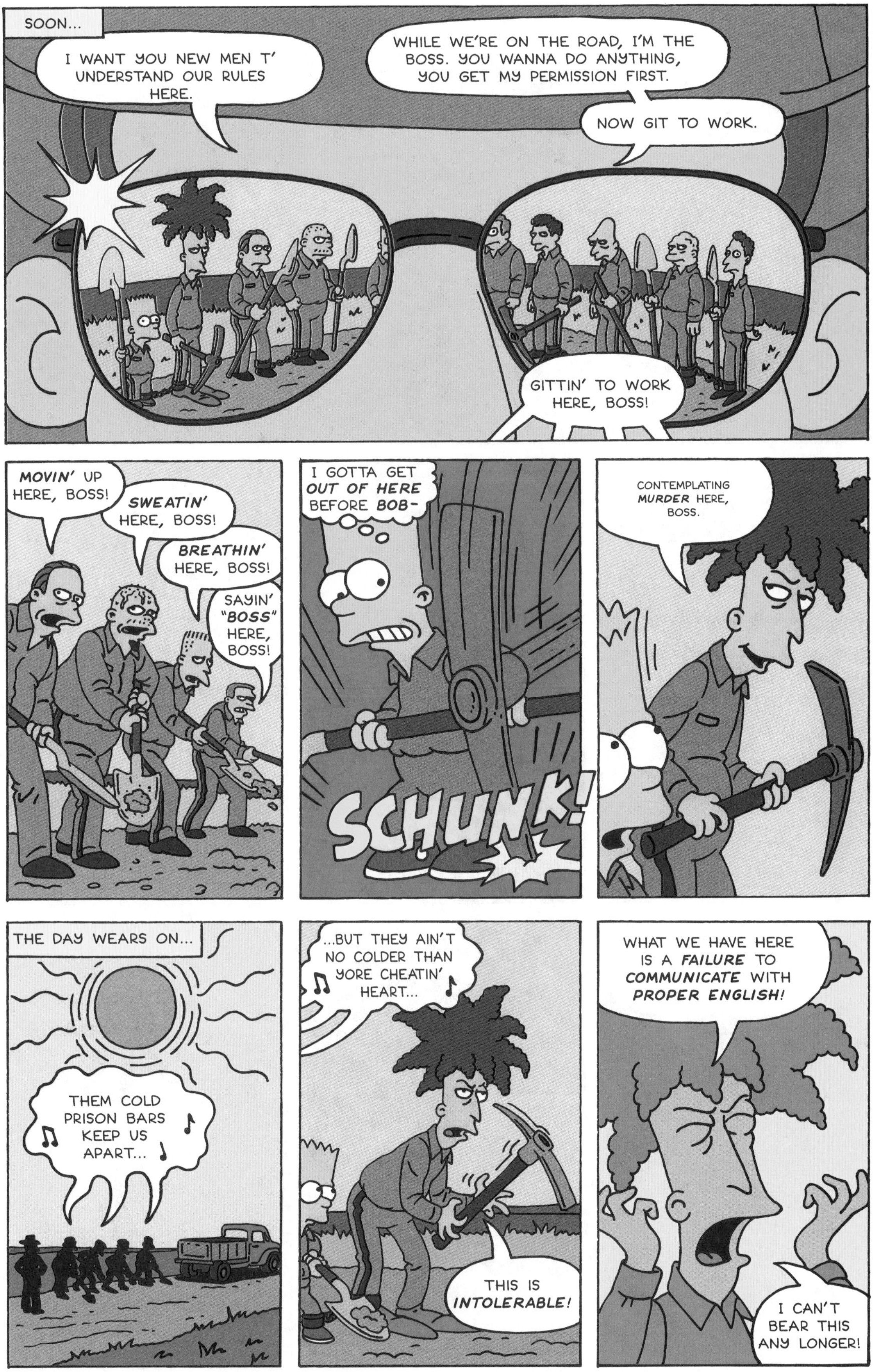

SOON...
I WANT YOU NEW MEN T' UNDERSTAND OUR RULES HERE.
WHILE WE'RE ON THE ROAD, I'M THE BOSS. YOU WANNA DO ANYTHING, YOU GET MY PERMISSION FIRST.
NOW GIT TO WORK.
GITTIN' TO WORK HERE, BOSS!
MOVIN' UP HERE, BOSS!
SWEATIN' HERE, BOSS!
BREATHIN' HERE, BOSS!
SAYIN' "BOSS" HERE, BOSS!
I GOTTA GET OUT OF HERE BEFORE BOB-
SCHUNK!
CONTEMPLATING MURDER HERE, BOSS.
THE DAY WEARS ON...
THEM COLD PRISON BARS KEEP US APART...
...BUT THEY AIN'T NO COLDER THAN YORE CHEATIN' HEART...
THIS IS INTOLERABLE!
WHAT WE HAVE HERE IS A FAILURE TO COMMUNICATE WITH PROPER ENGLISH!
I CAN'T BEAR THIS ANY LONGER!

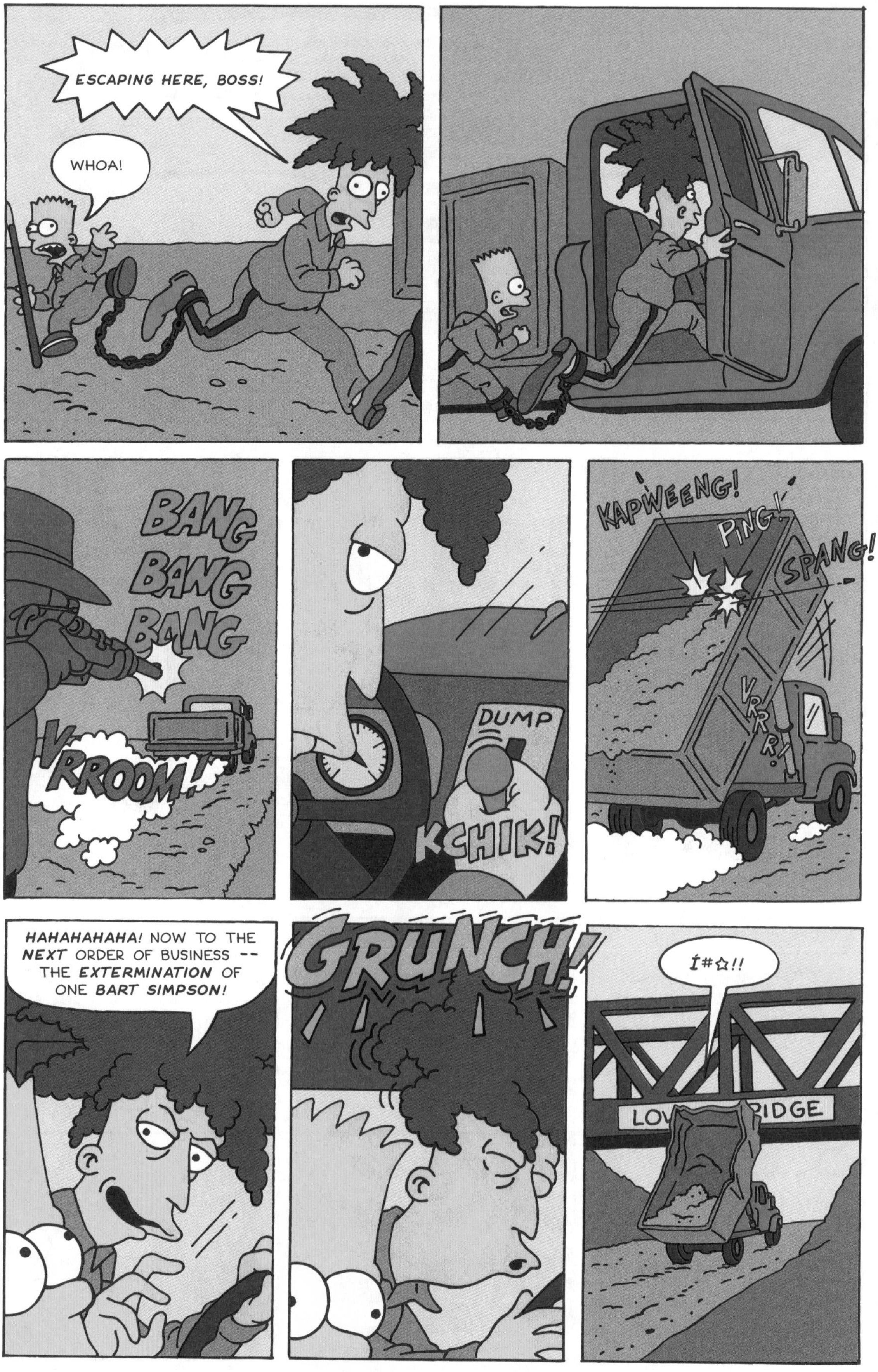
ESCAPING HERE, BOSS!
WHOA!
BANG
BANG
BANG
VRROOM!
DUMP
KCHIK!
KAPWEENG!
PING!
SPANG!
VRRRR!
HAHAHAHAHA! NOW TO THE NEXT ORDER OF BUSINESS -- THE EXTERMINATION OF ONE BART SIMPSON!
GRUNCH!
LOW
RIDGE
Í#☆!!

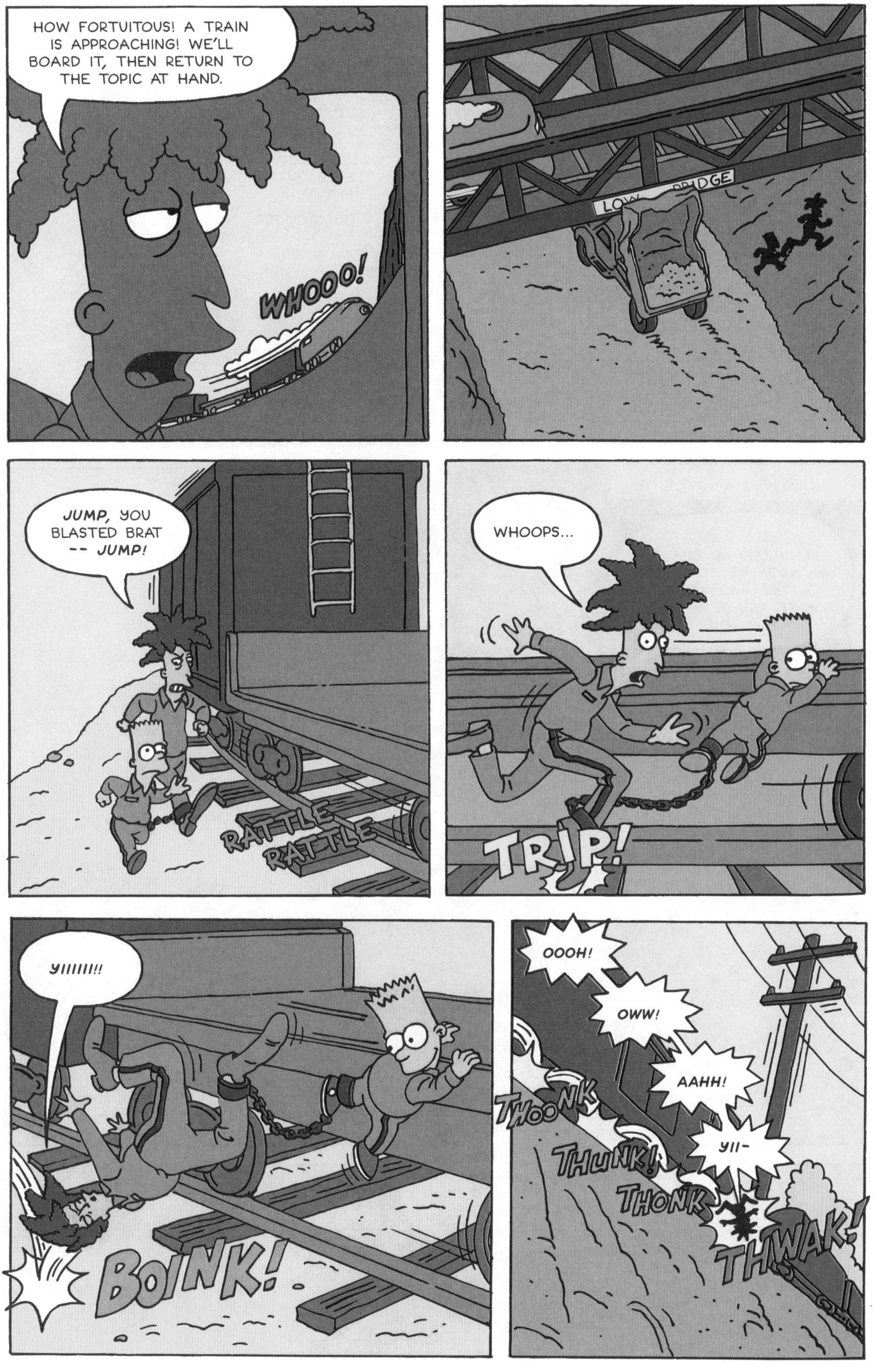
HOW FORTUITOUS! A TRAIN IS APPROACHING! WE'LL BOARD IT, THEN RETURN TO THE TOPIC AT HAND.
WHOOO!
LOW
JUMP, YOU BLASTED BRAT -- JUMP!
RATTLE RATTLE
WHOOPS...
TRIP!
YIIIIII!!
BOINK!
OOOH!
OWW!
AAHH!
THOONK
YII-
THUNK!
THONK
THWAK!

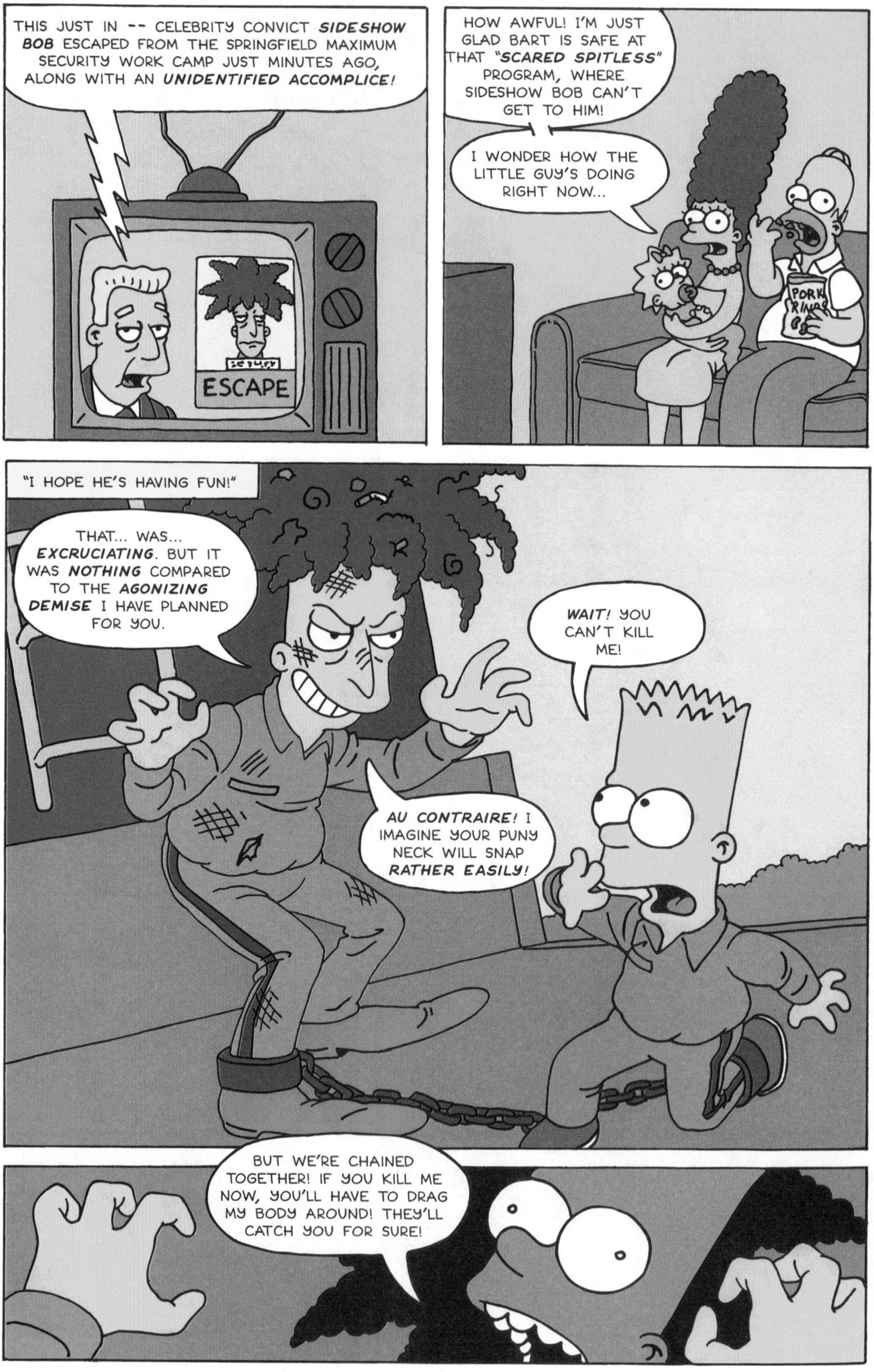
THIS JUST IN -- CELEBRITY CONVICT **SIDESHOW BOB** ESCAPED FROM THE SPRINGFIELD MAXIMUM SECURITY WORK CAMP JUST MINUTES AGO, ALONG WITH AN ***UNIDENTIFIED ACCOMPLICE!***
ESCAPE
HOW AWFUL! I'M JUST GLAD BART IS SAFE AT THAT ***"SCARED SPITLESS"*** PROGRAM, WHERE SIDESHOW BOB CAN'T GET TO HIM!
I WONDER HOW THE LITTLE GUY'S DOING RIGHT NOW...
"I HOPE HE'S HAVING FUN!"
THAT... WAS... ***EXCRUCIATING***. BUT IT WAS ***NOTHING*** COMPARED TO THE ***AGONIZING DEMISE*** I HAVE PLANNED FOR YOU.
WAIT! YOU CAN'T KILL ME!
AU CONTRAIRE! I IMAGINE YOUR PUNY NECK WILL SNAP ***RATHER EASILY!***
BUT WE'RE CHAINED TOGETHER! IF YOU KILL ME NOW, YOU'LL HAVE TO DRAG MY BODY AROUND! THEY'LL CATCH YOU FOR SURE!

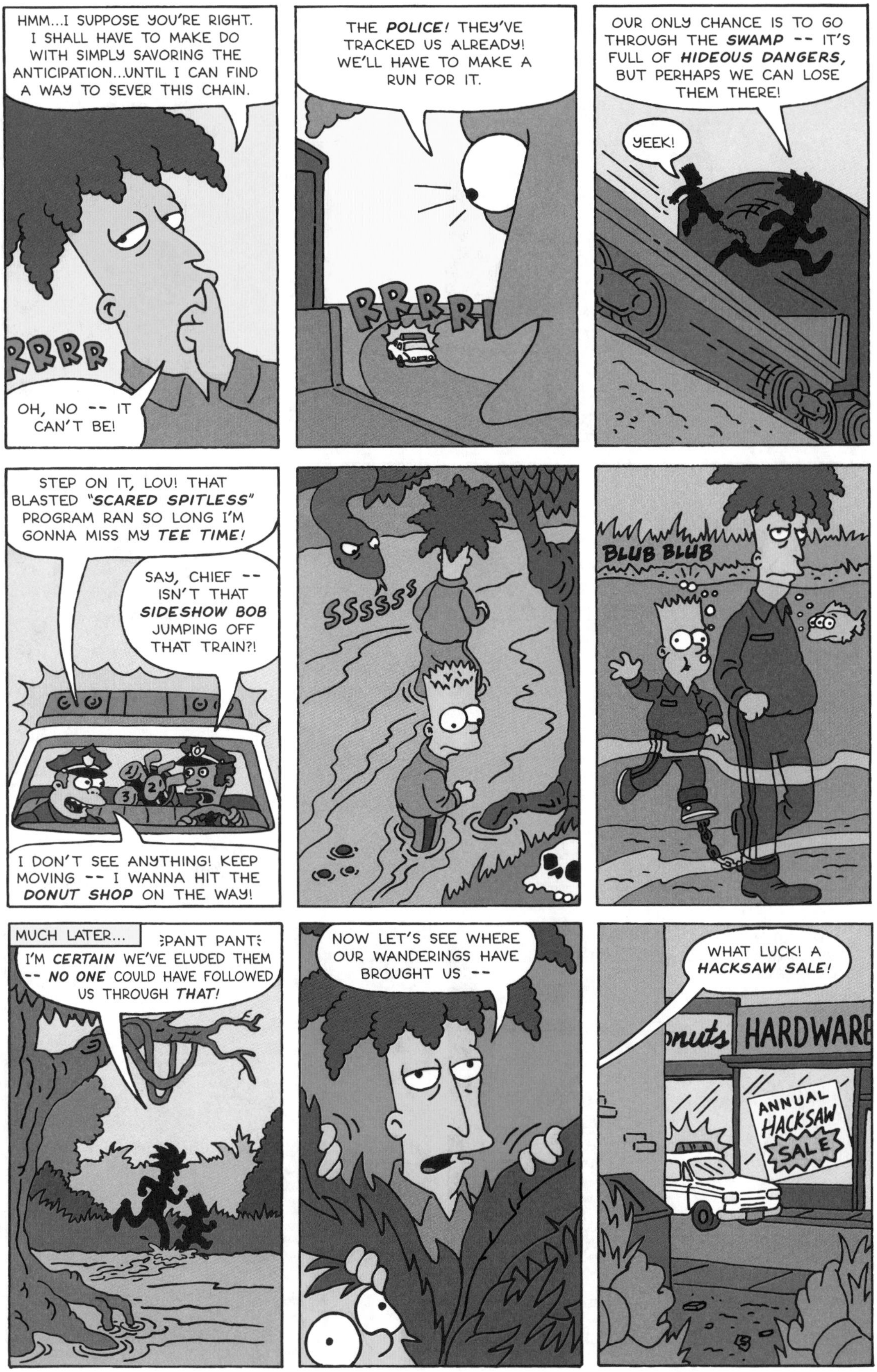
HMM...I SUPPOSE YOU'RE RIGHT. I SHALL HAVE TO MAKE DO WITH SIMPLY SAVORING THE ANTICIPATION...UNTIL I CAN FIND A WAY TO SEVER THIS CHAIN.
RRRR
OH, NO -- IT CAN'T BE!
THE POLICE! THEY'VE TRACKED US ALREADY! WE'LL HAVE TO MAKE A RUN FOR IT.
RRRRR
OUR ONLY CHANCE IS TO GO THROUGH THE SWAMP -- IT'S FULL OF HIDEOUS DANGERS, BUT PERHAPS WE CAN LOSE THEM THERE!
YEEK!
STEP ON IT, LOU! THAT BLASTED "SCARED SPITLESS" PROGRAM RAN SO LONG I'M GONNA MISS MY TEE TIME!
SAY, CHIEF -- ISN'T THAT SIDESHOW BOB JUMPING OFF THAT TRAIN?!
I DON'T SEE ANYTHING! KEEP MOVING -- I WANNA HIT THE DONUT SHOP ON THE WAY!
SSSSSS
BLUB BLUB
MUCH LATER...
PANT PANT
I'M CERTAIN WE'VE ELUDED THEM -- NO ONE COULD HAVE FOLLOWED US THROUGH THAT!
NOW LET'S SEE WHERE OUR WANDERINGS HAVE BROUGHT US --
WHAT LUCK! A HACKSAW SALE!
HARDWARE
ANNUAL HACKSAW SALE

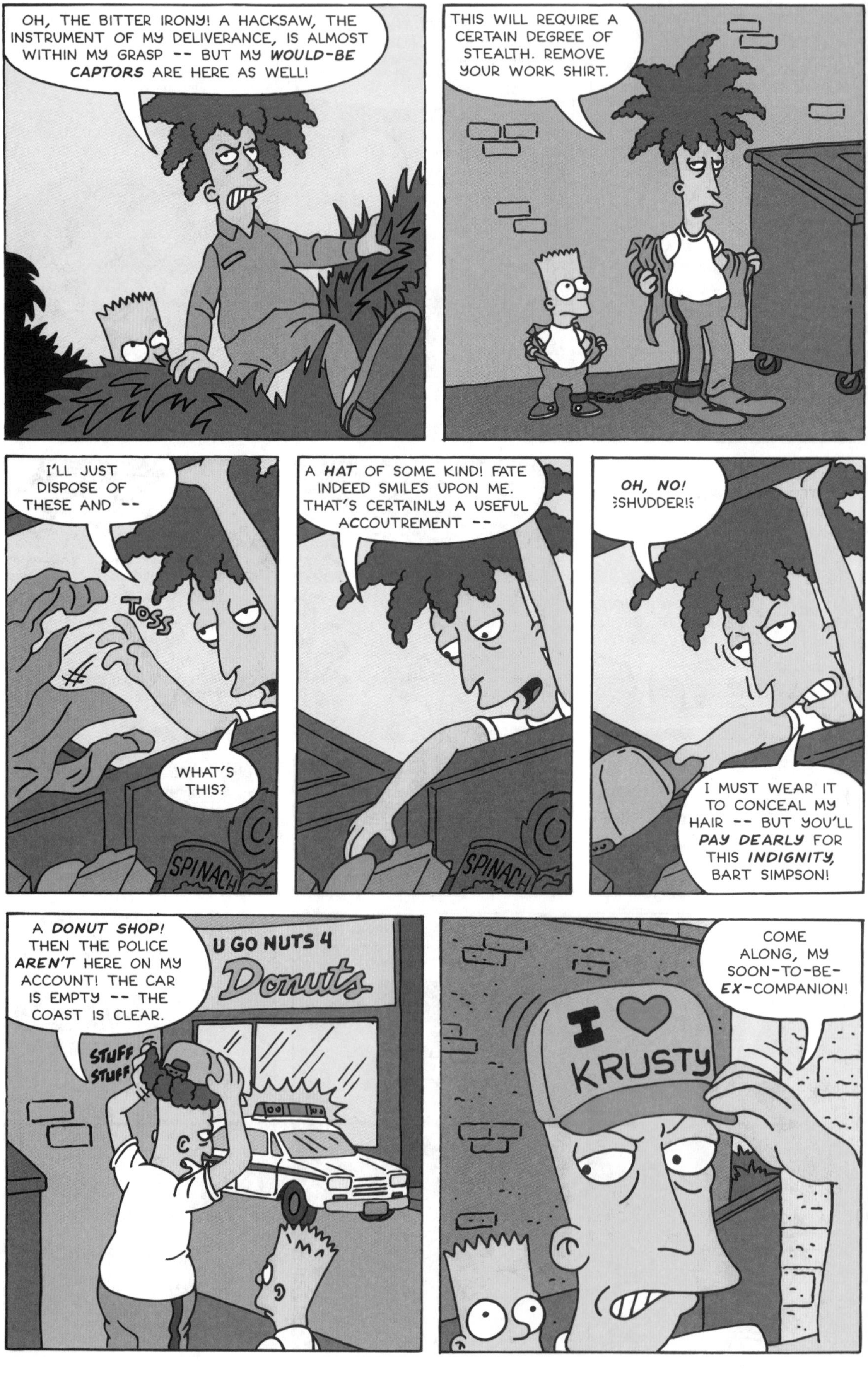
OH, THE BITTER IRONY! A HACKSAW, THE INSTRUMENT OF MY DELIVERANCE, IS ALMOST WITHIN MY GRASP -- BUT MY WOULD-BE CAPTORS ARE HERE AS WELL!
THIS WILL REQUIRE A CERTAIN DEGREE OF STEALTH. REMOVE YOUR WORK SHIRT.
I'LL JUST DISPOSE OF THESE AND --
TOSS
WHAT'S THIS?
SPINACH
A HAT OF SOME KIND! FATE INDEED SMILES UPON ME. THAT'S CERTAINLY A USEFUL ACCOUTREMENT --
SPINACH
OH, NO! :SHUDDER!:
I MUST WEAR IT TO CONCEAL MY HAIR -- BUT YOU'LL PAY DEARLY FOR THIS INDIGNITY, BART SIMPSON!
A DONUT SHOP! THEN THE POLICE AREN'T HERE ON MY ACCOUNT! THE CAR IS EMPTY -- THE COAST IS CLEAR.
U GO NUTS 4
Donuts
STUFF
STUFF
COME ALONG, MY SOON-TO-BE-EX-COMPANION!
I ♥ KRUSTY

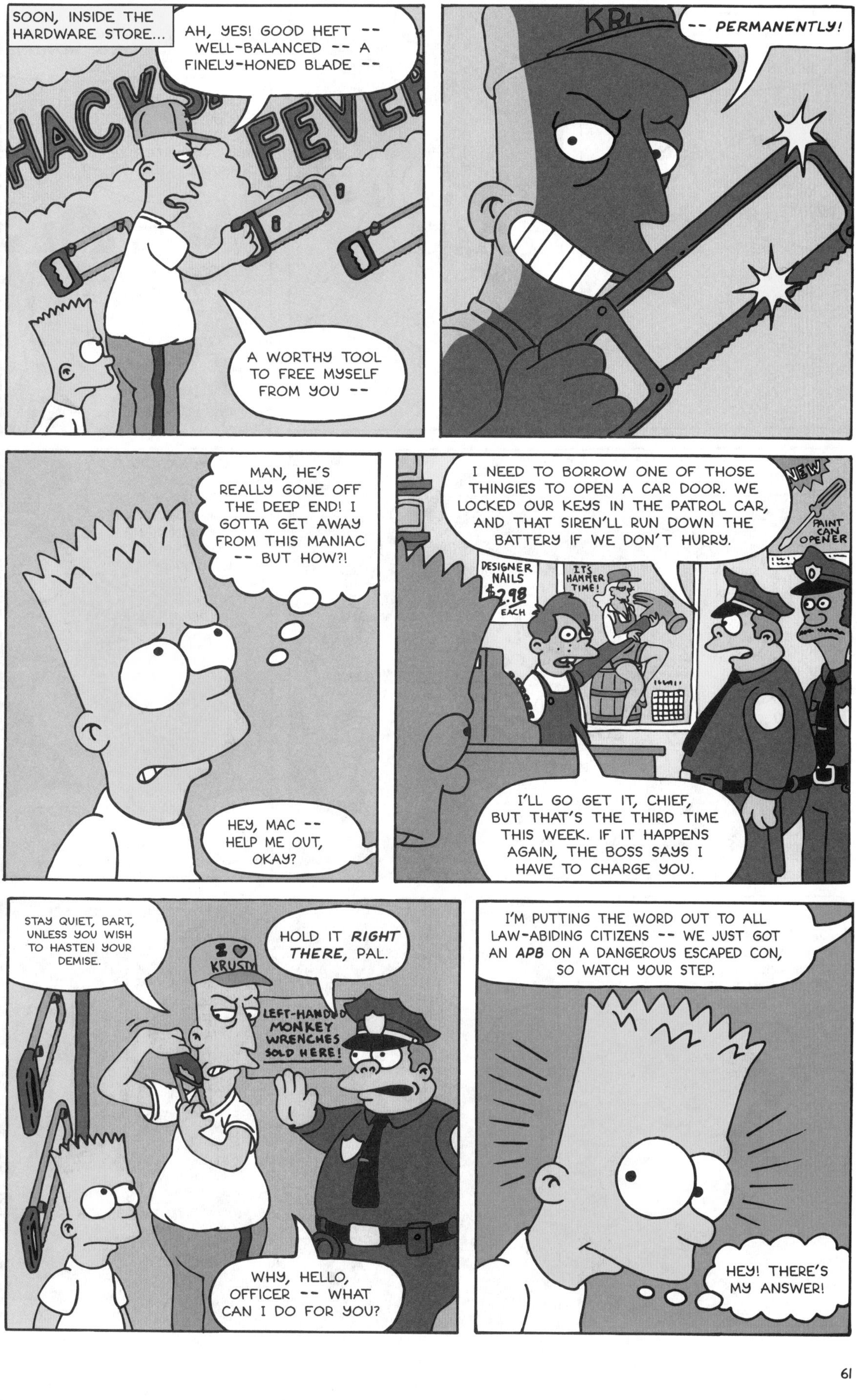
SOON, INSIDE THE HARDWARE STORE...
AH, YES! GOOD HEFT -- WELL-BALANCED -- A FINELY-HONED BLADE --
HACKSAW FEVER
A WORTHY TOOL TO FREE MYSELF FROM YOU --
-- PERMANENTLY!
MAN, HE'S REALLY GONE OFF THE DEEP END! I GOTTA GET AWAY FROM THIS MANIAC -- BUT HOW?!
HEY, MAC -- HELP ME OUT, OKAY?
I NEED TO BORROW ONE OF THOSE THINGIES TO OPEN A CAR DOOR. WE LOCKED OUR KEYS IN THE PATROL CAR, AND THAT SIREN'LL RUN DOWN THE BATTERY IF WE DON'T HURRY.
NEW
PAINT CAN OPENER
DESIGNER NAILS $2.98 EACH
IT'S HAMMER TIME!
I'LL GO GET IT, CHIEF, BUT THAT'S THE THIRD TIME THIS WEEK. IF IT HAPPENS AGAIN, THE BOSS SAYS I HAVE TO CHARGE YOU.
STAY QUIET, BART, UNLESS YOU WISH TO HASTEN YOUR DEMISE.
HOLD IT RIGHT THERE, PAL.
LEFT-HANDED MONKEY WRENCHES SOLD HERE!
WHY, HELLO, OFFICER -- WHAT CAN I DO FOR YOU?
I'M PUTTING THE WORD OUT TO ALL LAW-ABIDING CITIZENS -- WE JUST GOT AN APB ON A DANGEROUS ESCAPED CON, SO WATCH YOUR STEP.
HEY! THERE'S MY ANSWER!

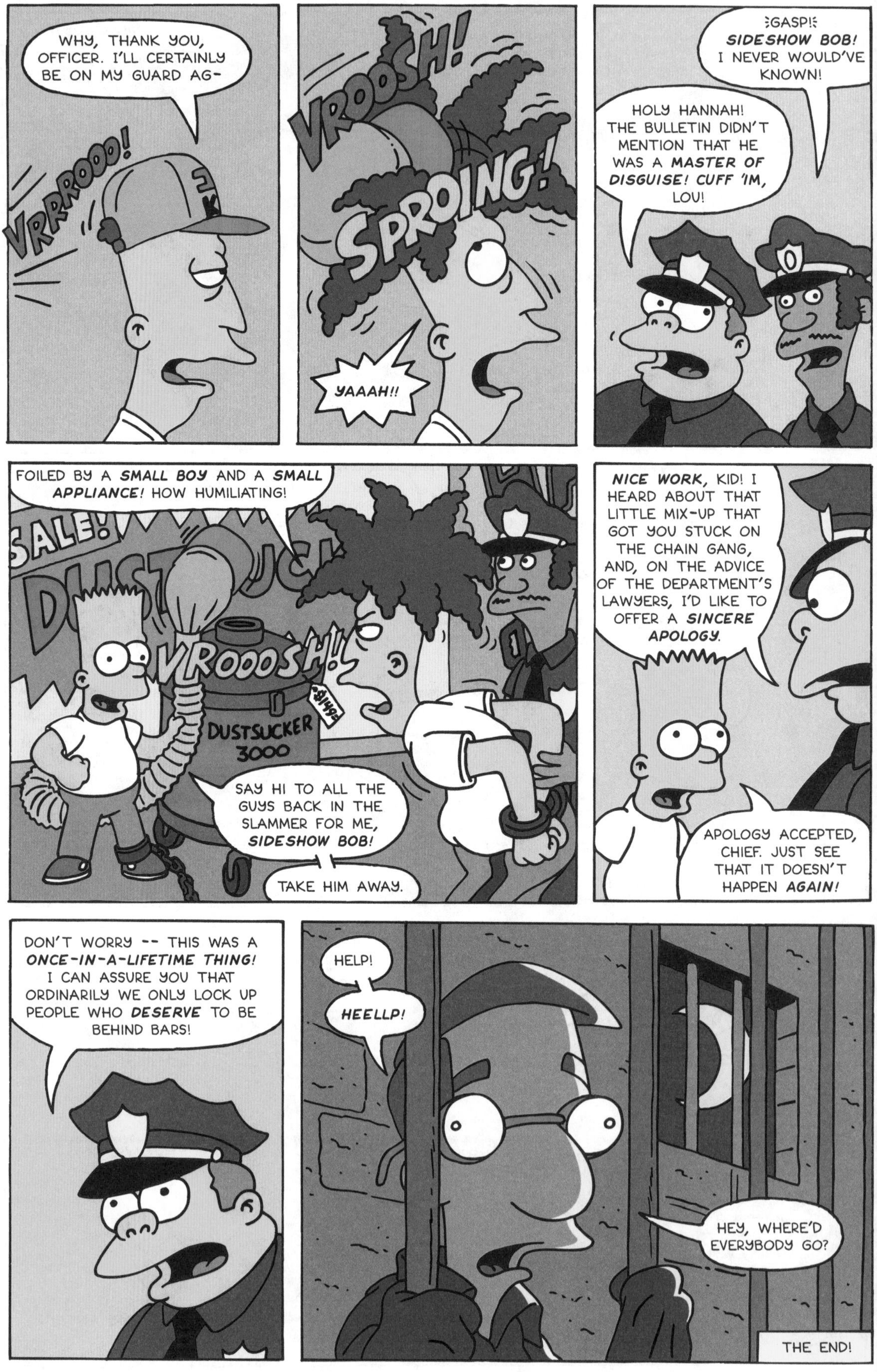
WHY, THANK YOU, OFFICER. I'LL CERTAINLY BE ON MY GUARD AG–
VRRROOO!
VROOSH!
SPROING!
YAAAH!!
GASP!
SIDESHOW BOB! I NEVER WOULD'VE KNOWN!
HOLY HANNAH! THE BULLETIN DIDN'T MENTION THAT HE WAS A MASTER OF DISGUISE! CUFF 'IM, LOU!
FOILED BY A SMALL BOY AND A SMALL APPLIANCE! HOW HUMILIATING!
SALE!
VROOOSH!
DUSTSUCKER 3000
SAY HI TO ALL THE GUYS BACK IN THE SLAMMER FOR ME, SIDESHOW BOB!
TAKE HIM AWAY.
NICE WORK, KID! I HEARD ABOUT THAT LITTLE MIX-UP THAT GOT YOU STUCK ON THE CHAIN GANG, AND, ON THE ADVICE OF THE DEPARTMENT'S LAWYERS, I'D LIKE TO OFFER A SINCERE APOLOGY.
APOLOGY ACCEPTED, CHIEF. JUST SEE THAT IT DOESN'T HAPPEN AGAIN!
DON'T WORRY -- THIS WAS A ONCE-IN-A-LIFETIME THING! I CAN ASSURE YOU THAT ORDINARILY WE ONLY LOCK UP PEOPLE WHO DESERVE TO BE BEHIND BARS!
HELP!
HEELLP!
HEY, WHERE'D EVERYBODY GO?
THE END!

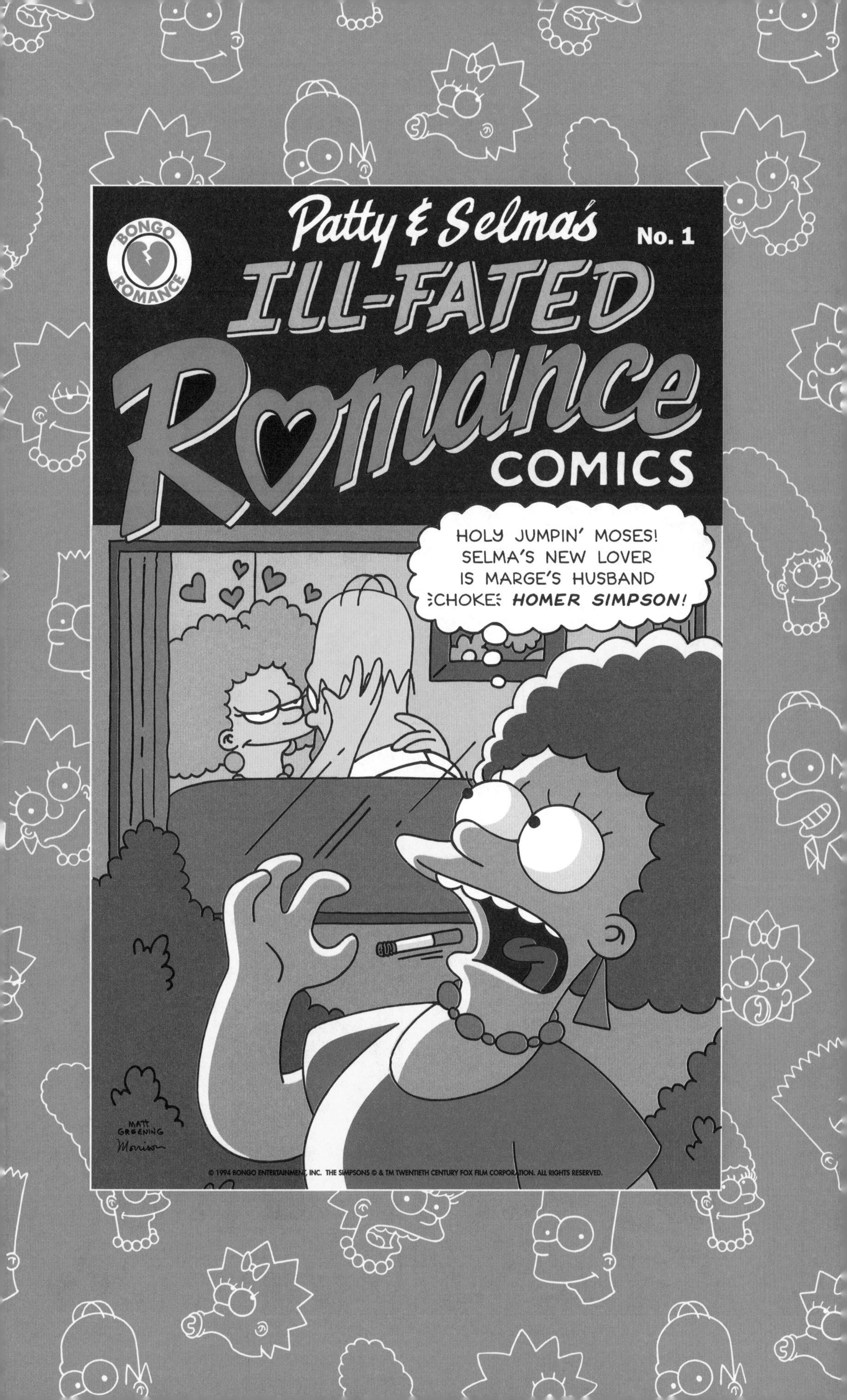
Patty & Selma's
No. 1
BONGO ROMANCE
ILL-FATED
Romance
COMICS
HOLY JUMPIN' MOSES!
SELMA'S NEW LOVER
IS MARGE'S HUSBAND
CHOKE HOMER SIMPSON!
MATT GROENING
Morrison
© 1994 BONGO ENTERTAINMENT, INC. THE SIMPSONS © & TM TWENTIETH CENTURY FOX FILM CORPORATION. ALL RIGHTS RESERVED.

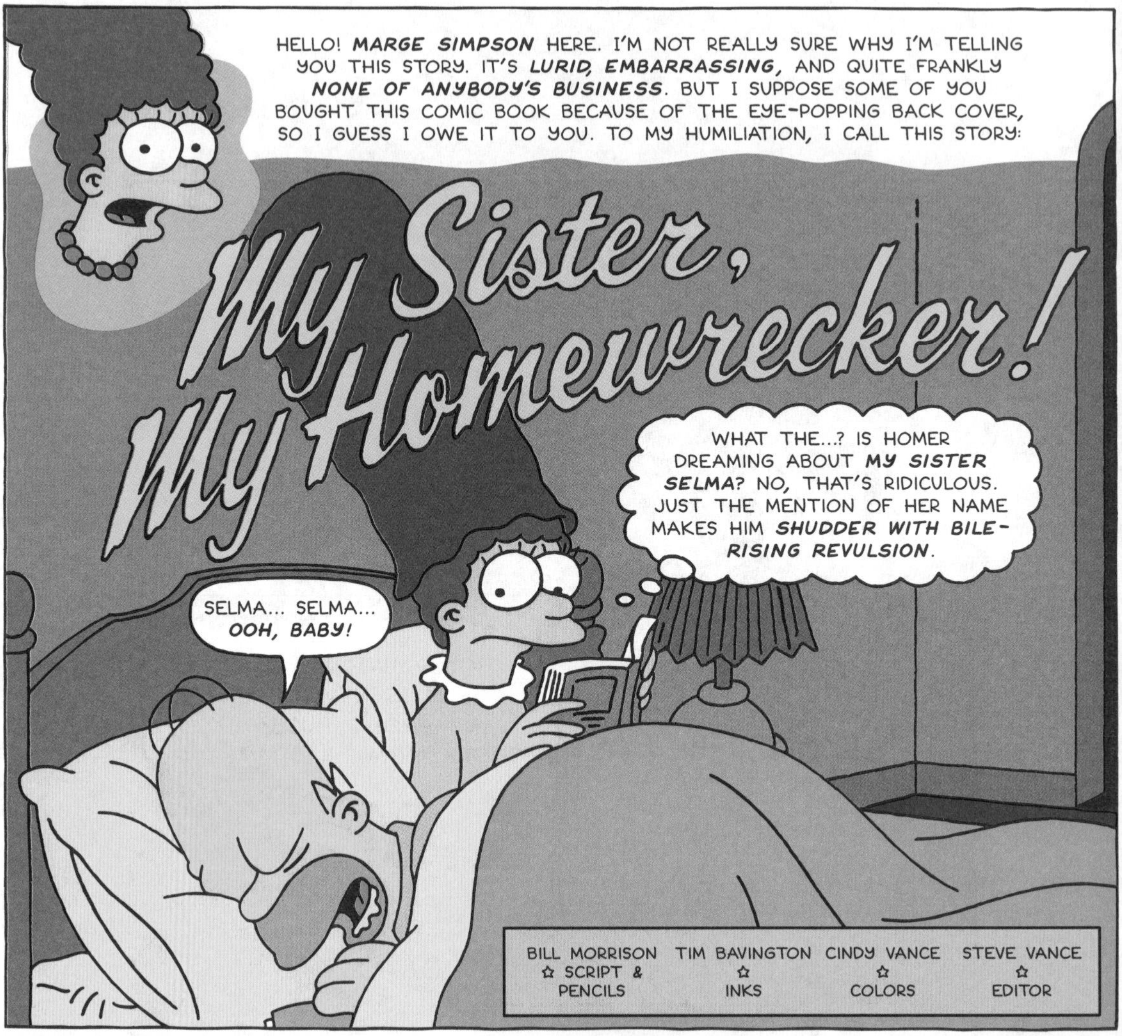
HELLO! MARGE SIMPSON HERE. I'M NOT REALLY SURE WHY I'M TELLING YOU THIS STORY. IT'S LURID, EMBARRASSING, AND QUITE FRANKLY NONE OF ANYBODY'S BUSINESS. BUT I SUPPOSE SOME OF YOU BOUGHT THIS COMIC BOOK BECAUSE OF THE EYE-POPPING BACK COVER, SO I GUESS I OWE IT TO YOU. TO MY HUMILIATION, I CALL THIS STORY:
My Sister, My Homewrecker!
WHAT THE...? IS HOMER DREAMING ABOUT MY SISTER SELMA? NO, THAT'S RIDICULOUS. JUST THE MENTION OF HER NAME MAKES HIM SHUDDER WITH BILE-RISING REVULSION.
SELMA... SELMA... OOH, BABY!
BILL MORRISON ☆ SCRIPT & PENCILS
TIM BAVINGTON ☆ INKS
CINDY VANCE ☆ COLORS
STEVE VANCE ☆ EDITOR

"OR SO I *THOUGHT.* THEN THE NEXT EVENING, I RECEIVED A VISIT FROM MY SISTER PATTY. WE WERE CHATTING LIGHTLY OVER COFFEE AND MAPLE LOGS WHEN PATTY ABRUPTLY BLURTED OUT THE WORDS WHICH YANKED MY ***DEEPEST, DARKEST FEAR*** FROM THE PIT OF MY STOMACH AND PULLED IT UP MY ESOPHAGUS AND INTO MY THROAT..."

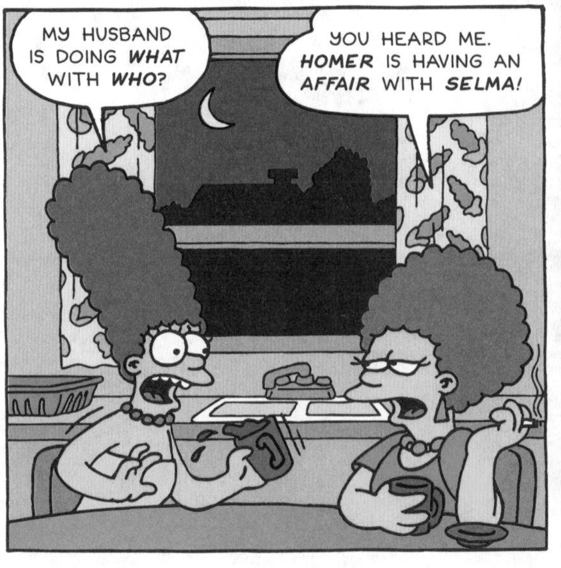
MY HUSBAND IS DOING WHAT WITH WHO?
YOU HEARD ME. HOMER IS HAVING AN AFFAIR WITH SELMA!

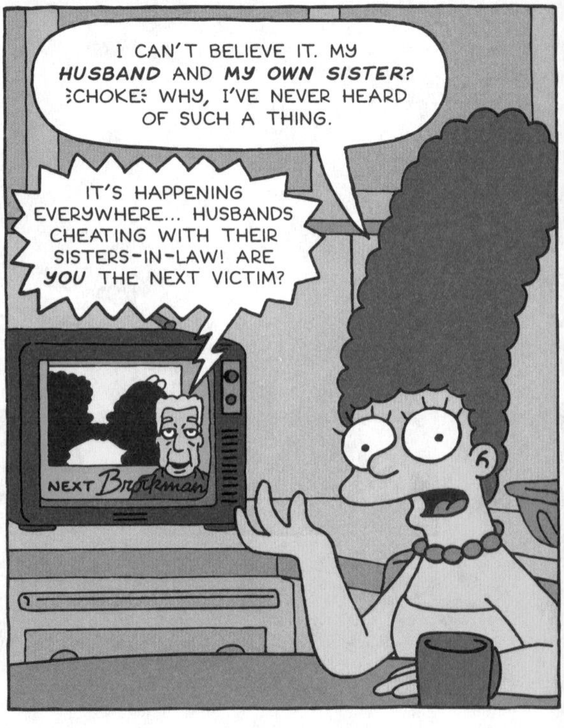
I CAN'T BELIEVE IT. MY HUSBAND AND MY OWN SISTER? ⁝CHOKE⁝ WHY, I'VE NEVER HEARD OF SUCH A THING.
IT'S HAPPENING EVERYWHERE... HUSBANDS CHEATING WITH THEIR SISTERS-IN-LAW! ARE YOU THE NEXT VICTIM?
NEXT Brockman

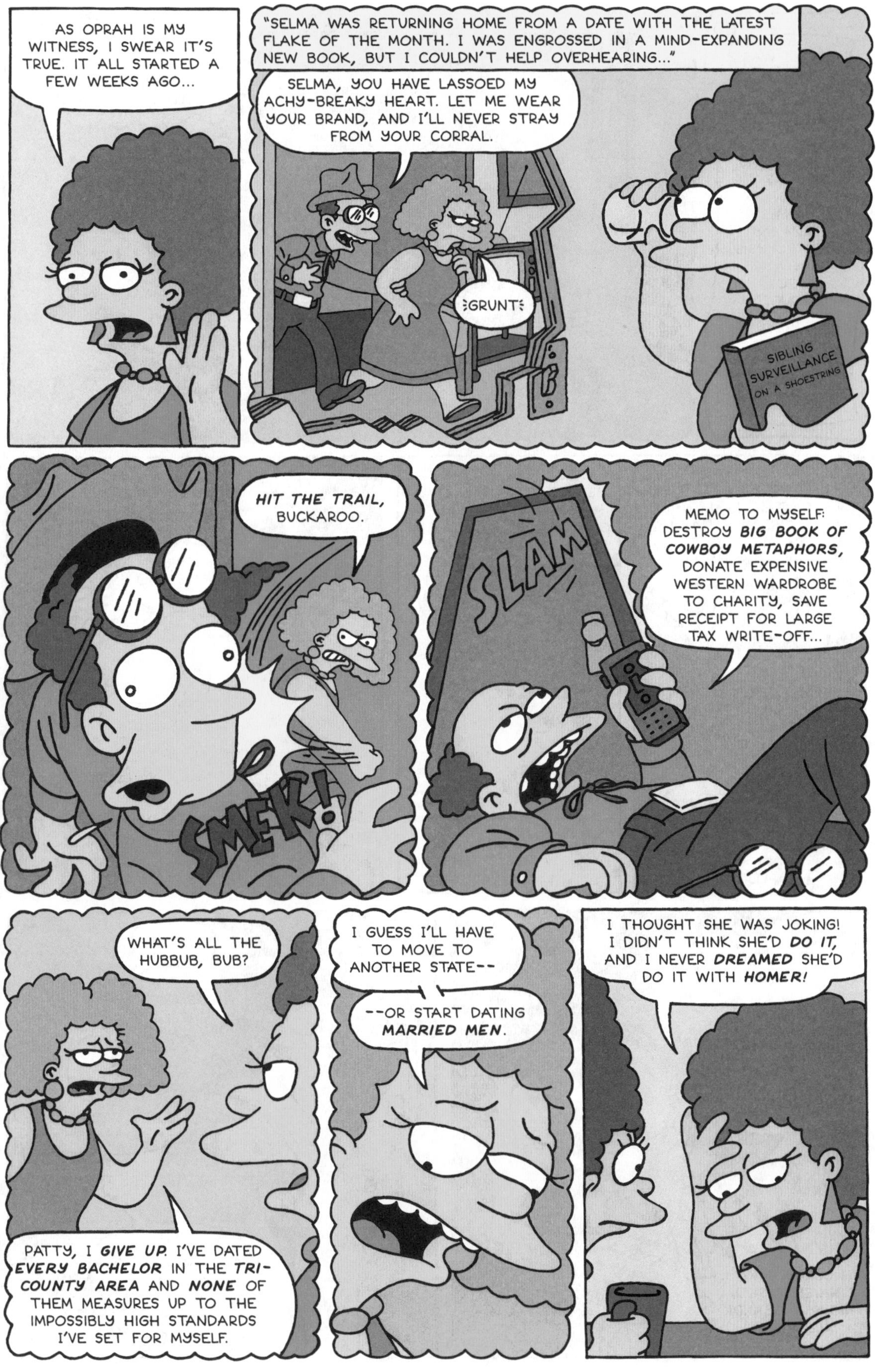
AS OPRAH IS MY WITNESS, I SWEAR IT'S TRUE. IT ALL STARTED A FEW WEEKS AGO...
"SELMA WAS RETURNING HOME FROM A DATE WITH THE LATEST FLAKE OF THE MONTH. I WAS ENGROSSED IN A MIND-EXPANDING NEW BOOK, BUT I COULDN'T HELP OVERHEARING..."
SELMA, YOU HAVE LASSOED MY ACHY-BREAKY HEART. LET ME WEAR YOUR BRAND, AND I'LL NEVER STRAY FROM YOUR CORRAL.
GRUNT
SIBLING SURVEILLANCE ON A SHOESTRING
HIT THE TRAIL, BUCKAROO.
SMEK!
SLAM
MEMO TO MYSELF: DESTROY BIG BOOK OF COWBOY METAPHORS, DONATE EXPENSIVE WESTERN WARDROBE TO CHARITY, SAVE RECEIPT FOR LARGE TAX WRITE-OFF...
WHAT'S ALL THE HUBBUB, BUB?
PATTY, I GIVE UP. I'VE DATED EVERY BACHELOR IN THE TRI-COUNTY AREA AND NONE OF THEM MEASURES UP TO THE IMPOSSIBLY HIGH STANDARDS I'VE SET FOR MYSELF.
I GUESS I'LL HAVE TO MOVE TO ANOTHER STATE--
--OR START DATING MARRIED MEN.
I THOUGHT SHE WAS JOKING! I DIDN'T THINK SHE'D DO IT, AND I NEVER DREAMED SHE'D DO IT WITH HOMER!

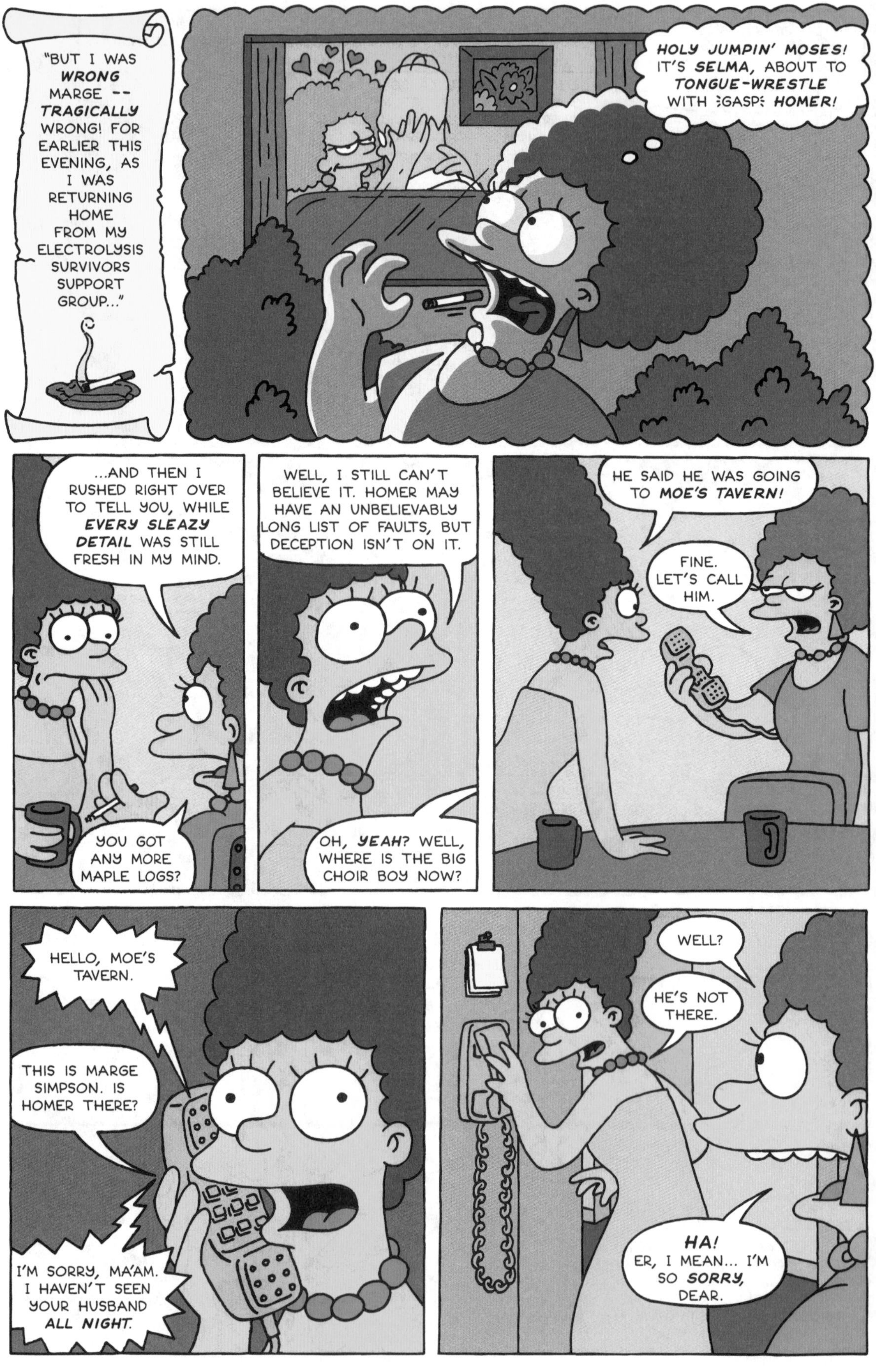
"BUT I WAS WRONG MARGE -- TRAGICALLY WRONG! FOR EARLIER THIS EVENING, AS I WAS RETURNING HOME FROM MY ELECTROLYSIS SURVIVORS SUPPORT GROUP..."
HOLY JUMPIN' MOSES! IT'S SELMA, ABOUT TO TONGUE-WRESTLE WITH *GASP* HOMER!
...AND THEN I RUSHED RIGHT OVER TO TELL YOU, WHILE EVERY SLEAZY DETAIL WAS STILL FRESH IN MY MIND.
YOU GOT ANY MORE MAPLE LOGS?
WELL, I STILL CAN'T BELIEVE IT. HOMER MAY HAVE AN UNBELIEVABLY LONG LIST OF FAULTS, BUT DECEPTION ISN'T ON IT.
OH, YEAH? WELL, WHERE IS THE BIG CHOIR BOY NOW?
HE SAID HE WAS GOING TO MOE'S TAVERN!
FINE. LET'S CALL HIM.
HELLO, MOE'S TAVERN.
THIS IS MARGE SIMPSON. IS HOMER THERE?
I'M SORRY, MA'AM. I HAVEN'T SEEN YOUR HUSBAND ALL NIGHT.
WELL?
HE'S NOT THERE.
HA! ER, I MEAN... I'M SO SORRY, DEAR.

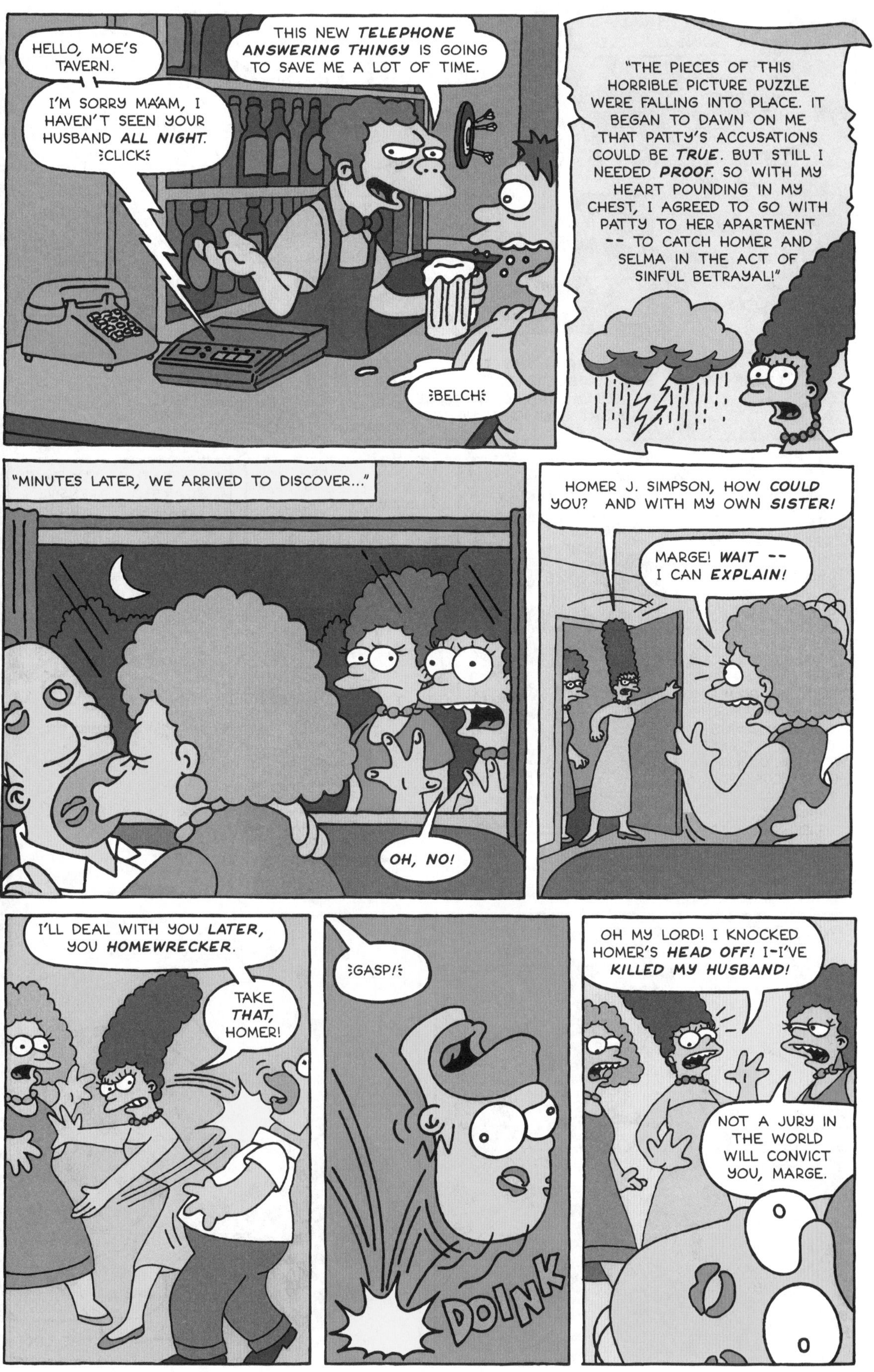
HELLO, MOE'S TAVERN.
THIS NEW TELEPHONE ANSWERING THINGY IS GOING TO SAVE ME A LOT OF TIME.
I'M SORRY MA'AM, I HAVEN'T SEEN YOUR HUSBAND ALL NIGHT. CLICK
BELCH
"THE PIECES OF THIS HORRIBLE PICTURE PUZZLE WERE FALLING INTO PLACE. IT BEGAN TO DAWN ON ME THAT PATTY'S ACCUSATIONS COULD BE TRUE. BUT STILL I NEEDED PROOF. SO WITH MY HEART POUNDING IN MY CHEST, I AGREED TO GO WITH PATTY TO HER APARTMENT -- TO CATCH HOMER AND SELMA IN THE ACT OF SINFUL BETRAYAL!"
"MINUTES LATER, WE ARRIVED TO DISCOVER..."
OH, NO!
HOMER J. SIMPSON, HOW COULD YOU? AND WITH MY OWN SISTER!
MARGE! WAIT -- I CAN EXPLAIN!
I'LL DEAL WITH YOU LATER, YOU HOMEWRECKER.
TAKE THAT, HOMER!
GASP!
DOINK
OH MY LORD! I KNOCKED HOMER'S HEAD OFF! I-I'VE KILLED MY HUSBAND!
NOT A JURY IN THE WORLD WILL CONVICT YOU, MARGE.

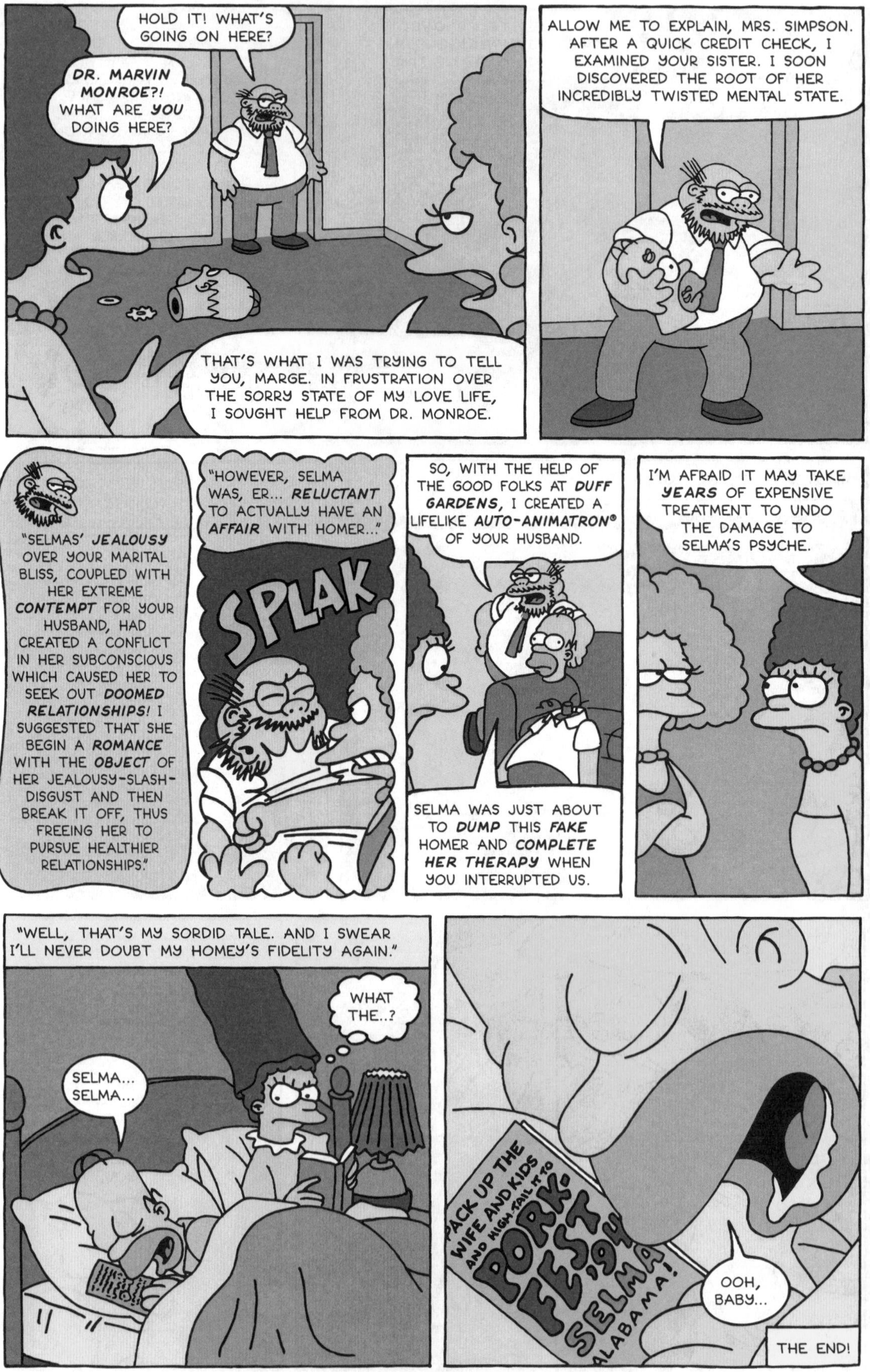
HOLD IT! WHAT'S GOING ON HERE?
DR. MARVIN MONROE?! WHAT ARE YOU DOING HERE?
THAT'S WHAT I WAS TRYING TO TELL YOU, MARGE. IN FRUSTRATION OVER THE SORRY STATE OF MY LOVE LIFE, I SOUGHT HELP FROM DR. MONROE.
ALLOW ME TO EXPLAIN, MRS. SIMPSON. AFTER A QUICK CREDIT CHECK, I EXAMINED YOUR SISTER. I SOON DISCOVERED THE ROOT OF HER INCREDIBLY TWISTED MENTAL STATE.
"SELMAS' JEALOUSY OVER YOUR MARITAL BLISS, COUPLED WITH HER EXTREME CONTEMPT FOR YOUR HUSBAND, HAD CREATED A CONFLICT IN HER SUBCONSCIOUS WHICH CAUSED HER TO SEEK OUT DOOMED RELATIONSHIPS! I SUGGESTED THAT SHE BEGIN A ROMANCE WITH THE OBJECT OF HER JEALOUSY-SLASH-DISGUST AND THEN BREAK IT OFF, THUS FREEING HER TO PURSUE HEALTHIER RELATIONSHIPS."
"HOWEVER, SELMA WAS, ER... RELUCTANT TO ACTUALLY HAVE AN AFFAIR WITH HOMER..."
SPLAK
SO, WITH THE HELP OF THE GOOD FOLKS AT DUFF GARDENS, I CREATED A LIFELIKE AUTO-ANIMATRON® OF YOUR HUSBAND.
SELMA WAS JUST ABOUT TO DUMP THIS FAKE HOMER AND COMPLETE HER THERAPY WHEN YOU INTERRUPTED US.
I'M AFRAID IT MAY TAKE YEARS OF EXPENSIVE TREATMENT TO UNDO THE DAMAGE TO SELMA'S PSYCHE.
"WELL, THAT'S MY SORDID TALE. AND I SWEAR I'LL NEVER DOUBT MY HOMEY'S FIDELITY AGAIN."
WHAT THE..?
SELMA... SELMA...
PACK UP THE WIFE AND KIDS AND HIGH-TAIL IT TO PORK FEST '94 SELMA, ALABAMA!
OOH, BABY...
THE END!

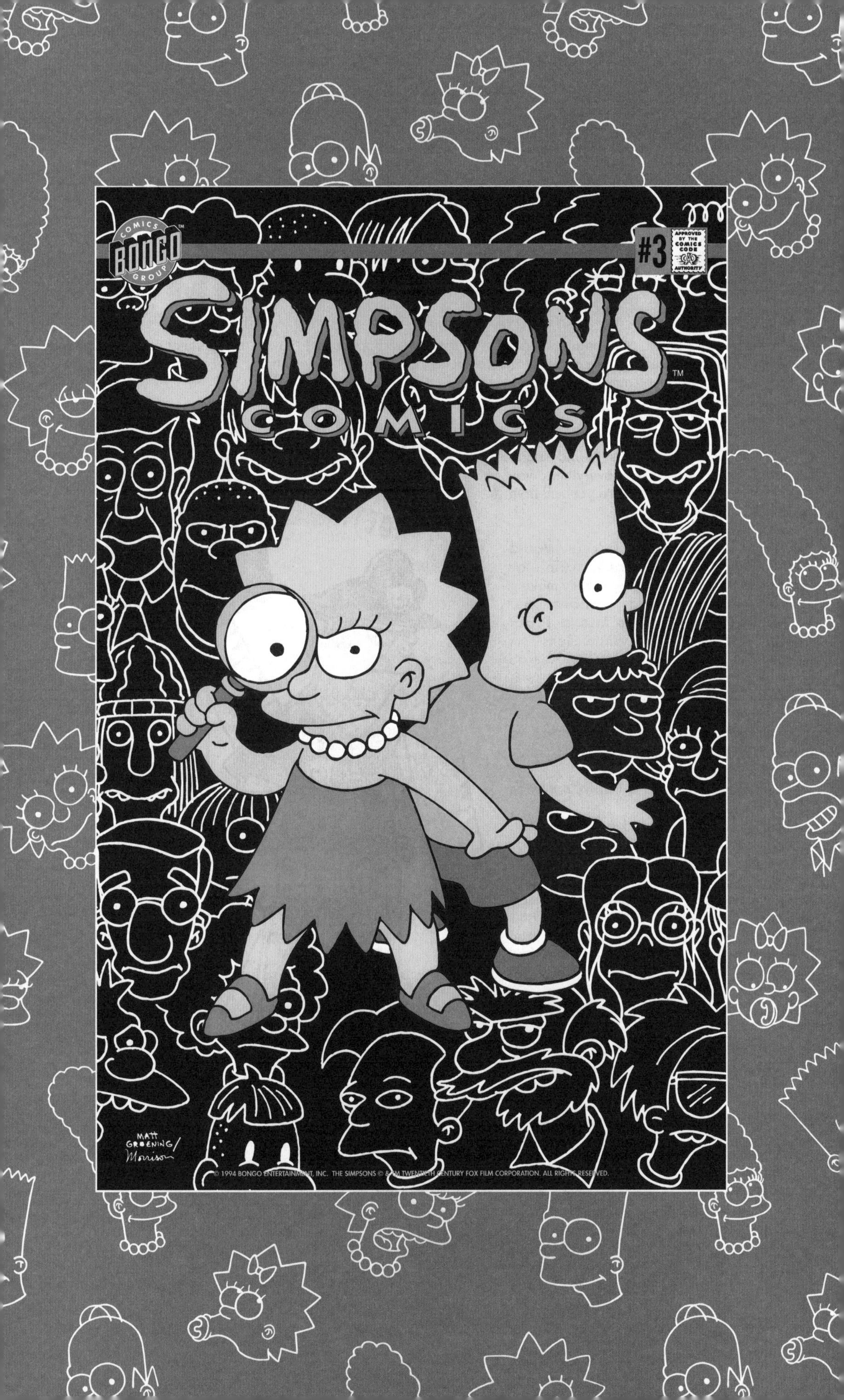
BONGO COMICS GROUP
#3
APPROVED BY THE COMICS CODE AUTHORITY
SIMPSONS COMICS
MATT GROENING/
Morrison
© 1994 BONGO ENTERTAINMENT, INC. THE SIMPSONS © & TM TWENTIETH CENTURY FOX FILM CORPORATION. ALL RIGHTS RESERVED.

SORRY, NOT A REAL ADVERTISEMENT

Apu Nahasapeemapetilon, successful entrepeneur, says:

"SO YOU ARE WANTING TO START A SMALL

Congratulations, my friend, on taking your first step on the road to opportunity! Now I, as proprietor of one of Springfield's most successful convenience-oriented retail establishments, am offering to you many helpful clues for the purpose of beginning an enterprise you may call your own. Now available for the first time anywhere outside of the Indian subcontinent is APU'S COURSE OF HOME STUDY FOR WOULD-BE ENTREPENEURS. In 17 easy-to-understand chapters, the course covers everything you need to know in order to liberate yourself from the dismal life of a wage slave.

Topics include:

• **"How Many Lottery Tickets Would You Care to Purchase, Sir or Madame?"** and other money-making questions with which to badger your customers.

• **Turning Video Games into a Profit Center.** Includes simple instructions for resetting 30 popular models so they will no longer give free games.

• **Your Gun vs. His:** When to Freeze, When to Fire.

• **From Simple Geometric Shapes to Incarceration:** Learning to Draw Robbery Suspects in Your Spare Time.

• **2¢ of Flavoring and a Penny's Worth of Ice:** The Slushie Miracle.

• Special chapter by noted psychologist Dr. Marvin Monroe, **"Stress Reduction for Convenience Store Operators,"** will hone your skills in dealing with the retail public.

You will find all this and many other closely guarded secrets of the retail trade in this program. By studying diligently the information provided to you, you could perhaps find yourself one day in a position of public trust

LOOK! AT WHAT YOU GET!

MY SECURITY CAMERA IS QUICK: THE THRILLING LIFE OF A CONVENIENCE STORE OWNER

• 385-page book, MY SECURITY CAMERA IS QUICK: THE THRILLING LIFE OF A CONVENIENCE STORE OWNER, written in Apu's own inimitable literary style!

• Life-size photo of uniformed policeman to place next to pastry display. Deterence value incalculable!

• Large-print, easy-to-read ruler to place at side of door. Most useful for determining height of fleeing suspects!

ACT NOW and receive this most handy brochure **FREE!**

HOW TO ALTER DAIRY PRODUCT EXPIRATION DATES FOR FUN AND PROFIT

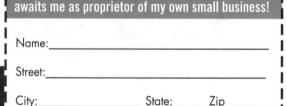

FOR FASTER SERVICE, CALL
(900) QUIZ-APU
95¢ a minute, 20-minute minimum

YES! Tell me more about the world of wonder that awaits me as proprietor of my own small business!

Name:_____

Street:_____

City:_____ State:_____ Zip_____

I understand that if I am not completey satisfied, it is my own damn problem.

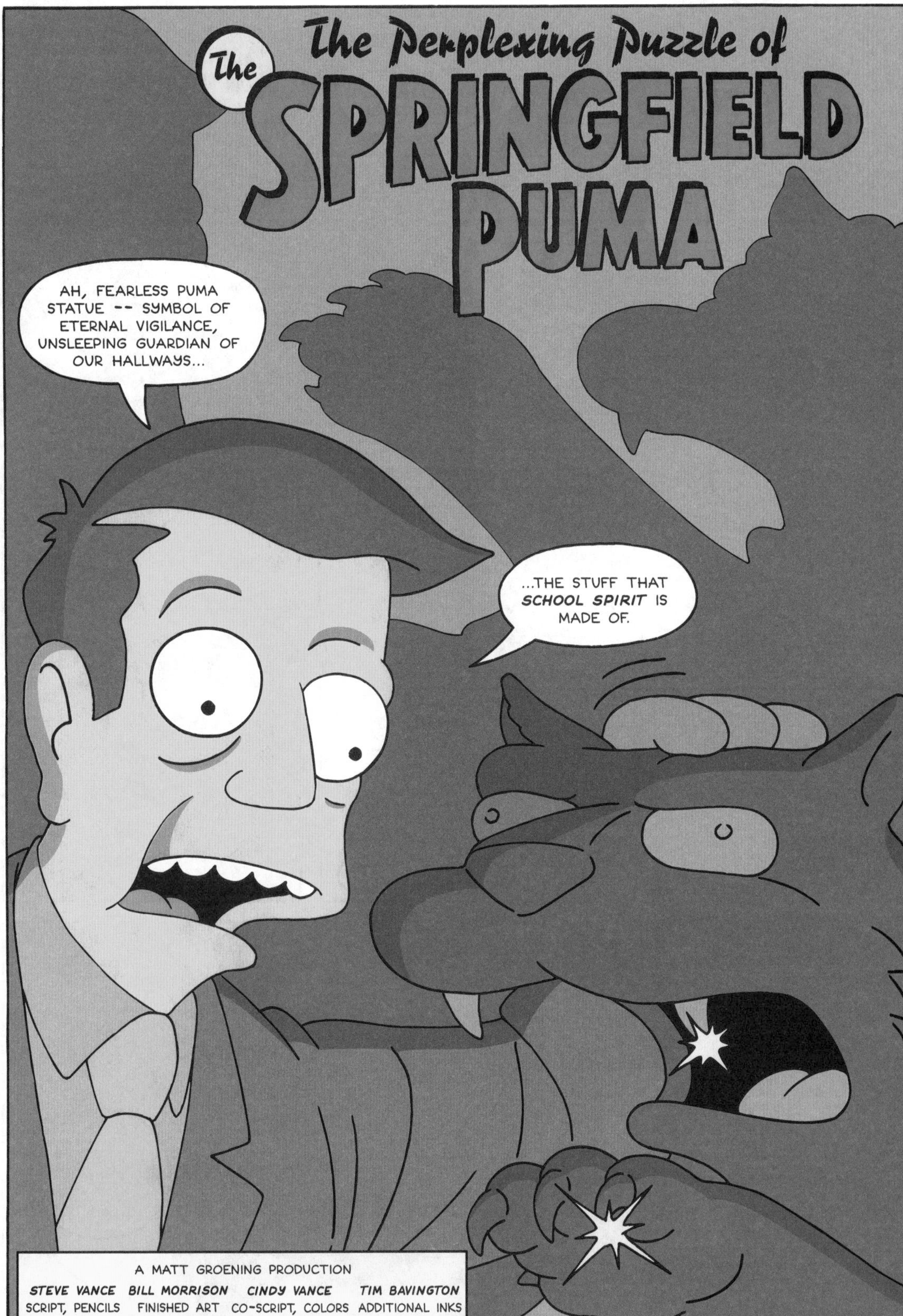
The Perplexing Puzzle of The SPRINGFIELD PUMA
AH, FEARLESS PUMA STATUE -- SYMBOL OF ETERNAL VIGILANCE, UNSLEEPING GUARDIAN OF OUR HALLWAYS...
...THE STUFF THAT SCHOOL SPIRIT IS MADE OF.
A MATT GROENING PRODUCTION
STEVE VANCE SCRIPT, PENCILS
BILL MORRISON FINISHED ART
CINDY VANCE CO-SCRIPT, COLORS
TIM BAVINGTON ADDITIONAL INKS

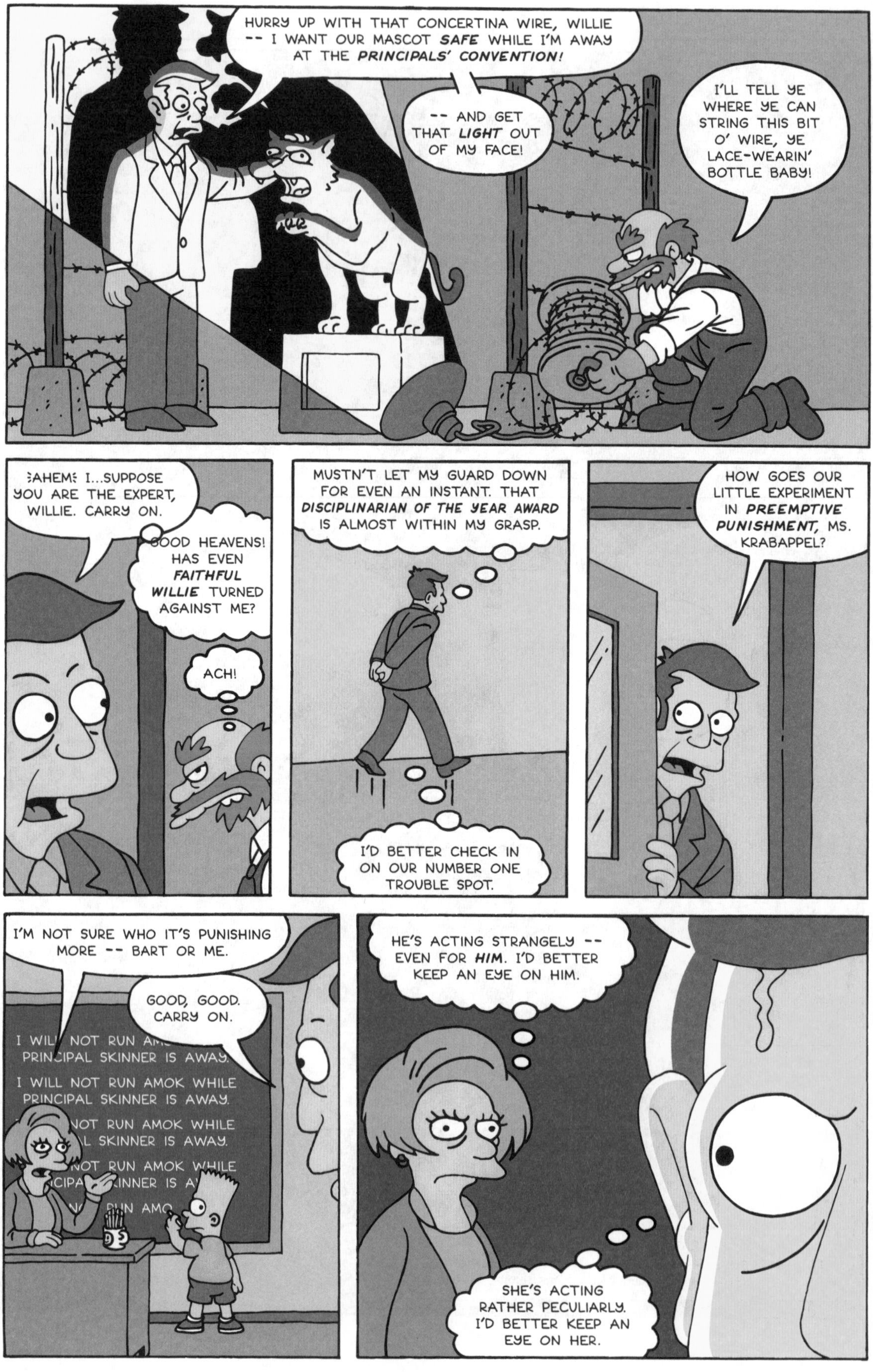
HURRY UP WITH THAT CONCERTINA WIRE, WILLIE -- I WANT OUR MASCOT SAFE WHILE I'M AWAY AT THE PRINCIPALS' CONVENTION!
-- AND GET THAT LIGHT OUT OF MY FACE!
I'LL TELL YE WHERE YE CAN STRING THIS BIT O' WIRE, YE LACE-WEARIN' BOTTLE BABY!
:AHEM: I...SUPPOSE YOU ARE THE EXPERT, WILLIE. CARRY ON.
GOOD HEAVENS! HAS EVEN FAITHFUL WILLIE TURNED AGAINST ME?
ACH!
MUSTN'T LET MY GUARD DOWN FOR EVEN AN INSTANT. THAT DISCIPLINARIAN OF THE YEAR AWARD IS ALMOST WITHIN MY GRASP.
I'D BETTER CHECK IN ON OUR NUMBER ONE TROUBLE SPOT.
HOW GOES OUR LITTLE EXPERIMENT IN PREEMPTIVE PUNISHMENT, MS. KRABAPPEL?
I'M NOT SURE WHO IT'S PUNISHING MORE -- BART OR ME.
GOOD, GOOD. CARRY ON.
I WILL NOT RUN AMOK WHILE PRINCIPAL SKINNER IS AWAY.
HE'S ACTING STRANGELY -- EVEN FOR HIM. I'D BETTER KEEP AN EYE ON HIM.
SHE'S ACTING RATHER PECULIARLY. I'D BETTER KEEP AN EYE ON HER.

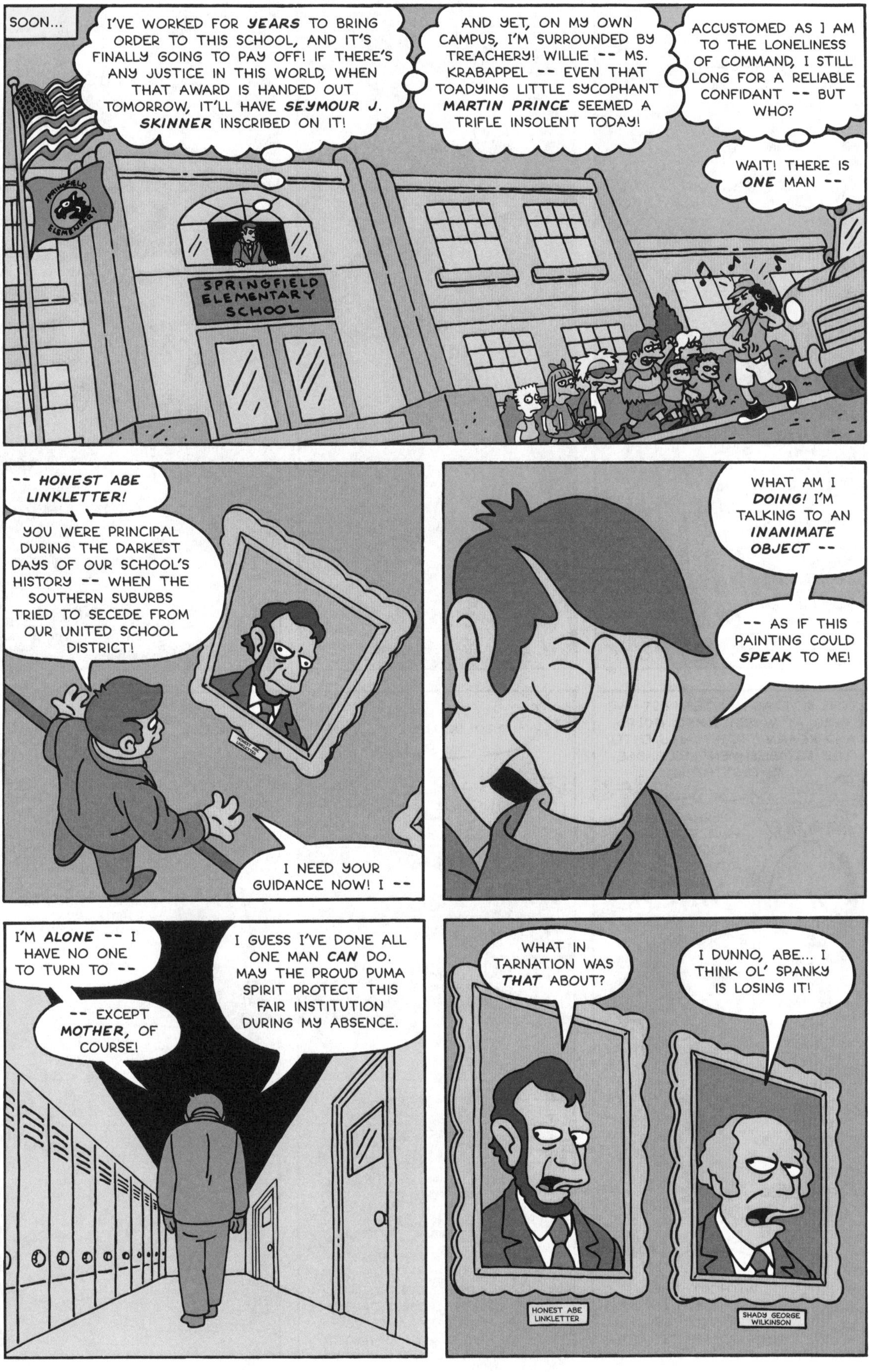
SOON...
I'VE WORKED FOR YEARS TO BRING ORDER TO THIS SCHOOL, AND IT'S FINALLY GOING TO PAY OFF! IF THERE'S ANY JUSTICE IN THIS WORLD, WHEN THAT AWARD IS HANDED OUT TOMORROW, IT'LL HAVE SEYMOUR J. SKINNER INSCRIBED ON IT!
AND YET, ON MY OWN CAMPUS, I'M SURROUNDED BY TREACHERY! WILLIE -- MS. KRABAPPEL -- EVEN THAT TOADYING LITTLE SYCOPHANT MARTIN PRINCE SEEMED A TRIFLE INSOLENT TODAY!
ACCUSTOMED AS I AM TO THE LONELINESS OF COMMAND, I STILL LONG FOR A RELIABLE CONFIDANT -- BUT WHO?
WAIT! THERE IS ONE MAN --
SPRINGFIELD ELEMENTARY
SPRINGFIELD ELEMENTARY SCHOOL
-- HONEST ABE LINKLETTER!
YOU WERE PRINCIPAL DURING THE DARKEST DAYS OF OUR SCHOOL'S HISTORY -- WHEN THE SOUTHERN SUBURBS TRIED TO SECEDE FROM OUR UNITED SCHOOL DISTRICT!
I NEED YOUR GUIDANCE NOW! I --
WHAT AM I DOING! I'M TALKING TO AN INANIMATE OBJECT --
-- AS IF THIS PAINTING COULD SPEAK TO ME!
I'M ALONE -- I HAVE NO ONE TO TURN TO --
-- EXCEPT MOTHER, OF COURSE!
I GUESS I'VE DONE ALL ONE MAN CAN DO. MAY THE PROUD PUMA SPIRIT PROTECT THIS FAIR INSTITUTION DURING MY ABSENCE.
WHAT IN TARNATION WAS THAT ABOUT?
I DUNNO, ABE... I THINK OL' SPANKY IS LOSING IT!
HONEST ABE LINKLETTER
SHADY GEORGE WILKINSON

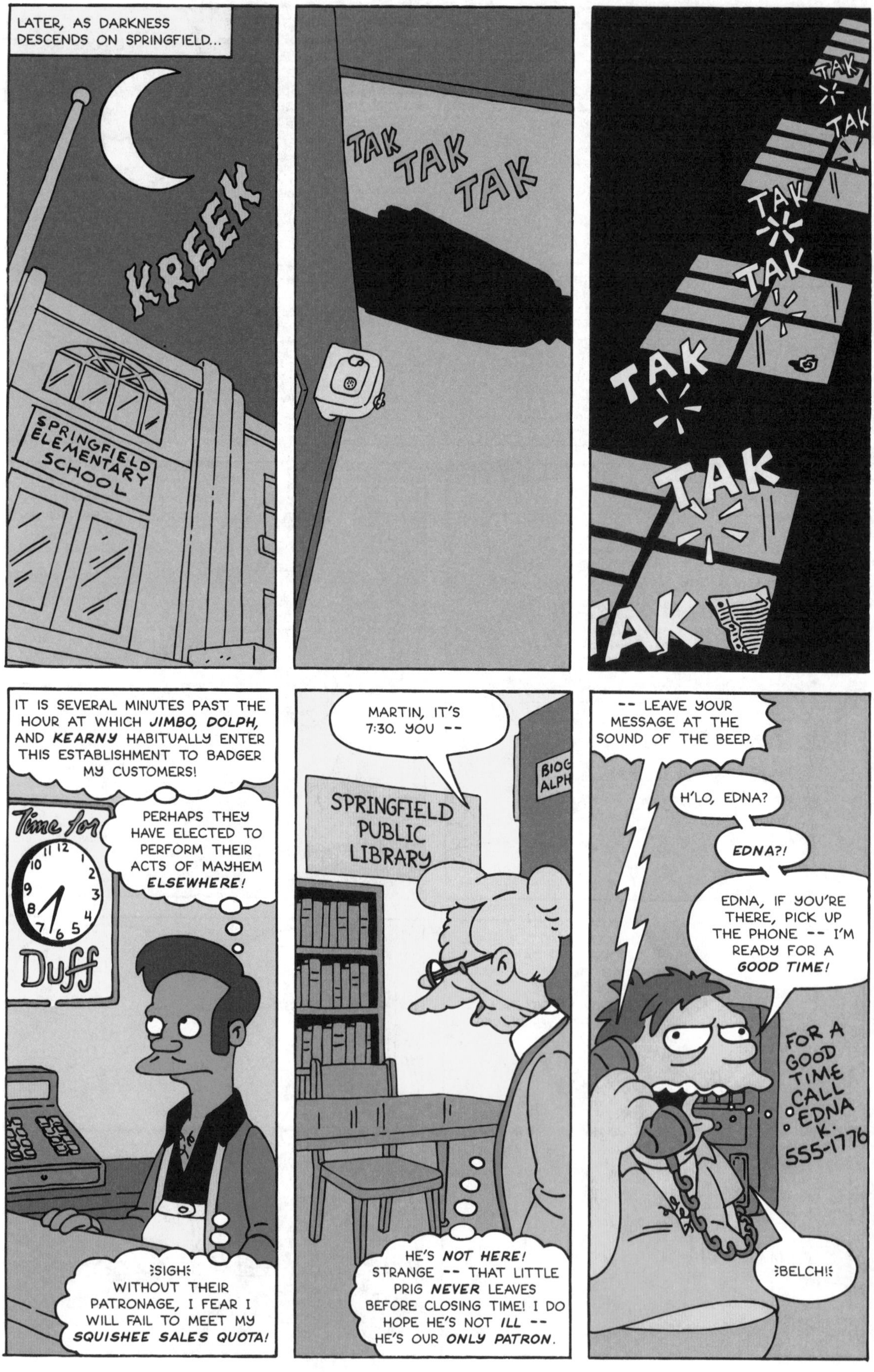
LATER, AS DARKNESS DESCENDS ON SPRINGFIELD...
KREEK
SPRINGFIELD ELEMENTARY SCHOOL
TAK TAK TAK
TAK
TAK
TAK
TAK
TAK
TAK
TAK
IT IS SEVERAL MINUTES PAST THE HOUR AT WHICH JIMBO, DOLPH, AND KEARNY HABITUALLY ENTER THIS ESTABLISHMENT TO BADGER MY CUSTOMERS!
PERHAPS THEY HAVE ELECTED TO PERFORM THEIR ACTS OF MAYHEM ELSEWHERE!
Time for
Duff
:SIGH: WITHOUT THEIR PATRONAGE, I FEAR I WILL FAIL TO MEET MY SQUISHEE SALES QUOTA!
MARTIN, IT'S 7:30. YOU --
SPRINGFIELD PUBLIC LIBRARY
HE'S NOT HERE! STRANGE -- THAT LITTLE PRIG NEVER LEAVES BEFORE CLOSING TIME! I DO HOPE HE'S NOT ILL -- HE'S OUR ONLY PATRON.
-- LEAVE YOUR MESSAGE AT THE SOUND OF THE BEEP.
H'LO, EDNA?
EDNA?!
EDNA, IF YOU'RE THERE, PICK UP THE PHONE -- I'M READY FOR A GOOD TIME!
FOR A GOOD TIME CALL EDNA K. 555-1776
:BELCH!:

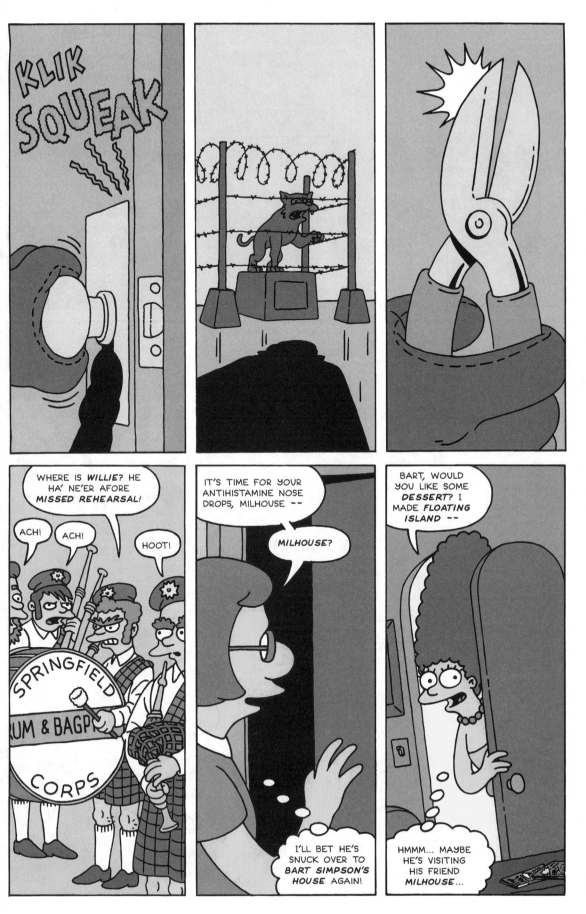

KLIK
SQUEAK

WHERE IS *WILLIE*? HE HA' NE'ER AFORE *MISSED REHEARSAL!*

ACH!

ACH!

HOOT!

SPRINGFIELD
RUM & BAGP...
CORPS

IT'S TIME FOR YOUR ANTIHISTAMINE NOSE DROPS, MILHOUSE --

MILHOUSE?

I'LL BET HE'S SNUCK OVER TO *BART SIMPSON'S HOUSE* AGAIN!

BART, WOULD YOU LIKE SOME *DESSERT?* I MADE *FLOATING ISLAND* --

HMMM... MAYBE HE'S VISITING HIS FRIEND *MILHOUSE*...

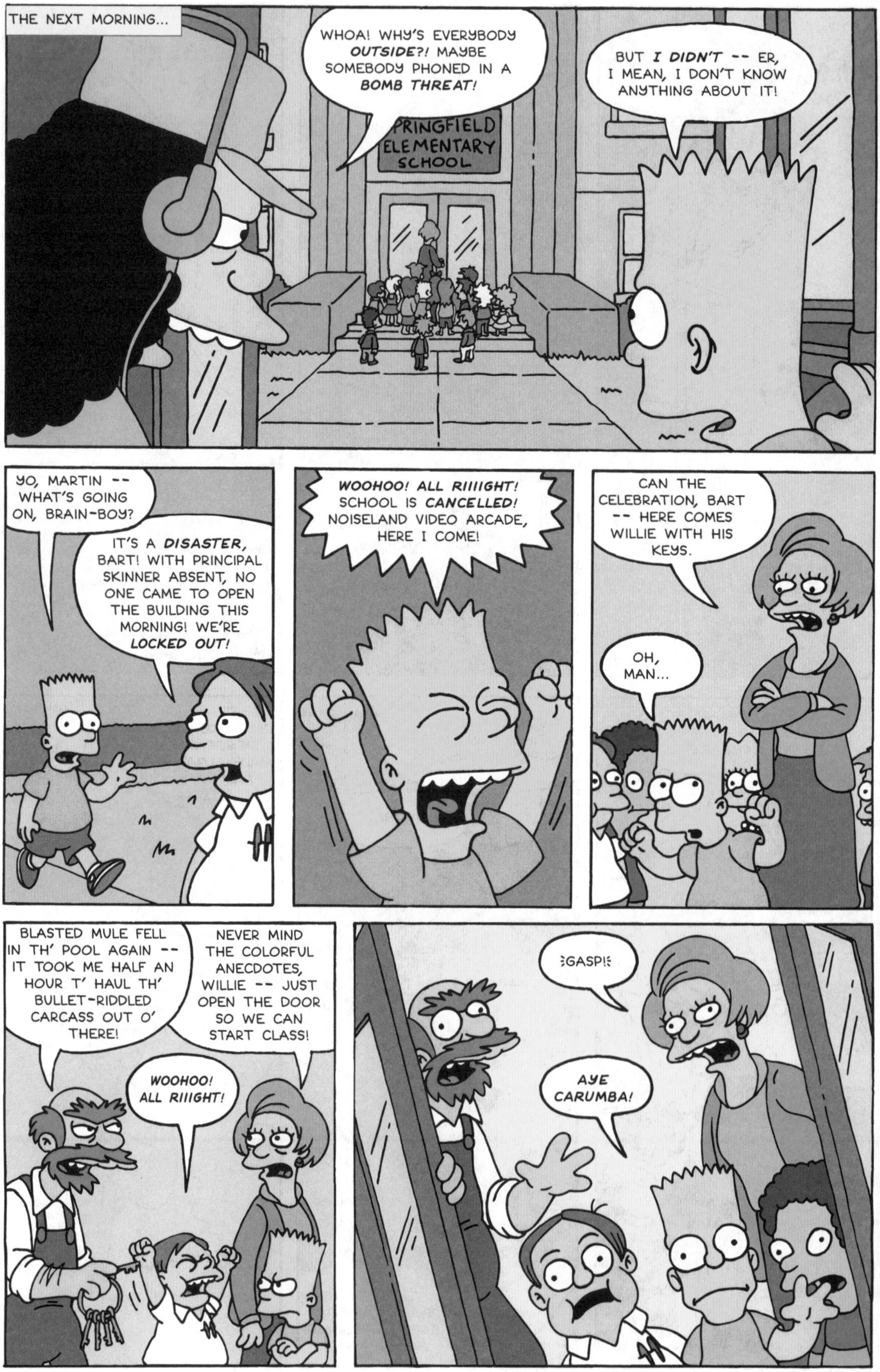
THE NEXT MORNING...
WHOA! WHY'S EVERYBODY OUTSIDE?! MAYBE SOMEBODY PHONED IN A BOMB THREAT!
PRINGFIELD ELEMENTARY SCHOOL
BUT I DIDN'T -- ER, I MEAN, I DON'T KNOW ANYTHING ABOUT IT!
YO, MARTIN -- WHAT'S GOING ON, BRAIN-BOY?
IT'S A DISASTER, BART! WITH PRINCIPAL SKINNER ABSENT, NO ONE CAME TO OPEN THE BUILDING THIS MORNING! WE'RE LOCKED OUT!
WOOHOO! ALL RIIIGHT! SCHOOL IS CANCELLED! NOISELAND VIDEO ARCADE, HERE I COME!
CAN THE CELEBRATION, BART -- HERE COMES WILLIE WITH HIS KEYS.
OH, MAN...
BLASTED MULE FELL IN TH' POOL AGAIN -- IT TOOK ME HALF AN HOUR T' HAUL TH' BULLET-RIDDLED CARCASS OUT O' THERE!
NEVER MIND THE COLORFUL ANECDOTES, WILLIE -- JUST OPEN THE DOOR SO WE CAN START CLASS!
WOOHOO! ALL RIIIGHT!
GASP!
AYE CARUMBA!

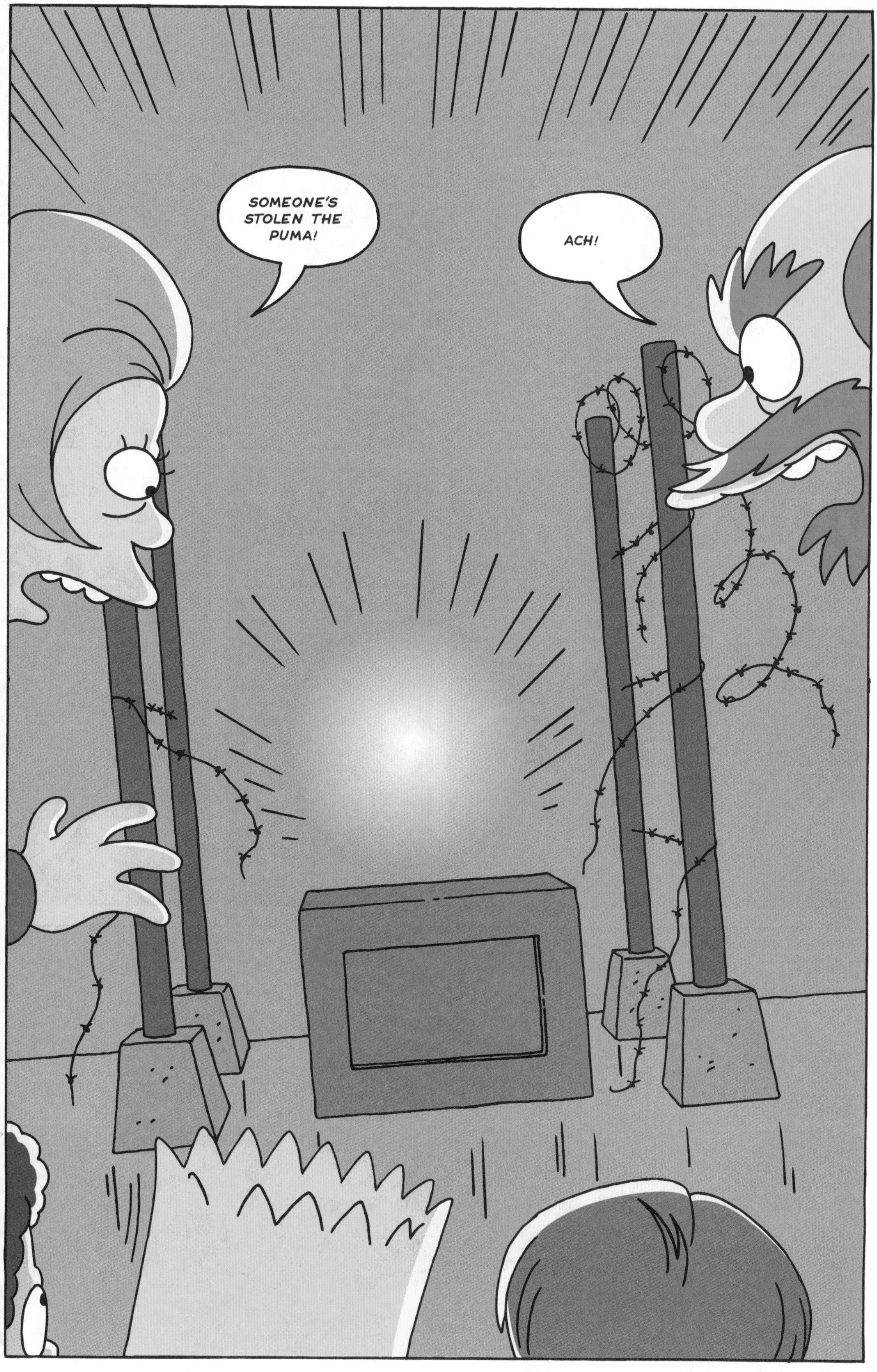
SOMEONE'S STOLEN THE PUMA!
ACH!

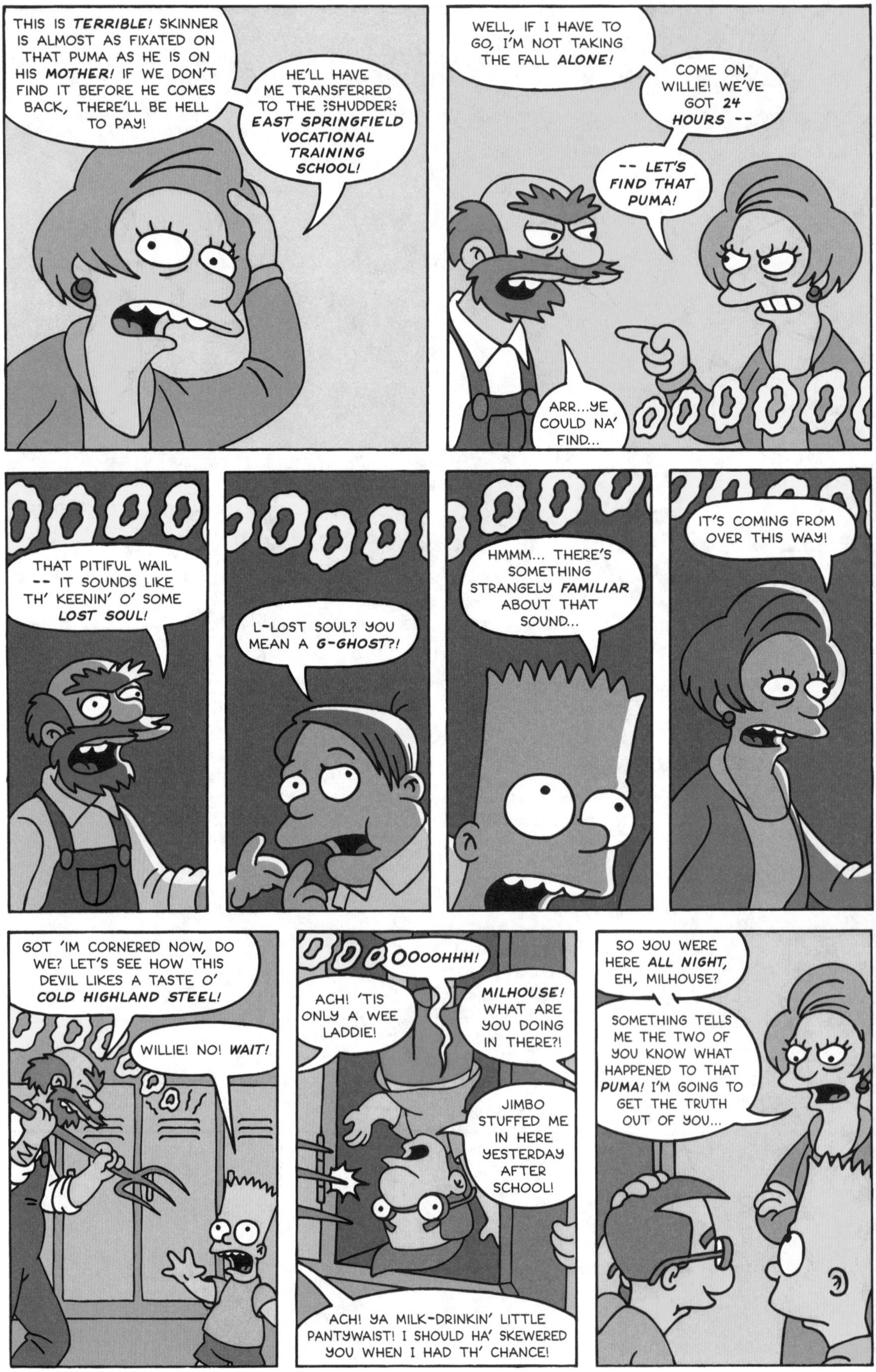

THIS IS TERRIBLE! SKINNER IS ALMOST AS FIXATED ON THAT PUMA AS HE IS ON HIS MOTHER! IF WE DON'T FIND IT BEFORE HE COMES BACK, THERE'LL BE HELL TO PAY!
HE'LL HAVE ME TRANSFERRED TO THE *SHUDDER* EAST SPRINGFIELD VOCATIONAL TRAINING SCHOOL!
WELL, IF I HAVE TO GO, I'M NOT TAKING THE FALL ALONE!
COME ON, WILLIE! WE'VE GOT 24 HOURS --
-- LET'S FIND THAT PUMA!
ARR...YE COULD NA' FIND...
THAT PITIFUL WAIL -- IT SOUNDS LIKE TH' KEENIN' O' SOME LOST SOUL!
L-LOST SOUL? YOU MEAN A G-GHOST?!
HMMM... THERE'S SOMETHING STRANGELY FAMILIAR ABOUT THAT SOUND...
IT'S COMING FROM OVER THIS WAY!
GOT 'IM CORNERED NOW, DO WE? LET'S SEE HOW THIS DEVIL LIKES A TASTE O' COLD HIGHLAND STEEL!
WILLIE! NO! WAIT!
OOOOHHH!
ACH! 'TIS ONLY A WEE LADDIE!
MILHOUSE! WHAT ARE YOU DOING IN THERE?!
JIMBO STUFFED ME IN HERE YESTERDAY AFTER SCHOOL!
ACH! YA MILK-DRINKIN' LITTLE PANTYWAIST! I SHOULD HA' SKEWERED YOU WHEN I HAD TH' CHANCE!
SO YOU WERE HERE ALL NIGHT, EH, MILHOUSE?
SOMETHING TELLS ME THE TWO OF YOU KNOW WHAT HAPPENED TO THAT PUMA! I'M GOING TO GET THE TRUTH OUT OF YOU...

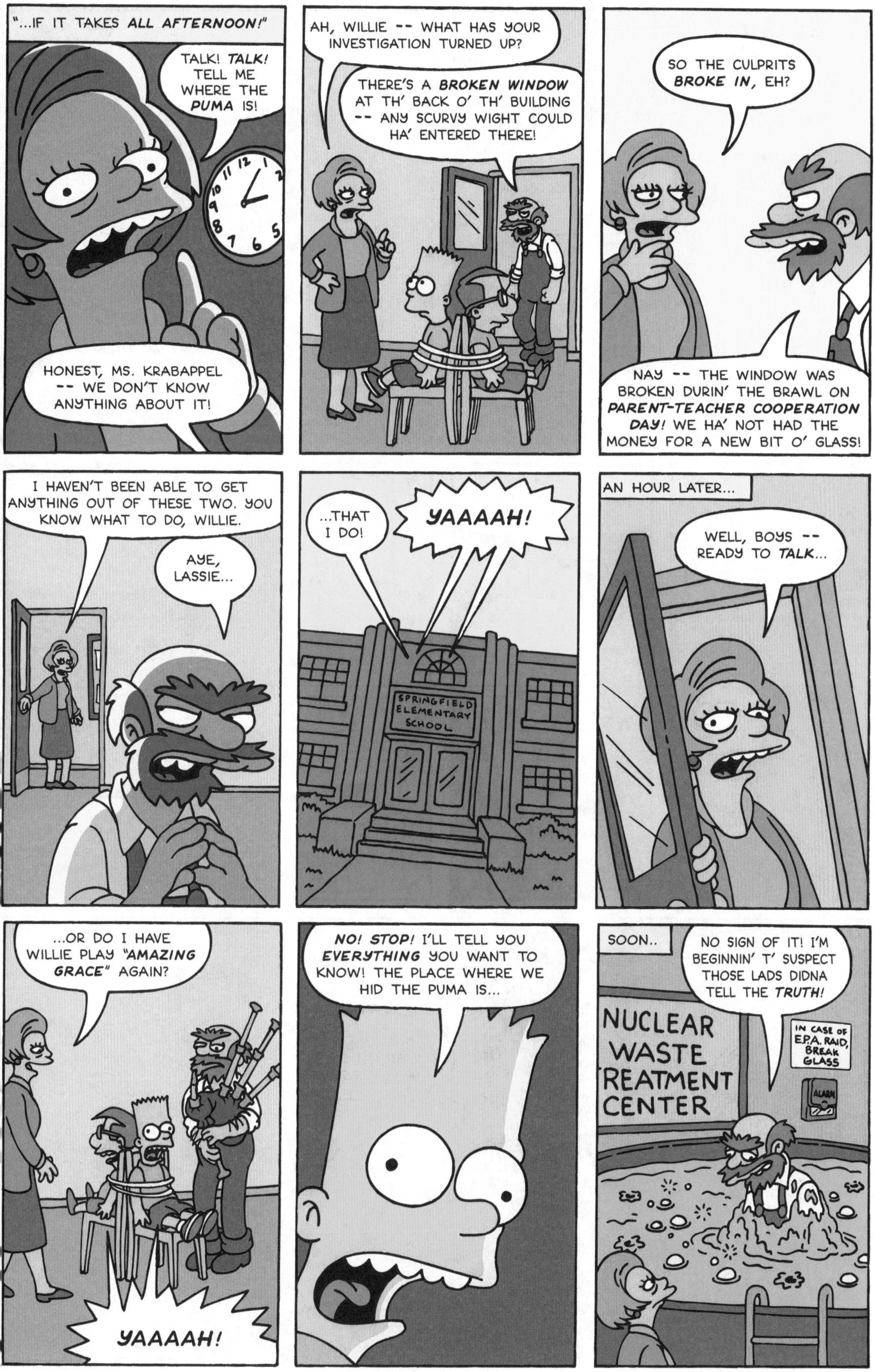
"...IF IT TAKES ALL AFTERNOON!"
TALK! TALK! TELL ME WHERE THE PUMA IS!
HONEST, MS. KRABAPPEL -- WE DON'T KNOW ANYTHING ABOUT IT!
AH, WILLIE -- WHAT HAS YOUR INVESTIGATION TURNED UP?
THERE'S A BROKEN WINDOW AT TH' BACK O' TH' BUILDING -- ANY SCURVY WIGHT COULD HA' ENTERED THERE!
SO THE CULPRITS BROKE IN, EH?
NAY -- THE WINDOW WAS BROKEN DURIN' THE BRAWL ON PARENT-TEACHER COOPERATION DAY! WE HA' NOT HAD THE MONEY FOR A NEW BIT O' GLASS!
I HAVEN'T BEEN ABLE TO GET ANYTHING OUT OF THESE TWO. YOU KNOW WHAT TO DO, WILLIE.
AYE, LASSIE...
...THAT I DO!
YAAAAH!
SPRINGFIELD ELEMENTARY SCHOOL
AN HOUR LATER...
WELL, BOYS -- READY TO TALK...
...OR DO I HAVE WILLIE PLAY "AMAZING GRACE" AGAIN?
YAAAAH!
NO! STOP! I'LL TELL YOU EVERYTHING YOU WANT TO KNOW! THE PLACE WHERE WE HID THE PUMA IS...
SOON..
NO SIGN OF IT! I'M BEGINNIN' T' SUSPECT THOSE LADS DIDNA TELL THE TRUTH!
NUCLEAR WASTE TREATMENT CENTER
IN CASE OF E.P.A. RAID, BREAK GLASS
ALARM

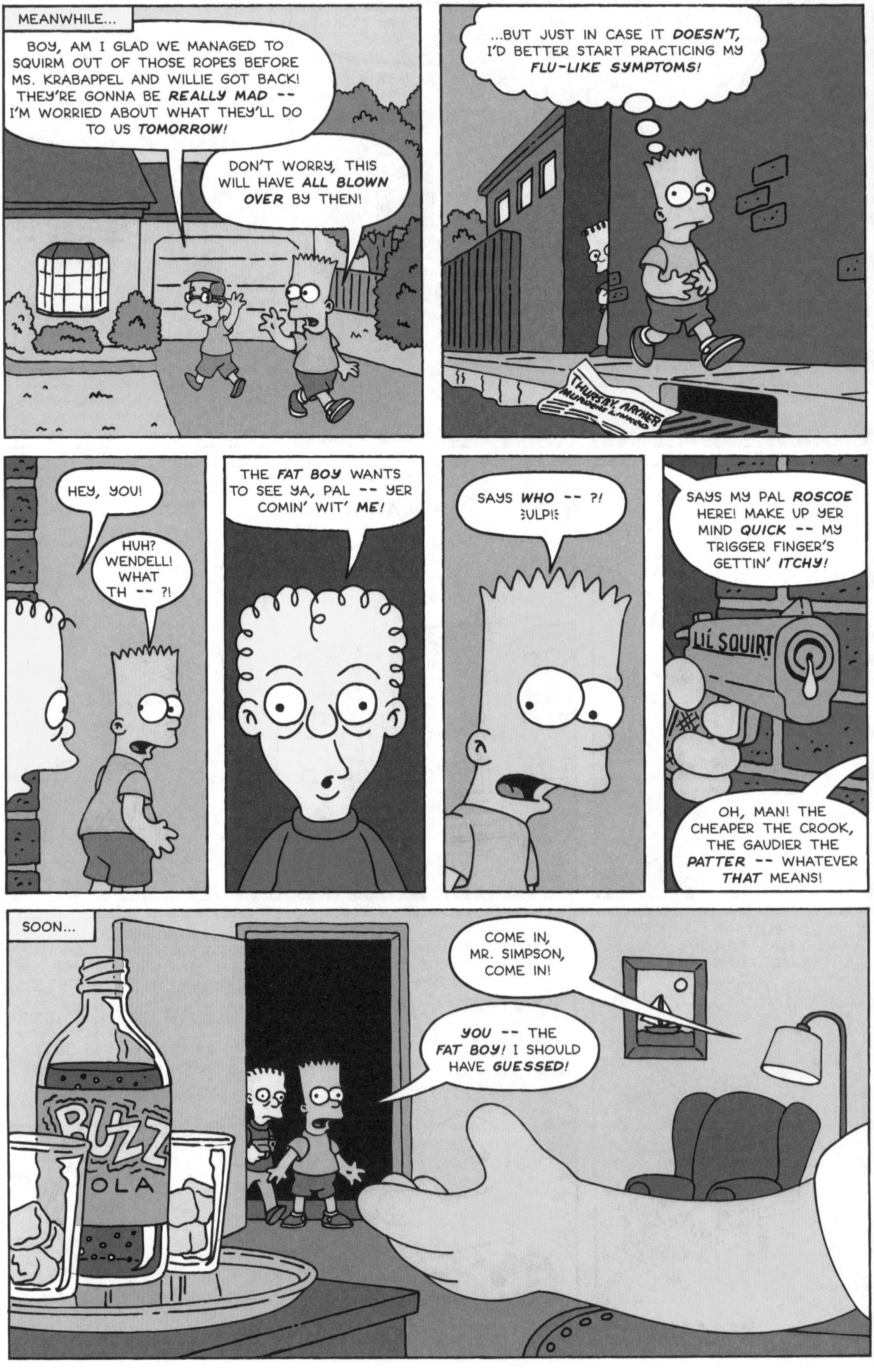
MEANWHILE...
BOY, AM I GLAD WE MANAGED TO SQUIRM OUT OF THOSE ROPES BEFORE MS. KRABAPPEL AND WILLIE GOT BACK! THEY'RE GONNA BE REALLY MAD -- I'M WORRIED ABOUT WHAT THEY'LL DO TO US TOMORROW!
DON'T WORRY, THIS WILL HAVE ALL BLOWN OVER BY THEN!
...BUT JUST IN CASE IT DOESN'T, I'D BETTER START PRACTICING MY FLU-LIKE SYMPTOMS!
THURSBY, ARCHER MURDERS LINKED
HEY, YOU!
HUH? WENDELL! WHAT TH -- ?!
THE FAT BOY WANTS TO SEE YA, PAL -- YER COMIN' WIT' ME!
SAYS WHO -- ?!
GULP!
SAYS MY PAL ROSCOE HERE! MAKE UP YER MIND QUICK -- MY TRIGGER FINGER'S GETTIN' ITCHY!
LI'L SQUIRT
OH, MAN! THE CHEAPER THE CROOK, THE GAUDIER THE PATTER -- WHATEVER THAT MEANS!
SOON...
COME IN, MR. SIMPSON, COME IN!
YOU -- THE FAT BOY! I SHOULD HAVE GUESSED!
BUZZ COLA

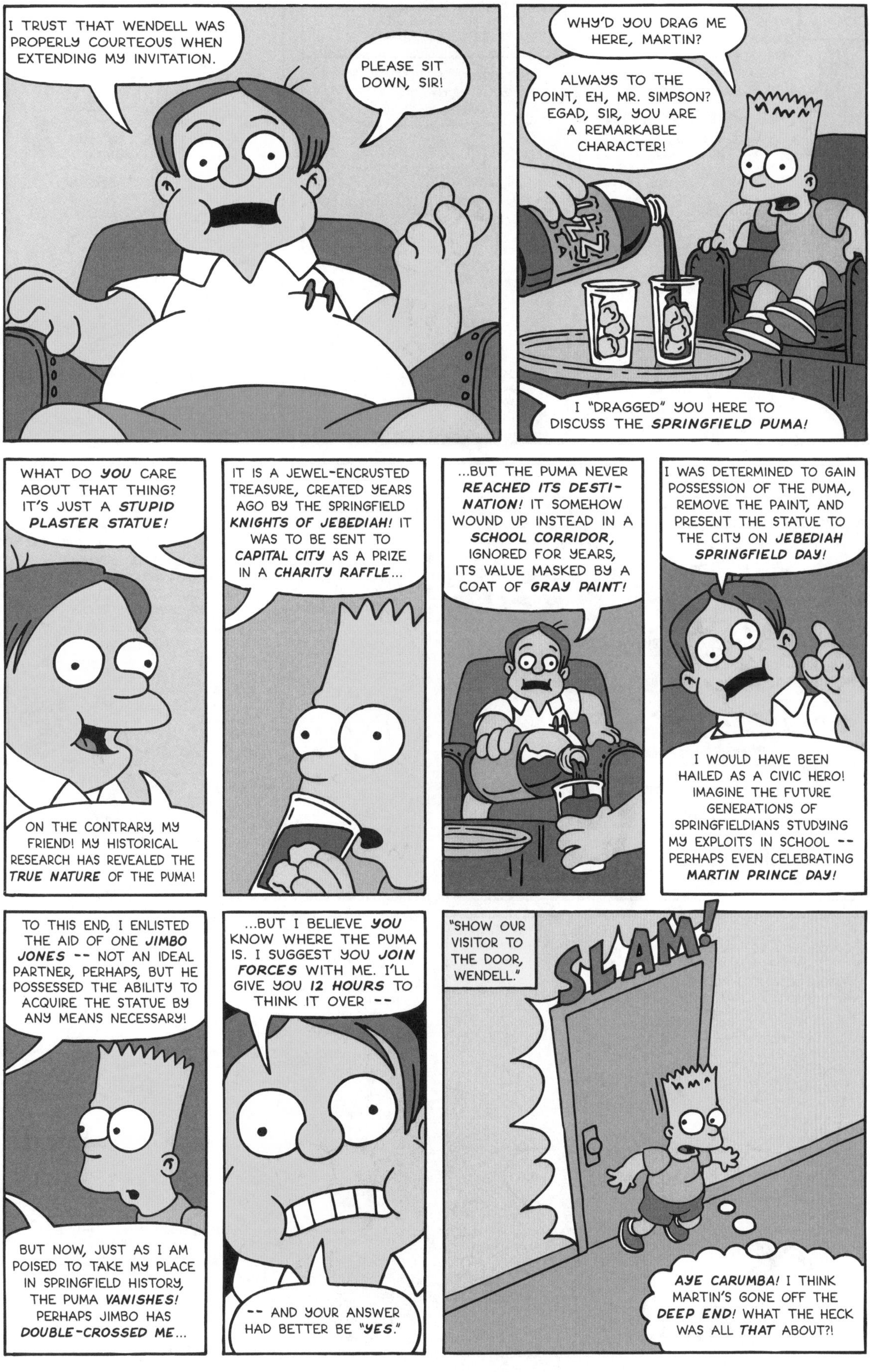
I TRUST THAT WENDELL WAS PROPERLY COURTEOUS WHEN EXTENDING MY INVITATION.
PLEASE SIT DOWN, SIR!
WHY'D YOU DRAG ME HERE, MARTIN?
ALWAYS TO THE POINT, EH, MR. SIMPSON? EGAD, SIR, YOU ARE A REMARKABLE CHARACTER!
I "DRAGGED" YOU HERE TO DISCUSS THE SPRINGFIELD PUMA!
WHAT DO YOU CARE ABOUT THAT THING? IT'S JUST A STUPID PLASTER STATUE!
ON THE CONTRARY, MY FRIEND! MY HISTORICAL RESEARCH HAS REVEALED THE TRUE NATURE OF THE PUMA!
IT IS A JEWEL-ENCRUSTED TREASURE, CREATED YEARS AGO BY THE SPRINGFIELD KNIGHTS OF JEBEDIAH! IT WAS TO BE SENT TO CAPITAL CITY AS A PRIZE IN A CHARITY RAFFLE...
...BUT THE PUMA NEVER REACHED ITS DESTINATION! IT SOMEHOW WOUND UP INSTEAD IN A SCHOOL CORRIDOR, IGNORED FOR YEARS, ITS VALUE MASKED BY A COAT OF GRAY PAINT!
I WAS DETERMINED TO GAIN POSSESSION OF THE PUMA, REMOVE THE PAINT, AND PRESENT THE STATUE TO THE CITY ON JEBEDIAH SPRINGFIELD DAY!
I WOULD HAVE BEEN HAILED AS A CIVIC HERO! IMAGINE THE FUTURE GENERATIONS OF SPRINGFIELDIANS STUDYING MY EXPLOITS IN SCHOOL -- PERHAPS EVEN CELEBRATING MARTIN PRINCE DAY!
TO THIS END, I ENLISTED THE AID OF ONE JIMBO JONES -- NOT AN IDEAL PARTNER, PERHAPS, BUT HE POSSESSED THE ABILITY TO ACQUIRE THE STATUE BY ANY MEANS NECESSARY!
BUT NOW, JUST AS I AM POISED TO TAKE MY PLACE IN SPRINGFIELD HISTORY, THE PUMA VANISHES! PERHAPS JIMBO HAS DOUBLE-CROSSED ME...
...BUT I BELIEVE YOU KNOW WHERE THE PUMA IS. I SUGGEST YOU JOIN FORCES WITH ME. I'LL GIVE YOU 12 HOURS TO THINK IT OVER --
-- AND YOUR ANSWER HAD BETTER BE "YES."
"SHOW OUR VISITOR TO THE DOOR, WENDELL."
SLAM!
AYE CARUMBA! I THINK MARTIN'S GONE OFF THE DEEP END! WHAT THE HECK WAS ALL THAT ABOUT?!

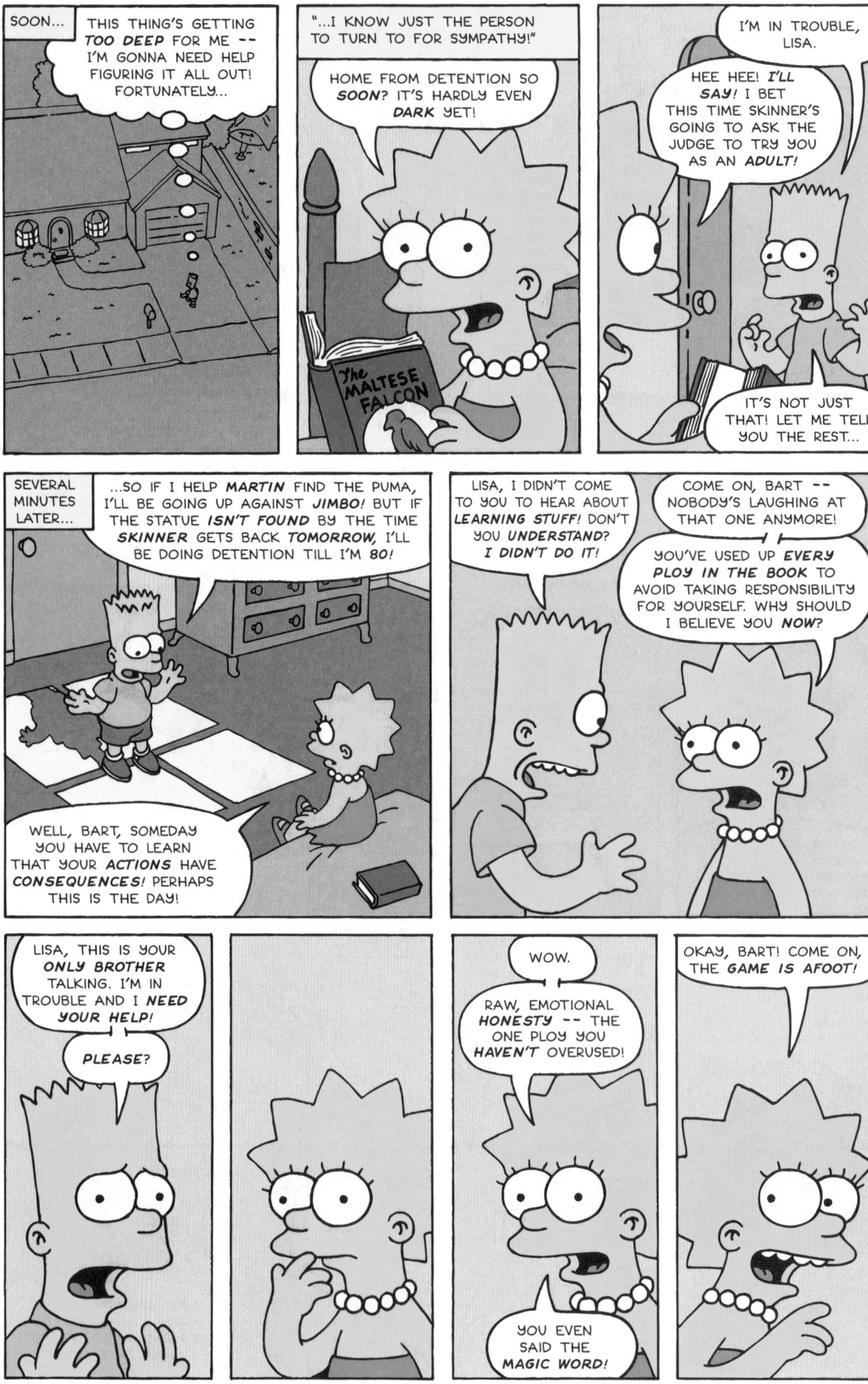
SOON...
THIS THING'S GETTING TOO DEEP FOR ME -- I'M GONNA NEED HELP FIGURING IT ALL OUT! FORTUNATELY...
"...I KNOW JUST THE PERSON TO TURN TO FOR SYMPATHY!"
HOME FROM DETENTION SO SOON? IT'S HARDLY EVEN DARK YET!
The MALTESE FALCON
I'M IN TROUBLE, LISA.
HEE HEE! I'LL SAY! I BET THIS TIME SKINNER'S GOING TO ASK THE JUDGE TO TRY YOU AS AN ADULT!
IT'S NOT JUST THAT! LET ME TELL YOU THE REST...
SEVERAL MINUTES LATER...
...SO IF I HELP MARTIN FIND THE PUMA, I'LL BE GOING UP AGAINST JIMBO! BUT IF THE STATUE ISN'T FOUND BY THE TIME SKINNER GETS BACK TOMORROW, I'LL BE DOING DETENTION TILL I'M 80!
WELL, BART, SOMEDAY YOU HAVE TO LEARN THAT YOUR ACTIONS HAVE CONSEQUENCES! PERHAPS THIS IS THE DAY!
LISA, I DIDN'T COME TO YOU TO HEAR ABOUT LEARNING STUFF! DON'T YOU UNDERSTAND? I DIDN'T DO IT!
COME ON, BART -- NOBODY'S LAUGHING AT THAT ONE ANYMORE!
YOU'VE USED UP EVERY PLOY IN THE BOOK TO AVOID TAKING RESPONSIBILITY FOR YOURSELF. WHY SHOULD I BELIEVE YOU NOW?
LISA, THIS IS YOUR ONLY BROTHER TALKING. I'M IN TROUBLE AND I NEED YOUR HELP!
PLEASE?
WOW.
RAW, EMOTIONAL HONESTY -- THE ONE PLOY YOU HAVEN'T OVERUSED!
YOU EVEN SAID THE MAGIC WORD!
OKAY, BART! COME ON, THE GAME IS AFOOT!

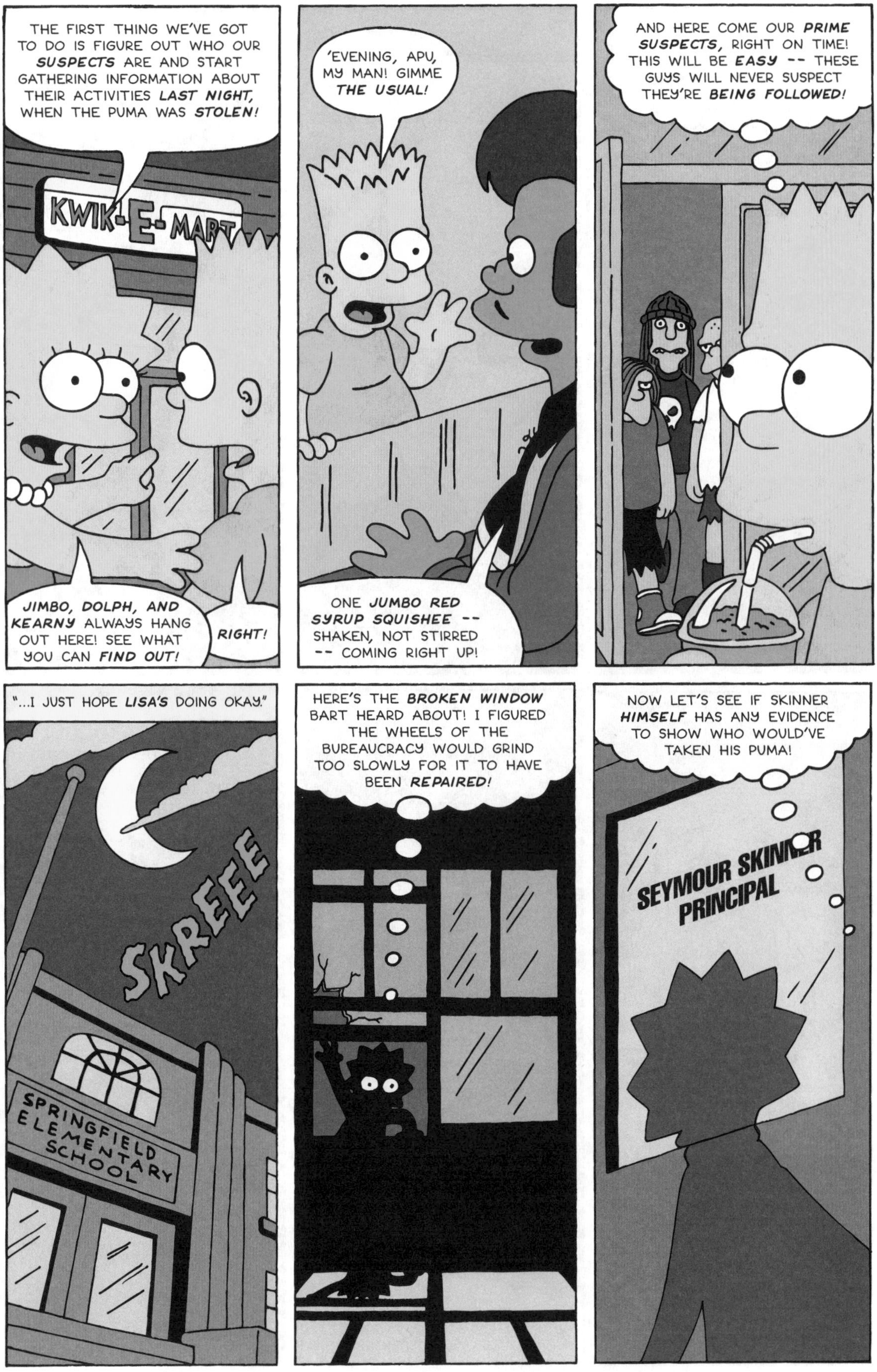
THE FIRST THING WE'VE GOT TO DO IS FIGURE OUT WHO OUR SUSPECTS ARE AND START GATHERING INFORMATION ABOUT THEIR ACTIVITIES LAST NIGHT, WHEN THE PUMA WAS STOLEN!
KWIK-E-MART
JIMBO, DOLPH, AND KEARNY ALWAYS HANG OUT HERE! SEE WHAT YOU CAN FIND OUT!
RIGHT!
'EVENING, APU, MY MAN! GIMME THE USUAL!
ONE JUMBO RED SYRUP SQUISHEE -- SHAKEN, NOT STIRRED -- COMING RIGHT UP!
AND HERE COME OUR PRIME SUSPECTS, RIGHT ON TIME! THIS WILL BE EASY -- THESE GUYS WILL NEVER SUSPECT THEY'RE BEING FOLLOWED!
"...I JUST HOPE LISA'S DOING OKAY."
SKREEE
SPRINGFIELD ELEMENTARY SCHOOL
HERE'S THE BROKEN WINDOW BART HEARD ABOUT! I FIGURED THE WHEELS OF THE BUREAUCRACY WOULD GRIND TOO SLOWLY FOR IT TO HAVE BEEN REPAIRED!
NOW LET'S SEE IF SKINNER HIMSELF HAS ANY EVIDENCE TO SHOW WHO WOULD'VE TAKEN HIS PUMA!
SEYMOUR SKINNER
PRINCIPAL

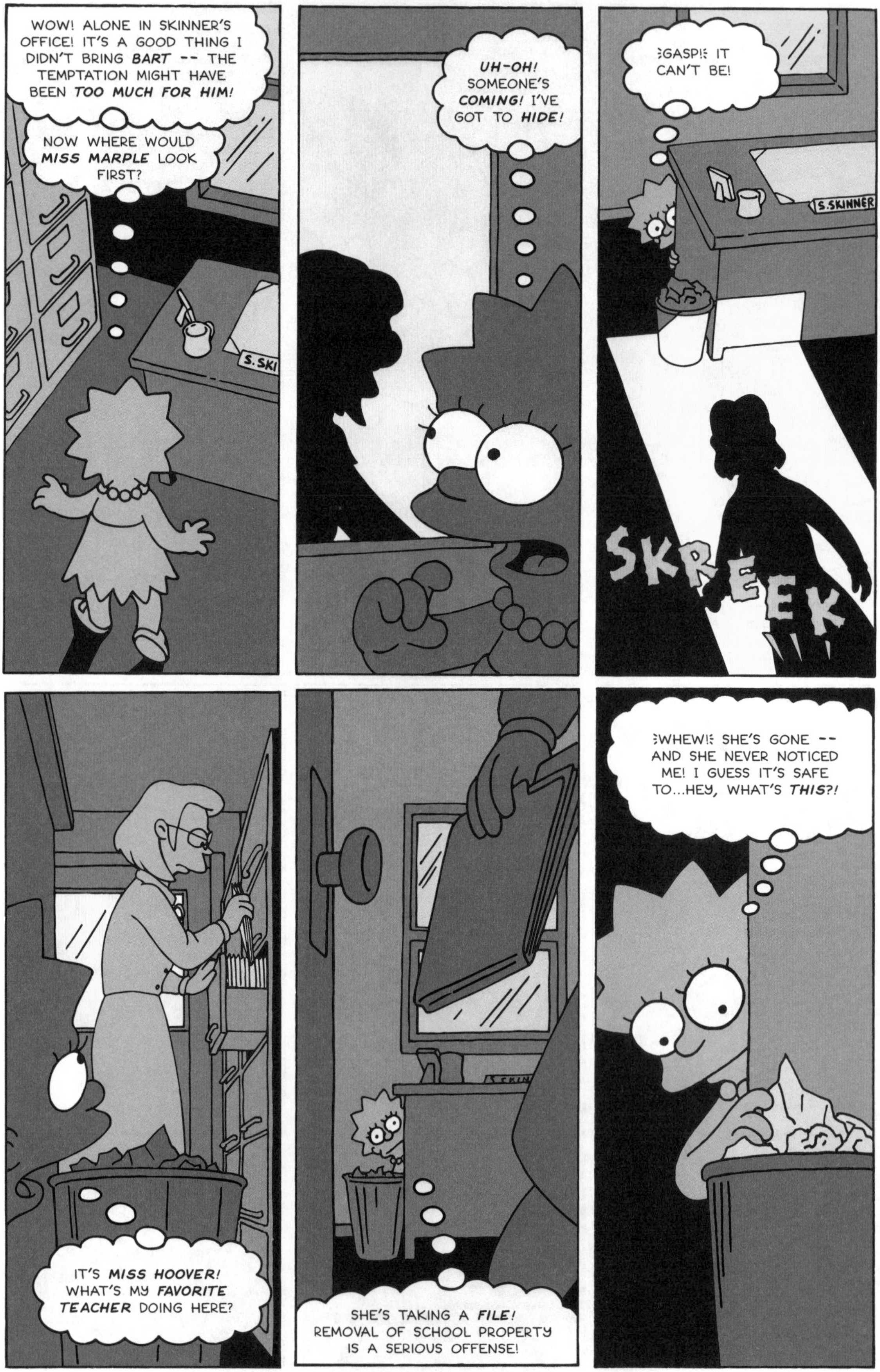
WOW! ALONE IN SKINNER'S OFFICE! IT'S A GOOD THING I DIDN'T BRING BART -- THE TEMPTATION MIGHT HAVE BEEN TOO MUCH FOR HIM!
NOW WHERE WOULD MISS MARPLE LOOK FIRST?
S. SKI
UH-OH! SOMEONE'S COMING! I'VE GOT TO HIDE!
GASP! IT CAN'T BE!
S.SKINNER
SKREEK
IT'S MISS HOOVER! WHAT'S MY FAVORITE TEACHER DOING HERE?
SHE'S TAKING A FILE! REMOVAL OF SCHOOL PROPERTY IS A SERIOUS OFFENSE!
WHEW! SHE'S GONE -- AND SHE NEVER NOTICED ME! I GUESS IT'S SAFE TO...HEY, WHAT'S THIS?!

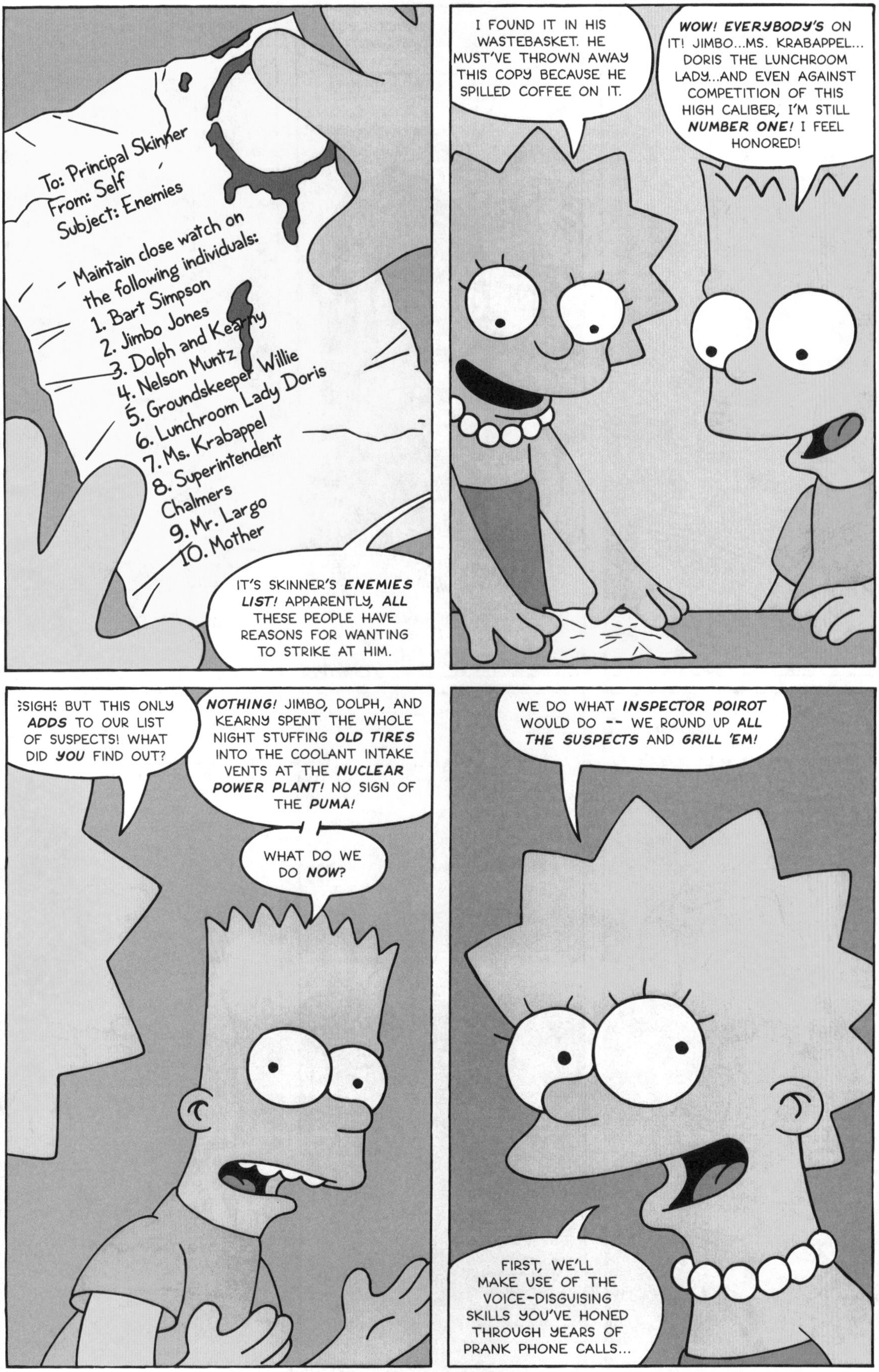
To: Principal Skinner
From: Self
Subject: Enemies
- Maintain close watch on the following individuals:
the Bart Simpson
1. Jimbo Jones
2. Dolph and Kearny
3. Nelson Muntz
4. Groundskeeper Willie
5. Lunchroom Lady Doris
6. Ms. Krabappel
7. Superintendent Chalmers
8. Mr. Largo
9. Mother
IT'S SKINNER'S ENEMIES LIST! APPARENTLY, ALL THESE PEOPLE HAVE REASONS FOR WANTING TO STRIKE AT HIM.
I FOUND IT IN HIS WASTEBASKET. HE MUST'VE THROWN AWAY THIS COPY BECAUSE HE SPILLED COFFEE ON IT.
WOW! EVERYBODY'S ON IT! JIMBO...MS. KRABAPPEL... DORIS THE LUNCHROOM LADY...AND EVEN AGAINST COMPETITION OF THIS HIGH CALIBER, I'M STILL NUMBER ONE! I FEEL HONORED!
:SIGH: BUT THIS ONLY ADDS TO OUR LIST OF SUSPECTS! WHAT DID YOU FIND OUT?
NOTHING! JIMBO, DOLPH, AND KEARNY SPENT THE WHOLE NIGHT STUFFING OLD TIRES INTO THE COOLANT INTAKE VENTS AT THE NUCLEAR POWER PLANT! NO SIGN OF THE PUMA!
WHAT DO WE DO NOW?
WE DO WHAT INSPECTOR POIROT WOULD DO -- WE ROUND UP ALL THE SUSPECTS AND GRILL 'EM!
FIRST, WE'LL MAKE USE OF THE VOICE-DISGUISING SKILLS YOU'VE HONED THROUGH YEARS OF PRANK PHONE CALLS...

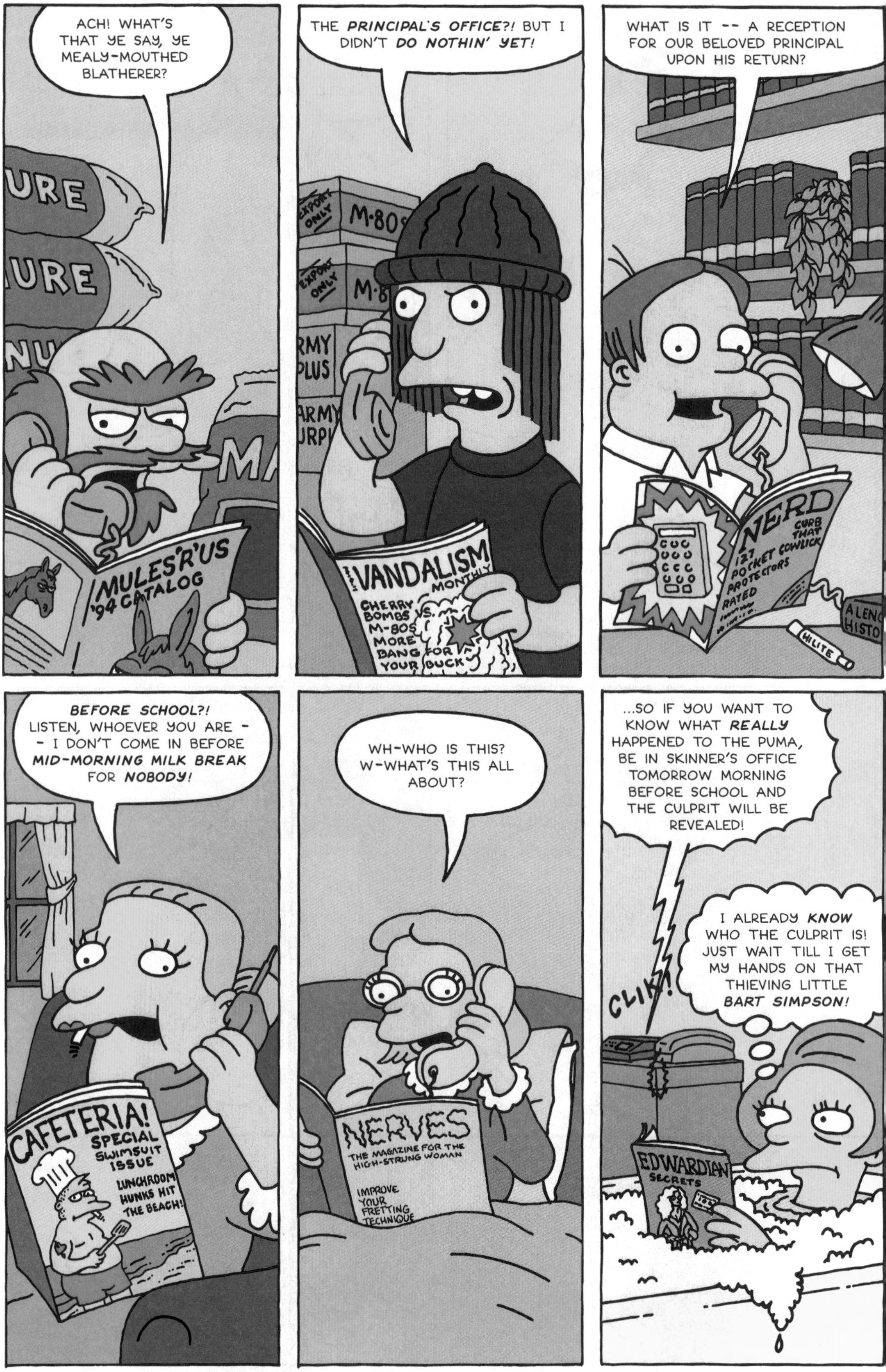
ACH! WHAT'S THAT YE SAY, YE MEALY-MOUTHED BLATHERER?
MULES'R'US '94 CATALOG
THE *PRINCIPAL'S OFFICE?!* BUT I DIDN'T *DO NOTHIN' YET!*
EXPORT ONLY
VANDALISM MONTHLY
CHERRY BOMBS VS. M-80S MORE BANG FOR YOUR BUCK
WHAT IS IT -- A RECEPTION FOR OUR BELOVED PRINCIPAL UPON HIS RETURN?
NERD
CURB THAT COWLICK
127 POCKET PROTECTORS RATED
HILITE
BEFORE SCHOOL?! LISTEN, WHOEVER YOU ARE -- I DON'T COME IN BEFORE *MID-MORNING MILK BREAK* FOR *NOBODY!*
CAFETERIA! SPECIAL SWIMSUIT ISSUE
LUNCHROOM HUNKS HIT THE BEACH!
WH-WHO IS THIS? W-WHAT'S THIS ALL ABOUT?
NERVES
THE MAGAZINE FOR THE HIGH-STRUNG WOMAN
IMPROVE YOUR FRETTING TECHNIQUE
...SO IF YOU WANT TO KNOW WHAT *REALLY* HAPPENED TO THE PUMA, BE IN SKINNER'S OFFICE TOMORROW MORNING BEFORE SCHOOL AND THE CULPRIT WILL BE REVEALED!
CLIK!
I ALREADY *KNOW* WHO THE CULPRIT IS! JUST WAIT TILL I GET MY HANDS ON THAT THIEVING LITTLE *BART SIMPSON!*
EDWARDIAN SECRETS

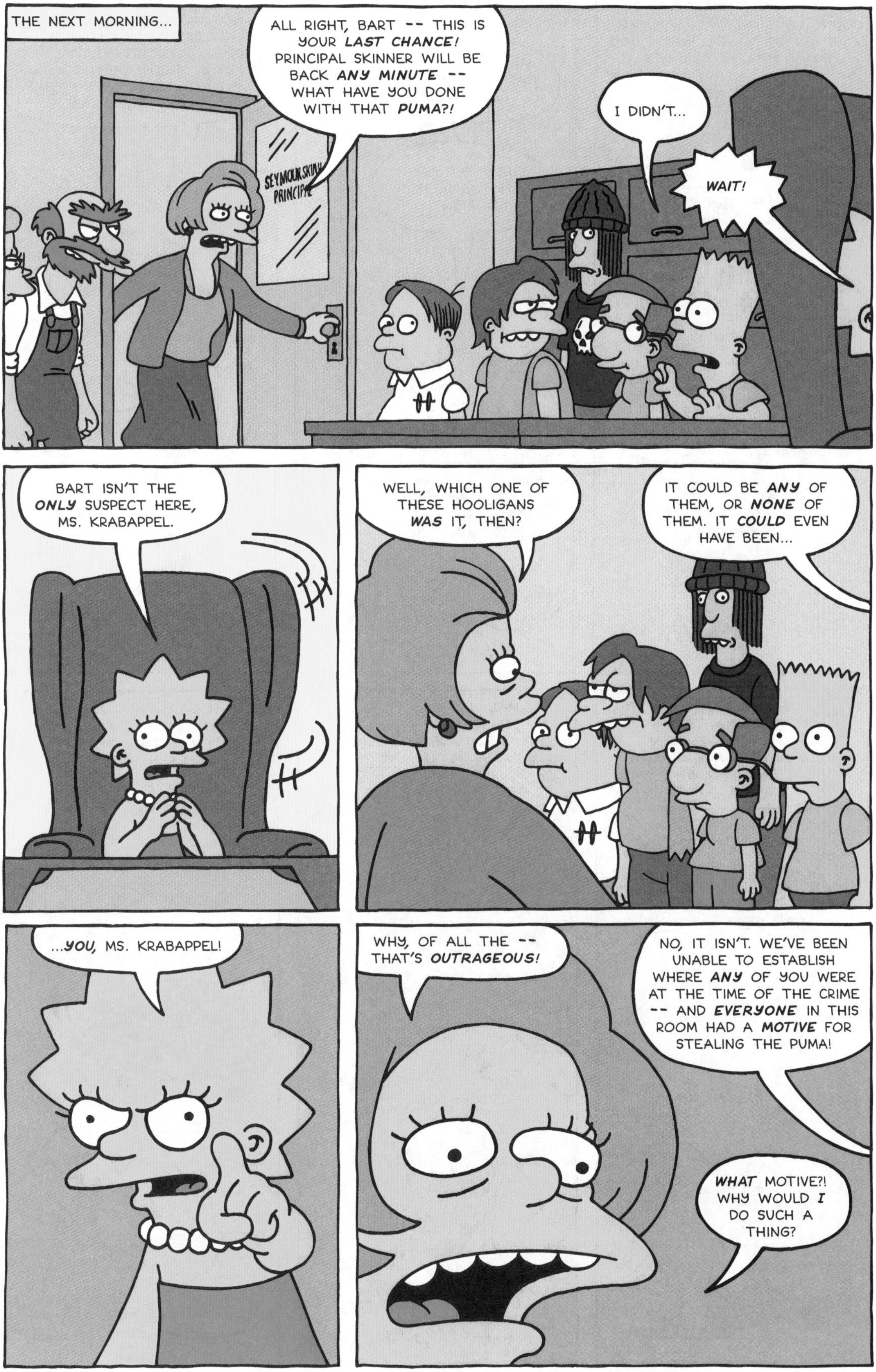
THE NEXT MORNING...
ALL RIGHT, BART -- THIS IS YOUR LAST CHANCE! PRINCIPAL SKINNER WILL BE BACK ANY MINUTE -- WHAT HAVE YOU DONE WITH THAT PUMA?!
I DIDN'T...
WAIT!
BART ISN'T THE ONLY SUSPECT HERE, MS. KRABAPPEL.
WELL, WHICH ONE OF THESE HOOLIGANS WAS IT, THEN?
IT COULD BE ANY OF THEM, OR NONE OF THEM. IT COULD EVEN HAVE BEEN...
...YOU, MS. KRABAPPEL!
WHY, OF ALL THE -- THAT'S OUTRAGEOUS!
NO, IT ISN'T. WE'VE BEEN UNABLE TO ESTABLISH WHERE ANY OF YOU WERE AT THE TIME OF THE CRIME -- AND EVERYONE IN THIS ROOM HAD A MOTIVE FOR STEALING THE PUMA!
WHAT MOTIVE?! WHY WOULD I DO SUCH A THING?

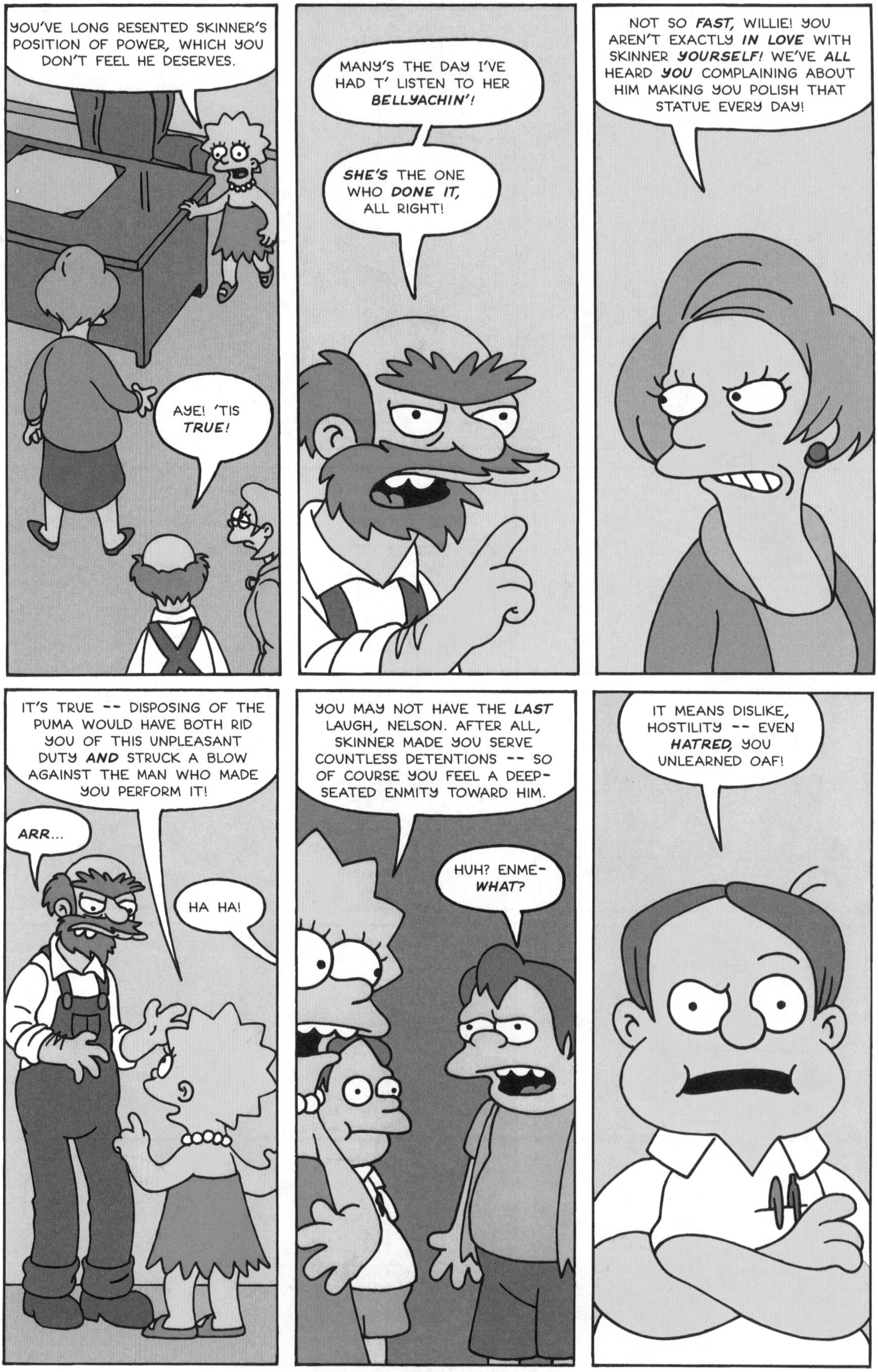

YOU'VE LONG RESENTED SKINNER'S POSITION OF POWER, WHICH YOU DON'T FEEL HE DESERVES.
AYE! 'TIS TRUE!
MANY'S THE DAY I'VE HAD T' LISTEN TO HER BELLYACHIN'!
SHE'S THE ONE WHO DONE IT, ALL RIGHT!
NOT SO FAST, WILLIE! YOU AREN'T EXACTLY IN LOVE WITH SKINNER YOURSELF! WE'VE ALL HEARD YOU COMPLAINING ABOUT HIM MAKING YOU POLISH THAT STATUE EVERY DAY!
IT'S TRUE -- DISPOSING OF THE PUMA WOULD HAVE BOTH RID YOU OF THIS UNPLEASANT DUTY AND STRUCK A BLOW AGAINST THE MAN WHO MADE YOU PERFORM IT!
ARR...
HA HA!
YOU MAY NOT HAVE THE LAST LAUGH, NELSON. AFTER ALL, SKINNER MADE YOU SERVE COUNTLESS DETENTIONS -- SO OF COURSE YOU FEEL A DEEP-SEATED ENMITY TOWARD HIM.
HUH? ENME-WHAT?
IT MEANS DISLIKE, HOSTILITY -- EVEN HATRED, YOU UNLEARNED OAF!

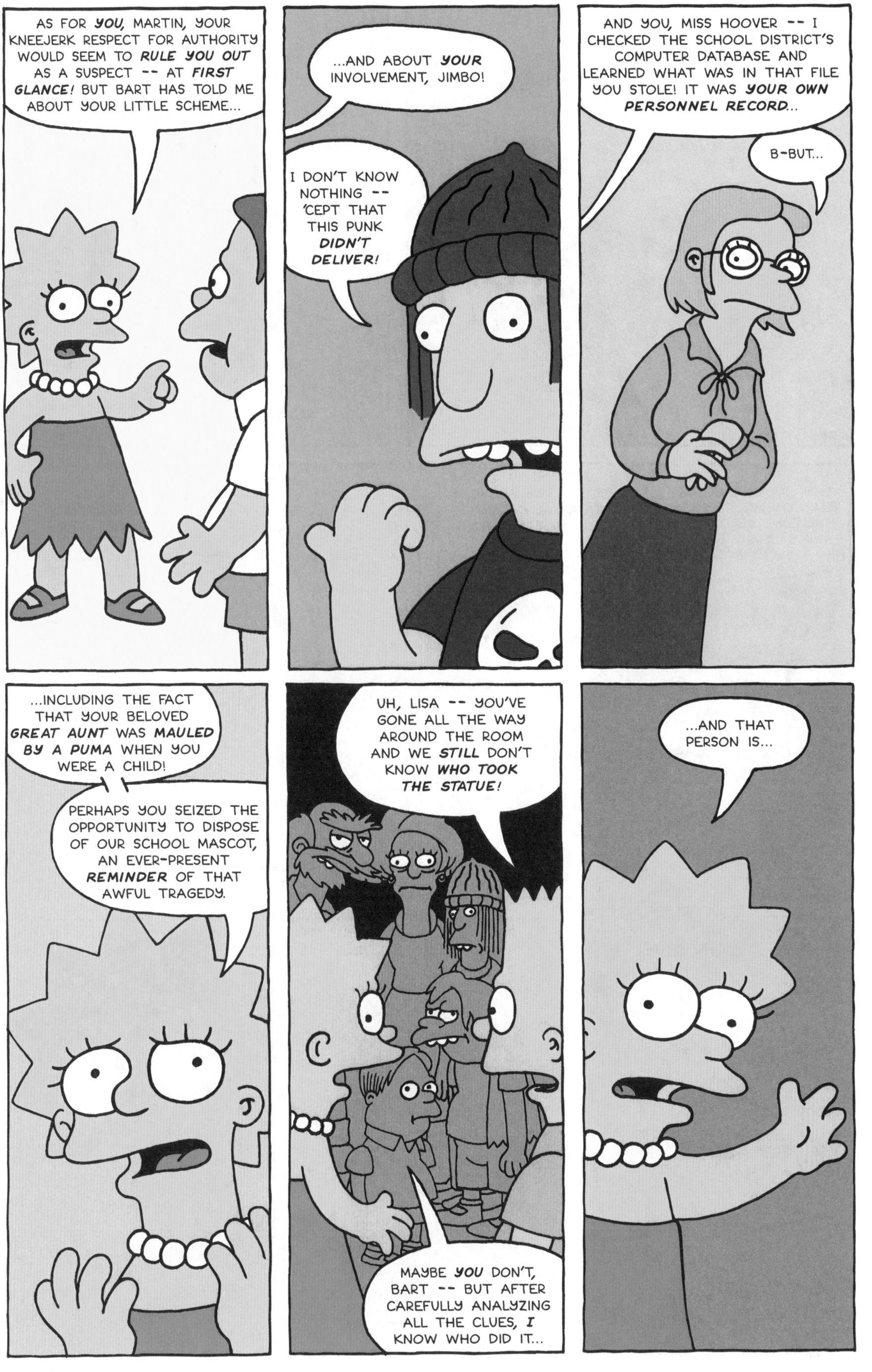
AS FOR YOU, MARTIN, YOUR KNEEJERK RESPECT FOR AUTHORITY WOULD SEEM TO RULE YOU OUT AS A SUSPECT -- AT FIRST GLANCE! BUT BART HAS TOLD ME ABOUT YOUR LITTLE SCHEME...
...AND ABOUT YOUR INVOLVEMENT, JIMBO!
I DON'T KNOW NOTHING -- 'CEPT THAT THIS PUNK DIDN'T DELIVER!
AND YOU, MISS HOOVER -- I CHECKED THE SCHOOL DISTRICT'S COMPUTER DATABASE AND LEARNED WHAT WAS IN THAT FILE YOU STOLE! IT WAS YOUR OWN PERSONNEL RECORD...
B-BUT...
...INCLUDING THE FACT THAT YOUR BELOVED GREAT AUNT WAS MAULED BY A PUMA WHEN YOU WERE A CHILD!
PERHAPS YOU SEIZED THE OPPORTUNITY TO DISPOSE OF OUR SCHOOL MASCOT, AN EVER-PRESENT REMINDER OF THAT AWFUL TRAGEDY.
UH, LISA -- YOU'VE GONE ALL THE WAY AROUND THE ROOM AND WE STILL DON'T KNOW WHO TOOK THE STATUE!
MAYBE YOU DON'T, BART -- BUT AFTER CAREFULLY ANALYZING ALL THE CLUES, I KNOW WHO DID IT...
...AND THAT PERSON IS...

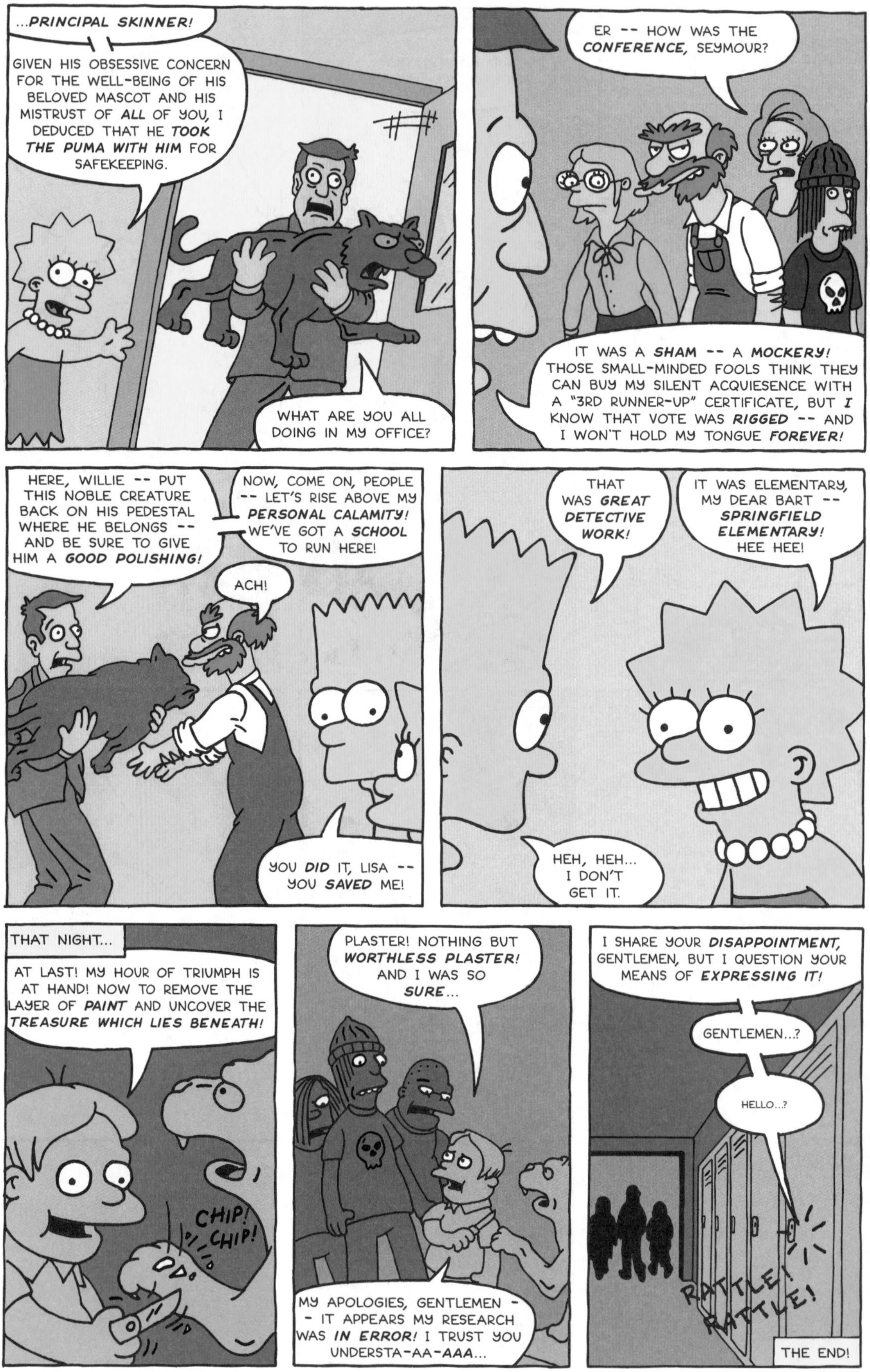
...PRINCIPAL SKINNER!
GIVEN HIS OBSESSIVE CONCERN FOR THE WELL-BEING OF HIS BELOVED MASCOT AND HIS MISTRUST OF ALL OF YOU, I DEDUCED THAT HE TOOK THE PUMA WITH HIM FOR SAFEKEEPING.
WHAT ARE YOU ALL DOING IN MY OFFICE?
ER -- HOW WAS THE CONFERENCE, SEYMOUR?
IT WAS A SHAM -- A MOCKERY! THOSE SMALL-MINDED FOOLS THINK THEY CAN BUY MY SILENT ACQUIESENCE WITH A "3RD RUNNER-UP" CERTIFICATE, BUT I KNOW THAT VOTE WAS RIGGED -- AND I WON'T HOLD MY TONGUE FOREVER!
HERE, WILLIE -- PUT THIS NOBLE CREATURE BACK ON HIS PEDESTAL WHERE HE BELONGS -- AND BE SURE TO GIVE HIM A GOOD POLISHING!
NOW, COME ON, PEOPLE -- LET'S RISE ABOVE MY PERSONAL CALAMITY! WE'VE GOT A SCHOOL TO RUN HERE!
ACH!
YOU DID IT, LISA -- YOU SAVED ME!
THAT WAS GREAT DETECTIVE WORK!
IT WAS ELEMENTARY, MY DEAR BART -- SPRINGFIELD ELEMENTARY! HEE HEE!
HEH, HEH... I DON'T GET IT.
THAT NIGHT...
AT LAST! MY HOUR OF TRIUMPH IS AT HAND! NOW TO REMOVE THE LAYER OF PAINT AND UNCOVER THE TREASURE WHICH LIES BENEATH!
CHIP! CHIP!
PLASTER! NOTHING BUT WORTHLESS PLASTER! AND I WAS SO SURE...
MY APOLOGIES, GENTLEMEN -- IT APPEARS MY RESEARCH WAS IN ERROR! I TRUST YOU UNDERSTA-AA-AAA...
I SHARE YOUR DISAPPOINTMENT, GENTLEMEN, BUT I QUESTION YOUR MEANS OF EXPRESSING IT!
GENTLEMEN...?
HELLO...?
RATTLE! RATTLE!
THE END!

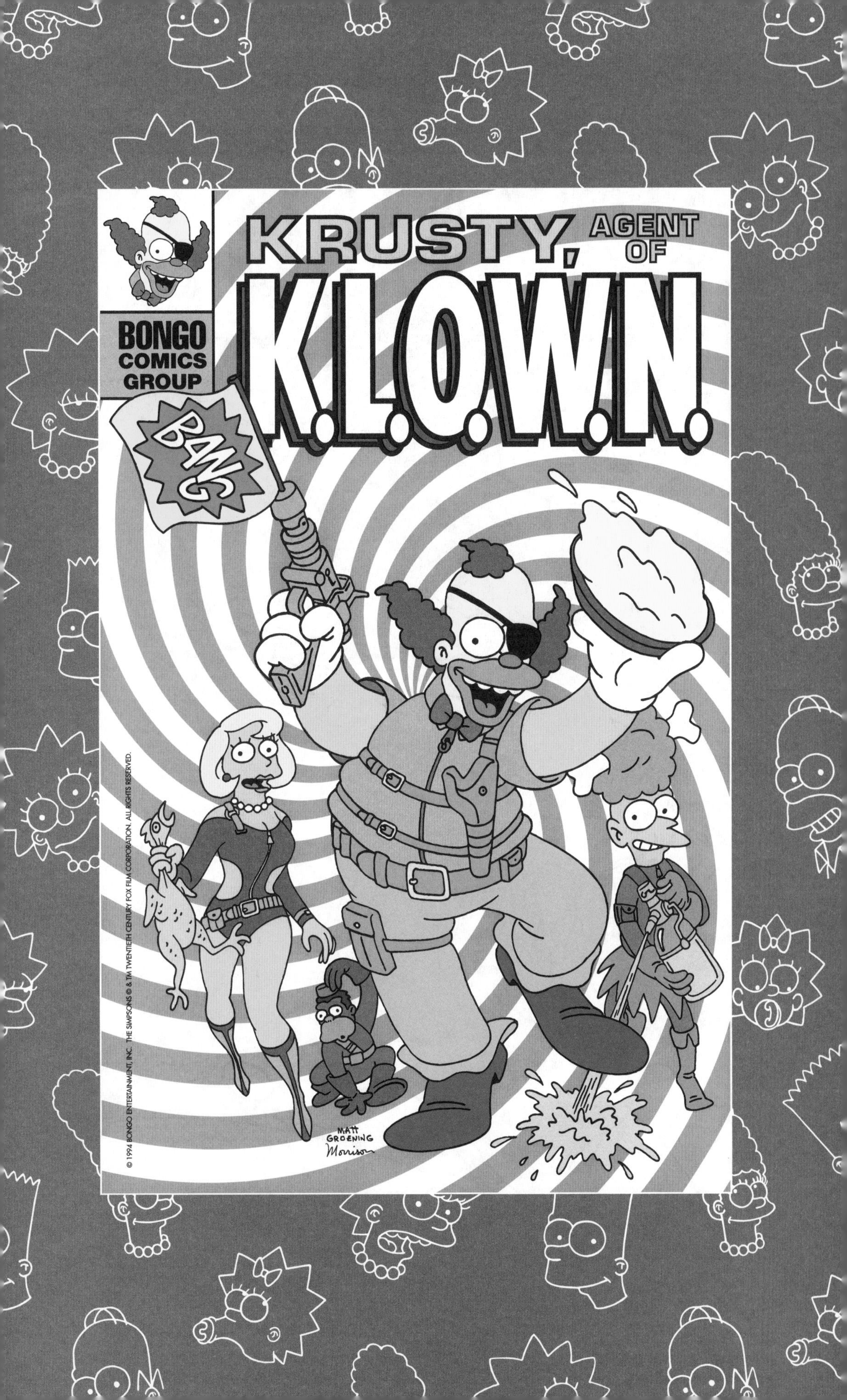
BONGO
COMICS
GROUP
KRUSTY, AGENT OF
K.L.O.W.N.
BANG
© 1994 BONGO ENTERTAINMENT, INC. THE SIMPSONS © & TM TWENTIETH CENTURY FOX FILM CORPORATION. ALL RIGHTS RESERVED.
MATT GROENING
Morrison

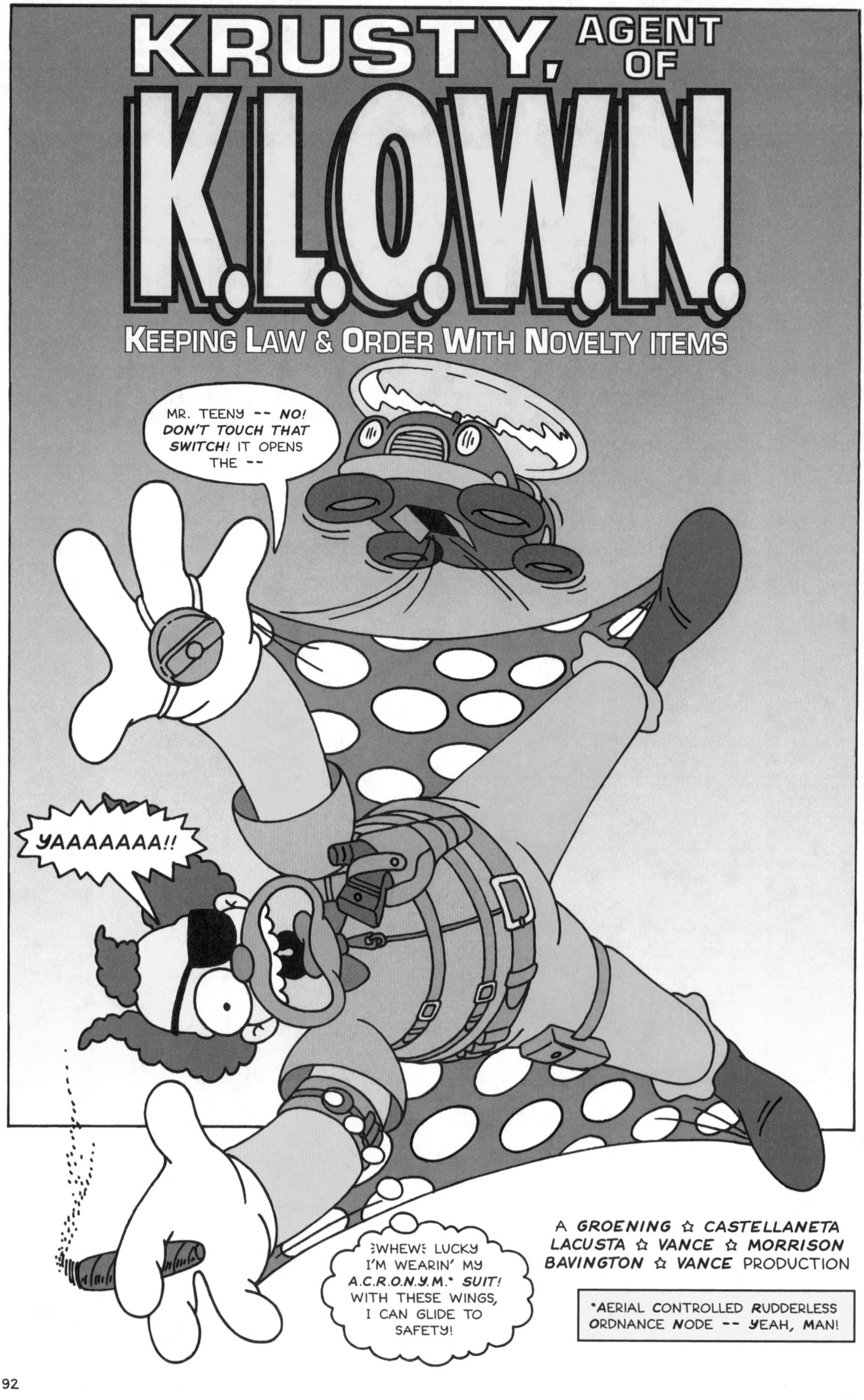
KRUSTY, AGENT OF K.L.O.W.N.
KEEPING LAW & ORDER WITH NOVELTY ITEMS
MR. TEENY -- NO! DON'T TOUCH THAT SWITCH! IT OPENS THE --
YAAAAAAA!!
A GROENING ☆ CASTELLANETA LACUSTA ☆ VANCE ☆ MORRISON BAVINGTON ☆ VANCE PRODUCTION
WHEW! LUCKY I'M WEARIN' MY A.C.R.O.N.Y.M.* SUIT! WITH THESE WINGS, I CAN GLIDE TO SAFETY!
*AERIAL CONTROLLED RUDDERLESS ORDNANCE NODE -- YEAH, MAN!

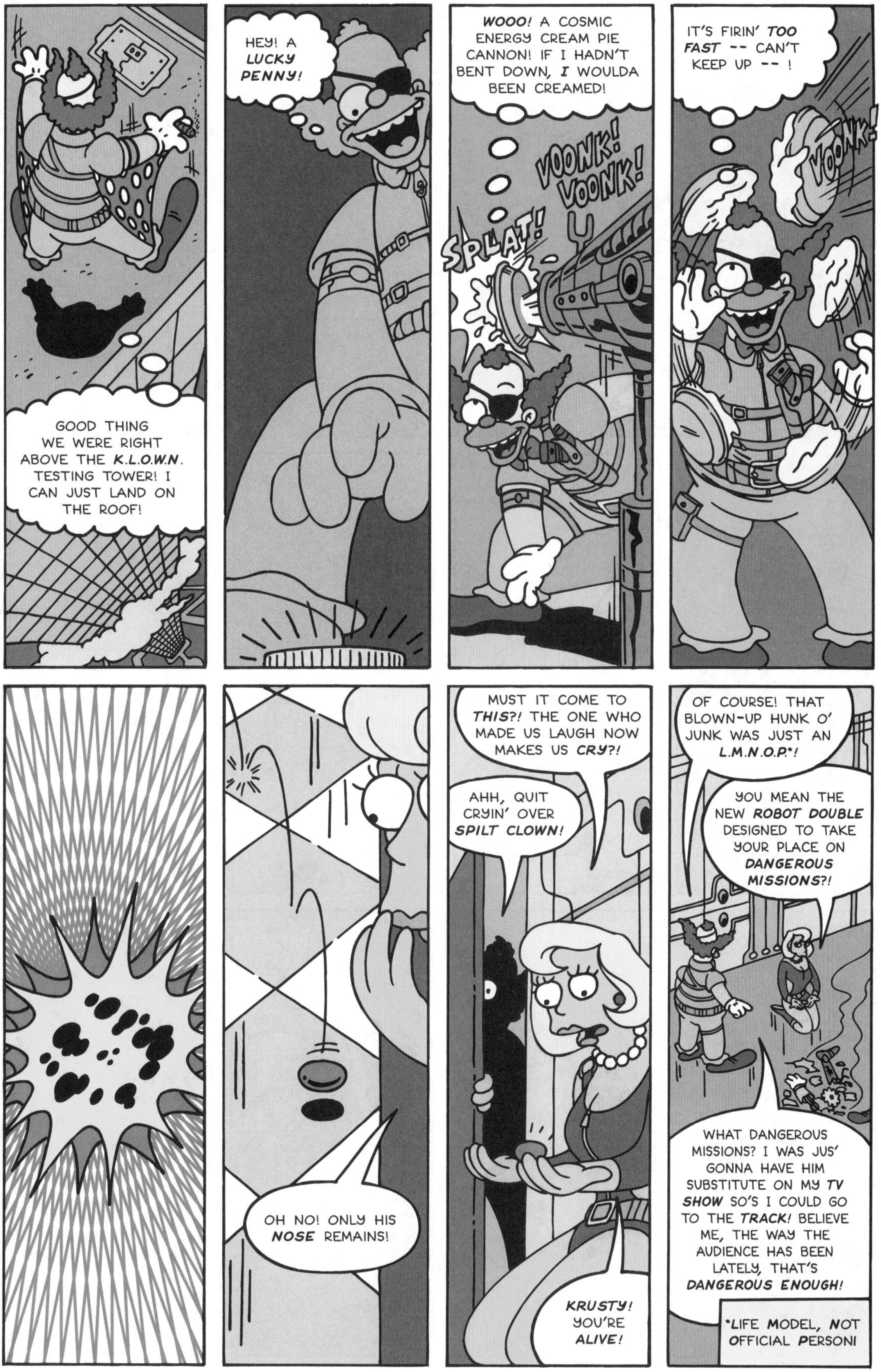
GOOD THING WE WERE RIGHT ABOVE THE K.L.O.W.N. TESTING TOWER! I CAN JUST LAND ON THE ROOF!
HEY! A LUCKY PENNY!
WOOO! A COSMIC ENERGY CREAM PIE CANNON! IF I HADN'T BENT DOWN, I WOULDA BEEN CREAMED!
VOONK! VOONK!
SPLAT!
IT'S FIRIN' TOO FAST -- CAN'T KEEP UP -- !
VOONK!
OH NO! ONLY HIS NOSE REMAINS!
MUST IT COME TO THIS?! THE ONE WHO MADE US LAUGH NOW MAKES US CRY?!
AHH, QUIT CRYIN' OVER SPILT CLOWN!
KRUSTY! YOU'RE ALIVE!
OF COURSE! THAT BLOWN-UP HUNK O' JUNK WAS JUST AN L.M.N.O.P.*!
YOU MEAN THE NEW ROBOT DOUBLE DESIGNED TO TAKE YOUR PLACE ON DANGEROUS MISSIONS?!
WHAT DANGEROUS MISSIONS? I WAS JUS' GONNA HAVE HIM SUBSTITUTE ON MY TV SHOW SO'S I COULD GO TO THE TRACK! BELIEVE ME, THE WAY THE AUDIENCE HAS BEEN LATELY, THAT'S DANGEROUS ENOUGH!
*LIFE MODEL, NOT OFFICIAL PERSON!

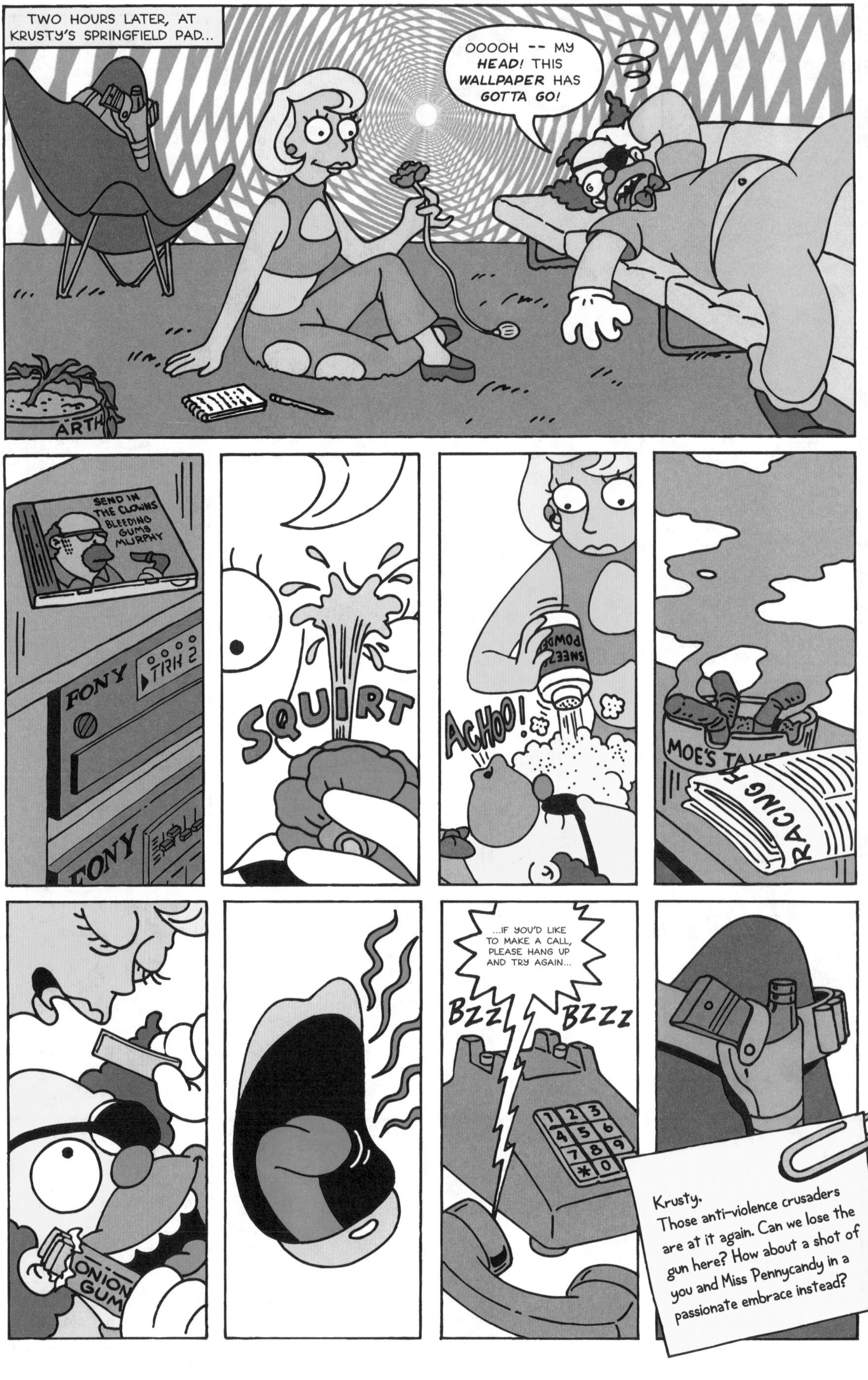

TWO HOURS LATER, AT KRUSTY'S SPRINGFIELD PAD...
OOOOH -- MY HEAD! THIS WALLPAPER HAS GOTTA GO!
SEND IN THE CLOWNS
BLEEDING GUMS MURPHY
FONY
TRK 2
FONY
SQUIRT
ACHOO!
RACING
ONION GUM
...IF YOU'D LIKE TO MAKE A CALL, PLEASE HANG UP AND TRY AGAIN...
BZZ
BZZZ
Krusty,
Those anti-violence crusaders are at it again. Can we lose the gun here? How about a shot of you and Miss Pennycandy in a passionate embrace instead?

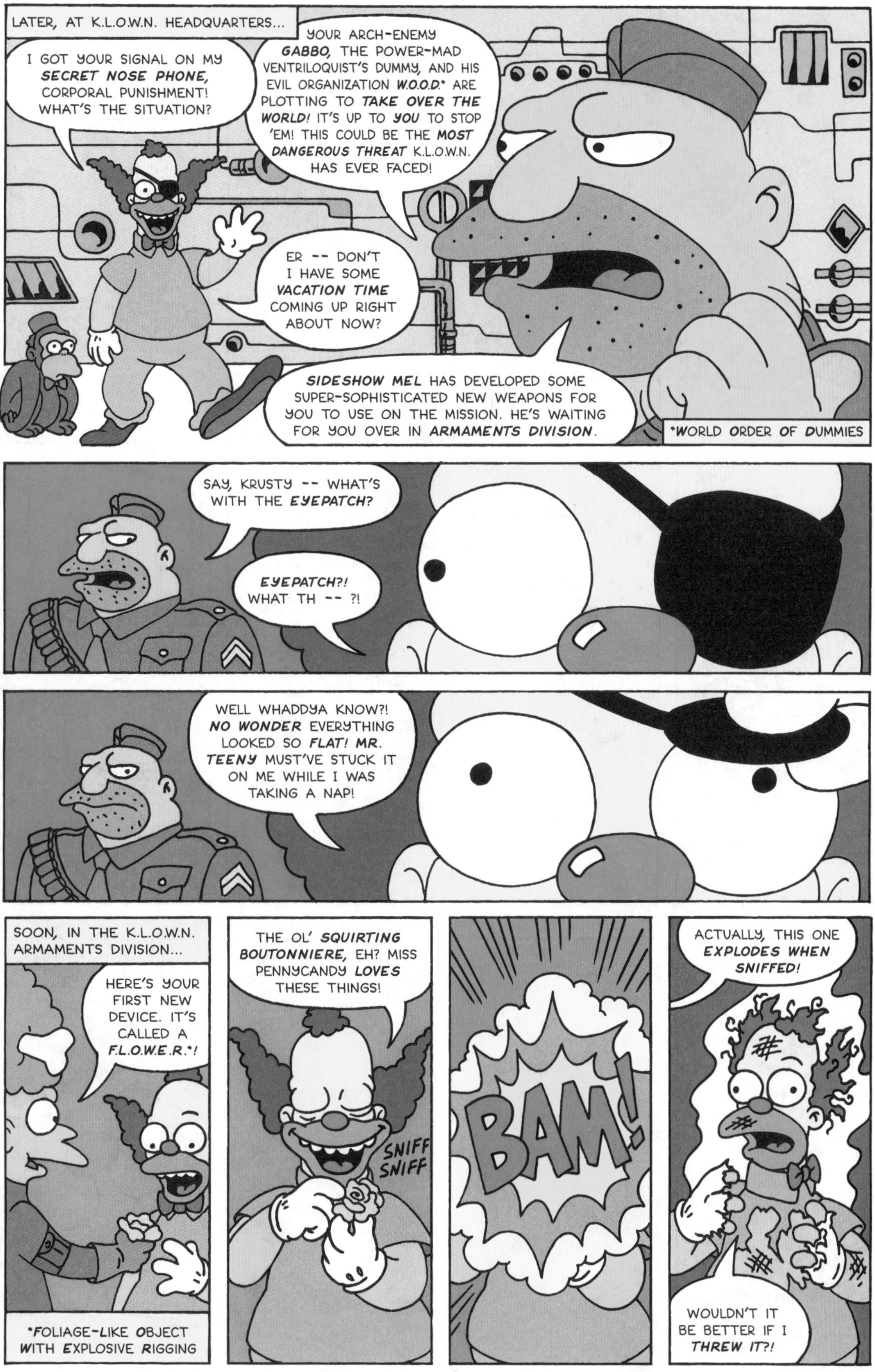

LATER, AT K.L.O.W.N. HEADQUARTERS...
I GOT YOUR SIGNAL ON MY SECRET NOSE PHONE, CORPORAL PUNISHMENT! WHAT'S THE SITUATION?
YOUR ARCH-ENEMY GABBO, THE POWER-MAD VENTRILOQUIST'S DUMMY, AND HIS EVIL ORGANIZATION W.O.O.D.* ARE PLOTTING TO TAKE OVER THE WORLD! IT'S UP TO YOU TO STOP 'EM! THIS COULD BE THE MOST DANGEROUS THREAT K.L.O.W.N. HAS EVER FACED!
ER -- DON'T I HAVE SOME VACATION TIME COMING UP RIGHT ABOUT NOW?
SIDESHOW MEL HAS DEVELOPED SOME SUPER-SOPHISTICATED NEW WEAPONS FOR YOU TO USE ON THE MISSION. HE'S WAITING FOR YOU OVER IN ARMAMENTS DIVISION.
*WORLD ORDER OF DUMMIES
SAY, KRUSTY -- WHAT'S WITH THE EYEPATCH?
EYEPATCH?! WHAT TH -- ?!
WELL WHADDYA KNOW?! NO WONDER EVERYTHING LOOKED SO FLAT! MR. TEENY MUST'VE STUCK IT ON ME WHILE I WAS TAKING A NAP!
SOON, IN THE K.L.O.W.N. ARMAMENTS DIVISION...
HERE'S YOUR FIRST NEW DEVICE. IT'S CALLED A F.L.O.W.E.R.*!
*FOLIAGE-LIKE OBJECT WITH EXPLOSIVE RIGGING
THE OL' SQUIRTING BOUTONNIERE, EH? MISS PENNYCANDY LOVES THESE THINGS!
SNIFF SNIFF
BAM!
ACTUALLY, THIS ONE EXPLODES WHEN SNIFFED!
WOULDN'T IT BE BETTER IF I THREW IT?!

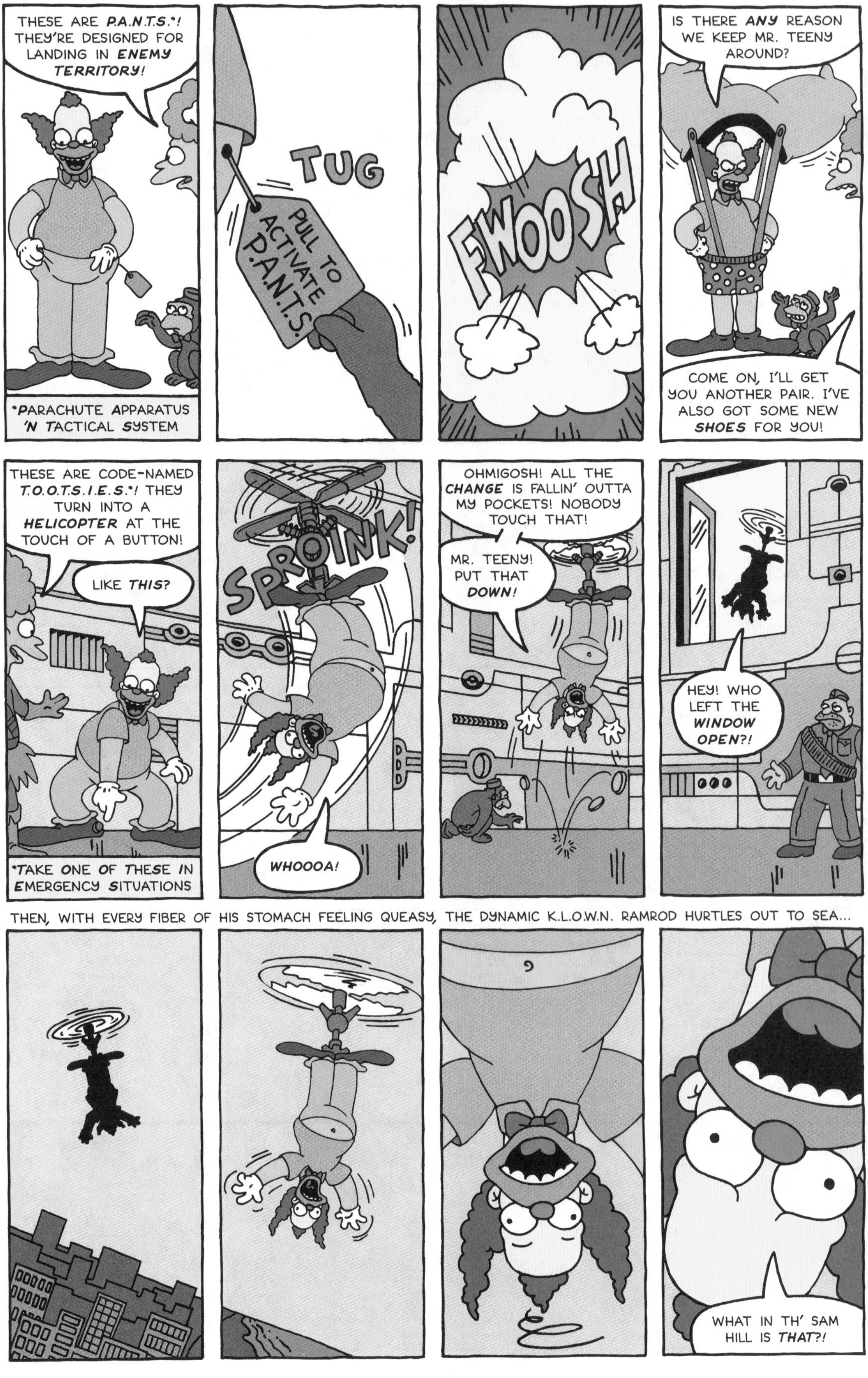

THESE ARE P.A.N.T.S.*! THEY'RE DESIGNED FOR LANDING IN ENEMY TERRITORY!
*PARACHUTE APPARATUS 'N TACTICAL SYSTEM
TUG
PULL TO ACTIVATE P.A.N.T.S.
FWOOSH
IS THERE ANY REASON WE KEEP MR. TEENY AROUND?
COME ON, I'LL GET YOU ANOTHER PAIR. I'VE ALSO GOT SOME NEW SHOES FOR YOU!
THESE ARE CODE-NAMED T.O.O.T.S.I.E.S.*! THEY TURN INTO A HELICOPTER AT THE TOUCH OF A BUTTON!
LIKE THIS?
*TAKE ONE OF THESE IN EMERGENCY SITUATIONS
SPROINK!
WHOOOA!
OHMIGOSH! ALL THE CHANGE IS FALLIN' OUTTA MY POCKETS! NOBODY TOUCH THAT!
MR. TEENY! PUT THAT DOWN!
HEY! WHO LEFT THE WINDOW OPEN?!
THEN, WITH EVERY FIBER OF HIS STOMACH FEELING QUEASY, THE DYNAMIC K.L.O.W.N. RAMROD HURTLES OUT TO SEA...
WHAT IN TH' SAM HILL IS THAT?!

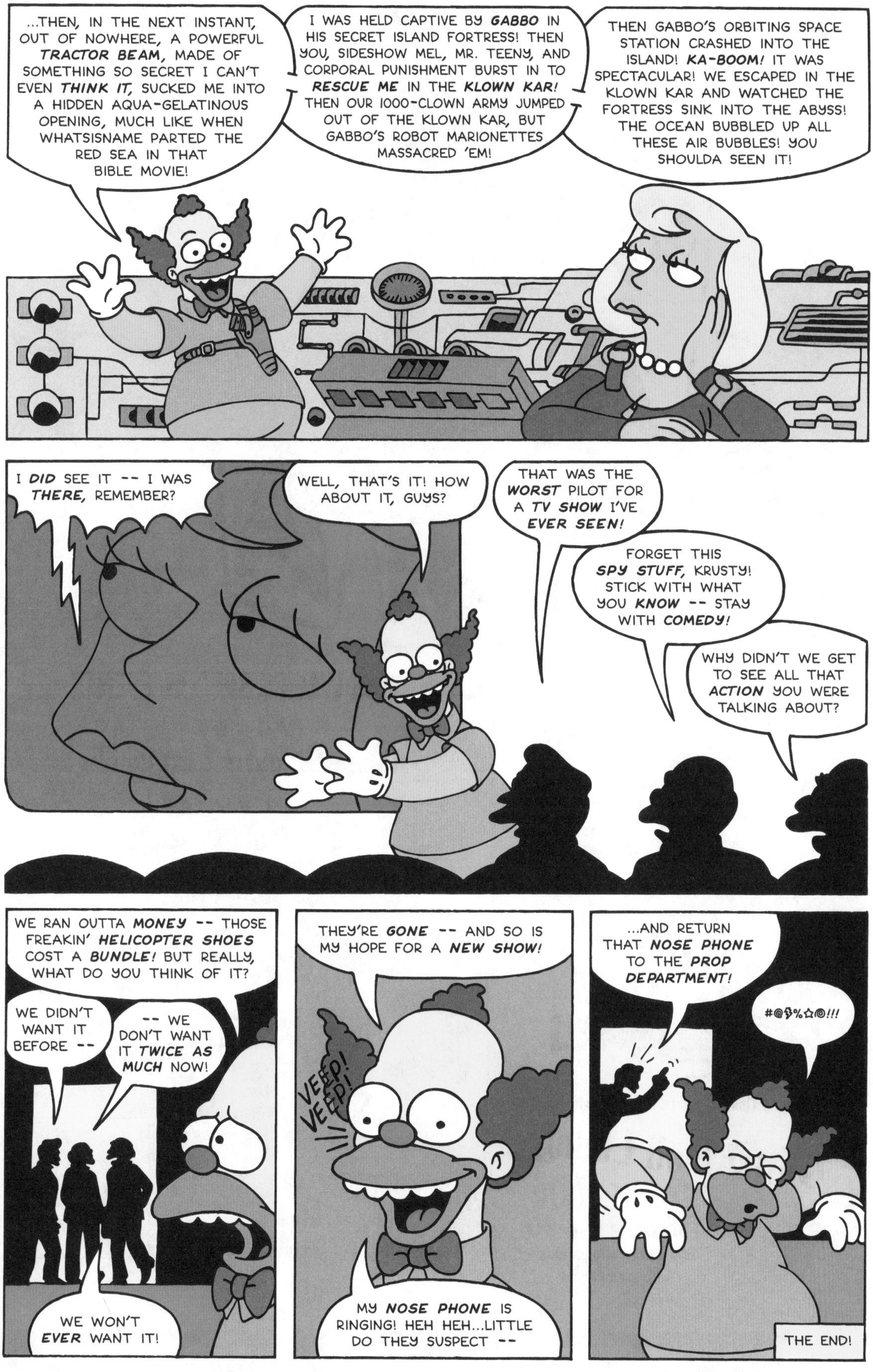
...THEN, IN THE NEXT INSTANT, OUT OF NOWHERE, A POWERFUL TRACTOR BEAM, MADE OF SOMETHING SO SECRET I CAN'T EVEN THINK IT, SUCKED ME INTO A HIDDEN AQUA-GELATINOUS OPENING, MUCH LIKE WHEN WHATSISNAME PARTED THE RED SEA IN THAT BIBLE MOVIE!
I WAS HELD CAPTIVE BY GABBO IN HIS SECRET ISLAND FORTRESS! THEN YOU, SIDESHOW MEL, MR. TEENY, AND CORPORAL PUNISHMENT BURST IN TO RESCUE ME IN THE KLOWN KAR! THEN OUR 1000-CLOWN ARMY JUMPED OUT OF THE KLOWN KAR, BUT GABBO'S ROBOT MARIONETTES MASSACRED 'EM!
THEN GABBO'S ORBITING SPACE STATION CRASHED INTO THE ISLAND! KA-BOOM! IT WAS SPECTACULAR! WE ESCAPED IN THE KLOWN KAR AND WATCHED THE FORTRESS SINK INTO THE ABYSS! THE OCEAN BUBBLED UP ALL THESE AIR BUBBLES! YOU SHOULDA SEEN IT!
I DID SEE IT -- I WAS THERE, REMEMBER?
WELL, THAT'S IT! HOW ABOUT IT, GUYS?
THAT WAS THE WORST PILOT FOR A TV SHOW I'VE EVER SEEN!
FORGET THIS SPY STUFF, KRUSTY! STICK WITH WHAT YOU KNOW -- STAY WITH COMEDY!
WHY DIDN'T WE GET TO SEE ALL THAT ACTION YOU WERE TALKING ABOUT?
WE RAN OUTTA MONEY -- THOSE FREAKIN' HELICOPTER SHOES COST A BUNDLE! BUT REALLY, WHAT DO YOU THINK OF IT?
WE DIDN'T WANT IT BEFORE --
-- WE DON'T WANT IT TWICE AS MUCH NOW!
WE WON'T EVER WANT IT!
THEY'RE GONE -- AND SO IS MY HOPE FOR A NEW SHOW!
VEEP! VEEP!
MY NOSE PHONE IS RINGING! HEH HEH...LITTLE DO THEY SUSPECT --
...AND RETURN THAT NOSE PHONE TO THE PROP DEPARTMENT!
#@$%☆@!!!
THE END!

Springfield's most "STRIKING" lanes!

BARNEY'S BOWL-A-RAMA

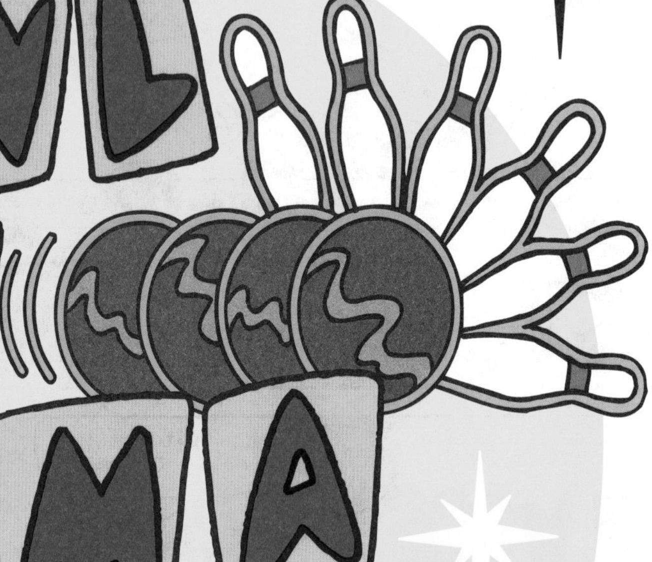

AND Coffee Shop

All items guaranteed 100% deep fried!

THIS WEEK'S SPECIAL EVENTS

MONDAY

Atomic Bombers League Night

THURSDAY

Blindfold Bowling

from 6:30 to 8 P.M.

$5 CASH PRIZE!

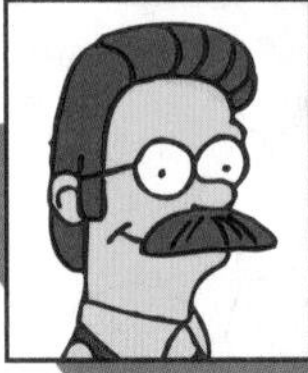

CONGRATULATIONS!

NED FLANDERS

FOR ROLLING A

PERFECT 300 GAME

ON JUNE 5!

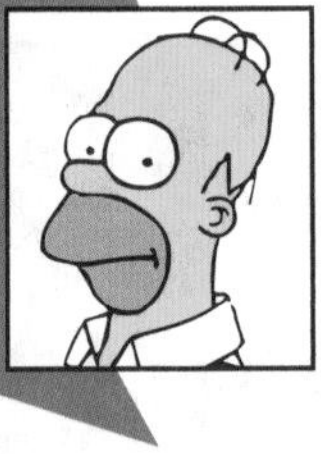

HUMER STIMSON

WINNER OF OUR

HIGH-HANDICAPPERS' CONSOLATION TOURNEY

After the final frame, refresh yourself at...

The Gutter Ball Lounge

"Home of the longneck Duff"

HAPPY HOUR

Thursdays 6-6:30

Free extra-salty peanuts with each pitcher

SUMMER LEAGUES FOR SULLEN TEENS

NOW FORMING!

Ladies! Sign up for our UNAPPRECIATED HOUSEWIVES CLASSES

For very personal instructions, ask for Jacques

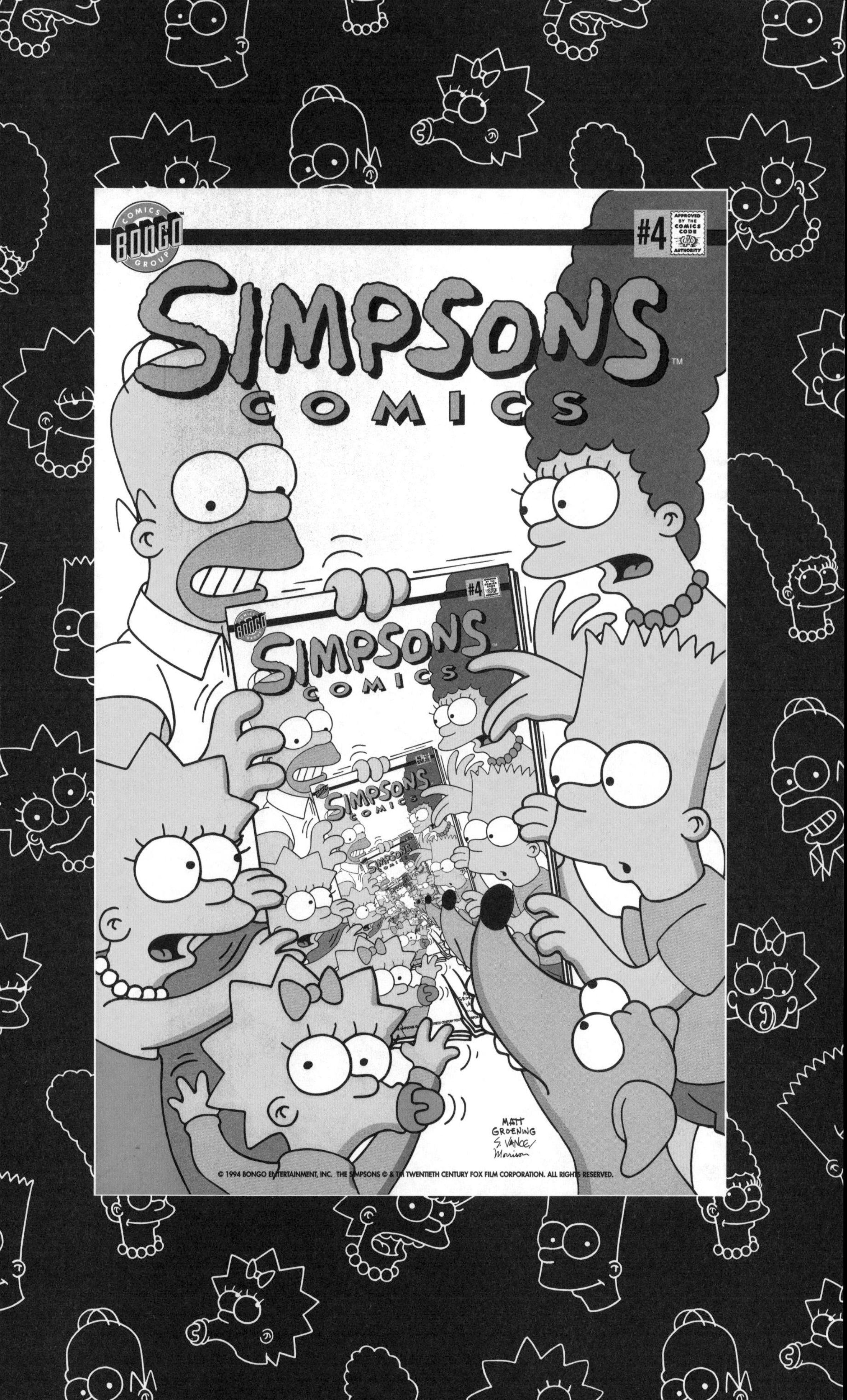
BONGO COMICS GROUP
#4
APPROVED BY THE COMICS CODE AUTHORITY
SIMPSONS COMICS
MATT GROENING
S. VANCE/ Morrison
© 1994 BONGO ENTERTAINMENT, INC. THE SIMPSONS © & TM TWENTIETH CENTURY FOX FILM CORPORATION. ALL RIGHTS RESERVED.

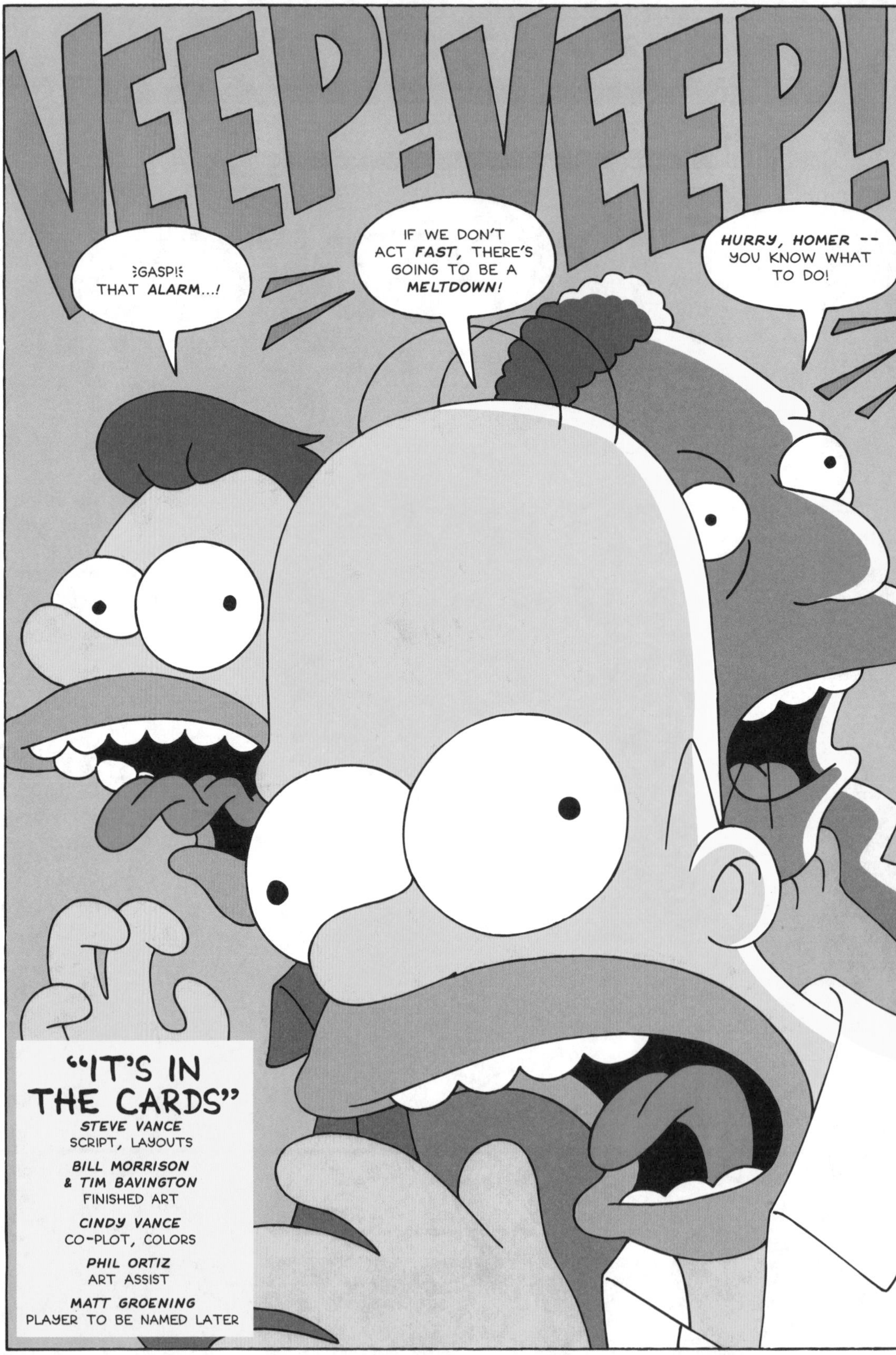
VEEP! VEEP!
ꟷGASP!ꟷ THAT ALARM...!
IF WE DON'T ACT FAST, THERE'S GOING TO BE A MELTDOWN!
HURRY, HOMER -- YOU KNOW WHAT TO DO!
"IT'S IN THE CARDS"
STEVE VANCE
SCRIPT, LAYOUTS
BILL MORRISON & TIM BAVINGTON
FINISHED ART
CINDY VANCE
CO-PLOT, COLORS
PHIL ORTIZ
ART ASSIST
MATT GROENING
PLAYER TO BE NAMED LATER

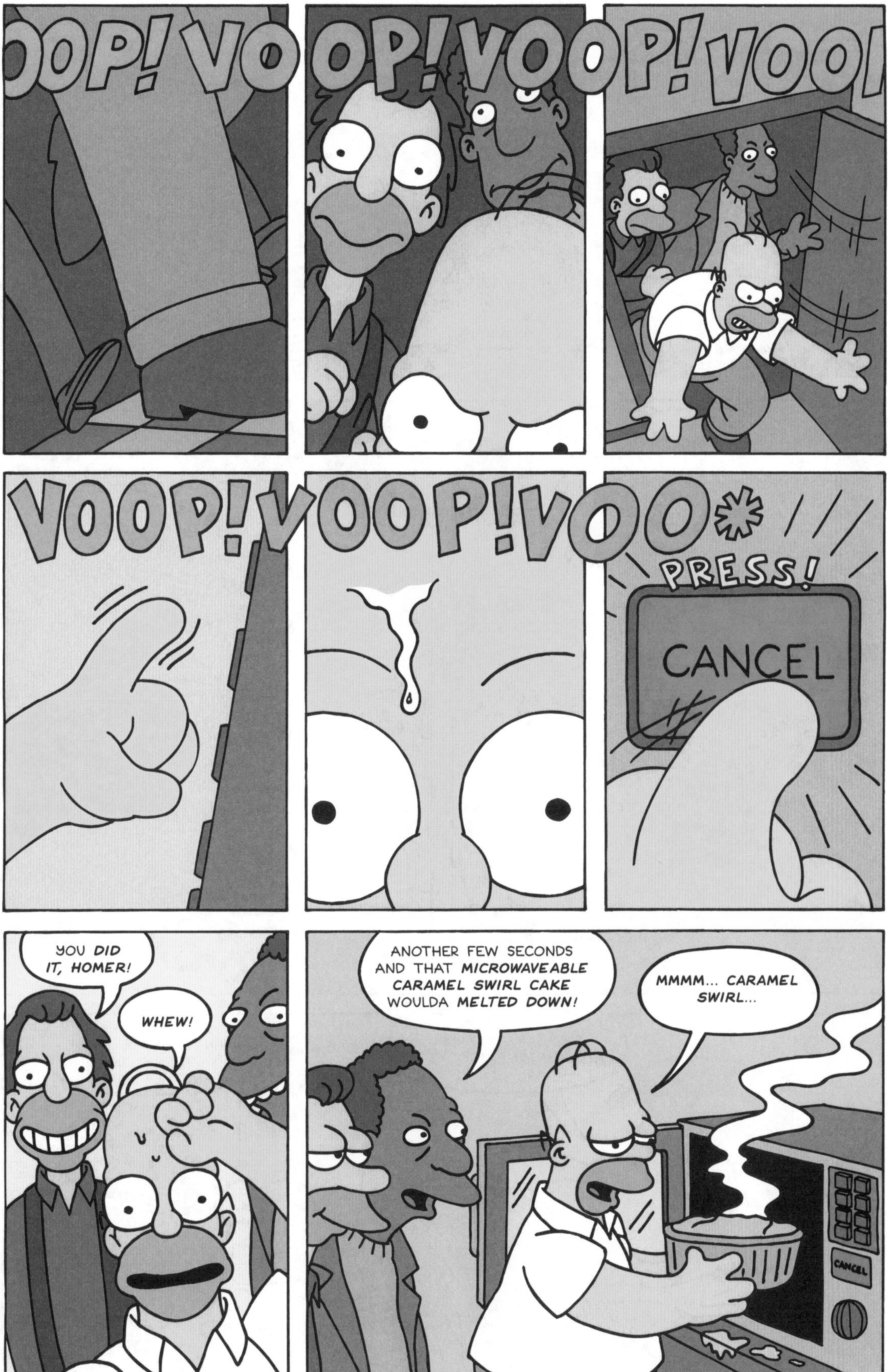
VOOP! VOOP! VOOP! VOOP! VOOP! VOOP! VOO*
PRESS!
CANCEL
YOU DID IT, HOMER!
WHEW!
ANOTHER FEW SECONDS AND THAT MICROWAVEABLE CARAMEL SWIRL CAKE WOULDA MELTED DOWN!
MMMM... CARAMEL SWIRL...

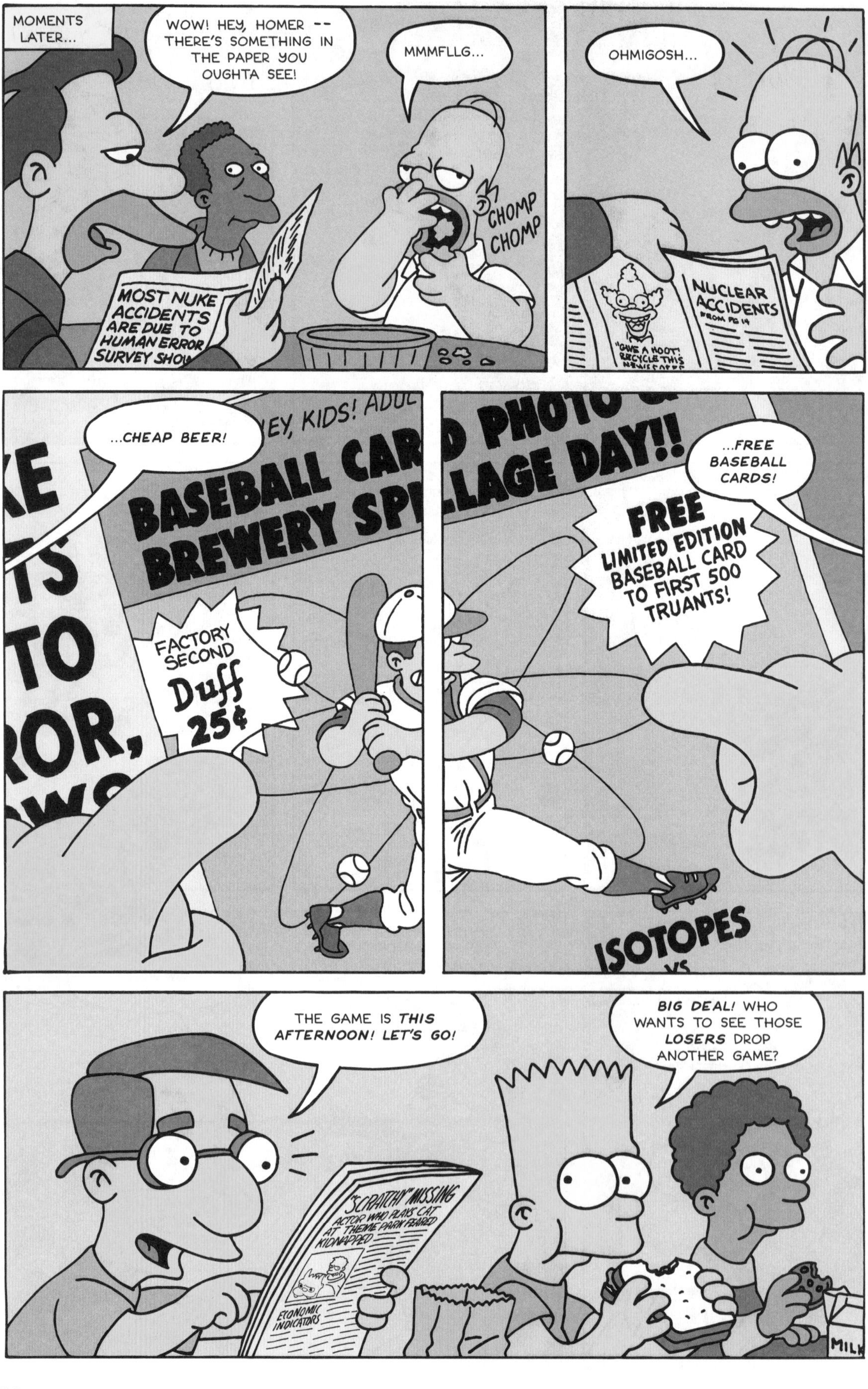

MOMENTS LATER...
WOW! HEY, HOMER -- THERE'S SOMETHING IN THE PAPER YOU OUGHTA SEE!
MMMFLLG...
CHOMP CHOMP
MOST NUKE ACCIDENTS ARE DUE TO HUMAN ERROR SURVEY SHOW
OHMIGOSH...
NUCLEAR ACCIDENTS
FROM PG 14
"GAVE A HOOT! RECYCLE THIS
...CHEAP BEER!
BASEBALL CAR
BREWERY SP
FACTORY SECOND Duff 25¢
D PHOTO &
LLAGE DAY!!
...FREE BASEBALL CARDS!
FREE LIMITED EDITION BASEBALL CARD TO FIRST 500 TRUANTS!
ISOTOPES
THE GAME IS *THIS AFTERNOON! LET'S GO!*
BIG DEAL! WHO WANTS TO SEE THOSE *LOSERS* DROP ANOTHER GAME?
"SCRATCHY" MISSING
ACTOR WHO PLAYS CAT AT THEME PARK FEARED KIDNAPPED
ECONOMIC INDICATORS
MILK

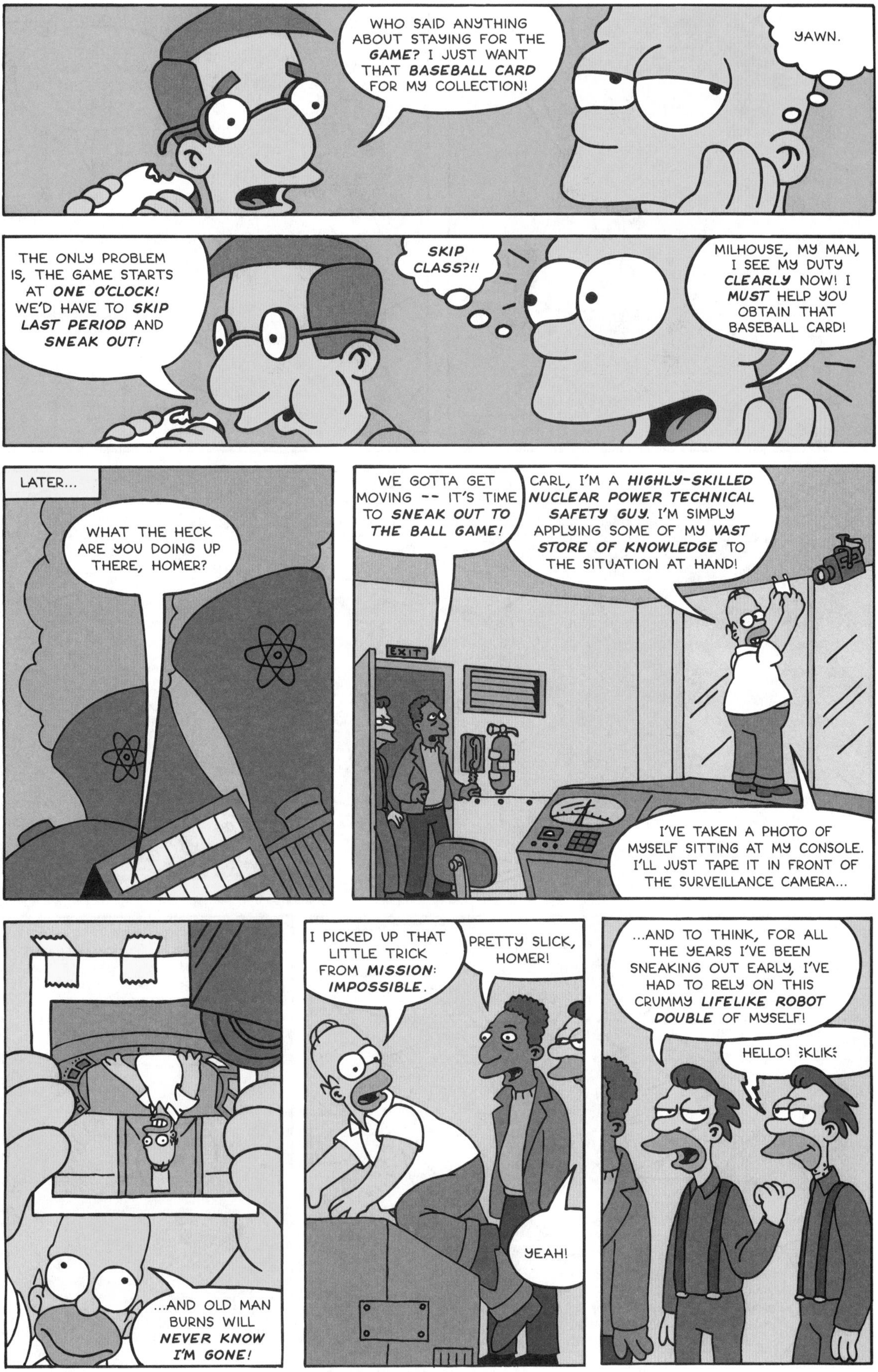
WHO SAID ANYTHING ABOUT STAYING FOR THE **GAME?** I JUST WANT THAT **BASEBALL CARD** FOR MY COLLECTION!
YAWN.
THE ONLY PROBLEM IS, THE GAME STARTS AT **ONE O'CLOCK!** WE'D HAVE TO **SKIP LAST PERIOD** AND **SNEAK OUT!**
SKIP CLASS?!!
MILHOUSE, MY MAN, I SEE MY DUTY **CLEARLY** NOW! I **MUST** HELP YOU OBTAIN THAT BASEBALL CARD!
LATER...
WHAT THE HECK ARE YOU DOING UP THERE, HOMER?
WE GOTTA GET MOVING -- IT'S TIME TO **SNEAK OUT TO THE BALL GAME!**
CARL, I'M A **HIGHLY-SKILLED NUCLEAR POWER TECHNICAL SAFETY GUY**. I'M SIMPLY APPLYING SOME OF MY **VAST STORE OF KNOWLEDGE** TO THE SITUATION AT HAND!
EXIT
I'VE TAKEN A PHOTO OF MYSELF SITTING AT MY CONSOLE. I'LL JUST TAPE IT IN FRONT OF THE SURVEILLANCE CAMERA...
...AND OLD MAN BURNS WILL **NEVER KNOW I'M GONE!**
I PICKED UP THAT LITTLE TRICK FROM **MISSION: IMPOSSIBLE**.
PRETTY SLICK, HOMER!
YEAH!
...AND TO THINK, FOR ALL THE YEARS I'VE BEEN SNEAKING OUT EARLY, I'VE HAD TO RELY ON THIS CRUMMY **LIFELIKE ROBOT DOUBLE** OF MYSELF!
HELLO! KLIK

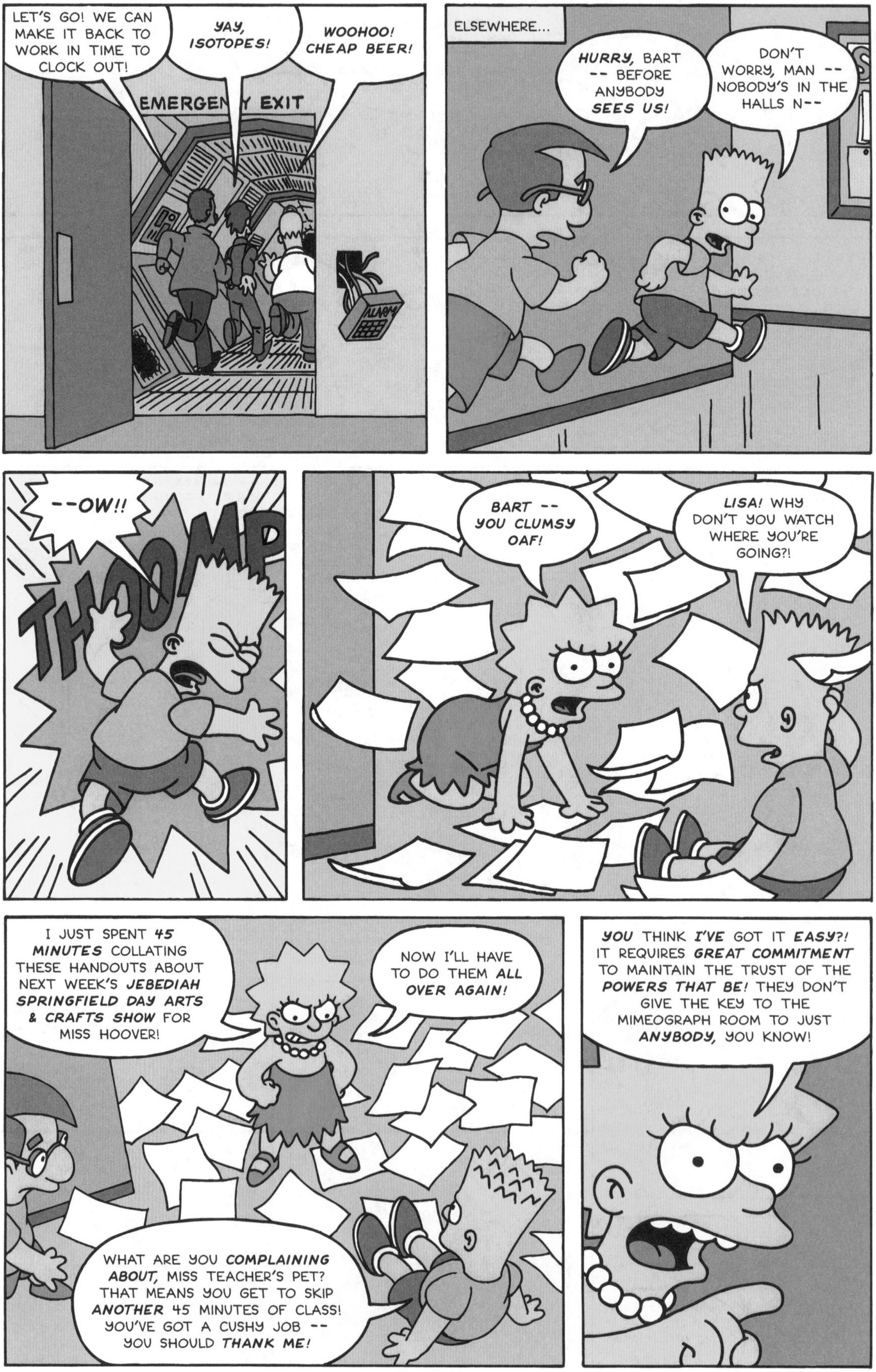
LET'S GO! WE CAN MAKE IT BACK TO WORK IN TIME TO CLOCK OUT!
YAY, ISOTOPES!
WOOHOO! CHEAP BEER!
EMERGEN Y EXIT
ALARM
ELSEWHERE...
HURRY, BART -- BEFORE ANYBODY SEES US!
DON'T WORRY, MAN -- NOBODY'S IN THE HALLS N--
--OW!!
THOOMP
BART -- YOU CLUMSY OAF!
LISA! WHY DON'T YOU WATCH WHERE YOU'RE GOING?!
I JUST SPENT 45 MINUTES COLLATING THESE HANDOUTS ABOUT NEXT WEEK'S JEBEDIAH SPRINGFIELD DAY ARTS & CRAFTS SHOW FOR MISS HOOVER!
NOW I'LL HAVE TO DO THEM ALL OVER AGAIN!
WHAT ARE YOU COMPLAINING ABOUT, MISS TEACHER'S PET? THAT MEANS YOU GET TO SKIP ANOTHER 45 MINUTES OF CLASS! YOU'VE GOT A CUSHY JOB -- YOU SHOULD THANK ME!
YOU THINK I'VE GOT IT EASY?! IT REQUIRES GREAT COMMITMENT TO MAINTAIN THE TRUST OF THE POWERS THAT BE! THEY DON'T GIVE THE KEY TO THE MIMEOGRAPH ROOM TO JUST ANYBODY, YOU KNOW!

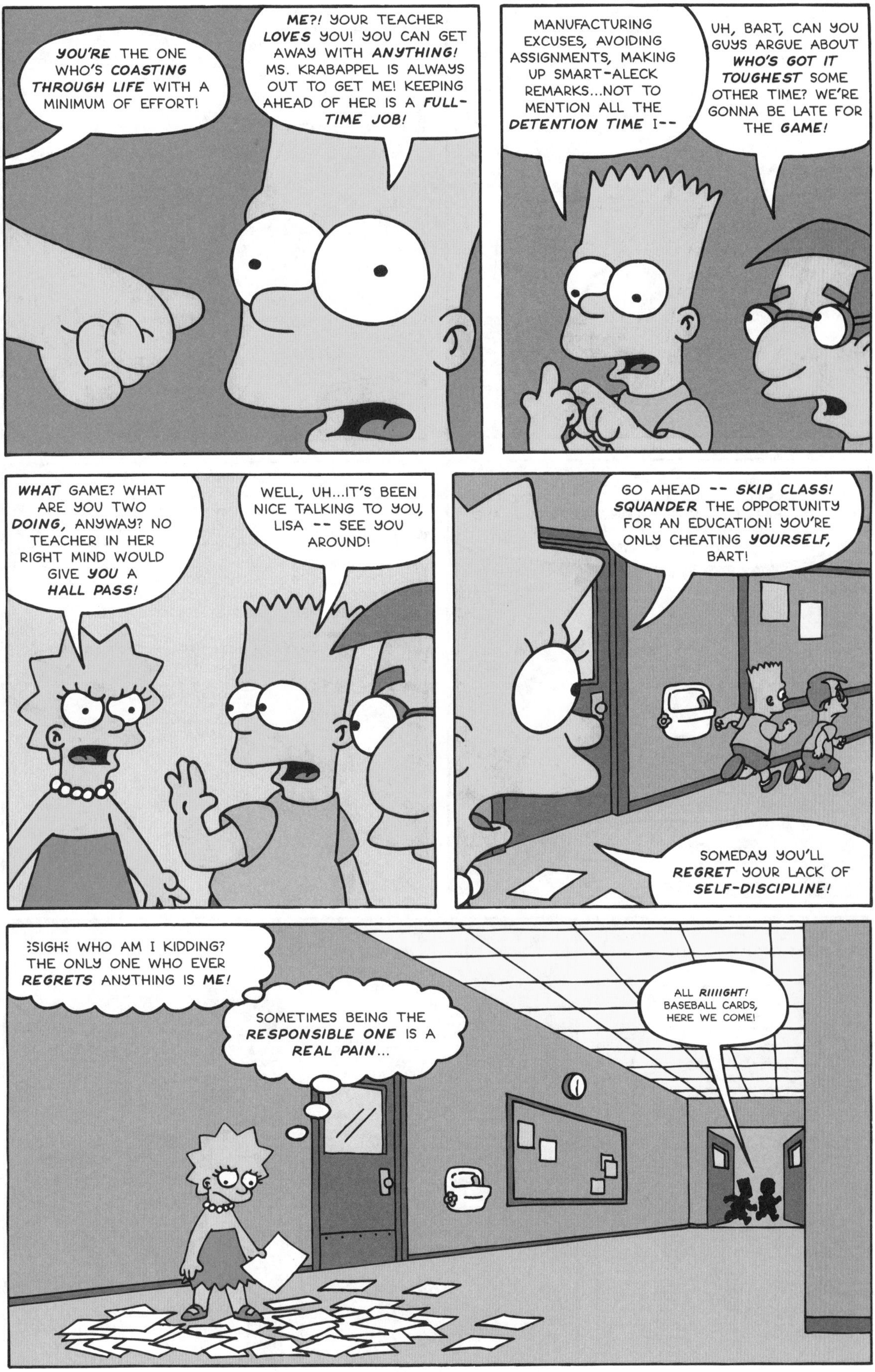
YOU'RE THE ONE WHO'S COASTING THROUGH LIFE WITH A MINIMUM OF EFFORT!
ME?! YOUR TEACHER LOVES YOU! YOU CAN GET AWAY WITH ANYTHING! MS. KRABAPPEL IS ALWAYS OUT TO GET ME! KEEPING AHEAD OF HER IS A FULL-TIME JOB!
MANUFACTURING EXCUSES, AVOIDING ASSIGNMENTS, MAKING UP SMART-ALECK REMARKS...NOT TO MENTION ALL THE DETENTION TIME I--
UH, BART, CAN YOU GUYS ARGUE ABOUT WHO'S GOT IT TOUGHEST SOME OTHER TIME? WE'RE GONNA BE LATE FOR THE GAME!
WHAT GAME? WHAT ARE YOU TWO DOING, ANYWAY? NO TEACHER IN HER RIGHT MIND WOULD GIVE YOU A HALL PASS!
WELL, UH...IT'S BEEN NICE TALKING TO YOU, LISA -- SEE YOU AROUND!
GO AHEAD -- SKIP CLASS! SQUANDER THE OPPORTUNITY FOR AN EDUCATION! YOU'RE ONLY CHEATING YOURSELF, BART!
SOMEDAY YOU'LL REGRET YOUR LACK OF SELF-DISCIPLINE!
SIGH WHO AM I KIDDING? THE ONLY ONE WHO EVER REGRETS ANYTHING IS ME!
SOMETIMES BEING THE RESPONSIBLE ONE IS A REAL PAIN...
ALL RIIIIGHT! BASEBALL CARDS, HERE WE COME!

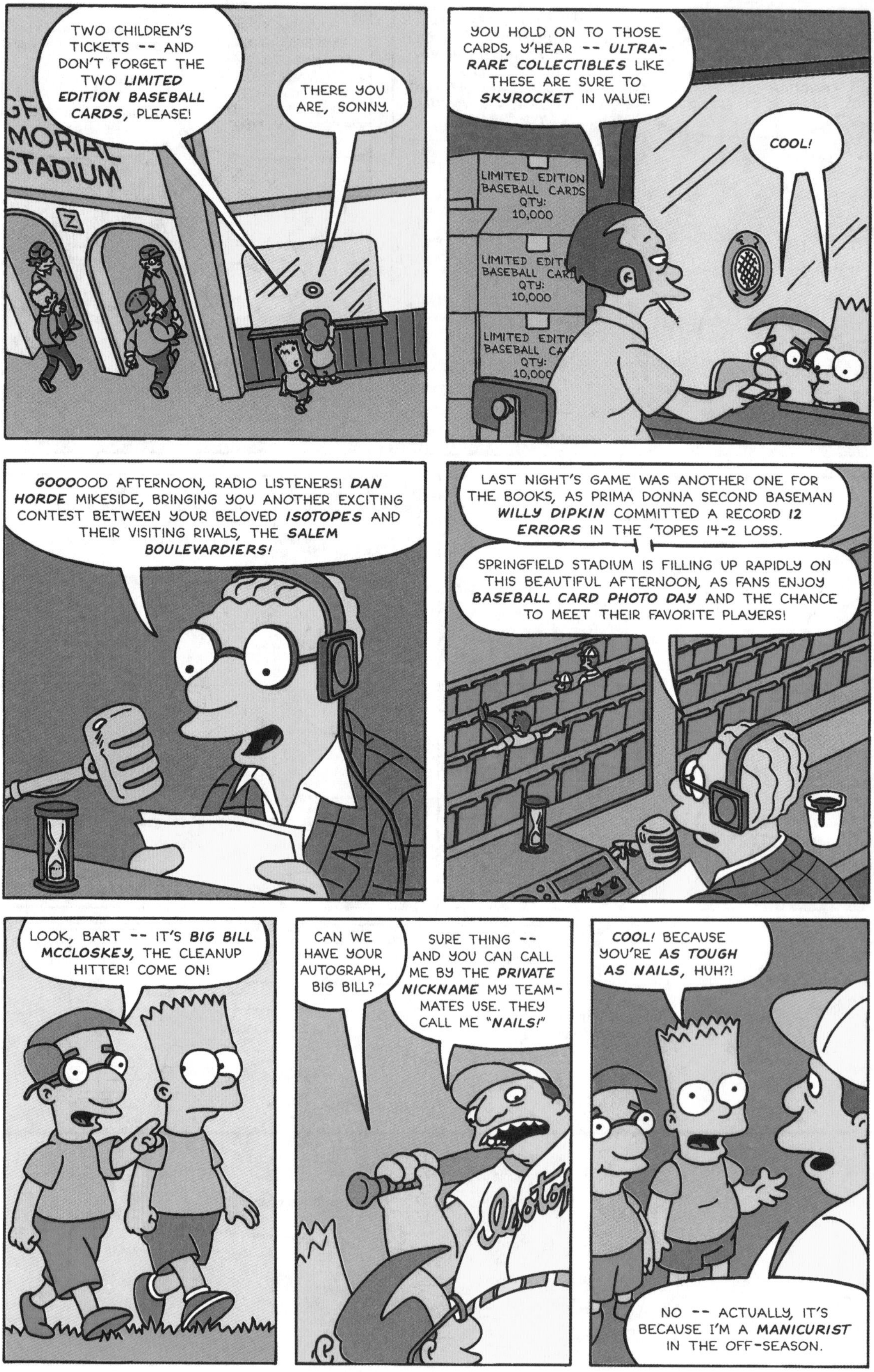
TWO CHILDREN'S TICKETS -- AND DON'T FORGET THE TWO LIMITED EDITION BASEBALL CARDS, PLEASE!
THERE YOU ARE, SONNY.
GF MORIAL STADIUM
Z
YOU HOLD ON TO THOSE CARDS, Y'HEAR -- ULTRA-RARE COLLECTIBLES LIKE THESE ARE SURE TO SKYROCKET IN VALUE!
COOL!
LIMITED EDITION BASEBALL CARDS QTY: 10,000
GOOOOOD AFTERNOON, RADIO LISTENERS! DAN HORDE MIKESIDE, BRINGING YOU ANOTHER EXCITING CONTEST BETWEEN YOUR BELOVED ISOTOPES AND THEIR VISITING RIVALS, THE SALEM BOULEVARDIERS!
LAST NIGHT'S GAME WAS ANOTHER ONE FOR THE BOOKS, AS PRIMA DONNA SECOND BASEMAN WILLY DIPKIN COMMITTED A RECORD 12 ERRORS IN THE 'TOPES 14-2 LOSS.
SPRINGFIELD STADIUM IS FILLING UP RAPIDLY ON THIS BEAUTIFUL AFTERNOON, AS FANS ENJOY BASEBALL CARD PHOTO DAY AND THE CHANCE TO MEET THEIR FAVORITE PLAYERS!
LOOK, BART -- IT'S BIG BILL MCCLOSKEY, THE CLEANUP HITTER! COME ON!
CAN WE HAVE YOUR AUTOGRAPH, BIG BILL?
SURE THING -- AND YOU CAN CALL ME BY THE PRIVATE NICKNAME MY TEAM-MATES USE. THEY CALL ME "NAILS!"
COOL! BECAUSE YOU'RE AS TOUGH AS NAILS, HUH?!
NO -- ACTUALLY, IT'S BECAUSE I'M A MANICURIST IN THE OFF-SEASON.

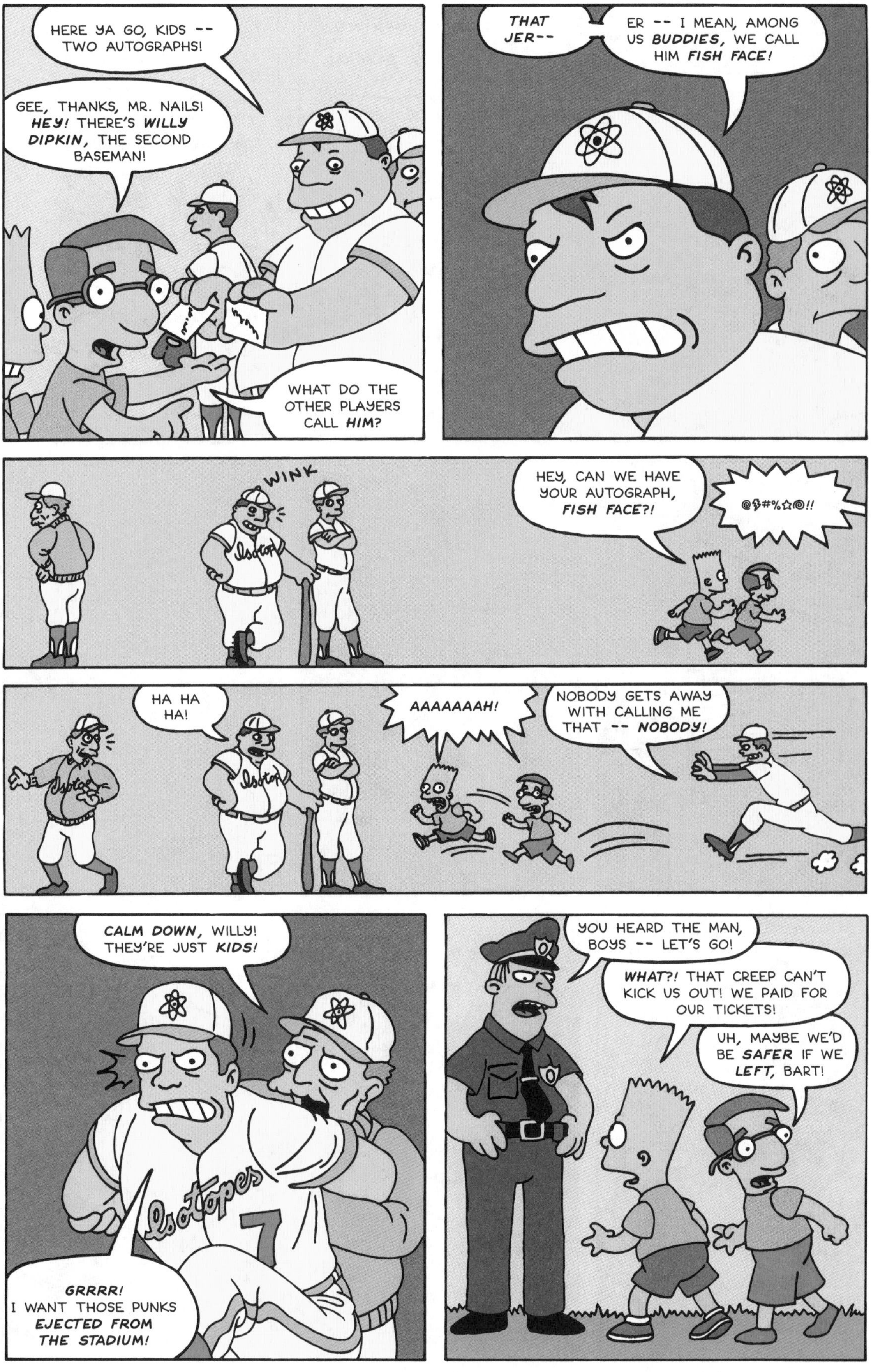
HERE YA GO, KIDS -- TWO AUTOGRAPHS!
GEE, THANKS, MR. NAILS! HEY! THERE'S WILLY DIPKIN, THE SECOND BASEMAN!
WHAT DO THE OTHER PLAYERS CALL HIM?
THAT JER--
ER -- I MEAN, AMONG US BUDDIES, WE CALL HIM FISH FACE!
WINK
HEY, CAN WE HAVE YOUR AUTOGRAPH, FISH FACE?!
@ϟ#%✩◎!!
HA HA HA!
AAAAAAAH!
NOBODY GETS AWAY WITH CALLING ME THAT -- NOBODY!
CALM DOWN, WILLY! THEY'RE JUST KIDS!
GRRRR! I WANT THOSE PUNKS EJECTED FROM THE STADIUM!
YOU HEARD THE MAN, BOYS -- LET'S GO!
WHAT?! THAT CREEP CAN'T KICK US OUT! WE PAID FOR OUR TICKETS!
UH, MAYBE WE'D BE SAFER IF WE LEFT, BART!

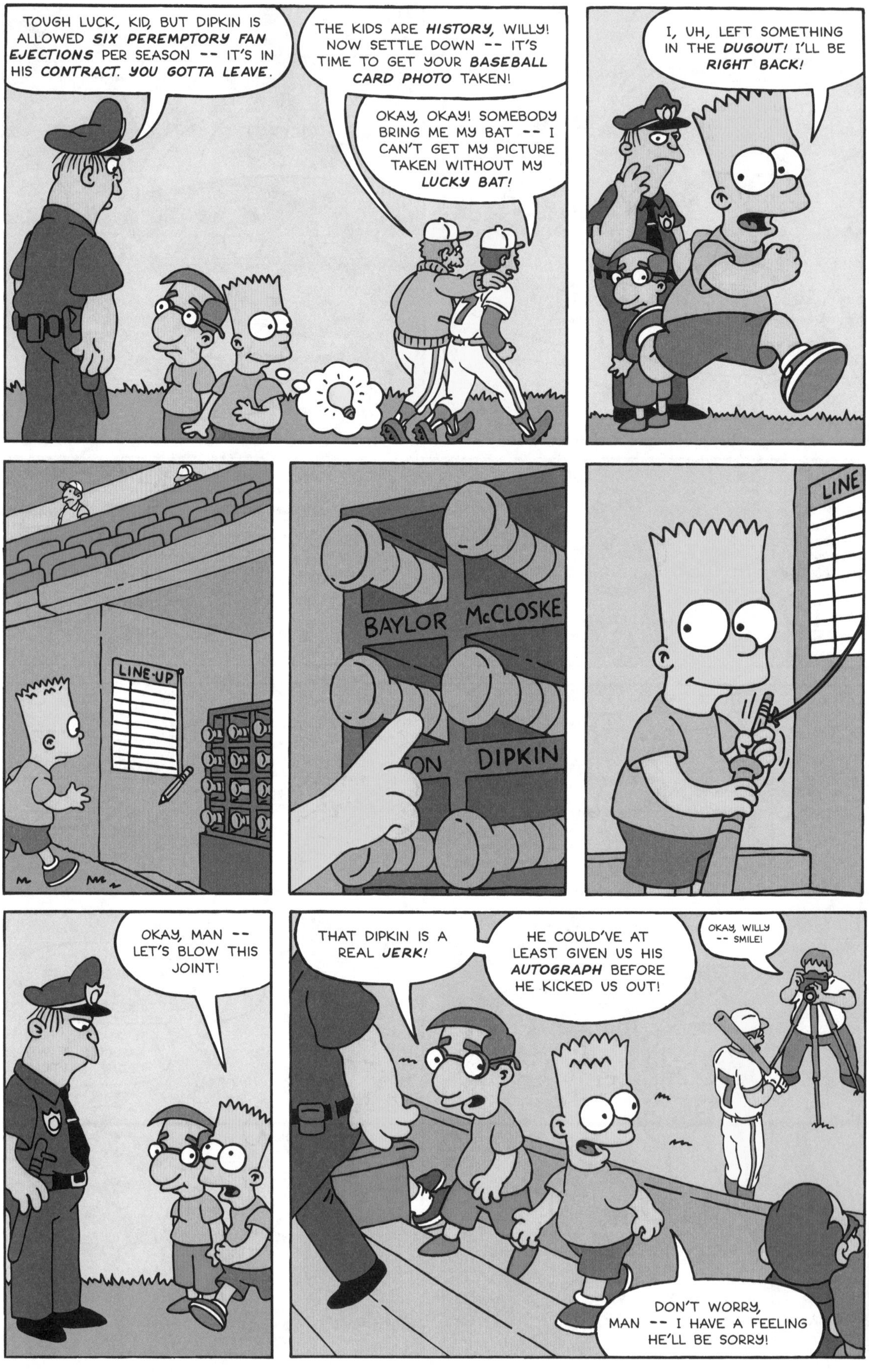
TOUGH LUCK, KID, BUT DIPKIN IS ALLOWED SIX PEREMPTORY FAN EJECTIONS PER SEASON -- IT'S IN HIS CONTRACT. YOU GOTTA LEAVE.
THE KIDS ARE HISTORY, WILLY! NOW SETTLE DOWN -- IT'S TIME TO GET YOUR BASEBALL CARD PHOTO TAKEN!
OKAY, OKAY! SOMEBODY BRING ME MY BAT -- I CAN'T GET MY PICTURE TAKEN WITHOUT MY LUCKY BAT!
I, UH, LEFT SOMETHING IN THE DUGOUT! I'LL BE RIGHT BACK!
LINE-UP
BAYLOR
McCLOSKE
DIPKIN
LINE
OKAY, MAN -- LET'S BLOW THIS JOINT!
THAT DIPKIN IS A REAL JERK!
HE COULD'VE AT LEAST GIVEN US HIS AUTOGRAPH BEFORE HE KICKED US OUT!
OKAY, WILLY -- SMILE!
DON'T WORRY, MAN -- I HAVE A FEELING HE'LL BE SORRY!

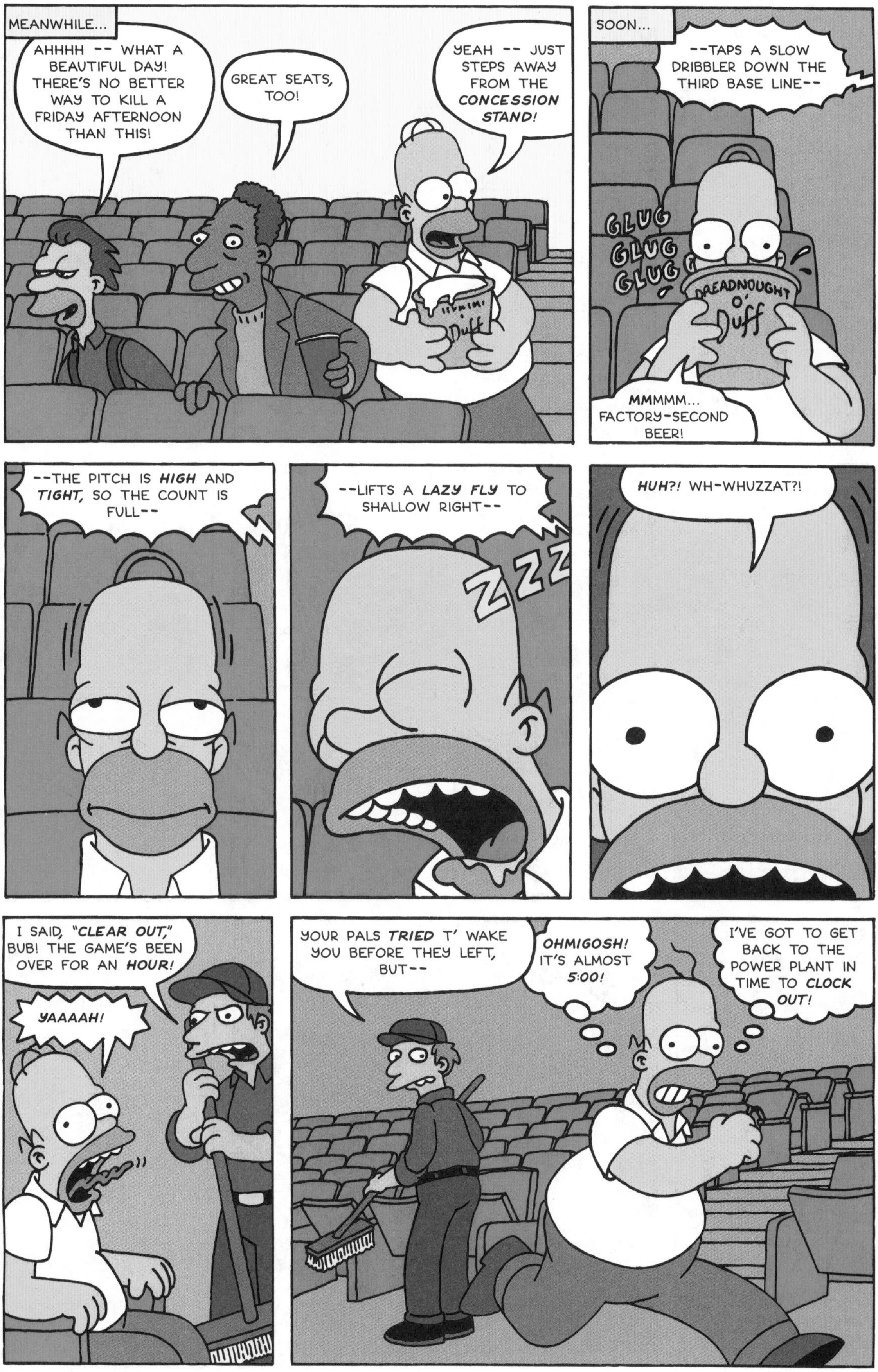
MEANWHILE...
AHHHH -- WHAT A BEAUTIFUL DAY! THERE'S NO BETTER WAY TO KILL A FRIDAY AFTERNOON THAN THIS!
GREAT SEATS, TOO!
YEAH -- JUST STEPS AWAY FROM THE CONCESSION STAND!
Duff
SOON...
--TAPS A SLOW DRIBBLER DOWN THE THIRD BASE LINE--
GLUG GLUG GLUG
DREADNOUGHT O' Duff
MMMMM... FACTORY-SECOND BEER!
--THE PITCH IS HIGH AND TIGHT, SO THE COUNT IS FULL--
--LIFTS A LAZY FLY TO SHALLOW RIGHT--
ZZZ
HUH?! WH-WHUZZAT?!
I SAID, "CLEAR OUT," BUB! THE GAME'S BEEN OVER FOR AN HOUR!
YAAAAH!
YOUR PALS TRIED T' WAKE YOU BEFORE THEY LEFT, BUT--
OHMIGOSH! IT'S ALMOST 5:00!
I'VE GOT TO GET BACK TO THE POWER PLANT IN TIME TO CLOCK OUT!

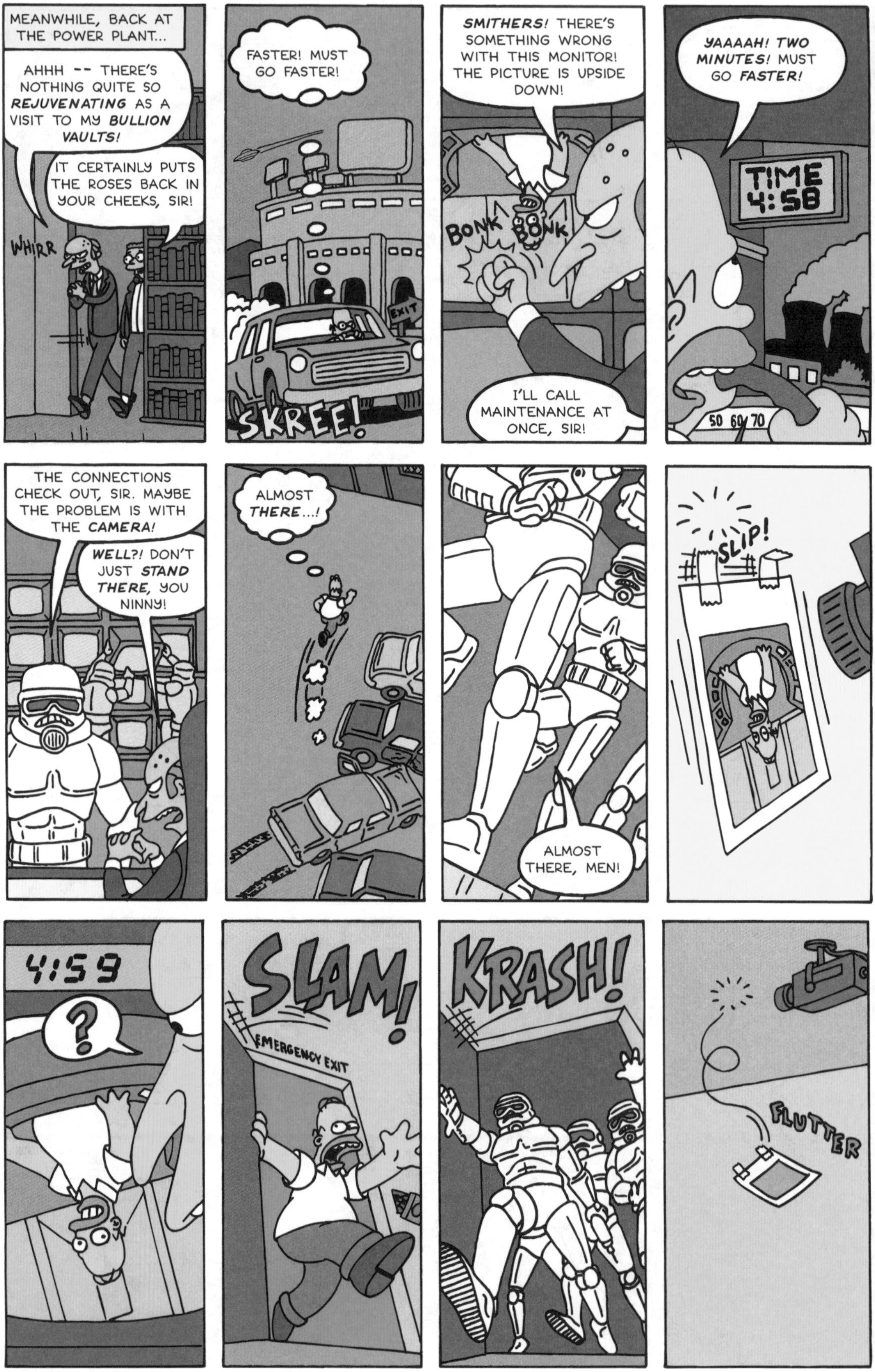
MEANWHILE, BACK AT THE POWER PLANT...
AHHH -- THERE'S NOTHING QUITE SO REJUVENATING AS A VISIT TO MY BULLION VAULTS!
IT CERTAINLY PUTS THE ROSES BACK IN YOUR CHEEKS, SIR!
WHIRR
FASTER! MUST GO FASTER!
EXIT
SKREE!
SMITHERS! THERE'S SOMETHING WRONG WITH THIS MONITOR! THE PICTURE IS UPSIDE DOWN!
BONK
BONK
I'LL CALL MAINTENANCE AT ONCE, SIR!
YAAAAH! TWO MINUTES! MUST GO FASTER!
TIME 4:58
50 60 70
THE CONNECTIONS CHECK OUT, SIR. MAYBE THE PROBLEM IS WITH THE CAMERA!
WELL?! DON'T JUST STAND THERE, YOU NINNY!
ALMOST THERE...!
ALMOST THERE, MEN!
SLIP!
4:59
?
SLAM!
EMERGENCY EXIT
KRASH!
FLUTTER

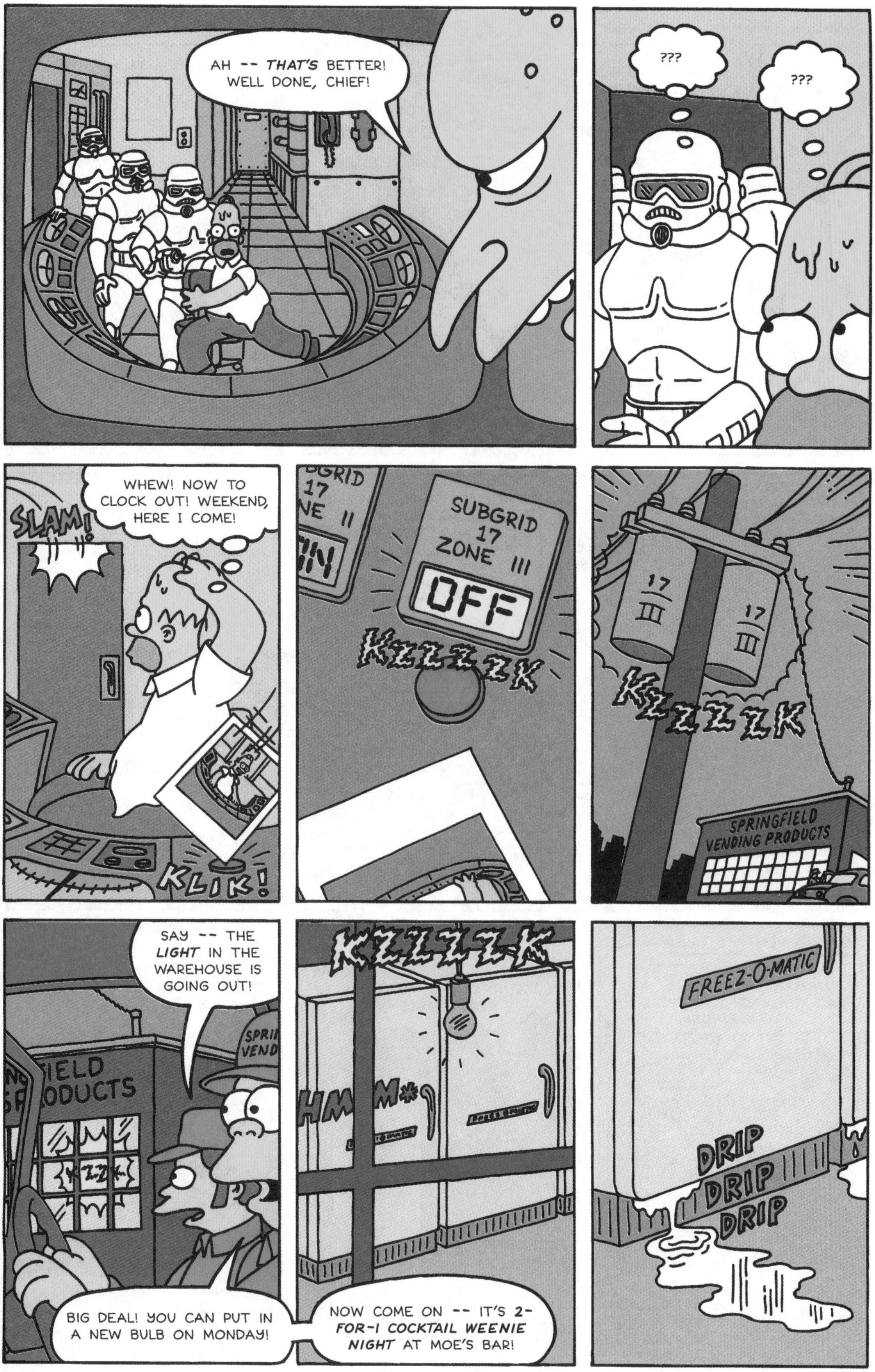
AH -- THAT'S BETTER! WELL DONE, CHIEF!
???
???
SLAM!
WHEW! NOW TO CLOCK OUT! WEEKEND, HERE I COME!
KLIK!
SUBGRID 17 ZONE III
OFF
KZZZZK
17 III
17 III
KZZZZK
SPRINGFIELD VENDING PRODUCTS
SAY -- THE LIGHT IN THE WAREHOUSE IS GOING OUT!
BIG DEAL! YOU CAN PUT IN A NEW BULB ON MONDAY!
KZZZZK
NOW COME ON -- IT'S 2-FOR-1 COCKTAIL WEENIE NIGHT AT MOE'S BAR!
FREEZ-O-MATIC
DRIP
DRIP
DRIP

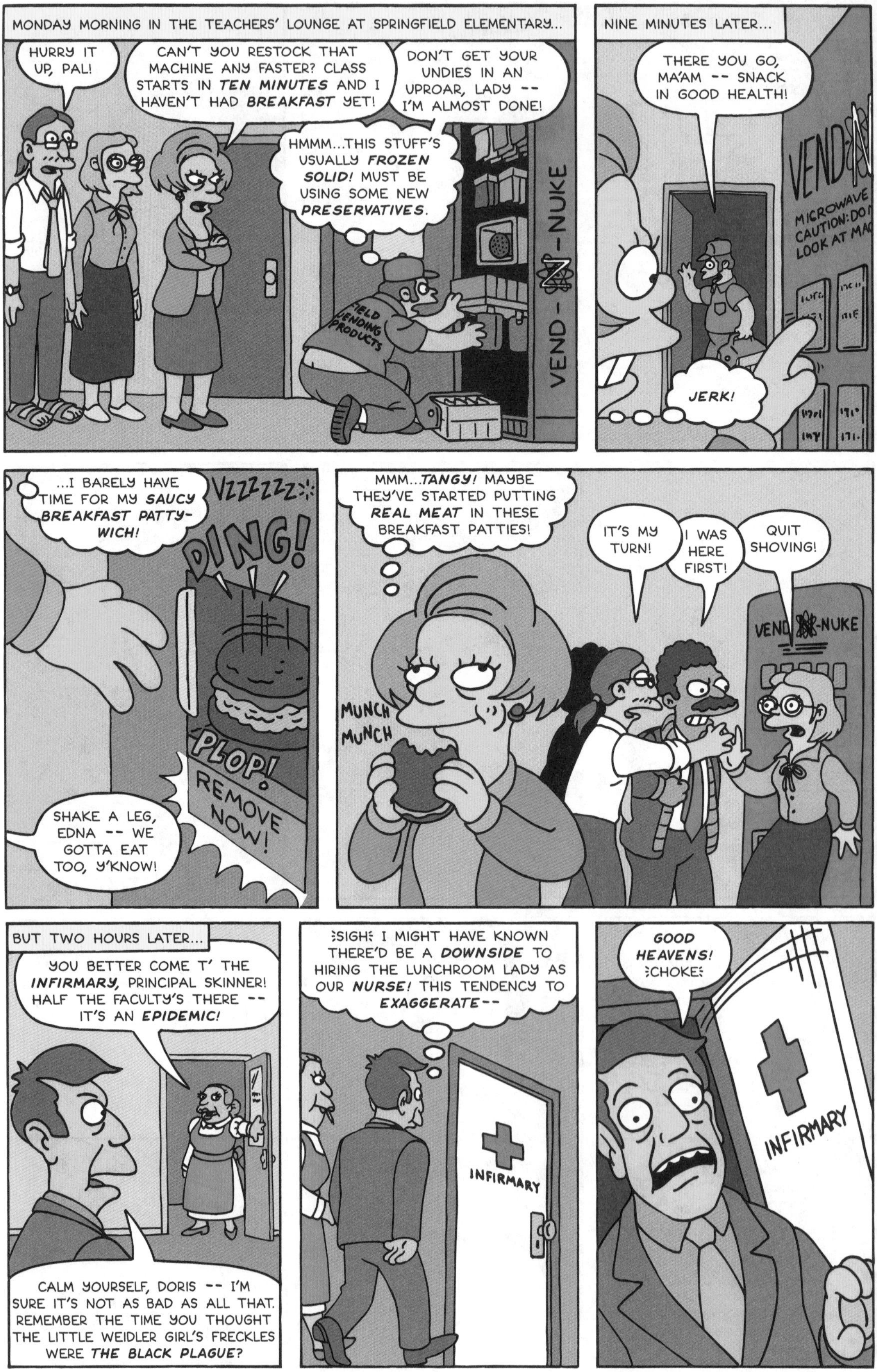
MONDAY MORNING IN THE TEACHERS' LOUNGE AT SPRINGFIELD ELEMENTARY...
HURRY IT UP, PAL!
CAN'T YOU RESTOCK THAT MACHINE ANY FASTER? CLASS STARTS IN TEN MINUTES AND I HAVEN'T HAD BREAKFAST YET!
DON'T GET YOUR UNDIES IN AN UPROAR, LADY -- I'M ALMOST DONE!
HMMM...THIS STUFF'S USUALLY FROZEN SOLID! MUST BE USING SOME NEW PRESERVATIVES.
VEND-N-NUKE
NINE MINUTES LATER...
THERE YOU GO, MA'AM -- SNACK IN GOOD HEALTH!
JERK!
...I BARELY HAVE TIME FOR MY SAUCY BREAKFAST PATTY-WICH!
VZZZZZZ
DING!
PLOP!
REMOVE NOW!
SHAKE A LEG, EDNA -- WE GOTTA EAT TOO, Y'KNOW!
MMM...TANGY! MAYBE THEY'VE STARTED PUTTING REAL MEAT IN THESE BREAKFAST PATTIES!
MUNCH MUNCH
IT'S MY TURN!
I WAS HERE FIRST!
QUIT SHOVING!
VEND-N-NUKE
BUT TWO HOURS LATER...
YOU BETTER COME T' THE INFIRMARY, PRINCIPAL SKINNER! HALF THE FACULTY'S THERE -- IT'S AN EPIDEMIC!
CALM YOURSELF, DORIS -- I'M SURE IT'S NOT AS BAD AS ALL THAT. REMEMBER THE TIME YOU THOUGHT THE LITTLE WEIDLER GIRL'S FRECKLES WERE THE BLACK PLAGUE?
:SIGH: I MIGHT HAVE KNOWN THERE'D BE A DOWNSIDE TO HIRING THE LUNCHROOM LADY AS OUR NURSE! THIS TENDENCY TO EXAGGERATE--
INFIRMARY
GOOD HEAVENS! :CHOKE:
INFIRMARY

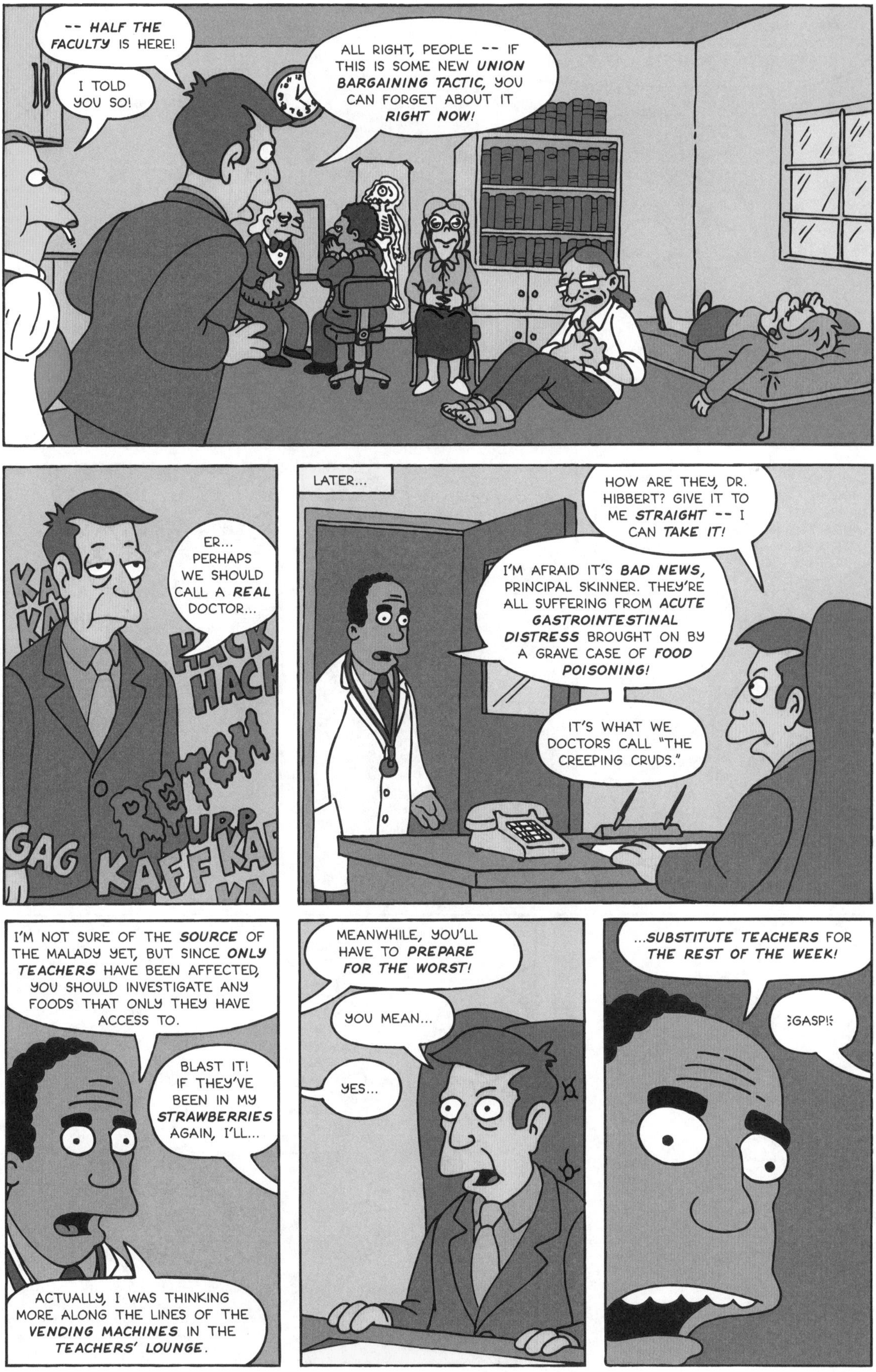

-- HALF THE FACULTY IS HERE!
I TOLD YOU SO!
ALL RIGHT, PEOPLE -- IF THIS IS SOME NEW UNION BARGAINING TACTIC, YOU CAN FORGET ABOUT IT RIGHT NOW!
ER... PERHAPS WE SHOULD CALL A REAL DOCTOR...
HACK
HACK
RETCH
URPP
GAG
KAFF
LATER...
HOW ARE THEY, DR. HIBBERT? GIVE IT TO ME STRAIGHT -- I CAN TAKE IT!
I'M AFRAID IT'S BAD NEWS, PRINCIPAL SKINNER. THEY'RE ALL SUFFERING FROM ACUTE GASTROINTESTINAL DISTRESS BROUGHT ON BY A GRAVE CASE OF FOOD POISONING!
IT'S WHAT WE DOCTORS CALL "THE CREEPING CRUDS."
I'M NOT SURE OF THE SOURCE OF THE MALADY YET, BUT SINCE ONLY TEACHERS HAVE BEEN AFFECTED, YOU SHOULD INVESTIGATE ANY FOODS THAT ONLY THEY HAVE ACCESS TO.
BLAST IT! IF THEY'VE BEEN IN MY STRAWBERRIES AGAIN, I'LL...
ACTUALLY, I WAS THINKING MORE ALONG THE LINES OF THE VENDING MACHINES IN THE TEACHERS' LOUNGE.
MEANWHILE, YOU'LL HAVE TO PREPARE FOR THE WORST!
YOU MEAN...
YES...
...SUBSTITUTE TEACHERS FOR THE REST OF THE WEEK!
GASP!

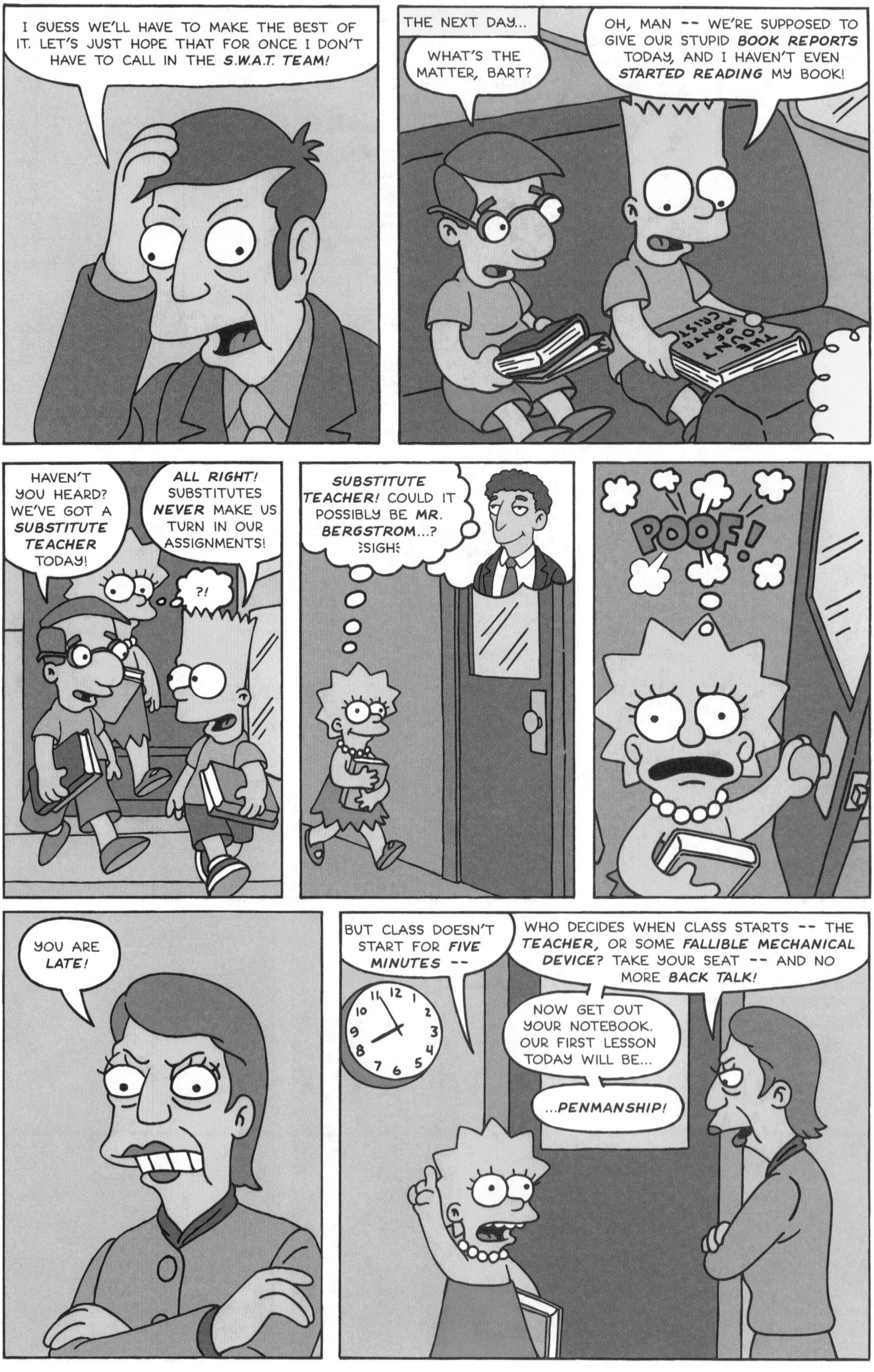
I GUESS WE'LL HAVE TO MAKE THE BEST OF IT. LET'S JUST HOPE THAT FOR ONCE I DON'T HAVE TO CALL IN THE S.W.A.T. TEAM!
THE NEXT DAY...
WHAT'S THE MATTER, BART?
OH, MAN -- WE'RE SUPPOSED TO GIVE OUR STUPID BOOK REPORTS TODAY, AND I HAVEN'T EVEN STARTED READING MY BOOK!
THE COUNT OF MONTE CRISTO
HAVEN'T YOU HEARD? WE'VE GOT A SUBSTITUTE TEACHER TODAY!
ALL RIGHT! SUBSTITUTES NEVER MAKE US TURN IN OUR ASSIGNMENTS!
?!
SUBSTITUTE TEACHER! COULD IT POSSIBLY BE MR. BERGSTROM...? SIGH
POOF!
YOU ARE LATE!
BUT CLASS DOESN'T START FOR FIVE MINUTES --
WHO DECIDES WHEN CLASS STARTS -- THE TEACHER, OR SOME FALLIBLE MECHANICAL DEVICE? TAKE YOUR SEAT -- AND NO MORE BACK TALK!
NOW GET OUT YOUR NOTEBOOK. OUR FIRST LESSON TODAY WILL BE...
...PENMANSHIP!

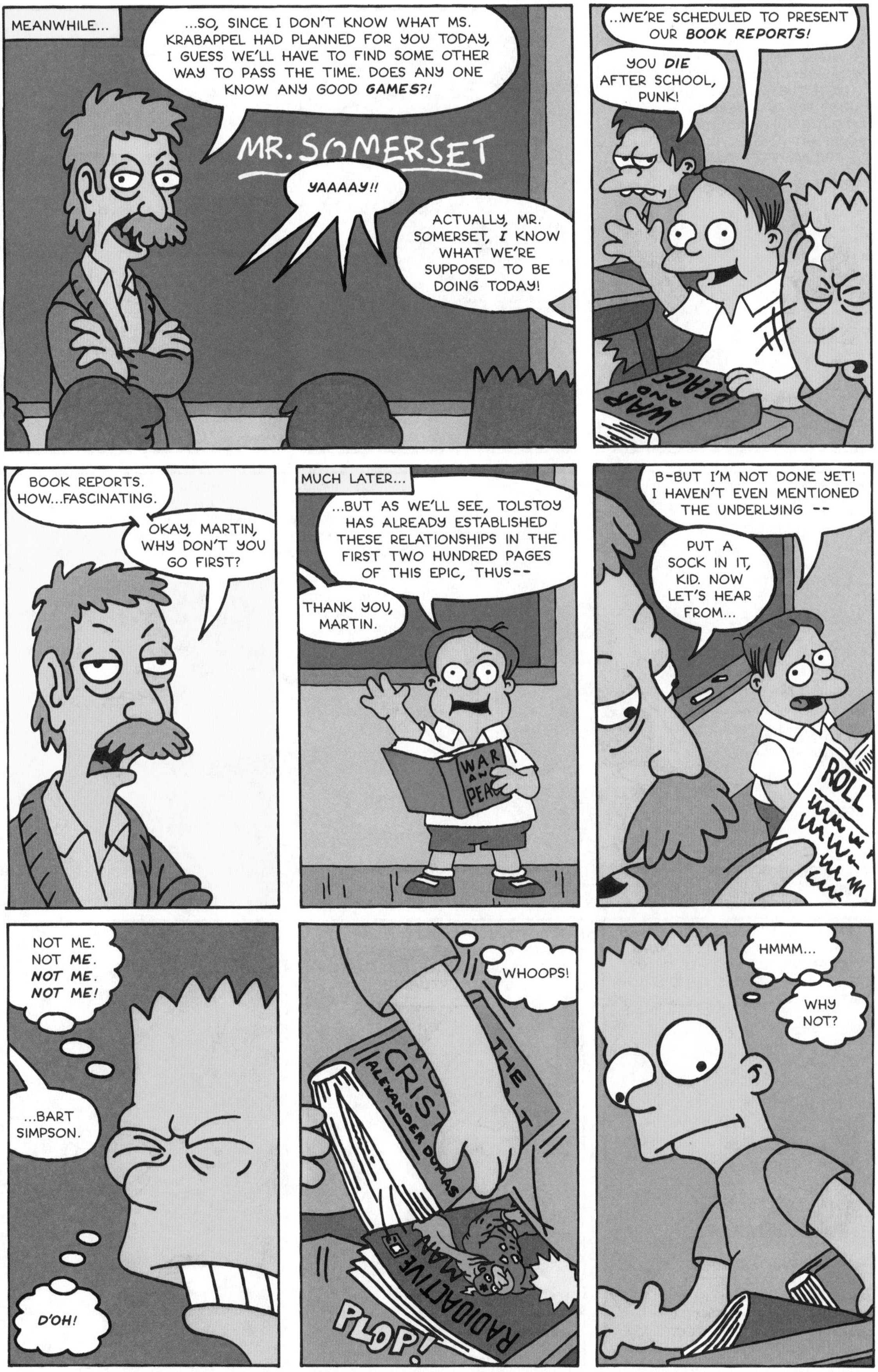
MEANWHILE...
...SO, SINCE I DON'T KNOW WHAT MS. KRABAPPEL HAD PLANNED FOR YOU TODAY, I GUESS WE'LL HAVE TO FIND SOME OTHER WAY TO PASS THE TIME. DOES ANY ONE KNOW ANY GOOD *GAMES*?!
MR. SOMERSET
YAAAAY!!
ACTUALLY, MR. SOMERSET, *I* KNOW WHAT WE'RE SUPPOSED TO BE DOING TODAY!
...WE'RE SCHEDULED TO PRESENT OUR ***BOOK REPORTS!***
YOU ***DIE*** AFTER SCHOOL, PUNK!
WAR AND PEACE
BOOK REPORTS. HOW...FASCINATING.
OKAY, MARTIN, WHY DON'T YOU GO FIRST?
MUCH LATER...
...BUT AS WE'LL SEE, TOLSTOY HAS ALREADY ESTABLISHED THESE RELATIONSHIPS IN THE FIRST TWO HUNDRED PAGES OF THIS EPIC, THUS--
THANK YOU, MARTIN.
WAR AND PEACE
B-BUT I'M NOT DONE YET! I HAVEN'T EVEN MENTIONED THE UNDERLYING --
PUT A SOCK IN IT, KID. NOW LET'S HEAR FROM...
ROLL
NOT ME. NOT **ME**. ***NOT ME***. ***NOT ME!***
...BART SIMPSON.
D'OH!
WHOOPS!
THE
CRIS
ALEXANDER DUMAS
RADIOACTIVE MAN
PLOP!
HMMM...
WHY NOT?

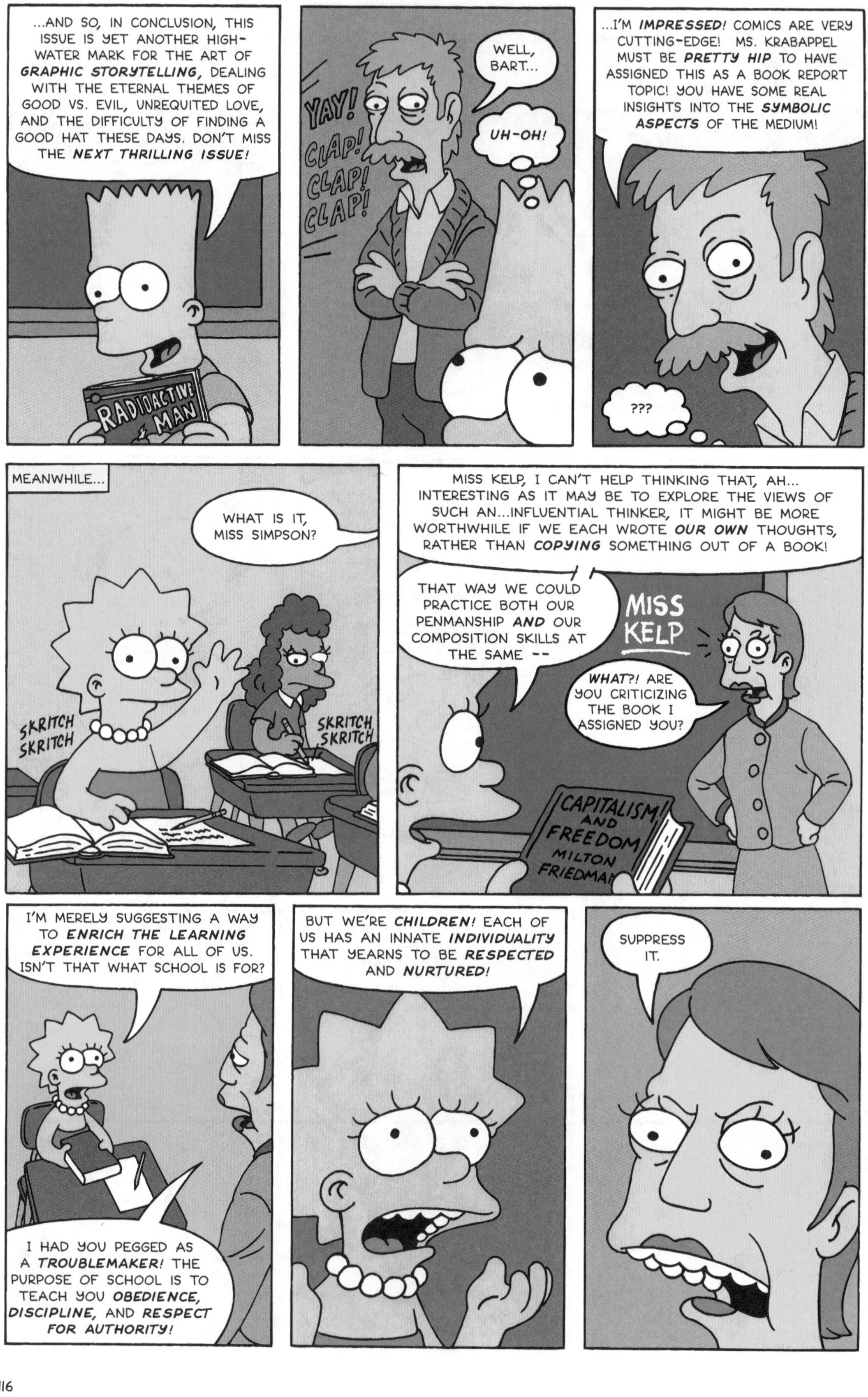
...AND SO, IN CONCLUSION, THIS ISSUE IS YET ANOTHER HIGH-WATER MARK FOR THE ART OF GRAPHIC STORYTELLING, DEALING WITH THE ETERNAL THEMES OF GOOD VS. EVIL, UNREQUITED LOVE, AND THE DIFFICULTY OF FINDING A GOOD HAT THESE DAYS. DON'T MISS THE NEXT THRILLING ISSUE!
RADIOACTIVE MAN
WELL, BART...
YAY! CLAP! CLAP! CLAP!
UH-OH!
...I'M IMPRESSED! COMICS ARE VERY CUTTING-EDGE! MS. KRABAPPEL MUST BE PRETTY HIP TO HAVE ASSIGNED THIS AS A BOOK REPORT TOPIC! YOU HAVE SOME REAL INSIGHTS INTO THE SYMBOLIC ASPECTS OF THE MEDIUM!
???
MEANWHILE...
WHAT IS IT, MISS SIMPSON?
SKRITCH SKRITCH
SKRITCH SKRITCH
MISS KELP, I CAN'T HELP THINKING THAT, AH... INTERESTING AS IT MAY BE TO EXPLORE THE VIEWS OF SUCH AN...INFLUENTIAL THINKER, IT MIGHT BE MORE WORTHWHILE IF WE EACH WROTE OUR OWN THOUGHTS, RATHER THAN COPYING SOMETHING OUT OF A BOOK!
THAT WAY WE COULD PRACTICE BOTH OUR PENMANSHIP AND OUR COMPOSITION SKILLS AT THE SAME --
MISS KELP
WHAT?! ARE YOU CRITICIZING THE BOOK I ASSIGNED YOU?
CAPITALISM AND FREEDOM MILTON FRIEDMA
I'M MERELY SUGGESTING A WAY TO ENRICH THE LEARNING EXPERIENCE FOR ALL OF US. ISN'T THAT WHAT SCHOOL IS FOR?
I HAD YOU PEGGED AS A TROUBLEMAKER! THE PURPOSE OF SCHOOL IS TO TEACH YOU OBEDIENCE, DISCIPLINE, AND RESPECT FOR AUTHORITY!
BUT WE'RE CHILDREN! EACH OF US HAS AN INNATE INDIVIDUALITY THAT YEARNS TO BE RESPECTED AND NURTURED!
SUPPRESS IT.

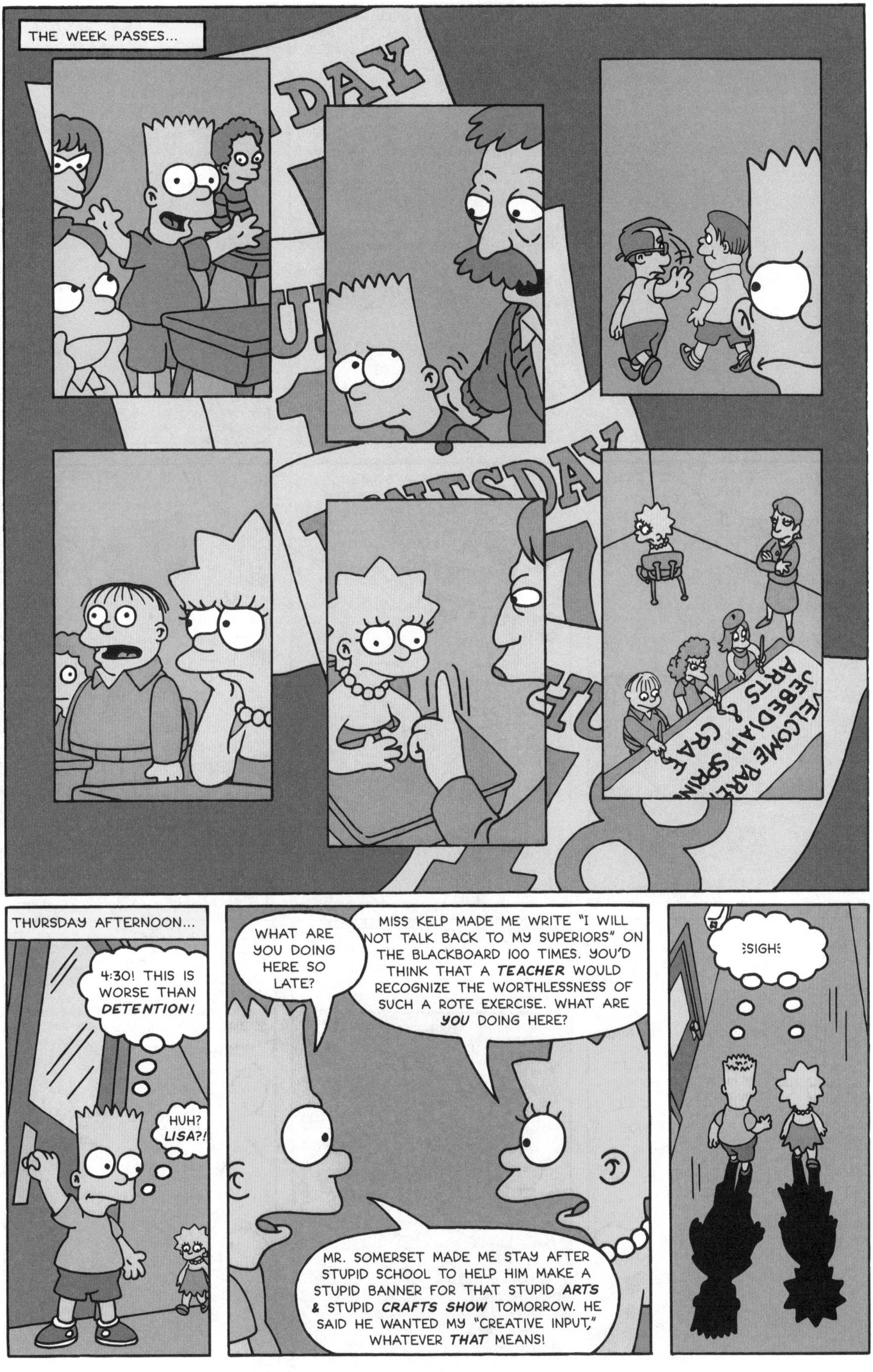
THE WEEK PASSES...
THURSDAY AFTERNOON...
4:30! THIS IS WORSE THAN *DETENTION!*
HUH? *LISA?!*
WHAT ARE YOU DOING HERE SO LATE?
MISS KELP MADE ME WRITE "I WILL NOT TALK BACK TO MY SUPERIORS" ON THE BLACKBOARD 100 TIMES. YOU'D THINK THAT A *TEACHER* WOULD RECOGNIZE THE WORTHLESSNESS OF SUCH A ROTE EXERCISE. WHAT ARE *YOU* DOING HERE?
MR. SOMERSET MADE ME STAY AFTER STUPID SCHOOL TO HELP HIM MAKE A STUPID BANNER FOR THAT STUPID *ARTS* & STUPID *CRAFTS SHOW* TOMORROW. HE SAID HE WANTED MY "CREATIVE INPUT," WHATEVER *THAT* MEANS!
SIGH

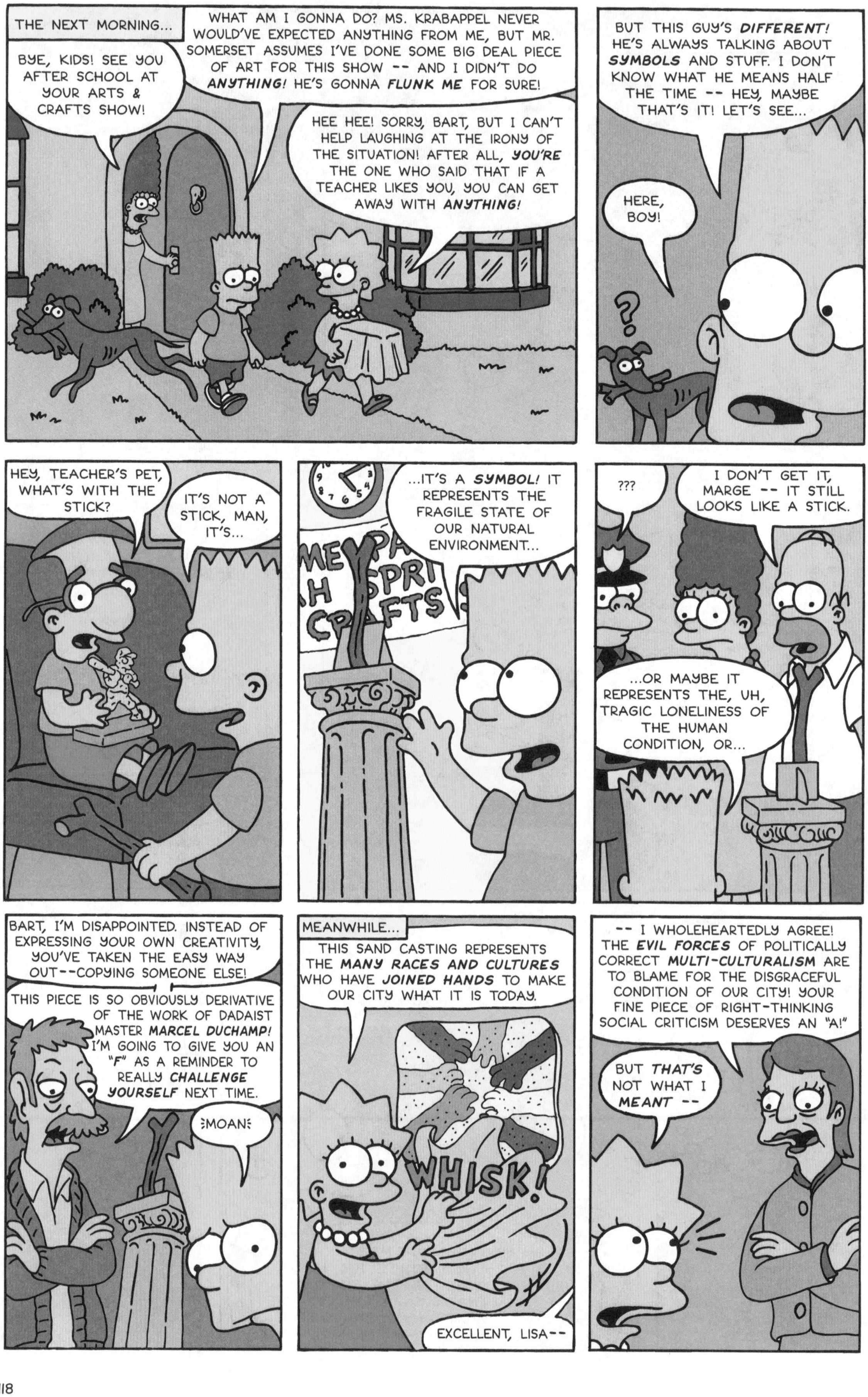

THE NEXT MORNING...
BYE, KIDS! SEE YOU AFTER SCHOOL AT YOUR ARTS & CRAFTS SHOW!
WHAT AM I GONNA DO? MS. KRABAPPEL NEVER WOULD'VE EXPECTED ANYTHING FROM ME, BUT MR. SOMERSET ASSUMES I'VE DONE SOME BIG DEAL PIECE OF ART FOR THIS SHOW -- AND I DIDN'T DO ANYTHING! HE'S GONNA FLUNK ME FOR SURE!
HEE HEE! SORRY, BART, BUT I CAN'T HELP LAUGHING AT THE IRONY OF THE SITUATION! AFTER ALL, YOU'RE THE ONE WHO SAID THAT IF A TEACHER LIKES YOU, YOU CAN GET AWAY WITH ANYTHING!
BUT THIS GUY'S DIFFERENT! HE'S ALWAYS TALKING ABOUT SYMBOLS AND STUFF. I DON'T KNOW WHAT HE MEANS HALF THE TIME -- HEY, MAYBE THAT'S IT! LET'S SEE...
HERE, BOY!
?
HEY, TEACHER'S PET, WHAT'S WITH THE STICK?
IT'S NOT A STICK, MAN, IT'S...
...IT'S A SYMBOL! IT REPRESENTS THE FRAGILE STATE OF OUR NATURAL ENVIRONMENT...
???
I DON'T GET IT, MARGE -- IT STILL LOOKS LIKE A STICK.
...OR MAYBE IT REPRESENTS THE, UH, TRAGIC LONELINESS OF THE HUMAN CONDITION, OR...
BART, I'M DISAPPOINTED. INSTEAD OF EXPRESSING YOUR OWN CREATIVITY, YOU'VE TAKEN THE EASY WAY OUT--COPYING SOMEONE ELSE!
THIS PIECE IS SO OBVIOUSLY DERIVATIVE OF THE WORK OF DADAIST MASTER MARCEL DUCHAMP! I'M GOING TO GIVE YOU AN "F" AS A REMINDER TO REALLY CHALLENGE YOURSELF NEXT TIME.
MOAN
MEANWHILE...
THIS SAND CASTING REPRESENTS THE MANY RACES AND CULTURES WHO HAVE JOINED HANDS TO MAKE OUR CITY WHAT IT IS TODAY.
WHISK!
EXCELLENT, LISA--
-- I WHOLEHEARTEDLY AGREE! THE EVIL FORCES OF POLITICALLY CORRECT MULTI-CULTURALISM ARE TO BLAME FOR THE DISGRACEFUL CONDITION OF OUR CITY! YOUR FINE PIECE OF RIGHT-THINKING SOCIAL CRITICISM DESERVES AN "A!"
BUT THAT'S NOT WHAT I MEANT --

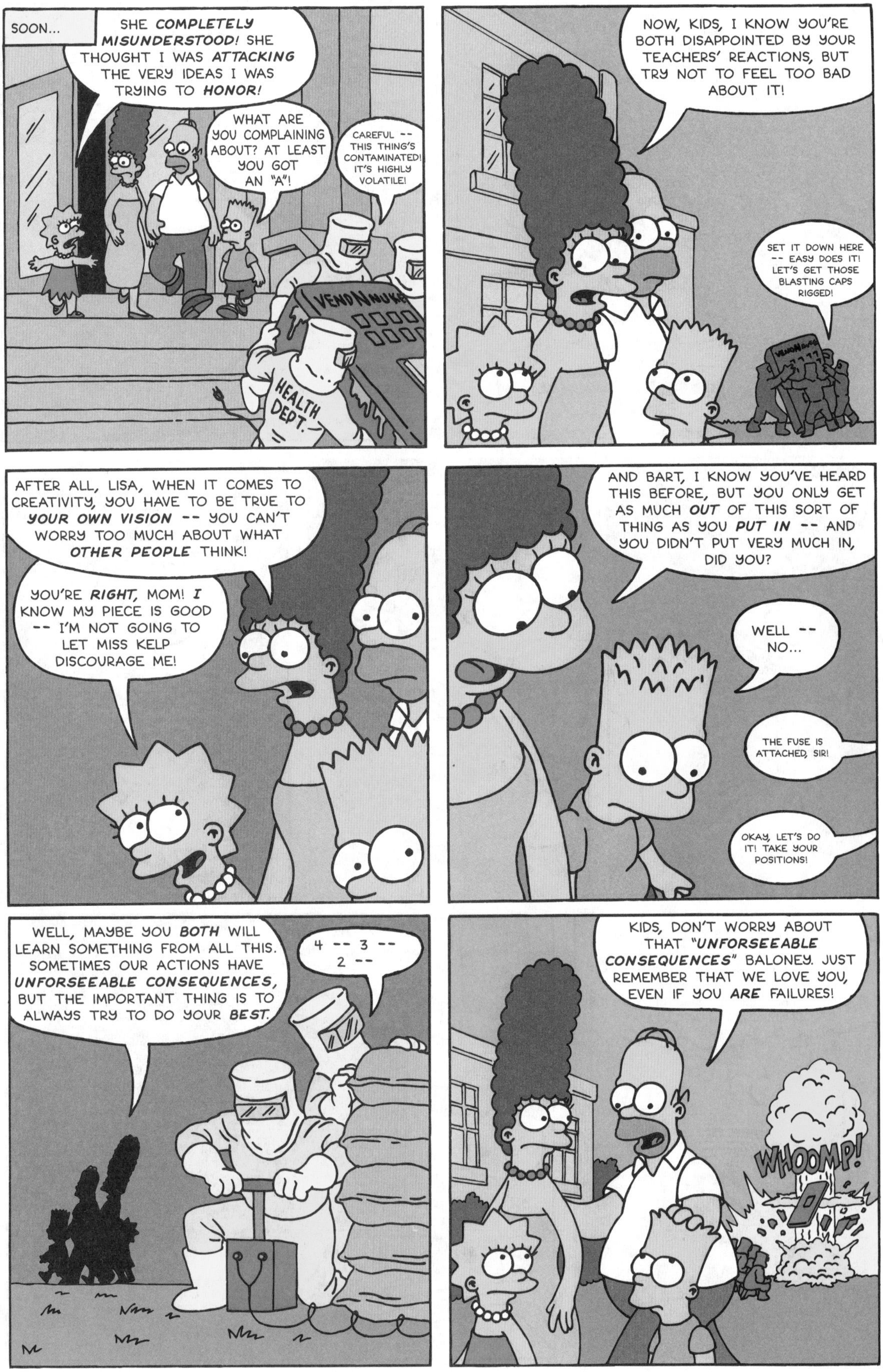
SOON...
SHE *COMPLETELY MISUNDERSTOOD!* SHE THOUGHT I WAS *ATTACKING* THE VERY IDEAS I WAS TRYING TO *HONOR!*
WHAT ARE YOU COMPLAINING ABOUT? AT LEAST YOU GOT AN "A"!
CAREFUL -- THIS THING'S CONTAMINATED! IT'S HIGHLY VOLATILE!
HEALTH DEPT.
NOW, KIDS, I KNOW YOU'RE BOTH DISAPPOINTED BY YOUR TEACHERS' REACTIONS, BUT TRY NOT TO FEEL TOO BAD ABOUT IT!
SET IT DOWN HERE -- EASY DOES IT! LET'S GET THOSE BLASTING CAPS RIGGED!
AFTER ALL, LISA, WHEN IT COMES TO CREATIVITY, YOU HAVE TO BE TRUE TO *YOUR OWN VISION* -- YOU CAN'T WORRY TOO MUCH ABOUT WHAT *OTHER PEOPLE* THINK!
YOU'RE *RIGHT,* MOM! *I* KNOW MY PIECE IS GOOD -- I'M NOT GOING TO LET MISS KELP DISCOURAGE ME!
AND BART, I KNOW YOU'VE HEARD THIS BEFORE, BUT YOU ONLY GET AS MUCH *OUT* OF THIS SORT OF THING AS YOU *PUT IN* -- AND YOU DIDN'T PUT VERY MUCH IN, DID YOU?
WELL -- NO...
THE FUSE IS ATTACHED, SIR!
OKAY, LET'S DO IT! TAKE YOUR POSITIONS!
WELL, MAYBE YOU *BOTH* WILL LEARN SOMETHING FROM ALL THIS. SOMETIMES OUR ACTIONS HAVE *UNFORSEEABLE CONSEQUENCES,* BUT THE IMPORTANT THING IS TO ALWAYS TRY TO DO YOUR *BEST.*
4 -- 3 -- 2 --
KIDS, DON'T WORRY ABOUT THAT *"UNFORSEEABLE CONSEQUENCES"* BALONEY. JUST REMEMBER THAT WE LOVE YOU, EVEN IF YOU *ARE* FAILURES!
WHOOMP!

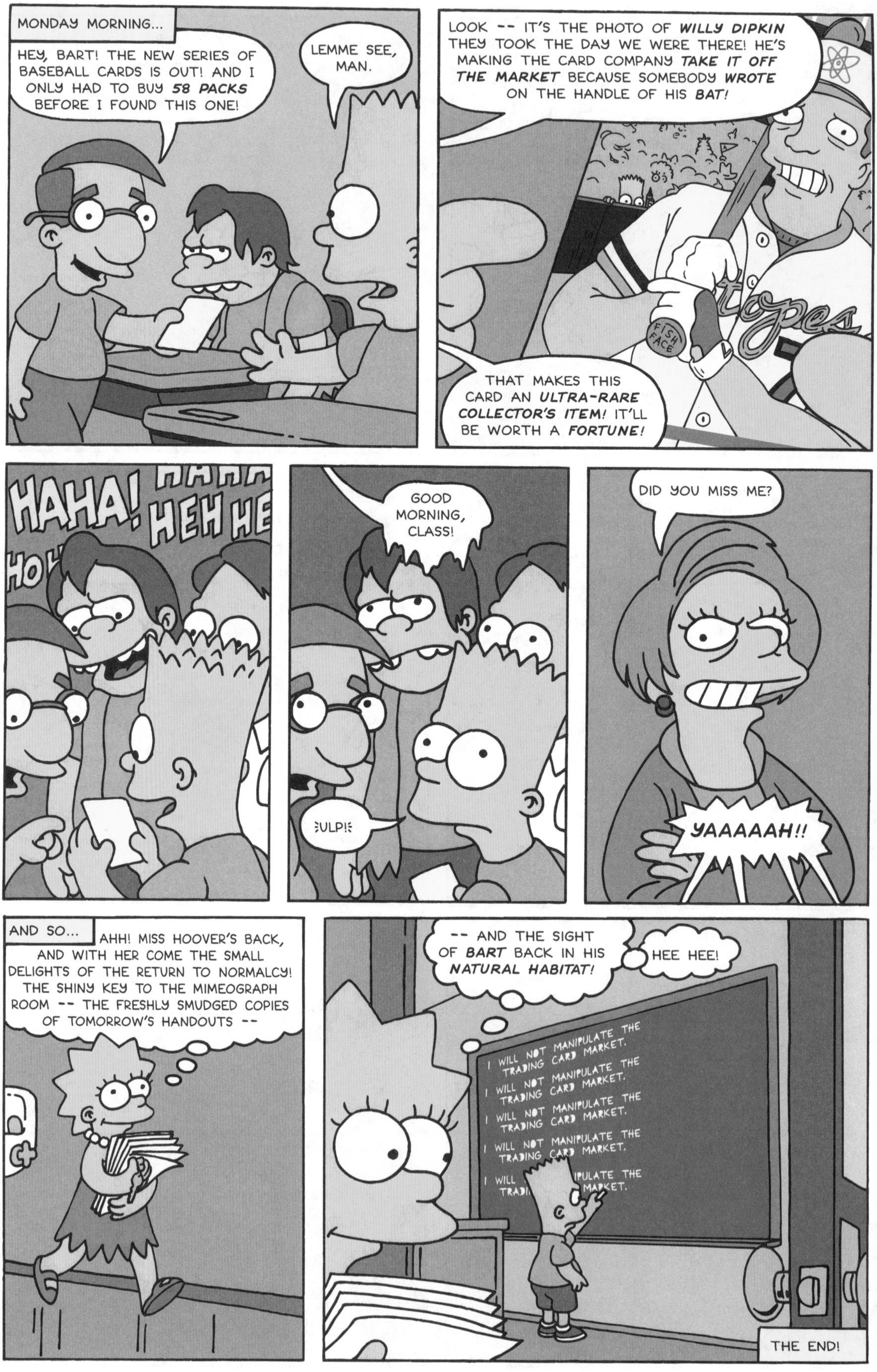

MONDAY MORNING...
HEY, BART! THE NEW SERIES OF BASEBALL CARDS IS OUT! AND I ONLY HAD TO BUY 58 PACKS BEFORE I FOUND THIS ONE!
LEMME SEE, MAN.
LOOK -- IT'S THE PHOTO OF WILLY DIPKIN THEY TOOK THE DAY WE WERE THERE! HE'S MAKING THE CARD COMPANY TAKE IT OFF THE MARKET BECAUSE SOMEBODY WROTE ON THE HANDLE OF HIS BAT!
FISH FACE
THAT MAKES THIS CARD AN ULTRA-RARE COLLECTOR'S ITEM! IT'LL BE WORTH A FORTUNE!
HAHA! HAHA HEH HE
GOOD MORNING, CLASS!
GULP!
DID YOU MISS ME?
YAAAAAH!!
AND SO...
AHH! MISS HOOVER'S BACK, AND WITH HER COME THE SMALL DELIGHTS OF THE RETURN TO NORMALCY! THE SHINY KEY TO THE MIMEOGRAPH ROOM -- THE FRESHLY SMUDGED COPIES OF TOMORROW'S HANDOUTS --
-- AND THE SIGHT OF BART BACK IN HIS NATURAL HABITAT!
HEE HEE!
I WILL NOT MANIPULATE THE TRADING CARD MARKET.
I WILL NOT MANIPULATE THE TRADING CARD MARKET.
I WILL NOT MANIPULATE THE TRADING CARD MARKET.
I WILL NOT MANIPULATE THE TRADING CARD MARKET.
THE END!

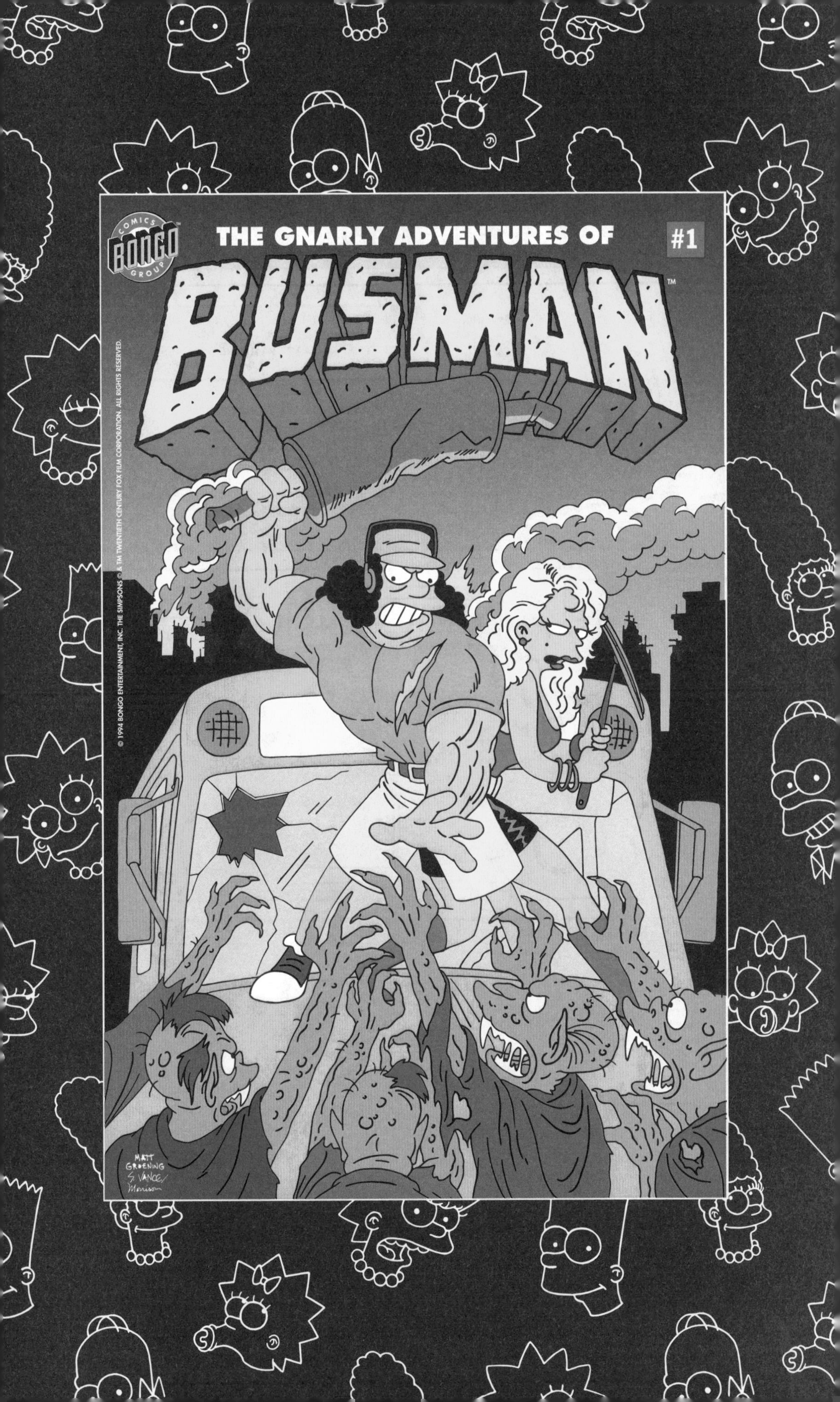

COMICS BONGO GROUP
THE GNARLY ADVENTURES OF
#1
BUSMAN™
© 1994 BONGO ENTERTAINMENT, INC. THE SIMPSONS © & TM TWENTIETH CENTURY FOX FILM CORPORATION. ALL RIGHTS RESERVED.
MATT GROENING
S. VANCE/ Morrison

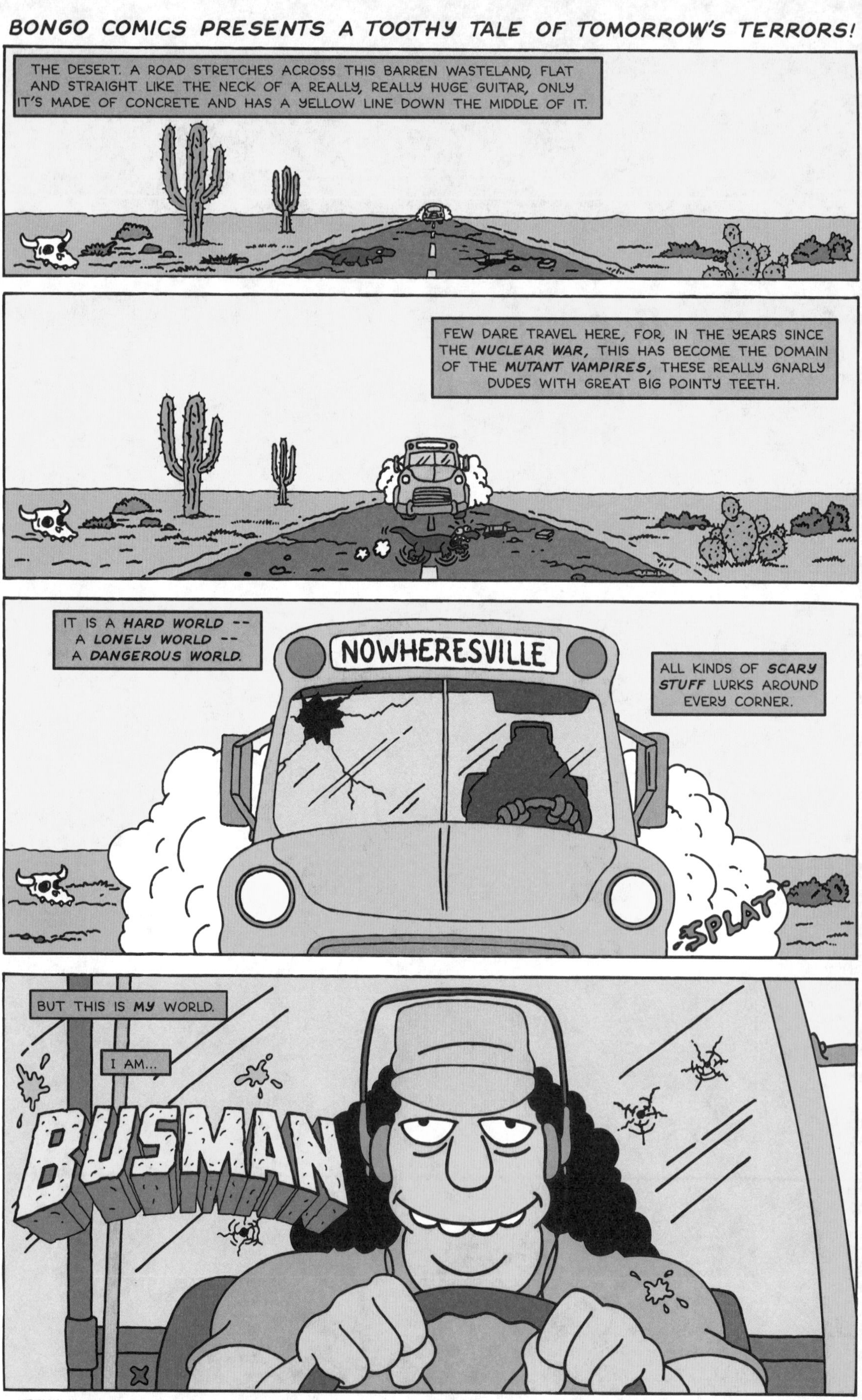
BONGO COMICS PRESENTS A TOOTHY TALE OF TOMORROW'S TERRORS!
THE DESERT. A ROAD STRETCHES ACROSS THIS BARREN WASTELAND, FLAT AND STRAIGHT LIKE THE NECK OF A REALLY, REALLY HUGE GUITAR, ONLY IT'S MADE OF CONCRETE AND HAS A YELLOW LINE DOWN THE MIDDLE OF IT.
FEW DARE TRAVEL HERE, FOR, IN THE YEARS SINCE THE NUCLEAR WAR, THIS HAS BECOME THE DOMAIN OF THE MUTANT VAMPIRES, THESE REALLY GNARLY DUDES WITH GREAT BIG POINTY TEETH.
IT IS A HARD WORLD -- A LONELY WORLD -- A DANGEROUS WORLD.
NOWHERESVILLE
ALL KINDS OF SCARY STUFF LURKS AROUND EVERY CORNER.
SPLAT
BUT THIS IS MY WORLD.
I AM...
BUSMAN

STEVE VANCE SCRIPT, LAYOUTS · **BILL MORRISON** PENCILS · **TIM BAVINGTON** INKS · **CINDY VANCE** COLORS · **MATT GROENING** FELLOW TRAVELLER

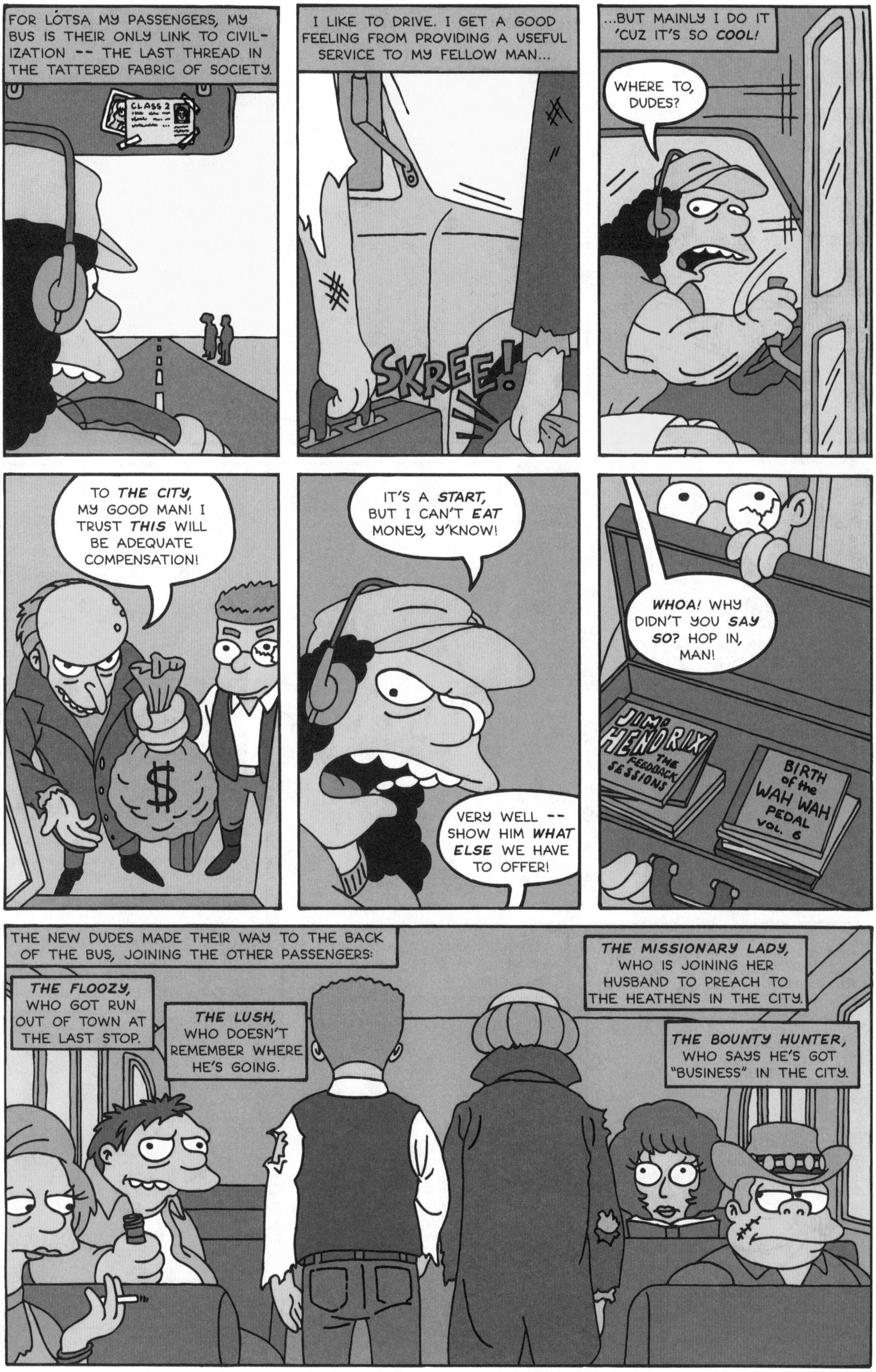
FOR LOTSA MY PASSENGERS, MY BUS IS THEIR ONLY LINK TO CIVILIZATION -- THE LAST THREAD IN THE TATTERED FABRIC OF SOCIETY.
CLASS 2
I LIKE TO DRIVE. I GET A GOOD FEELING FROM PROVIDING A USEFUL SERVICE TO MY FELLOW MAN...
SKREE!
...BUT MAINLY I DO IT 'CUZ IT'S SO COOL!
WHERE TO, DUDES?
TO THE CITY, MY GOOD MAN! I TRUST THIS WILL BE ADEQUATE COMPENSATION!
$
IT'S A START, BUT I CAN'T EAT MONEY, Y'KNOW!
VERY WELL -- SHOW HIM WHAT ELSE WE HAVE TO OFFER!
WHOA! WHY DIDN'T YOU SAY SO? HOP IN, MAN!
JIMI HENDRIX THE FEEDBACK SESSIONS
BIRTH of the WAH WAH PEDAL VOL. 6
THE NEW DUDES MADE THEIR WAY TO THE BACK OF THE BUS, JOINING THE OTHER PASSENGERS:
THE FLOOZY, WHO GOT RUN OUT OF TOWN AT THE LAST STOP.
THE LUSH, WHO DOESN'T REMEMBER WHERE HE'S GOING.
THE MISSIONARY LADY, WHO IS JOINING HER HUSBAND TO PREACH TO THE HEATHENS IN THE CITY.
THE BOUNTY HUNTER, WHO SAYS HE'S GOT "BUSINESS" IN THE CITY.

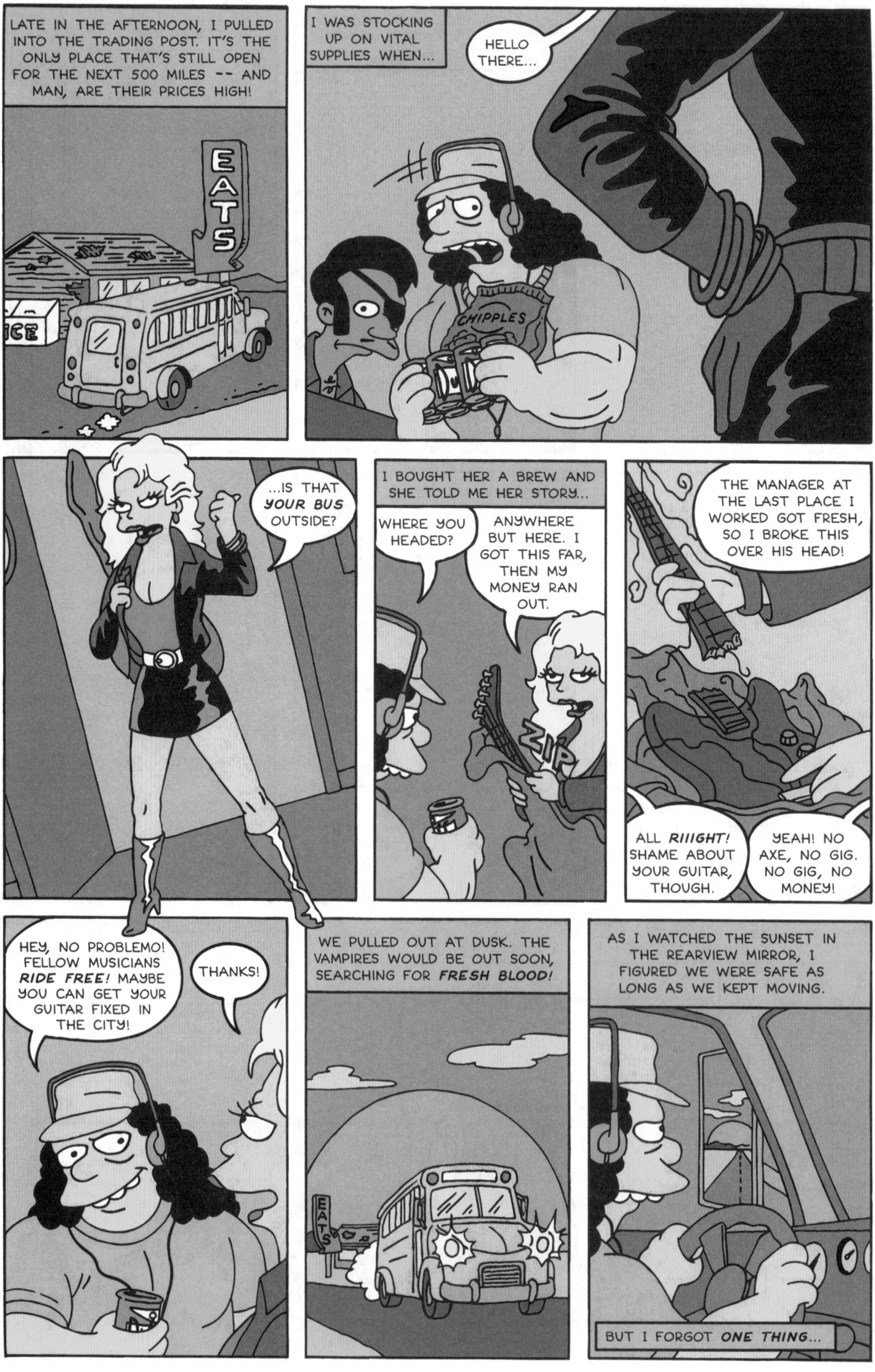
LATE IN THE AFTERNOON, I PULLED INTO THE TRADING POST. IT'S THE ONLY PLACE THAT'S STILL OPEN FOR THE NEXT 500 MILES -- AND MAN, ARE THEIR PRICES HIGH!
EATS
ICE
I WAS STOCKING UP ON VITAL SUPPLIES WHEN...
HELLO THERE...
CHIPPLES
...IS THAT ***YOUR BUS*** OUTSIDE?
I BOUGHT HER A BREW AND SHE TOLD ME HER STORY...
WHERE YOU HEADED?
ANYWHERE BUT HERE. I GOT THIS FAR, THEN MY MONEY RAN OUT.
ZIP
THE MANAGER AT THE LAST PLACE I WORKED GOT FRESH, SO I BROKE THIS OVER HIS HEAD!
ALL ***RIIIGHT!*** SHAME ABOUT YOUR GUITAR, THOUGH.
YEAH! NO AXE, NO GIG. NO GIG, NO MONEY!
HEY, NO PROBLEMO! FELLOW MUSICIANS ***RIDE FREE!*** MAYBE YOU CAN GET YOUR GUITAR FIXED IN THE CITY!
THANKS!
WE PULLED OUT AT DUSK. THE VAMPIRES WOULD BE OUT SOON, SEARCHING FOR ***FRESH BLOOD!***
EATS
AS I WATCHED THE SUNSET IN THE REARVIEW MIRROR, I FIGURED WE WERE SAFE AS LONG AS WE KEPT MOVING.
BUT I FORGOT ***ONE THING...***

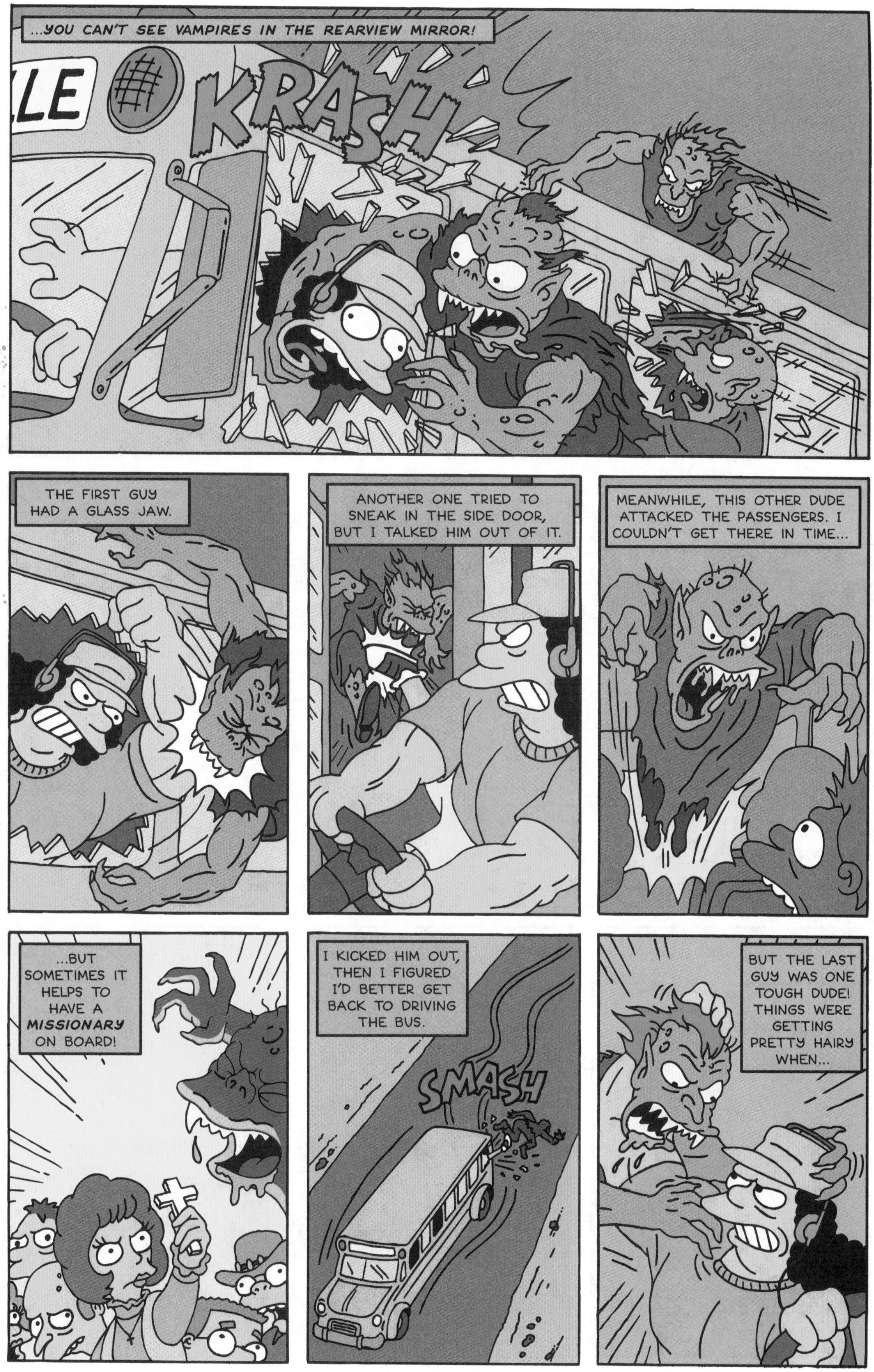
...YOU CAN'T SEE VAMPIRES IN THE REARVIEW MIRROR!
KRASH
THE FIRST GUY HAD A GLASS JAW.
ANOTHER ONE TRIED TO SNEAK IN THE SIDE DOOR, BUT I TALKED HIM OUT OF IT.
MEANWHILE, THIS OTHER DUDE ATTACKED THE PASSENGERS. I COULDN'T GET THERE IN TIME...
...BUT SOMETIMES IT HELPS TO HAVE A *MISSIONARY* ON BOARD!
I KICKED HIM OUT, THEN I FIGURED I'D BETTER GET BACK TO DRIVING THE BUS.
SMASH
BUT THE LAST GUY WAS ONE TOUGH DUDE! THINGS WERE GETTING PRETTY HAIRY WHEN...

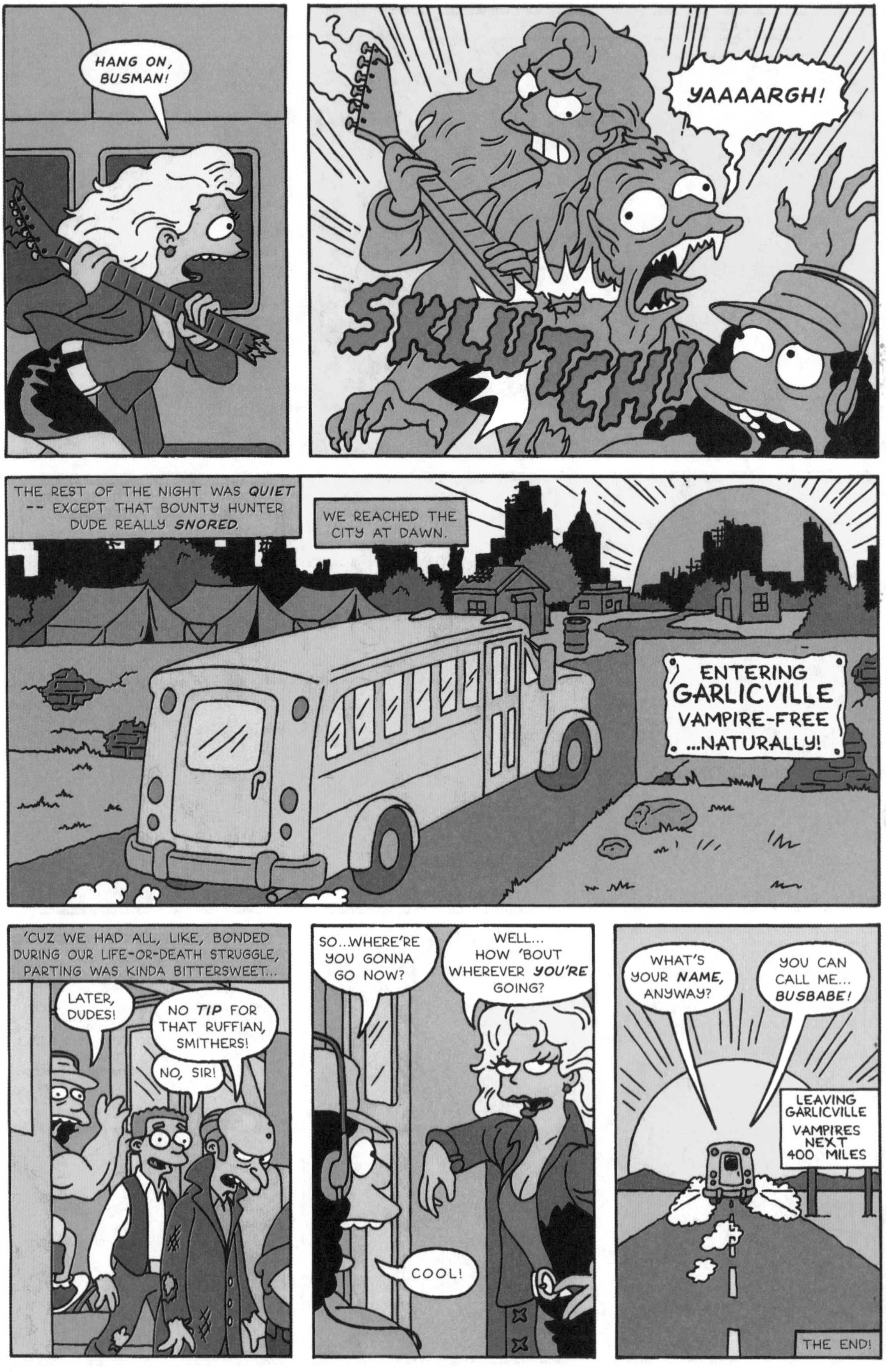
HANG ON, BUSMAN!
YAAAARGH!
SKLUTCH!
THE REST OF THE NIGHT WAS QUIET -- EXCEPT THAT BOUNTY HUNTER DUDE REALLY SNORED.
WE REACHED THE CITY AT DAWN.
ENTERING GARLICVILLE VAMPIRE-FREE ...NATURALLY!
'CUZ WE HAD ALL, LIKE, BONDED DURING OUR LIFE-OR-DEATH STRUGGLE, PARTING WAS KINDA BITTERSWEET...
LATER, DUDES!
NO TIP FOR THAT RUFFIAN, SMITHERS!
NO, SIR!
SO...WHERE'RE YOU GONNA GO NOW?
WELL... HOW 'BOUT WHEREVER YOU'RE GOING?
COOL!
WHAT'S YOUR NAME, ANYWAY?
YOU CAN CALL ME... BUSBABE!
LEAVING GARLICVILLE
VAMPIRES NEXT 400 MILES
THE END!

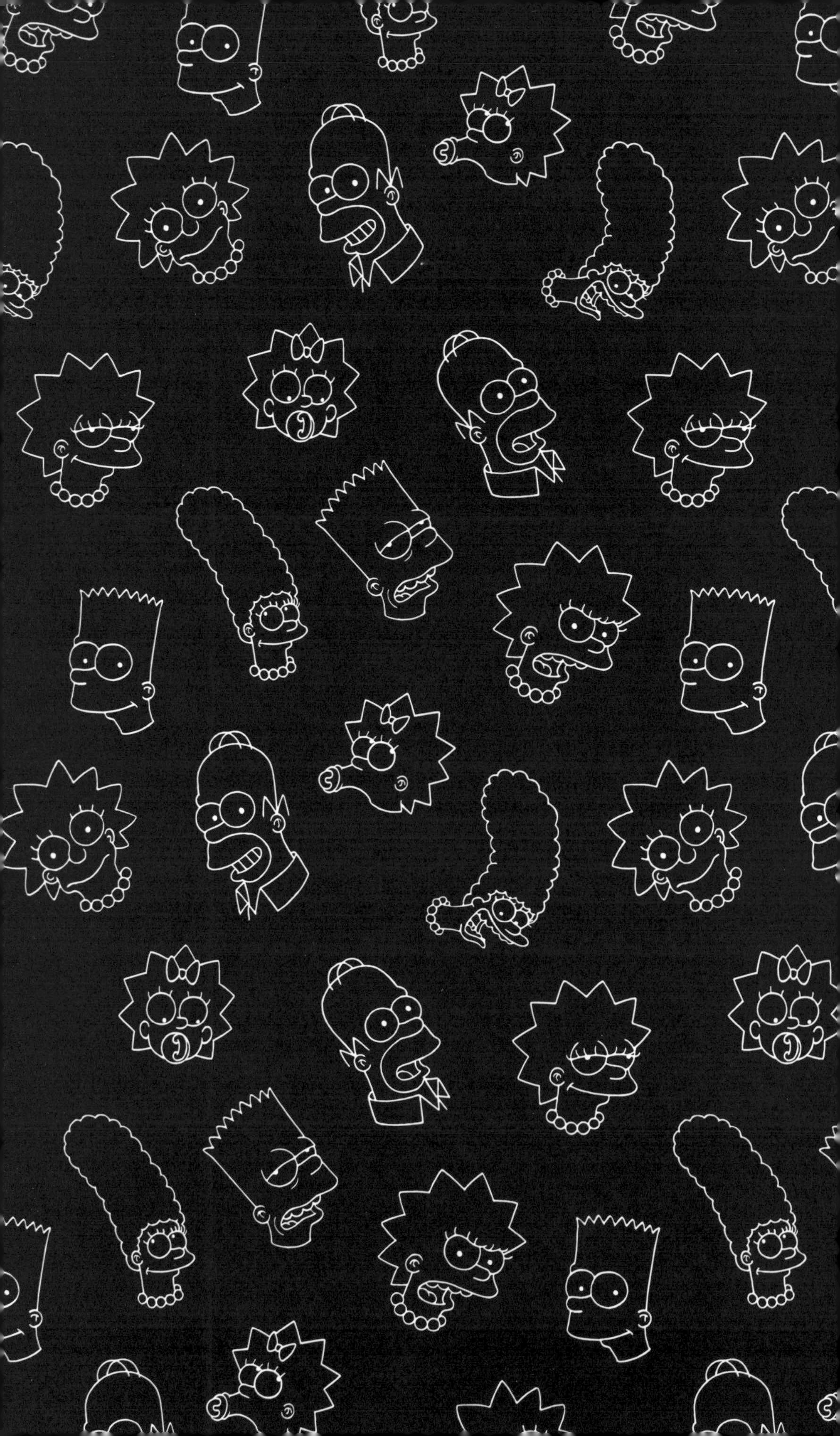